CAN'T BE LOVE

CAN'T BE LOVE

A Westin Pack Novel

By

Julie Trettel

Thanks and Acknowledgments

The final book. We made it!!! Thanks so much to everyone who has stuck it out through all 5 Westin Books. It's certainly been an exciting adventure, but while Westin Pack comes to close, the world that was started here will go on. I have you, the readers, to thank for that. Because of your love and support, I promise there will be many more shifter books to come!

Huge shout out to my fam, as always. They put up with so much so I can live my dream. I'm lucky to have found my one true mate at an early age and blessed by four amazing kids who are quickly turning into young adults I'm very proud and honored to have helped shape.

Special thanks to Beth Culver for coming in and joining my crazy editing family. Love this girl and greatly impressed by the dedication and hard work she put in to help shape Lily's story. Looking forward to working through many more books to come.

Lily

Chapter 1

Exiting the car, I stretched and smiled. There was something nice-smelling in the air that called to me, and I liked it. Collier territory was beautiful. I had visited here numerous times in my life, but something felt different this time.

Liam helped unload the car and I was bursting with excitement. It was the first time Maddie had been back to visit her home pack since my twin brother had found her. It was pretty cool that my oldest and dearest friend turned out to be my twin's one true mate, and I was really happy for them. All my siblings had found their true mates, and I couldn't wait till I found mine.

I was practically skipping and loving the wide-open space of Wyoming, when Liam gave me a concerned look. "What is wrong with you?"

Maddie laughed. "Leave her alone. This place just has that effect on people."

Madelyn looked happy, I thought.

"Sweetheart, are you okay?" Liam asked her, and I knew he was worried about her being emotionally overwhelmed by this trip. That's why he had asked me to tag along. I had a way of pulling her out of her shell.

Madelyn Amanda Collier Westin (sometimes we called her MC), was my very best friend in the entire world. We had met at summer camp when we were six years old and we were practically inseparable every year after, until the day that she had disappeared. Eight years later, my brother found her living a new life in the human world and brought her home.

Oscar, MC's son, bounded out of the car. He was clearly as excited as I was. It didn't take long before Maddie's sisters swarmed, fawning over Oscar and MC. She had five sisters, and one douchebag brother. I couldn't remember the last time I saw Thomas. He was a year younger than Maddie and me, and had been a pain when we were kids. He had disappeared and pulled away from the family after Maddie's disappearance. Asshole.

We headed for the Alpha house that Maddie had grown up in as everyone started grabbing our things and giving a round of welcome hugs.

There was something so familiar about the Collier Alpha house. It made me happy just to be there.

Cora and Zach Collier were good people. Zach was Alpha of the pack, and a great leader. Having shared the Alpha brat experience had helped Maddie and me become fast friends so many years ago. Few understood the pressures of that role, so it was a unique bond we had formed.

They had visited Westin a few times, but seeing Madelyn home was triggering a chain of tears and high emotions.

Sorry girl, I silently sent to Maddie. *I'm out of here!*

Leaving them to their reunion, I headed back outside. I breathed in the crisp mountain air, and it made my whole body start to tingle. *Mate,* I thought to myself.

I didn't want to freak out, and I could barely contain my excitement. I just knew my one true mate was here. He *had* to be a Collier, and I could live with that. I had waited my entire life to feel this tingly sensation that had the hair on my arms standing up.

My siblings had all fought their bond in some way, but I knew that would never be me. The magic of true mates was so romantic. It was something I had dreamed for and longed of my entire life.

There were several groups of people around. Unlike the Westin Alpha house that sat back in the woods and away from town, Collier's Alpha house literally sat on the main street of town.

People had obviously heard of Maddie's visit ahead of time and were anxious to catch a glimpse of her. I started walking around and saying hello to the people I passed, trying to make eye contact with every male in the area. I knew the moment our eyes met, I'd recognize him and everything was going to be perfect.

My senses were on full alert and I imagined my wolf was wagging her tail happily. He was here, this was it! There was even more of a spring in my step as I anxiously honed in on my mate, my one true mate! It took everything in my power not to "eek" out loud in excitement.

I channeled a little more of my wolf and let her guide me. We rounded a corner, and I saw a group of young men standing around talking. Every single one of them was super sexy hot. *Yes, please!* I was getting a super sexy hot mate. It was the greatest day of my life.

I looked at each of them, wondering which one he was. They all smiled and nodded as attention turned toward me. I was careful to make eye contact with each of them. Nothing. Then I noticed the one with his back turned stiffen. His shoulders sagged, and he took a deep breath. I was acutely aware of how his heart rate sped up and I was a million times positive that this was him, the man I had longed for my entire life.

I took a moment to check out and appreciate my mate. The thought alone had me grinning from ear to ear. He looked to have close-cropped brown hair. He was wearing a black flannel shirt tucked into tight jeans with a wide belt, completing the package with a pair of black cowboy boots. My very own cowboy. I quickly admired just how well his ass filled out those jeans. I already knew he was hotter than hot and he was all mine.

He slowly turned around and our eyes locked. It felt like my entire world tilted and he was the new gravity holding me in place. *Wow*, I thought. He had the most alluring chocolate-brown eyes. I was mesmerized. This was everything I had ever dreamed it would be.

Recognition flickered in his eyes first, breaking the fog I had found myself in.

"Lily Westin?" I heard him say in a deep, sexy voice that had my body trembling.

Surprised that he knew my name, I shook my head and took a closer look. Revulsion immediately set in. I couldn't believe what my eyes were telling me. I couldn't believe what my heart was telling me.

"Thomas?" I spit out, disgusted at the very thought. "Oh, hell no!"

I turned and ran as fast as I could. I had to get away from there. God was a good, loving, and kind God. There was no way he could possibly be cruel enough to condemn me to Thomas Collier as my one true mate. I had to have read things wrong. This could not be happening to me.

Thomas
Chapter 2

I had tried to ignore the tingling sensation alerting me to my mate's arrival—not just a compatible mate, but my one and only true mate. I wanted to identify her before I let on that she was there. I didn't even understand how it was possible. I knew every eligible woman in Collier Pack, so unless she was very young and recently turned, I didn't know how it could be happening.

I thought hard. My sister Maddie was coming to visit. I knew she was bringing her family, but Dad hadn't mentioned anyone else.

It was the oddest sensation. I felt her getting closer and imagined my wolf jumping up and wagging his tail in anticipation. I itched all over like I needed to shift.

Suddenly, there she was with big blue eyes that stared back at me in a dreamy way. It wasn't until recognition flashed on her face that I realized I knew her. I flinched when she spat out my name, cursed, and ran off.

Lily Westin. My one true mate was Lily freaking Westin. She had been my sister's best friend when they were kids. Every male wolf within at least three packs had lusted after her at some point in their life. Heck, she had starred in my first wet dream when I was only twelve. Even as a kid she was super hot and completely unattainable. And now she was mine.

I grinned at her retreating form. Lily freaking Westin. My mate.

She and Maddie had been inseparable every summer growing up and Lily often visited us throughout the year, too. I cringed, remembering how I'd tormented them. While I enjoyed playing the classic bratty baby brother role, I had always gone above and beyond in hopes of getting Lily's attention any way I could.

In truth, Maddie was only ten months older than me, and Lily only six. But they never let me forget that I was younger, just a little kid they were too cool to be bothered to hang out with. I thought as we got older maybe that would change, but when Maddie was sixteen she'd run away from home. We only recently found out what had happened to her when her true mate, Liam, who happened to be Lily's twin brother, had found her and brought her home. Apparently, she had kids now, too. Mom had talked about nothing else since the day Liam Westin had called my parents to tell them the news.

Madelyn and I had been close growing up. Whenever Lily wasn't around, she was cool. Being so close in age helped, too. I had five other sisters who constantly doted on me, the only boy in a house of six girls, and I was the baby of the family, which meant I had gotten away with pretty much everything, until Maddie disappeared.

Mom had smothered me, terrified something bad would happen to me, too. No one could truly understand what that was like. Ruby had come home to help out, but the others had all moved out and there was no one left to buffer my mother's fears.

They always somehow knew Maddie was alive. Mom had prayed for her and held on to that hope until the day of Liam's fateful call. I hadn't understood how it could be possible. If Madelyn was alive, why hadn't she just called or come home?

They said she'd been through something pretty traumatic, but I couldn't understand how anything could be so traumatic that you couldn't call or come home for eight years. I get she went through some deep stuff, but that's what family's supposed to be for, to pick you up at your lowest and carry you through the tough times. Maddie had chosen to reject us during that time in her life, and I was struggling to forgive her.

Shelby had made it to her wedding and said she was doing great. She was happy, in love, and had the cutest little family. The picture she painted only made me angrier. I was only fifteen when she'd disappeared. The little bit of life and freedom I was just beginning to experience had been ripped from me. For the first year

Mom had even insisted on homeschooling me, afraid to let me out of her sight for even a second. Naturally I rebelled, and Dad had eventually convinced her to let me return to school. I'd had to hold to a strict curfew though, so while my friends were out partying and enjoying high school, I was still tightly guarded.

The second I graduated, I took off and considered never returning. I knew my responsibility to the Pack, though. As the only son to the Alpha, I was the sole heir to the throne, so to speak, and they never let me forget it. I'd been groomed my entire life to take over as Alpha someday. It was a heavy burden, but it was mine alone to bear.

Every year on the anniversary of Maddie's disappearance, the Pack would hold this big vigil. I knew Lily always came—every year, except this most recent one. Turned out that was because she was busy reconciling with a ghost.

When we realized Maddie was gone, a full search was put into place. The best trackers around had been called in during the weeks following, but it was too late. She had been at a concert and heavily drinking from what the friend that had been with her told us about that night. The alcohol had made it difficult to catch her scent and only faint signs of her had ever come up, but it was enough to give them all hope. I couldn't deal with it.

As soon as I was old enough, I refused to come home during that week, or purposely planned whatever trip possible to ensure I was out of the country. I started to get a playboy reputation amongst the packs, which to my surprise made me quite desirable to the ladies. I had never struggled to find companionship, but it had always been empty, lonely. I longed for the connection of a mate, and suddenly, here she was, and from the look of disgust on her face, she had zero interest in me, but I was ready to do what I had done my entire life—chase Lily Westin. What did I have to lose?

A cocky grin spread across my face as I said goodbye to my friends and set off on the hunt for my mate. This was going to be fun, at the very least.

As I turned the corner, heading down the main strip of town towards my parents' house, there was a crowd forming in the middle of the street.

Maddie, I thought.

I knew it was an asshole move not to be there when she

13

arrived. I was happy my sister was alive, I was just still angry with her over the whole situation. It was a weight that had been pressing down on me my entire adult life and I didn't know how to let it go.

If it weren't for Lily I probably would have turned away and avoided the reunion, but my wolf and I were in predator mode with our eyes set on one thing.

"Thomas," my mother said, motioning for me to come over. She looked surprised to see me and it hurt. I didn't want to disappoint her, and yet I had for so long, and always where Madelyn was concerned. "Thomas, it's Maddie," Mom said, hugging my sister with tears streaming down her face.

When Mom finally let go of the woman, Maddie turned towards me. She had always been pretty, and it was clear that hadn't changed, but there was a grownup quality to her I couldn't overlook.

"Hi, baby brother," she told me with a hesitant smile.

Shit. I realized people must have warned her about me. I wasn't ready to forgive her, but I didn't want to upset Mom even further, so I pushed down my personal feelings and stepped forward to hug her. My wolf growled in my head and I struggled to maintain some semblance of control. She was my sister; my wolf shouldn't be reacting so strongly.

Mate. The word kept playing over and over in my head. My wolf was very distraught over Lily's earlier reaction.

"Welcome home," I told Maddie in a strained voice. The looks shot my way told me I sounded like an ass. I truly didn't mean to, I was just trying to get a grip on my wolf.

All Alpha wolves were strong and often overbearing, but mine had always been more powerful than most. In my wolf form, he was fierce and no one dared challenge me, but ever since my first shift we had struggled for dominance. The last thing I needed was Lily Westin in our territory.

"You remember Liam and Lily?" she asked. "And this is . . ."

"Patrick O'Connell, yeah, I know everyone, Mad."

"Oh," she said, seeming to struggle with what to say next, then she smiled up at me. "Bet you don't know these guys?" Maddie moved a blanket aside from the tiny bundle Liam was holding in his arms. "This is Sara, your niece, and your nephew. Oscar, this is your Uncle Thomas."

A boy with dark hair and dark eyes stepped out from behind

Liam Westin with a shy smile. "Hi," he said awkwardly.

I knew Maddie had a kid, but I wasn't prepared for the boy before me. He had to be eight or nine years old. I had somehow envisioned a baby or a toddler even, not a full grown child.

Liam nudged him toward me.

"I'm Oscar," he said, not quite making eye contact, and it dawned on me that he was sensing my wolf so close to the surface and recognizing me as an Alpha. I didn't want to scare the kid. I actually liked kids.

I chanced a look around and zeroed in on Lily, who was shooting me daggers, and I knew I had to calm down. Her look alone shot pain straight through my heart that I wasn't prepared for. Ignoring it as best I could, I bent down to Oscar's level. "It's nice to meet you Oscar," I said aloud, then bent over to whisper, "'Bout time we had another male in this family."

Oscar relaxed and smiled at me. He was a cute kid. I might still have been upset with his mom, but I wasn't about to take it out on a child.

Glancing up, I noticed that Lily looked like she was going to bolt again, but no longer appeared to wish me dead. Mom was smiling through her tears, and I straightened and shook hands with Liam and Patrick, welcoming them to my territory.

A larger crowd had gathered around us, leaving me feeling trapped. I knew most were there to welcome Madelyn home, but I suspected several were there to see how I was going to react. I'm sure I had disappointed the gossip mongrels with my civility.

Through my peripheral vision I saw Sydney Parker moving towards me. Sydney and I had been on again-off again for years. She honestly thought we'd end up together and was preparing herself to be Pack Mother someday. How the hell was I supposed to tell her that was never going to happen, because now that I'd scented my true mate, I knew I could never settle for anyone but Lily Westin.

My wolf was still highly agitated, and I didn't need an audience for that inevitable talk, so I did what any sane man would do. I turned and quickly left the scene before it could begin. I dared a glance back over my shoulder just in time to see Lily take notice of Sydney moving toward me, and the look on her face was a mix of sheer fury and confusion.

I headed straight for the one place I knew Syd wouldn't

follow, the Alpha house. I walked in and ran up the stairs, not stopping until I reached my old room. I collapsed down on my bed, my arm covering my face.

What the hell was I going to do?

At some point I'd have to sort out my feelings over my sister, but the more pressing crisis was Lily. My mate. I couldn't help the grin that spread across my face at the thought, but seeing Sydney and Lily together had thrown me for a loop. Syd and I had a past; there were expectations there. Sure, she knew I had messed around with nearly every eligible wolf across two packs, but she had also been the closest thing to a girlfriend I'd ever had. When all was said and done, I always went back to Sydney.

Just seeing Syd had messed with me. I couldn't imagine touching her after catching Lily's scent. I wasn't sure my wolf would allow me even if I wanted to. The constant images and reminders of Lily that my wolf kept flashing in my mind were going to drive me insane.

What I did know was that Lily Westin was my one true mate. I had an option to accept that or reject her. Truth was, I didn't really know Lily anymore, aside from her obvious dislike of me. Maybe that would change, maybe it wouldn't, but I knew with certainty that I would not get one bit of rest until I at least tried to see where things would go.

My decision was made. I would hang out for a few hours until the insanity outside calmed. I could even give Lily a day to settle in for her visit, and then I owed it to myself to find out what this mating stuff was truly about. She may not want it, she may not like it, but the chase was on and Lily didn't know what was coming for her, because now that I had her scent, I couldn't see anything else.

Lily

Chapter 3

My entire being had been painfully aware of Thomas when he'd come over to welcome Maddie home. He looked the part, he acted the part, but somehow it felt like a show. He had never been around for any of the vigils while Maddie was gone. I couldn't forgive him for that. He had given up on my best friend, his own sister.

How on earth could God possibly match the two of us? I had always tried to be a good person. I got carried away at times, but I wasn't a troublemaker or anything. I knew God was sitting up there in heaven laughing down at me. *Gotcha!*

All the expectations I'd had of my true mate had crumbled and exploded in a cloud of smoke. Thomas? I just couldn't believe it, yet when he'd passed near me to hug Maddie, every nerve in my body had been aware of him. Despite her being my best friend and his sister, for crying out loud, my wolf wanted to rip Maddie to pieces for touching our mate. My wolf's mate, I reminded myself. Thomas Collier could never be my mate.

Just that thought caused physical pain in my chest. What was I going to do?

A tall girl about my age bumped into me as she stood on her tip toes and strained to see above the gathering crowd. She stepped on my foot in the process.

"Ow," I complained.

"Oh, sorry," she apologized. "Did you happen to see where Thomas went?" she asked, clearly distracted.

"No," I lied. I had seen the look of panic on his face as he'd turned and headed for the house. I imagined he had likely exited out the back door and was long gone by now. If this girl was the cause of his quick exit, I should be thanking her. Instead I closed my eyes and bit back a growl as my wolf howled in my head, sending angry thoughts to my brain.

The girl sighed and stopped straining. She looked at me and surprise showed on her face. "Oh, hey, I'm Sydney. I don't think we've met."

"Lily," I said. "I'm here visiting with Maddie."

"Oh, so you're one of the Westin wolves?" she asked with obvious curiosity. "It's crazy about Maddie right? It's all the Pack talks about."

I cringed, knowing how much my friend hated being in the spotlight. It was one of the reasons she'd waited so long to return home.

I shrugged in response. "It was a shock at first, but I guess I've had awhile to get over it. I'm just glad Liam found her and brought her home."

"Oh, definitely—and Liam Westin as her true mate—wow, he's super hot," Sydney said.

I couldn't help it. I snorted. "Gross. He's my twin brother."

She looked surprised by my confession. "Really? You're Lily Westin?"

I nodded.

"Wow. That's so cool. Hey, would you like to get a drink and hang out some time?" she asked.

I looked at Maddie. Liam and Patrick were still running interference for her and I knew Sara would need to eat soon, giving her an excuse to get away from everyone's good intentions. I glanced up at the Alpha house, wondering if Thomas was still in there or not, deciding it was best not to chance it. I wasn't ready to face him.

"It's been a long day. I could really use a drink now. You free?"

She seemed surprised, but genuinely smiled. "Of course, come on."

Sydney linked her arm through mine and escorted me away from the crowd. We walked back down the main strip of town. I couldn't help but think that only moments ago I had practically skipped down this same street in search of my mate, so carefree and blissfully ignorant. It already felt like a lifetime ago. Recognizing Thomas as my mate was quickly changing me, and I was freaking out. I didn't want him for a mate. I needed a very stiff drink in hopes of passing out and waking up tomorrow to find it had all been one big nightmare.

She led me into a rustic looking building. The floor was planked wood and there were peanut shells crushed all over it.

"I know it's not much to look at, but it has a full bar and the best damn steaks you'll ever eat," Sydney admitted.

"Sounds heavenly," I told her.

"Hey Syd, you seen her yet?" the waitress asked. She was wearing a too-short skirt with a crop top, but she seemed friendly enough. I scolded myself for my bad habit of being a snob when it came to other people's attire. I never said it aloud, but I always judged them in my head.

"Yes, she looked good. Happy. I only saw her in passing though, didn't get to talk to her. Milly, this is Lily Westin, Madelyn's mate's twin sister." The ladies shared a knowing look that told me there wouldn't be any more talk of my best friend, which was probably best for everyone present.

"Hi," I said, smiling as pleasantly as I could muster.

"Hey, welcome to Collier. We're all really happy you're here and finally brought Madelyn home," Milly said before turning back to Sydney. "How's Thomas holding up? Everyone's been worried sick about him. You had a chance to talk to him?"

Sydney shook her head sadly. "No, he took off as soon as I got there and there were too many people around to chase him down. He didn't cause a scene or anything when he greeted her. So, hopefully that's a good sign. I'll see him tonight and judge for myself."

The insinuation Sydney was making regarding my mate had my body on fire as I bit back a growl. *My mate?* No, no, no, no, not Thomas. I couldn't think of him like that. The stupid bond was making me feel things I didn't want to feel. It had to stop. I took in a deep breath.

"So, you're close with Thomas then?" I asked innocently. Where the hell had that come from? I didn't care if this girl was close to him or not. I couldn't care. He was Thomas Collier. I hated him.

Milly laughed. "You're looking at our next Pack Mother right here, sweetie," she said proudly.

My eyes widened and flew to the girl before me. All I saw was red and there was a pounding in my ears. He couldn't have taken a mate, because he was my mate. *Mate,* my wolf growled in my head. I locked my jaw and ground my teeth as Sydney flushed.

"Someday, I hope," she confessed.

Milly grinned. "She's gonna make one hell of a Pack Mother, too. Those two have been inseparable since childhood. Now what can I get you ladies?"

"How about a beer," Sydney said.

"Whiskey, neat," I said. "Screw neat, just bring the bottle."

Milly stared for a second before heading off to fetch our order.

Sydney placed her hand on my arm. "Are you okay?"

I smiled. "It's been a long, crazy day. I'll be fine after a few drinks."

She nodded, but looked more concerned than anything. "Well, let's get you wasted then and I'll make sure you get back to the Alpha house safe and sound."

I snorted. A minute ago I secretly wanted to rip this girl's head off over a mate I didn't want. Now suddenly she was my new hero. *Oblivion, here I come!*

It took four drinks for me to work up the courage to ask Sydney about Thomas.

"So, you and Thomas?" I asked, trying not to slur my words. My tongue was beginning to feel thick and fuzzy, and my body was far too warm. I suddenly wished I had Milly's outfit instead of my own. She may look ridiculous in it, but I could totally rock that mini skirt.

"Thomas and I aren't true mates, if that's what you're wondering, but we are compatible. We've already been through the Council testing and approved last fall. But then word came in about his sister and he sort of retreated again." She sighed. "What happened to her was terrible, but it wasn't easy on him either. We decided to hold off starting a bond till things settled."

I had never really considered what it was like for Thomas

when Maddie disappeared, but I couldn't get past how he had disappeared and refused to participate in any of the vigils or searches for her. I didn't think I could ever forgive him that, yet hearing he was basically mated to this woman did all sorts of confusing things to my insides.

It's just the bond. It's just the bond, it'll pass when I break it, I kept reminding myself.

"I'm sure it'll happen soon, especially now that Madelyn is back," she said almost sadly.

"Aren't you worried he'll find his true mate?" I asked.

She laughed. "Trust me, as many women as that boy has chased, if his true mate were anywhere within five packs, he'd have known it long before now. Besides, what are the odds, really? Isn't it better to just be with someone you know makes you happy?"

I wasn't sure if she was trying to convince me or herself. I shrugged. "My siblings have all found their true mates. My parents preach that it's worth the wait." *But this time, they were wrong,* I thought, but didn't add.

"I guess, but what if you don't find him till you're both really old? Do you just miss out on life, family, and children in the hopes you'll find him? I don't really know many true mates our age."

It was true. Our generation had all but given up on true mates. Westin Pack was an exception. It had always meant the world to me to find mine. I poured another glass of whiskey and drank it down in one gulp, letting the burn tame the anxiety of my wolf. She was furious with my thoughts, and with me for not ripping the throat out of the woman across from us trying to claim our mate. The varying emotions with the added liquid courage was just confusing me.

"I never really thought of it, just honestly thought I'd find him one day," I said. I couldn't tell her I had. I suspected it would devastate her.

We never did order dinner, but somewhere along the line, I did manage to finish off that bottle of whiskey.

"I think you better get her home," Milly told Sydney as my head hit the table. I was starting to feel the pull of the liquor, and getting sleepy.

"Come on, Lily. I think you're good and wasted now. Time to go sleep it off," she told me.

"Good luck," Milly said, and I watched them share a look.

Outside, the cool air brought me back to life. I threw my arms out and started twirling until the whole world was spinning around me.

"Probably not your best idea, Lily," Sydney said, righting me and putting her arm around me.

I leaned into her heavily. "You are the best!" I said. "Sydney is the greatest!" I yelled. In my head I was speaking clearly and walking a straight line. I was invincible. A few guys walking by chuckled. "Do you know Sydney?" I asked them. "You should. She's great. I love her," I told them. "I love you, Sydney."

"I love you too, Lily," she told me.

"Do you need any help, Syd?" one of the guys asked.

"No, it's okay. She's staying at the Alpha house. We can make it."

"Alright. Holler if you change your mind," he said.

We walked on a little further. She helped me up the steps when I tripped. Without knocking, she opened the front door and I helped her inside. I knew she was drunk, and I was perfectly fine, unstoppable.

"Oh my gosh, what happened?" I heard Maddie ask.

"Sorry, Maddie," I slurred. "Sydney had a little too much to drink. She may need to sleep it off here."

"I'm fine," Syd told her. "I just wanted to make sure she got home okay."

"Thank you so much. She never drinks," Maddie told her.

"She said she had a really rough day and needed to get wasted, and that's exactly what she did. Do you need help getting her to bed?"

"I'm fine. I'm fine," I said, hugging Sydney. "I love you, Sydney!" Then I turned to Maddie and hugged her next. "And I love you, MC, the mostest, 'cause you're the best sister in the world. Now where's my room? I'm feeling a little tired."

"First door at the top of the stairs. Your stuff is already up there," Maddie directed.

"Make sure my friend gets home safely. She had a little too much to drink," I informed Maddie in what I thought was a whisper.

I turned and crawled up the stairs. The whole house smelled of Thomas. Stupid Thomas. My body was tingling and warm all over. *It's just the alcohol*, I lied to myself. I somehow managed to get the door open, and stumbled inside. I was hot. Too hot. Closing the door behind me, I stripped off my clothes, leaving only my bra and underwear on, and climbed into bed.

Thomas

Chapter 4

"What the hell?" I said aloud as I was jarred awake.

"Are you haunting my dreams now too?" Lily slurred.

A strong whiff of alcohol assaulted me. It took me a minute to get my bearings straight. I had been hiding in my old room, trying to process things. I must have fallen asleep. The room was dark, and only a sliver of moonlight showed through the window.

I took another deep breath, trying to calm myself. I was flooded with the scent of her. *Mate,* my wolf cried happily. An arm was wrapped around my abdomen. A leg pinned mine as a head nuzzled into my neck. My whole body froze. What the hell was happening?

My wolf was content. Far more content than he had been since the moment I had lain eyes on Lily Westin. I turned and sniffed the top of her head. *Lily.* I wrapped my arms around her as my body responded to the realization that she was naked, draped across me. Further inspection found she was in her underwear. As my hand stroked down her backside to confirm that, she moaned softly.

I chanced a look down and she was staring up at me with big blue eyes sparkling in the moonlight.

"I don't want you in my dreams," she pouted, then squeezed me closer and lay her head on my chest. "Why would God curse me with you as my mate?"

Her words were slurred, and it was evident she was drunk, but she cut me to the core. I didn't know words could hurt so much.

Her muscles flexed around me. "Mmm, I do love the way

you smell."

Just like that, my world seemed to right itself. It freaked me out, and yet I couldn't have moved if I'd wanted to. Okay, so she had me pinned to the bed, but I also didn't want to.

She started snoring softly. I grinned down at the sight, closed my eyes, and went back to sleep. It was the most restful sleep I could ever remember. For once there wasn't any nightmares. I didn't toss and turn, and my mind wasn't buzzing with a million things I needed to do, or Pack issues I needed to address.

A miserable sounding groan woke me from a solid sleep. I wasn't the best morning person and lying there, surrounded by the most alluring smell ever, I didn't want to move. Lily stirred beside me as memories of the night before came back to me.

I knew the moment she realized she wasn't alone in bed. I didn't even need to open my eyes to see the shock and confusion on her face.

"Shit," she whispered, reaching for her head. "What happened?" She started to sit up, then flopped down on me. "Uh, what the hell? What did I do?"

I opened my eyes just in time for her hands to fly to her neck. My wolf stirred in excitement as she confirmed we hadn't bonded.

"Thomas," she said, smacking me without even really looking at me. "What are you doing in my bed?"

"Actually, you climbed into my bed," I said, my morning voice was deep and husky, and I saw her respond favorably to it when those big blues finally looked at me.

"I-I would never do that," she said, sounding surer than she felt. It surprised me that I knew that with certainty. I could just feel it. I didn't want to stop and consider what that meant.

"You came in drunk as a skunk and climbed in my bed. You had me pinned, leaving me no choice but to stay," I confessed.

Lily sat up and stretched. I'd be lying if I said I didn't enjoy the view. She looked over towards the door and frowned like it hurt to think so hard.

"Maddie told me my bags were in my room at the top of the stairs. Those are my bags, you idiot. What are you doing here?"

I ignored the verbal jab, though I felt its impact. "I didn't know you were staying in here. I swear. I came in to lay down for a bit and fell asleep."

She snapped her fingers like things were starting to click into place and turned on me. "You were hiding from Sydney. I saw you run into the house. And you don't even live here. She told me that last night."

"Shit, you talked to Sydney?" I said, feeling the walls of my world closing in on me.

"Yes, we went out and bonded over drinks," she said, and I wasn't sure anything would have surprised me more. Lily and Sydney together could not happen.

"Lily, please tell me you did not tell Sydney you are my mate," I said as patiently as possible, trying not to freak the hell out.

I saw tears prick her eyes and she jumped up and ran for the first door she saw, frantically motioning as she leaned down and puked in my closet.

"Great," I said aloud, getting out of bed and walking over to her. When the first wave finished wracking her body, I scooped her up and carried her to the next door over, which was the bathroom I sure hoped she had been looking for. I lifted the toilet seat as she cradled around it and threw up some more. Three more times and she began retching, her stomach seemingly emptied.

I took a wash cloth from the cabinet and turned the water on, leaving it till it ran warm. I flushed the toilet even though she was groaning and still hugging it, then sat on the floor behind her and pulled her carefully back against my chest. She was miserable and complacent. I gently washed her face and hands as her head leaned back against my chest.

The feeling of holding my mate in my arms, caring for her for the first time, was overwhelming. I breathed in her scent, but was greeted by the smell of vomit.

"Okay, you really need to shower, and brush your teeth. Jesus, what did you drink last night?"

"A fifth of Jack," she surprised me by confessing.

"Huh, that much to rid yourself of the idea of being my mate?"

"Yes," she confessed. "But I didn't need to worry. You already have a mate."

I hadn't expected her to answer, let alone feel like she slapped me across the face with her response.

"Come on, slugger. Shower time."

"I don't think I can stand. The room's still spinning, and my head is pounding. Can you make me a bath instead?"

"Sure," I said. I needed to put some space between us to clear my head, so I left her on the floor to go and draw her bath. When I looked back over, she was crawling out the door. I rolled my eyes, praying she didn't puke anywhere else. I knew I still had the closet to contend with.

She stumbled back in on two feet and over to the sink, quickly brushing her teeth and gargling with some mouthwash she must have had in her bag.

"I'm never drinking again," she swore, holding her head in pain.

"Come on, let's get you settled in the tub and if you promise not to drown while I'm gone, I'll get you something for that headache."

"Really?" she asked, looking at me like I was the only life preserver in middle of the sea.

I gulped. "Really. Now come on,"

She quickly removed her bra and panties and I tried to do the right thing and not look, but damn! This was Lily Westin. This was my true mate. And at the end of the day, I was still a red-blooded American male and she had the body of a goddess.

I helped her down into the hot water, telling myself to ignore the way her breasts brushed against my arm. She moaned in pleasure as she sank into the warmth of the bath and I knew I had to get out of there quickly, lest I do something we both would regret. Okay, so my only regret would really be in acting while I was fairly certain she was still drunk.

Once I knew she was settled, I headed downstairs and into the kitchen. It seemed everyone in the house was there.

"Thomas?" my mother said in surprise. "What are you doing here, sweetheart?"

"Slept over last night," I said honestly.

"Oh, you did? Where?" she asked.

"My old room."

Out of the corner of my eye I saw Liam flinch.

"But I told Lily to sleep in there," Maddie admitted.

"Yeah, I noticed," I said as I dug around in the cabinet where I knew Mom kept bottles of medicine, and finally found some aspirin. I also grabbed two bottles of water off the counter before squatting down to reach under the sink to acquire wipes, some carpet cleaner, and a trash bag.

Liam was shooting daggers at me and his hands were balled into fists at his side when I stood and faced him.

"Dude, that's my sister," he warned.

A shit-eating smirk crossed my face before I could rein it in. I wanted so badly to say, *Yeah, well, you're doing my sister, guess it's my turn to do yours,* but that was the cocky kid that still resided in me.

"Whatever you're thinking, stop," Patrick warned.

I smiled and shrugged. "Look, nothing happened," I admitted. "I mean it was like sleeping with a three ton heater on my chest, but nothing happened. She crawled into bed in the wee hours of morning and passed out."

"And you couldn't just move her and do the right thing by leaving?" Liam challenged. The look he shot me would have made a lesser man quake in his boots.

I didn't want to, I thought, but didn't confess. Instead, I said, "I was asleep when she came in, and it barely even registered till this morning." Yeah, that was a big fat lie.

"Where is she now?" Maddie asked.

"Taking a bath." As Liam started to lunge towards me and Patrick moved to hold him back, I held up the aspirin bottle and shook it. "Think what you want, but even I'm not that big of a douche."

Liam snorted, realizing I was telling him that she was hungover and I was trying to help. "To hear Lily talk you are," he jabbed, and I tried not to let the pain it caused me show.

"Is Aunt Lily okay?" Oscar asked, sounding concerned.

I knelt to his level. "She'll be fine. She just has a really bad headache and an upset tummy. We need to stay quiet so she can relax and she'll be good as new in no time."

"Promise?" he asked.

"I promise, Oscar."

He wrapped his arms around my neck and hugged me tight. "Thanks for taking care of her, Uncle Thomas."

I watched as the others all shared a look between them.

"I can take them up," Maddie offered.

"Thanks. You going to clean up the puke in my closet, too?"
I asked as I held up the cleaning supplies, and she scrunched her
nose up in disgust.

"I don't do puke," she admitted.

"I'll handle it," Liam said with a huff as he passed the baby
to my mom.

"Great," I said, trying not to let my disappointment show.
"I'll run home and get cleaned up then."

I headed for the front door. Liam was already at the top of the
stairs, but Maddie hung back.

"I know Lily was completely wasted last night, Thomas. It's
honestly not like her at all. I've never seen her have more than two
drinks at any one time. I'm not sure what's going on with her, but
thanks for taking care of her. I really appreciate it," she said,
surprising me when she hugged me.

I was the guy with the sharp comebacks, but this time I didn't
have one. I hugged my sister back. "It was nothing," I finally said as
I let her go. She started to climb the stairs to care for my mate. It
should have been me, but if it couldn't be, I was glad at least it was
her. "Mad?" She stopped and turned to look at me. "I'm really glad
you're home."

She had tears in her eyes as she nodded. I turned and quickly
walked out the door. I needed to get home, make a really strong cup
of coffee, then take a long cold shower, because the sight of Lily
naked in my tub was not an image I would forget anytime soon.

Lily

Chapter 5

What had I done? And why was Thomas being nice to me? It went against everything I knew about him and was only causing me further confusion, but I couldn't stop to think about it, because it just made my head hurt more. I soaked down a little deeper in the tub and tried to relax.

The door to the bathroom creaked open.

"I'm fine, still alive, as promised," I said, without bothering to open my eyes.

"Well, that's good news," Maddie said.

I smiled, still refusing to open my eye and gave a halfway nod towards the door.

"Rough night?" she asked.

"You could say that."

"Thomas said you could use this," she said, shaking a bottle.

I opened my eyes and sat up a little with a groan as the pounding in my head grew. She passed me a couple of aspirin and a bottle of water.

"Thanks, you're a lifesaver," I said, setting the bottle on the side of the tub and sinking back into the hot water.

"What were you thinking?" she asked, and there was a hint of laughter in her voice.

"Clearly, I wasn't."

"Did you really pass out on Thomas? I didn't even think you liked him."

I silently cursed the tingling sensation that shot up my spine just at the mention of his name. "For the record, I don't. He's a douche. I just climbed into bed and fell asleep. I didn't even realize he was there till this morning."

Lies, all lies. I had been acutely aware of my mate. *Not my mate, not my mate*, I reminded myself. His scent had stilled all my nerves and confusion of the day, and when his arm wrapped around me and held me tightly, I had sighed and relaxed into him . . . and fortunately passed out hard. If I hadn't, who knows what would have happened.

All I remembered was my body literally buzzing with excitement. Was it the whiskey? Or was it him? I had never been so turned on in my life as I was just before the world turned black around me. Would I have had sex with Thomas Collier? Would I have bonded with him? The thought made me retch.

"Easy there," Maddie warned. "You really did have a rough night, huh?" She sat down on the floor beside the tub. "Want to talk about it?"

"There's nothing to talk about. I guess my wolf was stressed from being in a new territory with so many people crowded around. I met a new friend and we went to the bar. I had a little too much to drink. That's it."

"A little?" Maddie laughed. I grimaced as I laughed with her.

"Jesus Lily!" Liam yelled from the bedroom. "I'm never doing that again. Next time you decide to get bombed and throw up a year's worth of food, you can clean it up yourself."

My eyes grew wide. "I threw up? I mean I remember throwing up, but in the toilet."

"Apparently you thought the closet was the bathroom first."

I covered my face with my hands and groaned again.

"Thomas was on his way up to deal with it when Liam went all growly and protective over you. Serves him right," Maddie said.

"I heard that," Liam complained.

He peeked his head in, around the door, looking a little pale. MC closed the curtain enough that it covered me. Not that I really cared.

"Your clothes are literally thrown all over the room, Lil. Tell me you did not sleep with Thomas," he demanded.

I snorted. "As if I'd remember." Yeah, I would definitely have remembered, but I was not going to tell my overprotective brother that. "Nothing happened, Liam."

"He had to have seen you naked. Your underwear and bra are in the bedroom, Lil."

I laughed. "So what, Liam? We're shifters. Everyone in Westin Pack has seen me naked a million times. Why do I care if Thomas Collier did, too?"

Oh, but I did care, and I hated that I did. There was an internal war going on. The good guys wanted to push Thomas away and have him never look my way again, and the bad guys had been fully aware of his reaction to my naked body and liked it. I didn't want to like it.

Liam scrubbed his face with his hands in frustration. "You are going to be the death of me, I swear."

"Relax," I told him. "He already has a mate." I wasn't a hundred percent sure if I was referring to myself, or Sydney.

"He does?" Maddie asked. "No one told me that."

I shrugged. "I think it's still in limbo."

"Who?"

"Sydney, the girl I was hanging out with last night," I spit out, a little too harshly, but MC was too excited and curious to notice.

"Wow. I'm so happy for him. Is she his true mate?" she asked.

"No," I admitted. Sydney was definitely not his one true mate. I sighed and dipped my head under the water, the pain finally subsiding. "Can you grab my toiletry bag for me? I think the meds are starting to kick in. I may even feel almost human again soon."

Maddie laughed. "Should we be worried then?" Hearing baby Sara starting to cry, she excused herself. "Holler if you need me."

I lay there for a few more minutes, trying not to think about everything happening to me. The warm water was soothing, but my body was still buzzing from the intimacy of sleeping on my mate. I chastised myself for even allowing that to happen, but I couldn't go back and change it. I only hoped I hadn't sent Thomas the wrong signals. I had no intentions of completing a bond with him. I still couldn't forgive how he'd given up on Madelyn, and I didn't think I ever could. If a man like that could give up on his own sister, what was stopping him from giving up on me?

I washed up and got out. There was a towel waiting for me on the counter. I grabbed it and dried off, before heading back into the bedroom to dress. Even the scent of puke and cleaner couldn't mask the smell of him. I lay down on the bed and was consumed by it. He seemed to be everywhere, yet, I knew without a doubt he was no longer in the house. He had left. He would always leave, because that's how he was. It's what he did in a crisis and I needed to safeguard my heart with that memory, because I could already feel the pull of the bond. It clouded my judgement and made me want things I consciously didn't want.

No one had ever mentioned that part of the bond. I felt like I had no control, like some pre-determined destiny was dragging me along against my will. It was not at all the wonderful elation I had romanticized about my entire life.

Sighing, I got up. I needed some fresh air.

Walking downstairs, I could hear voices in the back of the house. I ignored them and headed outside. Once the door closed behind me, I took in a deep breath. Somehow, the entire town smelled just a little like Thomas. He was a Collier—not just a Collier, but *the* Collier, future Pack Alpha, and I was in his territory, so of course it did, but it certainly wasn't helping my situation one bit.

I decided a little shopping therapy was in order. I headed back down to the main street of town. Collier was actually the name of the town as well, so most of the stores were Collier this or Collier that. The main street was Collier Street and there were two parallel roads that basically comprised the entire town. Zachary Street to the left, Thomas Street to the right.

I rolled my eyes, wondering if all Colliers were so conceited as to name everything after themselves. I had never really gotten that impression from Zach, but in Thomas's case I chose to believe it was true.

I passed the bar at the end of Collier Street before turning right. I shook my head when I read the sign above the door, "Collier Steakhouse and Tavern." I also passed a post office, a drug store, and an ice cream parlor that reminded me a lot of Cold Shack back home, but nothing really grabbed my attention.

Turning onto Thomas Street, I saw one shop in the middle of it all that was painted a bright, cheerful yellow. It made it stand out from the drab wood tones of all the other stores. I was immediately drawn to it, and clapped in excitement as I got close enough to see clothes and shoes in the window.

A bell chimed as I opened the door. I looked towards the back but didn't see anyone. Unconcerned, I set about shopping, spying a very cute leather jacket. I knew I had to have it. I snatched it off the rack, along with several shirts and a pair of my favorite jeans. I had to order them online or make a trip into the city to find them, and even then only my favorite little boutique carried them. I squealed in delight, unable to believe they had such amazing things in Collier, of all places.

My arms were loaded down with treasures as I made my way through the store.

"Hello?" I called out.

"Just a minute," a lady called from the back. Her voice was familiar. A moment later, Sydney Parker rounded the corner. She stopped and grinned at the sight of me.

"Oh, hey Sydney. You work here?"

"I own it actually. Wow, you want to try some of that on?"

I hesitated. I really didn't need to, but it sounded like fun. It wasn't like I had any place to be, and a women's clothing store was a safe Thomas-free zone.

"I'd love that," I said, surprised that I genuinely meant it.

For the next two hours I tried on nearly everything in the store. Syd was working on a new online catalog for her store and asked if I'd mind modeling some outfits for the webpage. I was happy to help, and we laughed and enjoyed a stress-free morning.

"How are you feeling?" she finally asked. "Last night was insane."

"I didn't do or say anything weird, did I?" I could clearly remember her tale of love and long-time affair with Thomas. I didn't think I had confessed that he was my true mate, and I hoped I hadn't growled at her or anything. I snorted at that thought. Only the bond would have me growling at anyone over him. I didn't even like him.

My wolf hated when I thought that, and images of waking up in his arms suddenly filled my head.

"No, you were fine. Amazingly cool for a drunk," she teased.

I rolled my eyes. "I don't even know why I did it. My wolf was just so agitated. Probably the foreign territory," I lied.

I was changing back into my clothes and had a pile stacked on the counter when the door chimed.

"Be with you in just a moment," Syd said, without even looking up. To me she asked, "Do you really want all this? You don't have to feel obligated. I really appreciate you modeling them for me though."

"Are you kidding? I can't get this in San Marco. I want it all."

She looked at me like I was insane. "Lily, there's over three thousand dollars worth of clothes here."

"Don't forget the shoes," I reminded her. "I'm wearing them out."

"You're serious?"

"I never joke about fashion," I told her honestly.

Her eyes went wide in shock, but her excitement could probably be felt throughout the town. I guessed she didn't get a lot of large purchases. She had already admitted most of her sales came through her online store.

"Hey, Tamara," Sydney said, finally addressing the woman that had come in. "This is Lily Westin." We said pleasant hellos. "What can I do for you?"

"Lynn's birthday is coming up and I know there's a shirt in here she's been drooling over. Would you happen to know which one?" the woman asked.

"Excuse me," Syd said to me. "I'll only be a minute." I watched her walk around the counter and pull a blue flowered print shirt off a shelf and show it to her. They spoke and then moved to check out. "Do you mind, Lily? It will only take a second to ring this up, and then I'll get you out of here."

"Oh sure, it's fine. I'm not in any hurry."

I wandered around, checking out some jewelry she had near the register. I saw lots of nice things, but nothing I had to have.

Once Tamara left, Syd turned to me and apologized as she started checking me out. Her eyes almost bugged out of her head when I didn't even flinch at the price. I didn't want to tell her she was underselling herself. I'd have paid way more for the same in the city.

I smiled as I handed over my little black card, and she seemed to hold her breath as she ran the transaction, relaxing only when the accepted confirmation came through.

She bagged up all my new treats and asked if I wanted help getting it all home. I laughed and confessed I was a professional bag-carrying shopper. We stood there chatting a little longer until the bell tinkled again, signaling a new customer.

"You're busy today. I'll get out of your hair. Thanks for everything," I told her.

It wasn't until I started to turn around that his scent hit me. He stared at me with a startled look that quickly turned paranoid as he looked back and forth between me and Sydney. Good. Let him suffer. The knowledge that he was there to see her and not me should have been a relief, not a punch in the gut. Still, I liked Sydney and didn't want to see her hurt. I squared up my shoulders and raised my chin to exit, forgetting how that posture made my boobs stand out until his gaze dropped to stare at them.

"Thomas," I said in a polite voice, as I struggled with the internal battle of my wolf demanding we make our claim on the man right there for Sydney to see, and I quickly exited the building. *Don't do anything stupid, Lily*, I told myself.

Thomas

Chapter 6

I had spent the morning alone at home trying to get a grip on this new reality where I not only stood a chance with Lily, but Mother Nature was going to see to it that we ended up together. Now that the shock was wearing off, the idea excited me. She was Lily freaking Westin, my mate. I wanted to scream it from the top of the roof.

Only one thing held me back . . . Sydney. How was I going to tell her about Lily? I worried about it all morning long, trying to work up the courage to talk to her. She had a right to know. It wasn't like it was in my power here. I wasn't choosing one over the other; that choice had been made for me. It was something every shifter sought after their entire lives, as natural as breathing. So why did it feel like I was cheating on Syd?

I finally mustered up the courage to go and talk to her. It wasn't like I could hide forever. Collier wasn't that big, and my wolf was already fighting me for dominance. It was only a matter of time before I did something stupid that would alert the entire Pack to that fact I had a mate. She deserved to hear it from me before something like that happened.

But when I opened the door, instead of the familiar fragrance of Sydney, I was smacked in the face with Lily's scent. It was everywhere, and it called to me on such a visceral level that it took every ounce of willpower not to act on it.

What the hell was Lily doing here?

I caught sight of her loaded down with more shopping bags

37

than I'd ever seen one person juggle. My instinct was to go to her and help, but then I saw Syd and froze. I looked back and forth between them. Lily nodded in acknowledgement and I could see my wolf happily wagging his tail as she said my name.

Once the door closed I jolted back to the present. I wasn't entirely out of my Lily trance with her scent so prominent in the room, but it was enough for me to begin to think clearly at least.

"Hey, babe," Sydney called. She came around the counter with a smile on her face.

I didn't want to do it. I didn't want to sit her down and have the talk and watch her heart break before my eyes. I knew it was coming. She knew me too well. She'd know anyway because she was about to kiss me and my wolf was already growling in my head. I swallowed hard.

"Syd, we need to talk." My serious tone stopped her in her tracks.

"Um, okay. Let me lock up and we can talk," she said hesitantly.

"Not here," I said, and she turned questioning eyes my way. I couldn't explain to her how the smell of my mate was too fresh and distracting for the conversation we were about to have. "Can you lock up for lunch?"

"Yeah, sure," she said with uncertainty.

She locked up the store and we walked to my car. I held the door open, noticing she hadn't tried to kiss me or even reach out to me. I hated that. Syd and I had been friends our entire lives. I had hurt her before, but she'd always been so forgiving and loving. She always took me back no matter how many times I strayed from her. It was common knowledge that we had looked to pursue bonding as compatible mates. We'd even gone through the Pack Council and received permission, but then word came of Maddie being alive. It had shaken me to my core and in the chaos that followed, we'd dropped the idea.

What would have happened if we'd gone through with it? I'd never met a compatible mate who'd later found his true mate, never even heard of such a thing. What happened then? Would I have even recognized Lily if my wolf had already bonded with Sydney's? Would Lily have spent her entire life alone, looking for me? I had never much considered such things, but given the circumstances it was all I could think of.

"What's wrong, Thomas?" she asked as I drove us out of town.

I looked over at her sadly. I didn't know how to begin.

"Is it Madelyn?" she asked, sounding concerned.

I shook my head but remained quiet until I came to a clearing and pulled into a field. It overlooked only a part of our vast open land. Cows were roaming the area. Sydney had always loved it. Would Lily? Could she truly be happy living in Collier?

I turned in my seat to face Sydney, took a deep breath, and closed my eyes.

"I met someone, Syd," I finally said.

When I opened my eyes, she was nodding and there were tears in her eyes. We had been here before. I could see on her face she thought I wasn't ready to commit, that I'd changed my mind about being her mate so I didn't have to settle down. That wasn't exactly the same thing this time.

"It's not like that," I told her. "I—shit, I don't know how to talk about this."

She was openly crying now. "Just tell me, Thomas. You've never sugarcoated it before. Why start now?"

"That's not fair, Syd. This isn't the same."

"It's not?" she asked, sounding pissed. I could feel the anger bubbling up from her. She wasn't one to lose her temper, and I had never seen her so furious. "Look around, Thomas. Same field, same story, just a new day. I can't believe I was dumb enough to fall for it again. Which story is it this time? Huh? 'I'm just not ready to settle down.' 'I'm seeing someone else.' 'Can't you see you're better off without me?' Which excuse is it this time, Thomas? God, I can't believe after all you've put me through over the years that we're right back here. I love you. Don't you know that by now? What do I have to do to show you that I'm worth your love, too?"

I hated hurting her. It was tearing me up inside, but I knew this time it was final.

"I love you too, Sydney, always have. You know that. I don't want to hurt you."

"Well, take a good look around then, because that's exactly what you're doing." We sat in silence for a long time. I felt her anger begin to subside and acceptance replace it. "I can't do this with you again," she sniffed.

"It's not the same this time. I met someone."

"She better be the one, because I'm not going through this with you again."

I nodded sadly. "She is," I whispered.

Sydney's head whipped around in surprise. "What? She is what?"

"The one, Syd. I met my one true mate."

Her mouth fell open and the tears stopped flowing. "You met your true mate?" she repeated. "When? Where? How?"

"Yesterday."

"Yesterday? But you were here yesterday. There's no one new around that you didn't already know. How? Who?"

I wasn't ready to share details with her. I just needed her to know.

"It doesn't matter. It just happened and I'm trying to deal with it."

"Deal with it? Thomas, she's your true mate, what's to deal with? That trumps everything else in life. The world stops and your sole focus is now her. Why are we even having this conversation?"

I laughed in spite of the situation. "You deserved to hear it from me first. I do love you, Sydney. Always have. This is just, bigger than me. Bigger than us. I don't really know how to explain it."

She nodded like she could understand, but I knew that without having gone through it, there was no way she truly understood.

"So, wow. That's a lot to take in"

"I know."

"Have you talked to her about it? Are you happy?"

"Not really, and I don't know. I think I'm still in shock," I admitted. I'd never lied to Sydney before and I didn't see the point in starting now.

"So." She grinned over at me. "Who is she? Am I going to have to take her down in the challenges, or will she actually make you happy?"

I laughed. I shouldn't have been surprised by her quick acceptance—it was just who she was—but it never ceased to amaze me how big her heart was.

"I dunno how to answer that yet."

"You don't know who she is?"

"Oh, no, I know exactly who she is. Will she make me happy? I don't know. I fear she has a great potential to hurt me. She's not exactly thrilled with the idea of being stuck with me as a mate."

"Then she's an idiot. Don't ever think anything else. You're an amazing man, Thomas, and you're going to be a great Alpha someday. Any girl, who doesn't understand that, isn't worth your time. I'll take her in the challenges."

I grinned. "You're jumping ahead of yourself there. I'm not exactly confident it'll go that far. I'm not her favorite person. When I say she isn't thrilled about being stuck with me, that is putting it nicely. She hates me, Syd. She thinks I'm the biggest douche on the planet."

Her hands flew to her mouth as she covered a high-pitched squeal. "Oh my gosh, oh my gosh, Lily Westin is your true mate?!!!"

"What?" I asked, shocked that she guessed correctly on the first try. "Why would you think that?"

"You said douche. You said she thinks you're a douche. That's a very specific word and one that Lily used regarding you on more than one occasion last night."

"Shit," I said. "I can't believe you hung out with her all night. And why the hell did you let her get so drunk?"

Sydney shrugged. "She said she had a rough day and really needed to get wasted. I'm guessing now that rough day started with you. Don't worry, I watched out for her."

"Syd, I'm so sorry," I started, but she cut me off.

"No, you aren't going to do that, Thomas. I like Lily. She certainly won't put up with your shit the way I have, but I can see it. She'll be good for you, and wow, your true mate. I won't say it doesn't hurt, but I can't stay mad about that."

"Shit. I never even said she was . . ."

"You didn't have to."

Lily

Chapter 7

I wandered around town some more before heading back to the Alpha house to drop off my purchases. The thought of Thomas and Sydney together was too much for me to handle. I kept picturing all sorts of compromising things they were up to, and my wolf was more agitated than ever. I needed to shift and go for a run, but everywhere I went still smelled like Thomas. What I really needed was to just get away. Leave it all behind. Sydney was a good person. If she wanted that douchebag then who was I to get in her way? She deserved to be happy.

With my mind made up, I made arrangements for a car to take me to the airport and I waited until the last second to let Liam, Patrick, and Maddie know. They knew something was wrong, but none of them dared to ask.

"You're sure about this? We're only here a week," Maddie reminded me.

"I'm sure. I think it's just being in a foreign territory and all the strange smells," I lied. "It has my wolf on edge, and I just need to go home."

"I can escort you back," Patrick offered.

"No, I'll be fine. I called Kyle and he's arranging for someone to pick me up when I arrive. It'll be fine," I assured them.

I hugged each of them goodbye, thanked Zach and Cora for their hospitality, and then I ran like the chicken shit I was. The further away from Collier I got the more I expected to relax. In truth, the more distance I put between myself and Thomas, the more miserable I felt.

By the time my plane landed, I was an emotional mess. As I exited the airport, Cole Anderson stood by a car waiting. Cole was Kyle's second Beta and he sat on our Pack Council. He ran a tattoo parlor in town and he was the sexiest thing to ever set foot in Westin Pack. I had been crushing on him for as long as I could remember.

Every time I saw him, or caught a whiff of his scent, my heart would race. He was my idea of the perfect man, and he wouldn't touch me with a ten-foot pole. Oh, he liked to flirt, and I knew he hadn't gotten his bad boy heartbreaker image for nothing, but he had always kept me at arm's length despite my best efforts to change his mind.

I had been barely seventeen the first time I got the nerve up to proposition him. He was older, more experienced, and I had told him that's what I needed for my first time. He wisely turned me down, though seventeen-year-old Lily had been devastated.

The pain of that rejection was only a fraction of what was settling in my heart the further from I got Collier. No—the further away from Thomas. I didn't want it. I didn't even want to admit it, but the pull towards him was far greater than I had been prepared for.

"Hey, gorgeous," Cole said, opening his arms to hug me. Any other time I'd run into them, ecstatic for even that brief moment of connection. Now, my wolf was already snarling in my head at even the thought of any other man, especially Cole, touching me.

"Hey," I said, walking past him and putting my suitcases in the trunk.

"Okay," he drawled out before kicking into action. "Let me get those."

I left him to deal with my bags and settled into the front seat. I put my earbuds in and tried to tune out the world as he got into the driver's seat and pulled out.

"Wow, Patrick warned me something was off. I can't believe he didn't see it," Cole said.

I took out my headphones and turned to stare at him. I hated knowing they were talking about me, and even more that they were worried. They wouldn't have warned him otherwise.

"What exactly can't you believe?" I asked, feigning disinterest.

"There's only one reason I know of that Lily Westin wouldn't flirt with me anywhere, anytime."

"Sorry to bruise your ego, Cole. I'm just not in the mood right now. Not even for you."

"So why are you running?" he asked.

"Running from what?"

"Your true mate. You met him, right? He's a Collier wolf? Maddie suspected, so Kyle asked me to come check it out. You've been flirting with me since you were just a little pup, and not even a second glance today? I knew the day would come eventually, but I always thought you'd be screaming it from the rooftops for the whole world to hear, not running away."

"Who said I'm running away? I'm just having a bad day and want to go home," I lied, refusing to address the issue he'd just thrown in my face.

"Did something happen? Did someone hurt you?" he asked, changing his tone and going all Alpha overprotective on me.

I rolled my eyes. "In case you hadn't noticed, I'm a big girl now, Cole. I can handle myself."

"Oh, I'm fully aware of what of a big girl you are now." He gave me a smoldering look that should have had my panties melting, but I felt nothing. He stared at me for a few minutes. "Nothing? You're going to give me a complex here."

I punched him in the arm. "Stop teasing me."

"Then talk to me."

I looked at him like he'd lost his mind. "We've never really talked. Why do you think I'd start now?"

"Fair enough. But you're going to tell me anyway."

"I'm not talking about it," I said, crossing my arms over my chest defiantly. We drove in silence for a moment longer. I couldn't stand the silence and the lack of sexual tension between us was starting to freak me out. "You'd never understand anyway," I blurted out.

"Try me," he said. "You might be surprised."

I snorted. "Like you've ever dealt with a true mate before."

Cole pulled over on the side of the road and stopped the car. He turned in his seat and looked at me. "Yeah, I have, actually."

"Wh-what? You don't have a mate."

"I did once," he said, and I could see the pain in his eyes. "It's not something I talk about, Lily. Only two other people in this world even know about it."

"You ran from your one true mate?" I asked in astonishment.

"No, I didn't. She ran from me."

I felt his pain, and Thomas immediately flashed in my mind.

"When?" I asked.

"It was a long time ago."

"Does the pain get any easier?"

"You really want me to answer that honestly? 'Cause, no, I've never fully gotten over it."

"But you've never bonded either. Maybe it would help?" I offered.

"The thing is Lily, once you find your one true mate all others pale in comparison. Look at me. It's no secret you've always had a thing for me. I've never acted on it because I always knew you'd find your true mate someday and I didn't want to get in the way of that. You've always looked at me with stars in your eyes, gorgeous. Right now, there's nothing but sadness there."

"I don't want him, Cole. Anyone but him. Why did it have to be him?" All the confusion, pain, and heartbreak hit me full force, and I sat there and cried. Cole pulled me into his arms and I couldn't stop the growl that escaped. He laughed it off and continued to hold me as I cried.

"He's your true mate, Lily and you know what your mom says, God doesn't make mistakes choosing mates."

"But he did this time," I cried.

He let me have my cry and didn't speak again until I pulled away and wiped my face. I knew I must look awful, probably with black mascara running down my face, but I didn't care. I needed to cry, to mourn my idea of what my true mate should have been.

"Better?" he asked. I nodded. "Look, I don't want to upset you any further, but can I ask you something?" I nodded again. "Did you break the bond before you ran?"

"No. I didn't want to face him. He already found a compatible mate, Cole. He'll be fine." I knew I needed to truly believe that.

"He won't, Lil. You don't have to tell me who he is, but no one deserves to be left in limbo like that. I need you to understand that I've never been able to fully move on, because she never broke the bond. She chose someone else and denied our bond, but it was never broken, and I have to live with that. I don't care how disappointed you are in your mate, no one deserves that. It's no way to live."

"What? How do you break a bond? He may be a douche, but I don't hate him enough to make him suffer like that," I admitted, and realized I truly did mean it.

Cole was in the process of pulling out onto the road when he stilled and put it back in park, turning to look at me.

"Douche? Lily there's only one person in this world I've ever heard you call that. Are you telling me . . .?"

I cut him off. "Don't say it!"

"Thomas Collier is your true mate?"

"Ahh, don't say it! Somehow hearing it aloud just makes it more real. I don't want it to be real," I whined.

Cole stared at me and then burst out laughing. "I'm sorry. That's just priceless. As much time as you've spent at Collier all these years, how are you just finding this out?"

"He's always been away. I would visit for Maddie's vigil every summer, and he'd always make some excuse not to be there. Before yesterday I hadn't seen him since before she disappeared. We were just kids." I buried my face in my hands, knowing it was turning all shades of red.

"Wow. How'd he take the news?"

"I don't know, we didn't exactly talk about it."

"What? Between getting plastered at the bar last night and running away today, you didn't stop to talk to him?"

I knew he was only trying to lighten my mood, but I punched him in the arm anyway. It was like hitting a brick wall, but still satisfying. "Shut up. And seriously? It's not enough that there is no privacy in Westin Pack, must it filter over to everywhere I go?"

"When you act so out of character? Yup, it's talked about. Not like gossip, beautiful, just but there's a lot of people who worry and care about you."

He was biting back a smirk and I hit him again.

"They told you I slept on him, didn't they?"

He laughed a deep belly laugh. "And yet, no one suspected him."

I groaned.

"Are you sure this is what you want? I can turn around and stick your pretty little butt back on a plane," he offered.

"I know that's the right thing to do. And I know I need to break the bond and not leave us both in limbo, but I don't know if I can. Would you come with me?"

He gave me a haunted look. "Afraid not, gorgeous. Patrick's already there, and one of us Betas stays home, always."

"I know, but it didn't hurt to ask anyway."

"It'll eat you alive if you don't deal with this. Trust me on that, Lily."

Thomas
Chapter 8

Talking to Sydney had been easier than I thought. At the end of the day, we were still friends and that meant a lot to me. After talking with her I knew I had my work cut out for me where Lily was concerned, but I also knew I had the bond on my side. Westin wolves followed their hearts. They had more true mates than any other pack because it was important to them. I had to hold on to the hope that it was important to my mate, too.

I grinned just thinking of Lily. She'd come around. I truly believed that. I'd just have to prove to her I wasn't entirely the douchebag she seemed to think I was.

After dropping Syd back off at her store, I headed straight for my parents' house. There was a flurry of activity going on.

"Hey, Mom, what's up?" I asked, bypassing the commotion and heading for the kitchen. I had skipped lunch, anxious about the talk with Syd, and was suddenly starving.

"Hi, sweetie. Can I get you something to eat?" Mom asked.

"I'll never turn down your cooking," I said, kissing her cheek.

Liam and Madelyn walked into the room.

"I just can't believe she took off like that," Liam said.

"Oh, hey, Thomas." Madelyn acknowledged me while ignoring him.

"Did she make it home safely?" Mom asked, but I didn't know to who they were talking about.

"Yes. I got a call a few minutes ago that she had landed safely and one of our Betas picked her up at the airport," Liam said.

"Who?" I asked.

"Lily. Something was up with her, but she wouldn't talk about it. Said her wolf was agitated in Collier territory, so she went back to San Marco," Madelyn told me, and I felt like my entire world was crashing in around me. "I'm just worried about her. She hadn't been acting like herself since we arrived."

I tried not to growl or show my anger. She'd left? I knew I wasn't her idea of the perfect mate, but I was still her one true mate. How could she just leave? Just the thought of her gone caused a physical pain in my chest. I had to get out of there.

Without a word to the others I left, walking out the back door of the house. The second I was outside, I stripped and shifted. Sprinting, I ran for the woods on all fours. With the wind in my fur, I gave a little more control over to my wolf, until he immediately turned and tried to run back to the house in search of more information that would lead us to the woman who was haunting us both.

In a battle for dominance, I won. I always won, but my wolf felt stronger and more stubborn this time. He was very unhappy about our mate leaving. It was clear to me that Lily wasn't ready for us, and the best thing I could do was give her some space, no matter how much my instincts screamed to turn around, drop everything, and go after her.

I tried to think of anything but Lily. My thoughts turned to my sister. She was home, and she legitimately had this whole family thing going on. Seeing Oscar and how big he was freaked me the hell out. It was like I had heard of him and a part of my brain knew he existed, but I was having trouble reconciling the eight-year-old as my nephew. Still, he seemed like a good kid and I had no doubt Maddie was a great mom.

Mom? She was ten months older than me. That was it. We were essentially the same age. They used to call us Irish twins, but seeing her now, she seemed years ahead of me. I hadn't even begun to figure out my life and here she was living hers. The fact that she had done it without all of us hurt, but I knew I'd have to get over it. Mom and Dad were so excited to have her back. It was all they had talked about for months, and that had only made my resentment worse. I didn't want to feel that way, but I couldn't help it.

I saw sparks of my sister still there, and I was trying to put on a good face for Mom, but I still wasn't ready to completely forgive her.

My mind drifted back to Lily. I had been shocked at the realization she was my mate, but holding her and caring for her had felt so right, more right than anything ever had. Now she was gone. I still had to deal with my anger and disappointment with my sister, but now I had this anger, hurt, and disappointment concerning Lily. How could she just leave? My emotions were all over the place, and I was not a man used to dealing with this kind of shit.

Slowing my pace, I came to the river that ran the length of Collier territory. It was one of my favorite places on Earth. I shifted and walked over to sit on a large boulder looking out across the water. Whenever I had a problem to sort out or just needed to think and gain a new perspective, I'd end up here.

As future Alpha of Collier, I had a lot riding on my shoulders. The expectations alone would kill a lesser man. I had done my rebellion and come to terms with my position in the Pack. We were largely a farming community, and I took pride in that. My father had moved us from crop farming into cattle ranching. It suited me and I loved riding horses out into the valley to wrangle our cattle. Occasionally I would go in my fur. It spooked the cows at first, but the animals had grown accustomed to it over the years. The wolves did a great job of herding them, and I loved to run in the open fields. It was a simpler life than other packs led. Hard-working folks made Collier Pack strong. I didn't think Lily could possibly be a practical match for me because of that. She wasn't exactly simple, leaving me torn on what to do next.

I laughed. "Why?" I asked aloud. Lily Westin was no rancher's mate. She came from Westin Pack, where they had more money than God himself. While I loved the idea of taking this beautiful girl I'd terrorized much of my young life as my mate—I mean, who wouldn't?—I was also realistic enough to know that she was not cut out for a Collier life. Maybe her leaving was doing us both a favor, but it didn't stop the pain of rejection pulsating through my body.

My wolf growled in my head, angry at my thinking. He wanted our mate, period, end of story. Westins were well known for seeking out their true mates. They felt it made them stronger. My parents were true mates. I couldn't really argue the theory, but Colliers tended to keep to themselves, so compatible mates were more of the norm. It was rare for a Collier wolf to find his one true mate.

With that in mind, Sydney had seemed like a good, strong match for me, but now that I had caught Lily's scent, I knew I could never settle for less. I loved Sydney, but it wasn't enough. The pull of the bond between true mates was just too strong. I was glad Syd had taken the news well, but it didn't make it any less difficult. I hated seeing her hurt and crying, even if she was happy for me. How happy would she be when she heard Lily had rejected me by leaving? If Lily truly rejected me, would Syd take me back?

My wolf snarled and growled at the thought. No, it was too late. It would be Lily or no one for me. My natural instincts told me to go after her and enjoy every second of the chase, yet the ache in my chest made me stubbornly want to stay put and pray to God that she felt it too and came back to me.

I wasn't sure how long I had been sitting out there, sorting through my feelings and shit that day, but I eventually went home and threw myself into work. I left immediately on a cattle drive and for three days I worked myself to the bone. Clay and Austin had made the run with me and quickly learned that it was in their best interest to just stay out of my way.

The second I came home, I checked in at the Alpha house. I knew immediately Lily wasn't there. I don't know why I had even let myself hope she might be, but the realization that she hadn't come back, that she wasn't hurting as much as I was, both angered and terrified me.

The truth of the matter was that Lily was now in Westin territory. I couldn't even go to her without first getting permission from her brother, of all people.

Being out on the range and really having time to consider all my options made me realize one thing: our mating bond had already begun. That's just how it worked for true mates. I wasn't going to break that bond, only Lily could do that, but there was no way in hell I could just live in limbo like this for the rest of my life. It was a living hell. Something had to give.

I knew Maddie and Liam would be in town for another week.

I also knew that everyone expected me to run away from them. Though they were wrong, I knew I could use it to my advantage. I had never run away from Madelyn's vigils because I hated my sister and didn't want to support her, no matter how others assessed it. I did it for self-preservation. All signs said she was dead, and I couldn't live with the constant hope that maybe she wasn't. Maybe that was wrong of me, but that didn't mean it wasn't the best option I could live with while she was away.

I had been hurt, angry and I didn't want to believe Maddie was capable of being alive while the rest of us waited around not knowing anything. My mind flickered back to Lily. That's the same feeling she was leaving me stuck in. I wasn't going through that uncertainty again.

My mind made up, I headed down to my father's office. I entered and closed the door behind me. Someday that office would be mine, but it wasn't yet and made me feel like an intruder being there without Dad around.

I double checked to make sure his dampener was on. This was not a conversation I wanted anyone to overhear, especially not Maddie and Liam, who I knew were in the house.

Dad had the number on speed dial, as he did for all the Alphas of Collier's closest five packs. I hit the one labeled Kyle Westin and waited with bated breath.

"Zach," Kyle answered, sounding like he had a smile on his face. Collier and Westin packs had always been close. Would they still be when I confessed I was his sister's one true mate?

"Hey, Kyle, it's Thomas actually."

"Thomas? Good to hear from you, man. I hope everything's okay. Your father's well?"

"Yes, this isn't a pack call. It's personal."

I could hear him move around in his office and then settle before speaking again. "Alright, you have my undivided attention. It's not Maddie or Liam, right? Oscar and Sara are okay?"

He sounded nervous and concerned. I liked that about Kyle. He was a strong Alpha, not someone even I'd be dumb enough to cross, but he had compassion too, and it was obvious how much he cared for his family and his pack.

"They're all fine, I promise. This has to do with your sister."

He let out a sharp breath. "What did Lily do?"

"What?"

"Look, you said Maddie was fine. I know it can't be Elise, because she's been here working her butt off staffing a new project Liam dropped on her before leaving. To the best of my knowledge, you've never met Jenna, and I just spoke with Chase this morning so if there was a problem he'd have told me. That leaves Lily. Look, whatever it is, I can fix it."

I wanted to laugh at his assumption that Lily had done something wrong, like he was used to her getting in trouble. I considered that for a moment. Was he used to Lily getting herself in trouble?

"Thomas, you there? Just give it to me straight. How bad is it? I know she was only there a short time. She won't even talk to MC about it." I smiled at the affection he used. Only the Westins had ever called Maddie that. "I know she got pretty drunk while there. Tell me she didn't do something stupid. Is that why she ran home with her tail between her legs? She's been avoiding me and nearly everyone else since she got home. Best of my knowledge, she's only really talked to Cole Anderson about it, and he advised I wait until she was ready to tell me herself. So how bad are we talking here?"

I bit back a growl at the thought of her discussing our bond with another man. I knew who Cole Anderson was, and that made it even worse. The possessiveness that gripped me was all consuming. I had to get through this call and get to my mate soon or I was going to lose it.

"It's really not what you think, Kyle," I assured him, still stalling. How do you tell an Alpha as strong as Kyle Westin that you were mated to his sister?

He blew out another breath. "Is this about her crawling into bed with you? Yeah, Liam told me. He wasn't happy and I assume he spoke to her about it already. I'm really sorry about that. She gets, well, flirty and touchy-feely when she's drinking. Shit," he said, more to himself than to me. "Of all the people, she had to pick an Alpha heir. I'm so sorry, man."

I growled at the insinuation that my mate would crawl into bed with just anyone because she was drunk. Despite all her bravado, and Kyle's assumptions, I knew for a fact Lily was as pure as the day she was born. It wasn't exactly like there was some special smell to a virgin, though our wolves could often sense it, heightened by the bond, and I knew with certainty that Lily wasn't as wild as she might act.

"Uh, Thomas?" Kyle asked with a hint of aggression in his voice. Shit, I had to tone it down.

"It wasn't like that, Kyle. I don't even know how to say this, but she freaked out and took off, because—because I'm her mate." I held my breath and waited. Just like with telling Sydney, there was a weight lifted off my shoulders just speaking it aloud.

Nothing but silence on the end of the phone.

"Come again?" he finally said.

"Lily's my true mate, Kyle. It wasn't like I was her favorite person to begin with, but I had been in the process of settling down with a compatible mate, who, as my luck would have it, she befriended. I know she knows about it, but she left before I could talk to her about it. I've tried to put her out of my mind, but I can't. I just can't. And now she's back in your territory, so I can't just pack up and go after her, unless you give me permission to enter your territory."

"And that's why you're calling?"

"Yes."

"Because you mated my baby sister?"

I cringed. "Yes."

I expected him to be angry. I was prepared for him to tell me no. What I wasn't expecting was the loud, full belly laugh coming through the phone.

"I'm sorry, you're gonna have to give me a minute to catch my breath," he finally said.

"Kyle, what's wrong?" I heard a female ask through the phone, and guessed it was his mate, Kelsey.

"Lily has found her mate. That's what she's running from," he told the woman.

"What? Who?" she asked.

"Thomas Collier."

"Thomas? Maddie's brother?"

"Yup," Kyle said, as I sat there listening to their conversation.

"The douchebag?" she sort of whispered.

"That's the one, Kels. The one and only," Kyle confessed. I wasn't sure how I felt about that.

"Oh, this is rich! Is he coming for her?" Kelsey asked.

"Yes, he is," Kyle confirmed. "Hey, Thomas?"

"Yeah," I said, my heart lifting just a little.

"Let me know if you need a lift from the airport. I'll happily pick you up myself. You're more than welcome on Westin land."

Lily

Chapter 9

I had been wallowing for days. The scary part was that with distance, I wondered what was really so bad about Thomas. *No, no, no*, I couldn't think like that. I knew all the reasons I had left. They had been a mantra in my head, but it didn't stop the physical pain or the emptiness in my heart. Why didn't anyone warn me about this part of the bond?

Since my return to San Marco I'd mostly locked myself up in the room. I couldn't help thinking, with disgust, how I had criticized Elise for doing the same thing. I'd called her a chicken for not facing her mate. I kept waiting for her to burst through the door to laugh in my face, but I hadn't told her or anyone, aside from Cole, that I had found my true mate.

Today was the day I returned to the real world, no matter how hard it was or how much it hurt. I didn't understand how I could physically ache for someone I hated. It didn't make sense to me how that douchebag had weaseled into my heart. *No, no, no.* This couldn't be love. Hearts aren't involved here, it's the physical connection caused by the bond and nothing more. In time it would lessen.

I dragged myself from bed, cringing at my own funk. It was bad enough that I didn't remember the last time I'd showered. I made quick work to rectify the situation, taking extra care in applying my makeup and picking out my outfit.

I was heading over to Cole's tattoo shop for my first ink. It was exciting. In the days since leaving Collier, I had spent a lot of time with Cole. He'd opened up and told me about his past. He had also told me about the therapy in tattoos as he'd shown me each one and explained me the story behind it. All but one, at least. I was determined to get to the bottom of that one, but he could be a tough nut to crack when he dug his feet in. I already suspected it had something to do with his mate.

I grinned and shook my head. Cole Anderson had a true mate who had rejected him. Nothing could have been more shocking. I cringed at the realization that there must be plenty of eligible females that would think the same thing of Thomas Collier.

I sighed. The purpose of today was rejuvenation. A cleansing of sorts. Cole had made it painfully clear that I couldn't just push Thomas out of my mind and ignore the situation. I knew from the misery I was experiencing that he was telling the truth. Eventually I'd have to deal with it, but today I would grieve the loss of a true mate. The tattoo I was getting represented that grief. With it permanently in place as a reminder, I would face Thomas and officially break the bond so he would be free to mate Sydney. I needed to be the one to break it, because I wasn't one hundred percent certain he would, and because I worried it might destroy me entirely if he did.

I swung into the kitchen and grabbed a piece of toast that just popped up before Mom could get to it. She started to scold me, but took notice of my appearance and the fact I no longer stank, and smiled.

"Much better," Mom said. "Now where is my beautiful girl off to today?"

"Cole's. I'm getting a tattoo," I confessed, even though I knew it caused her to snarl just a little.

Mom threw her hands up in the air and shook her head. "I don't even want to know."

I hugged her and headed out to my car. The drive to town was far too short, and nervous butterflies took flight in my stomach. I didn't like needles or pain, but Cole had told me he'd gotten most of his tattoos after his mate's rejection because he had been equal parts numb and miserable. The pain of the needles had shown him life again, made him feel something other than the pain and loss of the bond. He'd admitted he'd gotten a little addicted to it for a while.

I understood the pain and numbness he had described. Mine

was also combined with anger. I was angry that of all the wolves in the world, heck of all the shifters in the world, even of all the men in the world, my true mate had to be him. Him! The one person I had vowed to hate forever.

The bell over the door of the shop jingled when I entered.

"Cole? You here?" I yelled.

Giggling came from down the hall and my senses went on high alert. The whole place smelled like sex. I shook my head in disgust. A perky blonde with just-got-laid hair appeared in the doorway. She turned and wiggled her fingers. "Call me later," she said before noticing me for the first time with a look of pure hatred, and then left.

"Human? Really?" I said as the door closed behind her.

"Much less complicated," Cole said in a deep voice from behind me.

I shook my head. "You're a manwhore."

He shrugged and gave me a lazy smile that should have had me wet between my legs. I frowned and sighed. Nothing.

"How long do you think I'm going to remain entirely unaffected by you?" I asked him.

He gave me a sad smile. "Probably for a really long time, Lil, especially if you don't go back and deal with it."

"But I don't want to deal with it. I just want it to go away," I whined, even knowing I sounded like a bratty child.

"I know, gorgeous, but it just doesn't work that way. Now come on, are we still doing this or what?" he asked.

"Yeah, I'm ready."

"Great." He gave me a sultry look. "Shirt off, bra off."

I laughed. "So you have any idea how long I've waited to hear *the* Cole Anderson tell me that?" I turned away from him before I caught myself. Ugh, the bond worked in crazy ways. I wasn't shy about my body. I didn't ever turn around and cover myself, yet I had, and I knew it was because Thomas wouldn't like another man seeing me naked, not with the bond so new and fresh.

"Argh, why do I even care?" I said, more to myself than Cole.

"You can't help it. Best advice you ever gave anyone was don't fight it. So why are you?" he asked as he directed me to a chair to lie down. I did, with my back to him, laying on my side. He reached down and pulled my right arm up and over my head. I braced for the spark that had always shot through me from his touch, even knowing it wasn't coming.

"Well, come on, spill it. Why are you fighting your bond so hard? Is it just because of who he is? Are you worried about being a Pack Mother?"

"What? No. Why would that bother me?"

"I don't know. I mean, I get he's been a bit of a douchebag in the past, but did you even stop to give him a chance to explain why?"

"And why would I do that? Actions speak louder than words, and his spoke volumes."

"You don't really know what he's been through, Lily. Aren't you even the slightest bit curious?"

"No," I said stubbornly.

He started rubbing my skin down with alcohol as he continued to talk.

"So that's it then?"

"What do you want me to say Cole? He didn't stop me from leaving. He hasn't bothered to track me down. Clearly this is what he wants, too." The pain of that realization was overwhelming, and I hoped Cole would get a move on it so I could get lost in the physical pain of the needle like he'd described to me.

"You didn't exactly give him a chance to stop you, and you ran home to Westin territory so he couldn't follow you without telling your brother about the bond," Cole pointed out.

I rolled back to look up at him. "Whose side are you on, anyway?"

"I'm not on anyone's side here, Lily. Just a minute," Cole yelled as the front door bell chimed. "Now lie back down and be a good girl. You have to stay still or I will hurt you," he said before turning to see to his customer out front.

An aggressive, low guttural growl had Cole frozen in place. I couldn't see around him.

"Lily, just stay calm," Cole said in what I thought was meant to be a calming voice.

"What the hell is going on?" Kyle's voice boomed down the hallway.

I turned and pushed Cole aside, just in time to see Thomas

standing in the doorway. His hands were clenched into fists at his sides. His face was contorted in anger and his wolf was very close to the surface, enough that he was already sprouting fur on his hands and neck.

"Shit. Thomas, calm down," Kyle said, and I felt his Alpha power thick in the air.

All it appeared to do was make Thomas even angrier. His eyes were glued on Cole with a look of death gleaming behind them. I had no doubt Thomas was seeing red, and while it infuriated me, it excited my inner wolf.

"Lily, I can't control him. You have to calm him down," Kyle ordered. "His wolf's too strong, it won't surrender to mine."

I jumped from the table, forgetting I wasn't wearing a shirt until his wild eyes swept over my body and another growl erupted from him.

"Jesus. What are you doing?" Kyle muttered under his breath.

"Thomas, I'm right here. I'm fine. What the hell am I supposed to do, Kyle?"

"Go to him."

"Kyle's right. You have to touch him; his wolf needs to know you're okay. I really don't want to fight a mating Alpha male, Lily. Please. Just do it," Cole said, his eyes never leaving Thomas's as the smell of testosterone cranked up another notch in the room.

I walked up to him and ran my hands down his arms. "Thomas, look at me. Look at me," I said, a little gentler, and when my hand touched his cheek he finally turned. When our eyes met, he relaxed a little and leaned into my hand. I was mesmerized by his power, and my own to control him.

"I'm okay," I told him.

Strong arms wrapped around me and crushed me to him. With our bodies intimately touching all over, he finally relaxed. As he did, Kyle's and Cole's wolves backed down too, significantly lowering the aggression in the room.

Thomas shook beneath my arms as I wrapped them around him and squeezed him tightly. My body relaxed for the first time since I'd woken up next to him the morning after our bond had showed. I didn't want to think about what it meant.

When his heart rate started slowly returning to normal, he

released me, but only long enough to remove his jacket and wrap it around me. We were still standing in the doorway so Cole was trapped in the room and Kyle just behind in the hallway. Kyle's worried eyes sought out mine. I felt his disappointment and hated it.

I couldn't let myself think about what could have happened, all because I was too chicken to face my mate.

"I'm sorry," Thomas finally said in a soft but gruff voice. I could tell he was back in control, though. "I've never lost control like that before."

Kyle clapped a hand on his back. "Welcome to the wonderful world of mating."

I choked on my own spit and started coughing. When I finally caught my breath, I stared into Thomas's eyes. "You told him?" I shrieked.

Cole started laughing from behind me.

"How else was I going to get permission to come after you?" Thomas admitted with a grin. Still staring at him, I noticed it was just a little crooked. How had I never seen that before?

Before the realization of what he said fully sank in, Kyle was talking again.

"What are you even doing here, Lil? The whole place smells like sex, and you're sprawled out half naked with Cole Anderson. I know you've always had a thing for him, but seriously, you choose now to act on it?"

I knew Kyle was frustrated and not thinking clearly, and when Thomas started growling again he knew he needed to rein it in, too. Talking candidly to me was one thing, but he was only agitating Thomas further.

I snorted and rubbed his back. "Simmer down. Nothing happened. I was getting a tattoo, if you guys must know, hence the lack of shirt. And the sex smell, well you'll have to discuss that with your human-loving manwhore of a Beta over there."

I chanced a look back at Cole, but he just grinned and shrugged as he turned to start putting the stuff away.

I pouted. "No tattoo?"

"Not today, gorgeous. I think this place has seen enough action for one day. Kyle, how about a beer?"

"You're ditching me?" I asked, suddenly panicking at the thought of being alone with Thomas.

"Take your own advice on this one," Cole recommended as Thomas moved out of the way and let him pass.

"Good luck," Kyle called out as they left.

"Thanks," I hollered back.

"Oh, he wasn't talking to you," Cole said, laughing.

"Traitors!" I yelled behind them, nervous when the door chimed shut behind them, leaving me all alone with Thomas.

The last time I'd been alone with him I was severely hung over, maybe still a little drunk, which meant this was the first time I was thinking clearly and truly alone with Thomas since we were kids. And I was standing way too close. The heat from his body radiated off him, and I was fully aware of every part still pressed against me. It made my body warm. I took a step back, putting space between us.

"You ran away," he challenged. I had expected we'd need to have the talk, but I didn't think it would be quite so soon.

"I did," I said. Why deny it?

"Why?"

"Seriously? You're going to ask me that? You have a mate already, Thomas, or have you forgotten?" I said sarcastically, even knowing that was the least of my concerns regarding this man before me.

"That's not fair, Lily. What? You want me to apologize. Okay, I'm sorry," he said.

"Wait, what? What are you sorry for?"

"I'm sorry that I went through the compatibility testing with Syd. I'm sorry I didn't have enough faith to wait for you. I'm sorry I tormented you as a kid, and for whatever else I've done to give me the title of biggest douchebag on the planet."

I grimaced. "You know about that?"

"Yeah, well, your family seems to take great humor in letting me know it. Look, I get you aren't happy with this situation, but the truth is, you don't even know me. We haven't seen each other since we were kids, and you can hardly fault me for tagging along with you and Maddie. You were the hottest girl at camp and I was the lucky kid with the connections to be close to you. Of course I took advantage of that."

"What are you talking about? You really think you earned biggest douchebag title just because you and all your friends had a crush on me and your sister at camp for a few summers?"

"I don't know, Lily. I've been wracking my brain trying to figure that out, because you don't know me, and I don't know you. And I don't know how to do this mating stuff. If I did, I probably would have already been mated to Syd, but I'm not, and since the moment I saw you standing there staring at me, I knew I never could. She's one of my best friends. She's happy for me. She's happy for us."

"You told her?" I asked, wondering if there was anyone he hadn't told already.

"I had to. I'm sorry if that bothers you, but I had to do the right thing. You were busy leaving town while I did it."

Guilt punched me in the gut. I had been a chicken while he was clearing up his past to make room for me. And he had come. He was here, for me.

"What do you want, Thomas?"

"I want you to come home."

"I am home," I said, cutting him off in a knee-jerk reaction. I closed my eyes and took a deep breath. "Sorry. Continue."

"I want you to come back to Collier with me. I've seen what happens with unresolved true mates, so unless you're telling me right now that you're breaking the bond without even giving us a chance, then I'm asking you to come back with me. Maddie and Liam leave in one week. Give us that time to get to know each other, before you make your final decision, because make no mistake, Lily, it is your decision."

"You do have a choice in this," I pointed out sensibly.

"No, I don't. My heart already knows where it belongs."

Huh? How do you come back from that one? I wondered.

"One week, slugger. That's all I'm asking. If at that time I'm still the biggest douche on the planet, I'll mutually break the bond and you'll be free of me forever."

My heart rose into my throat, and I thought I might be sick just from considering breaking the bond. I stared at him, searching his eyes for some clue he was the man I thought he was. I started to protest, but Cole's words came back to me. *Take your own advice for once.*

"Okay," I whispered.

"Okay to what?" he asked.

"All of it. I'll go back with you." I swallowed hard. "I'd like to get to know you before making such a monumental decision."

He grinned, and I knew that crooked smile was about the sexiest thing I'd ever seen.

Thomas
Chapter 10

My body was still shaking from the reality of what had happened. I was calming under Lily's touch, but my wolf was still on edge. The fact that she had agreed to go back home with me and give us a chance had me elated, and my wolf was slowly finding contentment even while still on full alert.

I had heard about mating males losing it, but never in a million years had I thought it could happen to me. I shuddered and tried to push it all from my mind.

"We have to go by the house before leaving. I need to explain things to my parents and pack," she said softly. A part of her looked defeated and it worried me. She had agreed too quickly and too easily.

"Are you okay?" I asked, sincerely concerned.

She looked at me and smiled. "I'm fine."

She surprised me further when she reached over and took my hand, linking our fingers together.

"Sorry. I don't mean to send mixed singles. And I did mean it when I said I would give it a try. It's just that my wolf is still edgy, and it helps her to touch you."

I smiled and squeezed her hand. I didn't want to admit just how happy such a small gesture made me feel.

"It helps mine, too," I admitted instead.

She led me to a car and let go of our hands as she walked around to the driver's side. We sat in silence as she drove us to the Alpha house, then parked and walked in unannounced. Logically I knew that was normal, but it felt a little odd for me being a visiting Alpha-heir.

"Come on," she encouraged as if sensing my hesitation.

"Mom?" she yelled when we entered.

"Kitchen," the woman returned.

As we walked through the living room I didn't even noticed the dark-haired woman sitting on the couch until she spoke.

"Thomas Collier?" she asked.

"Jesus, E, you scared me half to death. I didn't see you there," Lily said, and I noticed she was blushing. "Thomas, this is my sister, Elise."

Elise bit back a grin as she said hello.

Lily walked into the kitchen, returning with her mom, who eyed me suspiciously.

"Hello, Thomas."

"Hi, Mrs. Westin," I said, feeling like an awkward little boy again.

"It's Mary," she corrected.

Another woman came into the room, her belly protruding with child. Lily wrapped her arms around her and I stared, envisioning her swollen with my child. I would never have pegged Lily Westin as the family type, yet seeing her with her own family made me wonder why.

A small child came running into the room and didn't hesitate as he launched himself at Lily. She didn't miss a beat as she snatched him up and snuggled him close. It made my heart hitch at the sight.

"I wuv you, Aunt Weewee," the little boy said, causing my mate to gush over him.

"I love you too, Z-man," she said, tickling his neck and making him squeal and wiggle until she set him down again. He was off and running quickly.

Everything I thought I knew about Lily changed in that moment. I didn't just see her as my mate, but also for the first time I could see her clearly as a future Pack Mother.

"Hi, I'm Kelsey," the pregnant woman said, though I had already suspected, knowing Kyle's mate was with child.

"Thomas," I said.

Lily turned back to me. "It won't take me long. I didn't really unpack," she confessed before disappearing.

"Wait up," Elise yelled, running after her and grabbing Kelsey's arm and dragging her along with them. I watched them leave, knowing they were talking about me. I tried to do the right thing and tune them out even though curiosity kept one ear open, until I heard *douchebag* and then I forced myself not to listen anymore.

I took a seat on the couch, knowing it could take her a while. Jason Westin wandered in. He feigned surprise to see me there as he greeted me, but from the shared look with his mate, I knew he was well aware of my presence.

"What brings you to Westin, son?" Jason asked.

I snorted. "I think you already know the answer to that, sir." I looked at Mary, who tried and failed to hide that knowing smirk again.

They each took a seat on either side of me, successfully trapping me in place.

"Lily will make you a fine mate, Thomas," Mary finally said.

I blew out a breath I didn't realize I was holding as she forced us all to confront the elephant in the room. I nodded, not really sure what to say. My initial reaction had been that there was no way Lily Westin was cut out to be Pack Mother of Collier, but after seeing her with her family for only a few moments, I wasn't so sure about that after all.

"I hope so. She's very reluctant," I said, cautiously.

Jason laughed. "I can imagine. She must have been shocked out of her mind, the way she came running home with her tail between her legs. That girl has dreamed of her one true mate her entire life."

"And I clearly have not lived up to that dream," I finished for him, knowing it was true.

From upstairs Kelsey's voice drifted down below. "He didn't look like a douchebag at least." And all the girls burst out in giggles.

I nodded my head and wiped my sweaty palms on my jeans.

"You're aware the only time the words douche or douchebag are used in this house, it's affectionately in reference to you?" Jason said, not even bothering to hide the humor from his voice.

"Yup, she hates me," I admitted.

"She doesn't hate you, Thomas," Mary jumped in to defend

her daughter.

"The thing is," I said, "I don't even know why. She doesn't even know me. Was I that terrible to her as kids?"

Mary and Jason shared a concerned look.

"Oh, dear, it's not that. It's, well, it's probably best that she explains her reasoning. In truth, we think you've just always been the scapegoat she's channeled her anger towards."

"That's what I don't understand. I can't even remember the last time I saw her. I couldn't have been more than fourteen, maybe younger even." That was the part that had bothered me so much.

Jason clapped a hand on my shoulder. "That's really the problem, now isn't it?"

"Huh?" I asked, not really following.

"Did you know that Lily has gone to Collier nearly every year for the annual vigil since Maddie's disappearance?"

I shook my head. I didn't know that. "Not really. I knew she had been to some, but I had stayed as far away from there as possible."

"That's the point," her father said. "You weren't there, and the rumors of the harem of women you were entertaining instead certainly helped contribute to your specific title."

I was stunned silent, trying to process everything they had just said—and what they hadn't. Lily thought I had abandoned my family in their time of need. Had I? I couldn't evaluate it in that moment, and so did what I always did, and shoved the thought into a box to meditate on later. That was a big one, but it explained a lot.

How was I going to reverse nearly nine years of pent-up anger and speculations in just one week?

"Well," I said aloud. "I guess I have one week to change her opinion."

Mary's full smile reached all the way to her eyes. "That's the attitude! Now remember, Lily is a romantic at heart." I cringed and Mary smacked me in the arm. "I'm serious here, so pay attention. She's always been in love with the idea of her one true mate. That's you, so use it to your favor."

"She's also fiercely loyal and protective of those she cares about, and that very much includes your sister. If you haven't settled things yourself with Maddie, you may want to start there," Jason added.

"Okay, that was already on my to-do list," I admitted, trying to make a mental note of all the tips they were giving me. "Why are you telling me this?" I wondered aloud.

"Simple, because you're her one true mate," Mary said, looking at Jason with glassy eyes. "You are what's best for her. God makes no mistakes in that. That also means she's what's best for you. It won't be easy, our Lily-girl loves hard, but she also could use some taming. Her father has spoiled her for years, and she gets away with too much." I chanced a look at Jason, who just shrugged and smiled, not even bothering to deny it. "No filter on that one, so often whatever she's thinking pops right on out of her mouth. That's not always a bad thing. You'll always know where you stand with her. You just might not always like it."

"We're rooting for you," Jason whispered as we heard the girls coming back down the stairs.

"Ready?" Lily asked as she walked into the room. She had changed into tight skinny jeans and a blue T-shirt that highlighted her eyes. It was more casual than anything I'd seen her in, and she looked stunning. My mouth went dry and I couldn't speak, only nod.

We said goodbye to her family as Jason shook my hand and wished me good luck. I loaded three suitcases and two overnight bags into the back of her car and offered to drive. She seemed to hesitate, but conceded, handing over the keys.

She was quiet on the drive to the airport, staring out the window, lost in her own thoughts. I longed to hear what she was thinking. Maybe someday, if I were lucky enough, we'd have a bond strong enough for that.

The Collier plane was waiting at the small airport at the bottom of the mountain. She raised her eyebrows at me, but didn't ask. I retrieved our bags from the trunk, wondering, not for the first time, if she was already planning to stay for more than a week. Dropping them off to be loaded, I led her over to the plane.

As we headed up the stairs I muttered under my breath, "Collier may not be as prestigious as Westin, but we do well enough. It's not just some little hick pack."

Lily turned quickly, almost knocking me backwards as I grabbed for the bars and she grabbed for me. "I would never call it a hick pack, Thomas. I love Collier."

Her vehement tone threw me for a loop. "You looked

surprised to see the plane. I shouldn't have assumed."

"You're right, you shouldn't have," Lily spat back before storming up the stairs. She took a calming breath and sat down. "At first I expected to see a Westin Foundation logo on the side, but realized it wasn't one of ours. It wasn't that I thought Collier couldn't afford a plane or anything, I just didn't realize you had one. You and Maddie always flew commercial. So yes, I was surprised to see the plane."

I rubbed my temples, realizing how very little I knew about my mate.

"I'm sorry. I'm very proud of my Pack and all we've accomplished. We may not have all the luxuries you're used to at Westin, but we have enough, and everything we need," I said.

Lily softened and reached for my hand. "Thomas, I'm an Alpha's kid, too. I'm not as pampered and sheltered as you seem to think. Spoiled, yes, I'll admit that, but not sheltered. I've visited many Packs. I know what a hick pack looks like, and Collier definitely isn't that. Besides, Sydney's store is amazing. That place alone elevates Collier above Westin even. I have to drive an hour to get labels like that."

I groaned. Of all my packmates, why did Lily have to befriend Sydney?

Conversation took a turn into lighter territory as she asked me a thousand questions during the flight, everything from my favorite food to the color of my favorite car. It was fun and I felt like I was finally starting to get to know her, the real Lily, instead of the one I'd assumed, imagined, or dreamed about.

Unlike Westin, Collier had plenty of space for our own airfield, so we didn't have another long, awkward drive, though I suspected it wouldn't have been quite so awkward or quiet if we had. I drove us straight home after we unloaded. It wasn't until we were walking in the door and Lily started checking things out that I realized she might prefer to stay at the Alpha house.

"So, this is my home. I don't need much, and chose it for its views, not its size, especially knowing that I'll eventually move back into the Alpha house when my turn comes around," I admitted.

I took her hand and led her away from the bedroom she was heading for and instead toward the back of the house, where off the kitchen lay a sunroom made entirely of floor-to-ceiling windows.

The view was stunning, overlooking the river and the mountains on either side.

Her breath hitched at the sight and it warmed me.

"It's beautiful," she said in awe. "It doesn't even look real. I could grab a cup of coffee and get lost in my own world, just sitting here staring at that all day."

I smiled down at her.

"Unfortunately, I have this long-lost sister that's been really worried about you, so I think we should head over to the Alpha house and check in."

"Does she know?" Lily asked.

I shook my head. "I didn't tell anyone, well, except Sydney." I hesitated. "And Kyle. I kind of had to tell them, you understand?"

"Thomas, it's fine. I just wanted to know what I'd be walking into. Dealing with Kelsey and Elise today wasn't all that bad, but it did make it a little less awkward that they already knew."

I laughed. "So you want me to tell her?"

"I don't know. I don't really want anyone to know unless we know it's going to work."

Her short hair was cut at an angle, and it cascaded down into her face. I brushed it back so I could look at her.

"Do you want us to work, Lily?"

She stilled, and I wasn't sure she was breathing. "I don't know," she finally whispered.

It felt like another punch in the gut. I tried to brush it off with a smile. "Come on, slugger. Everyone knows you took off in a hurry, and three days later I did too, both of us without warning. It's a small pack, they're already talking, I guarantee it, so let's just get it over with."

"You want to announce it to the pack?" she asked.

"Isn't that what mating couples do?"

"Trial, Thomas, we agreed to a trial. Shouldn't we wait until the week's up at least?"

"Fine," I conceded a little too quickly. "But . . ."

"There's a 'but?'"

"There's always a 'but,' Lily. But, if someone asks, I won't deny it. If you decide to get drunk again and flirt with a guy, I won't be able to not react to that, and judging by the Cole Anderson situation, it won't be pretty."

She giggled. "No drinking. No flirting. No denying. Got it. Anything else?"

"Yeah," I grinned, pulling her so close to me I could feel her heart beat against my chest. All I had to do was look down and I knew our mouths would align perfectly. "I didn't say no flirting. I said no flirting with other men."

"Oh," she said, breathlessly. "Okay then."

I begrudgingly let her go. "Anything you'd like to add?"

"Just some questions."

"Go ahead."

"First, is it okay with you if I hang out with Sydney? Outside of the bar, of course." She shot me a wicked grin.

"Sydney's great, I think that would be fine with her."

"I wasn't asking if she'd be okay with it, I'm asking if you're okay with it. If it's too weird during our trial period, I'll steer clear of her."

My heart expanded at the realization she was worried about my feelings, not Syd's. In a lot of ways it felt like she'd just punched me again, only this time instead of the gut it went straight to the heart. "It's not a problem for me."

"Great. Okay, next, you brought me here first. Does that mean I'm staying here?"

The air sizzled around us as my wolf perked up at the thought.

"I'll leave that up to you. You're welcome to have my room at the Alpha house if that's more comfortable for you," I said, when really I wanted to beg her to stay. Nothing in my life felt more right than having Lily in my home.

"You're sure?" she asked.

"Yeah, it's fine. We can take your stuff over now," I said, trying not to let my disappointment show.

"No, I meant are you sure it's up to me? You know, that you don't want a say in it?"

"Lily, I'd never force you to do anything. Of course it's your decision."

"Then I'd rather stay here," she said simply.

"What? You're serious?"

"I said I'd give us a chance. I don't half-ass things. If I'm in, I'm all in. I told you, you have a week to convince me you're not the douchebag I've built you up as." She said it with a smile on her face for the first time. That had to be progress already, right?

"How am I doing so far?" I asked.

She shrugged. "Verdict's still out."

"Any other questions?" I asked as I escorted her back out to the car.

"Just one more. Why do you keep calling me 'slugger?'"

I laughed. "Why do you keep calling me 'douchebag?'"

"I have my reasons," she said.

"Ditto," I told her, suddenly excited for the week ahead.

Lily

Chapter 11

I was nervous going back to Collier's Alpha house. I'd just left without giving any real explanation. I knew it was a dumb thing to do, but at the time it felt like the only thing to do.

I fidgeted with the bracelets on my wrist, running them up my arm and letting them clink back together as we drove. Thomas finally reached over and stilled me. He took my hand confidently and my wolf started to settle, as did my nerves. It amazed me, the effect his touch had on my emotions.

We got to the house and I started to get out of the car.

"Wait," Thomas said. "I know you don't want a big pack announcement, yet, but don't you think we need to tell them? Maddie's going to get it out of you eventually, you know she will. Then she'll tell Mom, and I'll have to explain to Dad why I didn't go to him with this, and . . ."

"We'll tell them," I said, watching relief wash over him.

"You're sure?"

"My family already knows. Yours should too, especially if you decide to go all psycho wolf on me again. Best your dad be ready to subdue you," I teased him as I got out of the car.

"I'm not even sure my wolf would have submitted to my father in that incident. Just, try to keep your clothes on around other guys this week."

I snorted. "You make it sound like it's a common occurrence."

"Is it?" he asked, and I didn't think he was entirely joking.

We were still bantering back and forth when we walked into the house. Maddie was in the living room sitting on the floor playing a game with Oscar while holding a sleeping baby.

"Is it what?" she asked without looking up.

"Am I in the habit of running around naked in front of guys?" I asked her as casually as if I'd never left at all.

Surprised at my voice, she looked up. Considered it for a moment. "Depends. Is alcohol involved? How about Cole Anderson? You'd definitely get naked for that."

She was laughing when an aggressive growl rumbled through Thomas, who was standing next to me. His hand tightened around mine until pain shot up my arm.

"Ow," I cried out, causing him to let go so fast you'd think he'd just touched fire.

"Question mark?" Maddie asked. "You're back, and holding hands with my brother?"

"Fine. Thomas is my one true mate. I freaked out a little. It's Thomas!" I said, feeling a weight lifting from my chest confessing it to my bestie. I needed some time with MC to help me sort it all out.

"I am right here, you know," he pointed out, but I ignored him.

Madelyn laughed so hard, she woke the baby. Liam came running in to find out what all the commotion was about, and Oscar scolded us all for disturbing Sara's nap. He gently took the baby from his mother and went to sit in the rocking chair and soothe her back to sleep.

"What's wrong?" Liam asked, though his total focus was on his mate.

She pointed up at me, still laughing so hard she couldn't speak. Annoyed, I crossed my arms over my chest and waited for it all to pass.

"Lil? When did you get back?" my brother finally asked.

"A couple hours ago," I sighed.

"She . . . mated . . . Thomas," Maddie managed through tears and laughter. "She mated Thomas!"

Liam looked at us both in shock.

"You took my sister as a mate?" Liam demanded.

I stepped in front of Thomas without even realizing I was doing it.

"Not yet, not that it's any of your business. Plus, technically you took his sister as your mate first. Just pointing that out," I said as he snarled at me, causing Thomas to tense behind me. I wasn't sure how I knew that exactly, but I did. "Would you relax, both of you? He's my true mate, Liam," I told him.

"Thomas Collier? The biggest do—" Liam stopped himself before finishing the statement.

"Biggest douchebag on the planet," Thomas finished for him. "Yeah, yeah, yeah, I've heard that one a few times already."

I cringed, suddenly hating the nickname I'd long ago reserved just for him.

Our voices must have summoned the others, because the next thing I knew the entire Collier family was standing around gawking at me and Thomas.

"Hi," I squeaked, wanting to crawl into a hole and die. It was not how I'd imagined his family finding out when I agreed we should probably tell them. It didn't help that MC was grinning like a fool.

"What's all this about?" Zach Collier asked.

My mouth dropped open to speak, but nothing came out.

"Mom, Dad, sisters, meet my mate," Thomas said, sounding proud and looking much too smug.

"Your mate? Lily? But she doesn't even like you," Shelby blurted out.

"If she was your true mate, don't you think we'd know that by now?" his sister Ruby asked.

"Settle down and hear them out," Zach ordered, and the whole room went quiet, staring at the two of us.

Thomas started to talk, but I cut him off.

"Trust me, no one here is more shocked than I am. Truth is, until I arrived here, last week, I hadn't seen Thomas since I was what? Maybe fourteen years old? A long time. Coming here was the first time I'd seen him since either of our wolves surfaced. I know, it's still sinking in for us too, but it is true and we're trying to make the most of it with a trial run. I've said some pretty horrible things about him over the years. Really hoping he doesn't prove me right on any of them, but we'll see. Now can we please try not to make a big deal out of this?"

Thomas had six sisters: Lizzy, Clara, Peyton, Ruby, Shelby,

and Madelyn. He was the baby of the family. Of course I knew this, but seeing the six of them staring at me under scrutiny was very unnerving. Maddie kept laughing about it, but Lizzy and Peyton had always been overprotective of Thomas and they didn't look too happy about our situation. They had spoiled him rotten as a small pup, and even though I'd felt part of their family my entire life, I suddenly found myself the outsider.

Thomas must have sensed my discomfort, because he wrapped his arm around my waist and pulled me tightly against his side. My wolf calmed immediately and my entire body relaxed as I melted against him.

Peyton's eyes nearly bugged out of her head. "It's true then?" she asked. "She really is your one true mate?"

Thomas nodded. "Yes, she really is."

"How odd is that? I mean Liam and Lily are twins, what are the odds that you and Maddie would be their true mates? Heck, you and Mad are practically twins. So weird," Ruby assessed.

"I wish I'd find my true mate, sooner rather than later," Clara sighed, sinking down on the couch and grabbing a pillow to hug. "I think it stinks that the two youngest found theirs first. How unfair is that really?"

Shelby came over and hugged me. "Welcome to the family, Lily. Though really it's kind of gross. You were sorta already like a sister and now you're mating our brother." She crinkled up her nose and Maddie laughed some more.

Cora stroked Madelyn's hair with glassy eyes. "How I've missed that laugh in this house. And Shelby's right, Lily. You've always been a part of this family. 'Bout time we made it for real, and for keeps."

I gave Thomas a comical look that made everyone laugh.

"We're still dealing with the shock factor. Let's not jump ahead too quickly," I reminded them.

Cora and Zach shared a knowing look and grinned. I knew that look. It was the one where I could swear they saw into the future and knew everything would work out. I wasn't sure if that made me feel better or worse, though.

While the girls all ganged up on Thomas with question after question that I knew he didn't want to answer, Maddie snuck over and we disappeared. I felt only mildly guilty for leaving Thomas to fend for himself, but mostly I was grateful to not be center stage for it all. We didn't say a word as I followed her out of the house and down the street.

We headed off into the woods not far from the house and came to an embankment that overlooked the river. I had been there many times as a child, and even more by myself as an adult in the years after Maddie had disappeared.

We sat on the rocks, but the peaceful serenity didn't last long before MC started attacking with questions.

"So, you and Thomas, huh? How are you handling that?"

I snorted. "Poorly."

We both laughed before sobering.

"It's weird, right? I don't mean you and Thomas. I mean the feel of the bond. It was hard to talk about it with you before, because I knew you couldn't fully understand, but if you need to talk about it, I'm here."

I put my arm around her and squeezed. "Thanks. I'm not even sure where to begin. When I first sensed him when we arrived, it was the greatest feeling ever. I couldn't believe it and I was so happy, and then my wolf led me to him. It was like every dream I'd ever had about my future mate crumbled in an instant. And I feel terrible about that. If it were anyone else, I'd be spending every waking moment getting to know him and falling in love, but I've built Thomas up into this enemy inside my head and I'm not sure I could ever truly love him, Mad. When I'm not thinking and I just feel, I think maybe things will be okay, but then I remember. I remember how he was never there for your family when they needed him. I remember how he disappeared at every vigil. Why would he do that? How can I trust he'd ever be there for me?"

"Oh, hon. I'm so sorry. Thomas and I have talked a little, but nothing about what happened. I'm sure he knows what happened to me and all. Heck, the whole Pack probably knows by now, but things are still pretty tense with us. I can see how much my leaving affected him. I'm sure he had his reasons for all of that, Lil."

"I just can't come up with one single scenario that would have made it okay. Actions speak so much louder than words, and despite agreeing to give us a shot and see how things go, I'm not sure I can fully let my guard down with him. A part of me will always worry that he'd leave me both physically and emotionally, like if something serious ever happened."

"It's not the same Lily," Maddie insisted.

"Isn't it, though?"

"Thomas isn't the boy we used to know. I think we both need to give him the benefit of the doubt and find out who he really is now as a man."

"You can really do that?" I questioned.

She nodded and smiled. "Yes, and so can you. He's my brother, Lil. I love him. And he's your mate. That's not something you just turn your back on. What is it your mother is always saying?"

"God never makes mistakes, especially when pairing mates," I said, rolling my eyes.

"Exactly!"

After a moment of silence, I told her about everything that had happened since the moment I'd arrived in Collier, including how much time I'd spent with Cole and the invaluable advice he'd given me. She got a good laugh as I painted the picture of my tattoo attempt that Thomas had interrupted, and I confessed how much it had turned me on seeing the aggressive side of my mate.

"Eww, Lily! There are some things I do withhold from you regarding your brother out of respect to you. Please do the same."

I laughed. "MC, I lived in the same house with you and Liam. Trust me, you overshared plenty. Next time, use a freaking dampener, will ya?"

Maddie's cheeks heated to a dark red.

We talked for several more hours about anything and everything, and I could finally breathe again. I felt Thomas's presence even before he cleared his throat, and I knew by the look on MC's face that Liam was with him. It unnerved me a little to see our bond strengthening in that way.

"We really didn't want to interrupt, but Sara is screaming for her mommy," Thomas said.

"Oh, no. We completely lost track of time. Is she okay? Where is she?" Maddie started asking.

"She's fine sweetheart. Her big brother isn't going to let anyone near her while she's upset. You know how he is," Liam chuckled. "She just started fussing. We wanted to give you guys as much time as possible."

She jumped up and gave him a quick peck on the cheek. "Thanks."

They left, leaving me alone with Thomas.

"It's getting late. So, how about three options?" he asked.

"Um, okay," I agreed wondering what he was up to.

"An awkward dinner at my parents' where my sisters will no doubt continue to gawk and snicker, because once the shock started wearing off they all decided our, uh, situation, is quite hilarious. Option two, we walk into town and grab some dinner. Or, option three, I can order to go and we can head home and have dinner alone."

He had an uncertain look in his eyes as he said option three, but there was also obvious heat behind them that made me gulp. I weighed all three options and sighed.

"If we head into town together everyone will start talking. I think I've had enough of that for one day, and obviously that omits your parents' place, too, so dinner at home, I guess it is," I said, uncertainty evident in my voice.

I couldn't tell if that pleased him or disappointed him. Maybe a little of both, but he quickly shook it off. "Subs okay?" he asked as I nodded my head and he dialed a number on his cell.

In no time at all we walked to the sub shop, where he went in and picked up our order while I waited outside.

The shop was just across from Sydney's store, and as my luck would have it, she was closing up for the night. She spotted me before it even registered, and was quickly crossing the street heading right for me. I took a deep breath. This meeting was bound to happen sooner or later. I had hoped I'd have a little more time to prepare for it, though.

Syd walked right up to me and, shocking me more than anything, wrapped her arms around me, pulling me into a tight embrace.

"I always knew it was a possibility I'd lose him, but I'm so happy it was to you," she whispered.

"You are?" I blurted out. "Why?"

She pulled back and looked me in the eyes and I saw absolutely no animosity there.

"Look, I know how you feel about him, but you really should give him a chance, Lily. Thomas Collier is one of the best men I know. Get to know him and you'll see I'm right."

"But Sydney, you were supposed to be his mate," I reminded her. "I know you love him, but I don't feel that way about him."

"A part of me will always love Thomas, but if you could see how happy he was to find you, his true mate, I knew I'd never be enough, and I also know that I deserve my true mate, too. I didn't really understand the difference until I saw how he lit up talking about you. I want a man that thinks the moon shines on me that way too. I don't deserve to settle for second best, and neither do you. Maybe you're not in love with him yet, but I'm willing to bet your bond is strong and will only continue to grow. I truly hope we can still be friends," she said hesitantly.

I nodded, trying to absorb what she had said. Thomas lit up just talking about me? I thought he was as disappointed in our mating as I had been. I hugged Sydney again, unable to formulate any words.

Thomas came out with our food at that moment.

Thomas
Chapter 12

Lily refused to go inside with me, worried someone would see us. The last thing I expected to find was her hugging Sydney when I came back out.

"Uh, hey, Syd," I said, awkwardly. I hated the uncertainty the bond gave me at times, but this would have been a bad situation regardless.

"Hey, Thomas," Sydney returned without letting go of my mate. When she finally did, she turned and grinned at me. I knew that look—it was the one that always meant trouble. She had seemed genuinely happy for me when I last saw her, but that look told me she was up to something. She rose on her tip toes and kissed my cheek as she walked by.

A loud, angry growl ripped through Lily, shocking us both. Sydney just grinned.

"Dammit, Sydney, you did that on purpose," Lily accused.

"Just proving my point." She laughed. "See you two later."

As she left, I stared at Lily, trying to hide my happiness that she had growled at Syd over me. It was a start at least, some little sign that she felt the bond as strongly as I did.

"So, what was her point exactly?" I finally asked Lily as we got back to the Alpha house and retrieved my car.

"Nothing," she said, a little too quickly, and I didn't ask again as her cheeks matched the pink streaks in her hair.

We drove back to my house in silence. I carried the food in when we arrived and held the door open for Lily. She sat on the sofa and I assumed that's where she wanted to eat. I dropped the bag of food on the coffee table and went to grab some plates from the kitchen. Returning and passing her one, she filled it and began to eat in silence.

I kicked off my shoes by the front door and hung my hat on the rack before joining her. It should have been uncomfortable, but it wasn't at all. Just having her there gave me peace.

"Was your meal okay?" I asked, as she finished eating and rose to take her plate to the kitchen.

"It was great, thanks," she said as she washed her plate and set it on a dish towel on the counter to dry before returning to clean up our mess and take my plate, too.

"You don't have to do that," I told her, not wanting her to feel she had to wait on me.

"Don't be silly. It'll only take a minute," she said, brushing it off like it was nothing, but it sure felt like everything. "I was a little nervous about running into Sydney, but honestly I'm glad it's done and over with," she chatted as she cleaned. "Are you sure it won't bother you if we stay friends?"

"No," I said, then grinned at her and couldn't resist myself. "As long as you remember your way back to my bed the next time the two of you decide to go out and get drunk again."

She turned around in surprise, wet dishrag still in her hand. I was gloating over shocking her and didn't notice her wrapping it up until she snapped the wet rag at my leg. It stung, but the surprise attack only lasted a second before I grabbed a towel and began rolling it up, too.

"Don't you dare!" Lily warned, but there was a hint of humor behind her threat. "You'll regret it, Thomas."

The sound of my name so easily rolling off her lips warmed me and only encouraged me to press on. I snapped the rag, just missing her. She retaliated quickly, the sting hitting my upper arm this time.

"Oh, it's on now," I told her.

She squealed as I made my attack and bolted for the next room. The chase was on. It made my wolf excited to see the playful side of our mate. I had visions of him happily wagging his tail and yipping in my head.

Lily tore off down the hall. I heard door after door slam shut.

I laughed. She was fast, I'd give her that. When I caught up, every door in my house was shut. *Two can play at this game*, I thought. Taking a deep breath, I called my wolf to the surface. My senses immediately heightened, and I followed the trail of our mate.

Slowly, I opened the door to my bedroom with a grin, but Lily was nowhere to be found. I turned on the lights and looked around. There was no sign of her. I moved to another room, checking each of them. I couldn't find my mate.

Confused and getting frustrated, I tuned back into my wolf. He led me to my bedroom once again. I walked in and sniffed the air, following her scent up the ladder to my loft, but Lily wasn't there, either.

A scratching just outside my window drew my attention as I was heading down the ladder. I climbed back up and examined the area closer. The window was not quite closed. My wolf was anxious, fighting to shift. I could feel fur starting to sprout on my hands as I opened the window and looked around.

"About time. You really suck at tracking, don't you?" Lily said.

I took a deep breath before peeking my head out the window. Lily was sitting on the roof, looking up at the stars in the sky. She patted the space next to her in invitation to join her, so I climbed out of the window and sat next to her. Her proximity began to calm my wolf.

"That was kind of cheating, don't you think?" I asked.

She turned and grinned at me. Her eyes were full of mischief, and I knew life with Lily would never be dull.

"There were no rules, Thomas."

I grinned back at her. "I do much prefer Thomas to douchebag."

I watched her cringe.

"Yeah, about that. Look, it's just . . ." she started, and I raised my hand to cut her off.

"You don't have to explain. I'm sure you have your reasons." And I wasn't certain I was ready to hear them all. Her parents had already given me plenty to consider. "Tomorrow I have a few things I have to do. You're welcome to tag along if you want, or I'm sure Maddie or Sydney would be thrilled to spend the day with you.

"I won't lie and say I'd rather hang out with you, because we both know that's not true. But, I did make a promise, and if nothing else, that means something to me. If we're going to give this a go, I think we should stick together, get to know each other, and try to put aside old judgements. Besides, I would like to see the territory and meet the people here, too. After all, I could be their Pack Mother someday."

Lily sighed and laid her head on my shoulder. I turned and kissed the top of her head like it was the most natural thing in the world. "Someday," I whispered.

I wasn't sure how long we sat there in comfortable silence staring out into the night's sky. After the turmoil I'd felt when she'd left, I didn't care. I needed her near to comfort my wolf. It scared me just how much I needed her.

My dad once told me that your mate was your biggest treasure, your greatest weakness, and she must always be protected. I scoffed at him at the time. *No woman would ever weaken me,* I had told him. I truly believed it then.

Lily shivered, and without hesitation or even thought, I wrapped my arm around her and tucked her close to my side. In that moment, I knew exactly what my father had meant about a mate.

Much too soon, Lily wiggled away from me and stretched, yawning.

"Come on, let's get you to bed, slugger. It's been a hell of a day," I said, trying to keep things light between us, but not really wanting the day to end.

The sexy way she moved when she stretched was making me uncomfortable in all the right places. I had made huge steps in the last twenty-four hours with her and I didn't want to scare her off by acting rashly. If she stretched again and her shirt pulled up one more time, exposing the smooth skin across her stomach, I wasn't sure I could be held responsible for my actions. My body still vividly remembered how soft her skin was and how perfectly my large hand fit in the curve above her hip.

She begrudgingly agreed, not seeming to want the night to end either. I sniffed the air and smelled the nerves wafting off her. Perhaps my little slugger was just nervous about what happens next.

She led the way back through the window and down the ladder from the loft into my bedroom. Crossing her arms over her chest in a defensive move, she waited for me to descend behind her.

I wasn't sure how I knew it, but despite her act, I knew she was checking out my butt.

Lily

Chapter 13

One thing that equally bothered and excited me was just how well Thomas had filled out over the years we hadn't seen each other. If I were honest he was never that hard to look at. But the kid I remembered was tall and lanky with big teeth he hadn't quite grown into yet, nothing like the man before me with his bulging leg muscles and that firm ass . . . I had always loved a nice butt, but dang if his wasn't the best I'd ever seen in a pair of nice tight jeans. It made my hands twitch to reach out and touch him, but I quickly clasped my fingers together behind my back to fight the urge.

Thomas jumped down to the floor, skipping the last few rungs of the ladder, and turned to me with a smirk on his face like he had known exactly what I was thinking. *Don't blush, don't blush*, I scolded myself even as I felt the heat rising in my cheeks.

Feeling like it was safe to let go of my own hands, I crossed my arms back across my chest. As Thomas's eyes dropped lower, my body felt like a live wire sparking with electricity.

I cleared my throat. "Where would you like me to sleep?" I asked.

His pupils dilated as they met my own eyes.

"I have five sisters. I know a loaded question when I hear one. I'll tell you what your options are and then you have to choose," he said, his voice deeper than it had been previously. "The couch in the living room. Either of the two guest rooms. Or, my bed," he said, like he had just issued me a challenge.

I raised my chin in defiance and looked him straight in the

eyes. "Fine. I'll take your bed then."

Turning on my heels, I left him in shock while I went to the living room to retrieve my suitcase. When I walked back into the room, Thomas was pulling up a pair of sweatpants and his shirt was nowhere in sight.

"What are you doing?" I squeaked.

"Getting ready for bed," he informed me as he sat down on the big king-sized bed.

"I told you, I'm sleeping there," I said defiantly.

"And where did you think I was going to sleep?" he challenged.

I hefted my suitcase onto the opposite side of the bed to retrieve my stuff.

"I don't know. The couch? Either of the two guest rooms," I said in my snarkiest voice.

Thomas rose from the bed and walked around to me, placing his hands on either side of the bed, effectively trapping me as I turned to face him. I gulped at the look of desire in his eyes. "That's not what's going to happen here," he said, lowering his head and kissing my neck.

"That's not fair. You aren't playing by the rules," I said in a shaky voice.

Thomas pulled back and grinned. "There are no rules, Lily," he said, throwing my own words back at me.

I started to laugh and push him away, but not fast enough. His lips crashed down on mine possessively. I stiffened in surprise, but my body quickly took over before my brain could even register what was happening.

He gently lifted me on to the bed. I wrapped my legs around his waist, pulling him closer to me. My fingers wound through his hair. But then my brain engaged as reality set in like whiplash. I jerked away abruptly and breathlessly.

My palms were now flat against his chest, his hard, rigid bare chest, so I shook my head, trying to clear my thoughts as I unwrapped my legs from around him and gave him a slight push.

"I'm sorry, Thomas. I don't know what came over me. I'm still confused and unsure about us, and I don't want to lead you on," I told him honestly. "This mating pull is just so damn strong sometimes."

I saw the hurt in his eyes, but it quickly disappeared as that crooked grin appeared on his face. He stepped back. "Don't worry about it, slugger. It's been a long day. Go get ready for bed and we'll call it a night."

My mouth was dry and my nerves high, but I managed to smile and nod as I turned and pulled out my pajamas and travel case and took them to the bathroom, closing the door behind me.

I stared at my reflection in the mirror. I still looked like me, but I definitely didn't feel like me. I had no clue what had come over me to make me act so, well, primal towards that kiss. It wasn't like I've never kissed a guy before. My fingers felt my swollen lips as I remembered. God, Thomas knew how to kiss.

I considered a quick shower, but my wolf protested, enjoying the scent of our mate on me. I was too tired and confused to argue. After changing, I brushed my teeth and washed my face before quietly exiting the bathroom.

Thomas lay on top of the covers, his arms tucked behind his head. *When the hell did he get all those muscles?* I wondered as I tried not to stare.

The only light remaining was the lamp next to my side of the bed. He had pulled back the covers for me, though he remained on top of them. I acknowledged for a brief moment what a sweet thought that was as I slithered in and pulled the sheets up around me. Reaching over to the nightstand, I turned off the light. "Goodnight," I whispered.

"Goodnight Lily," he said in a husky voice that made my body tremble.

I scooted a little further away and turned on my side so my back was toward him. We didn't say another word, and as his breathing began to even out in a steady rhythm, I was lulled to sleep.

My next coherent memory was the unique and intoxicating scent of my mate. A smile tugged at my lips before my eyes even opened. Thomas. There was a part of me that still didn't trust him. The part that wanted to hate him, but I had seen a different side to him already, and it was waging war with everything I thought I had known about him.

A loud snore rumbled through Thomas. It surprised me, but even more so that I actually felt it. I stretched alongside his hard body and froze. I slowly opened my eyes and realized I was using him as my own personal body pillow. I lifted my head and looked around.

Great, I thought. He was in exactly the same position and I was on the wrong side of the bed. Me, not him. To make matters worse, I was horrified to see a small puddle of drool on his chest where my head had just been. I quickly wiped it off as he continued to snore loudly, and I tried to roll back to my side of the bed. With any luck he'd never even know I'd breached the gap between us in my sleep.

As I moved, so did he. He rolled to his side, and without opening his eyes, snagged me mid-escape and pulled me back to him. He nuzzled my hair, taking a deep breath like he was memorizing my scent.

"Good morning," he said.

I wiggled to try to get away, but he just wrapped his arms around me even tighter, pulling me flush against him as he spooned me from behind. I could feel every inch of him, including the hard erection poking me in the backside.

"Oh my God!" I squealed, trying to pull away from him.

"What?" he asked, on full alert as I dramatically motioned towards his lower half.

He laughed, brushing it off like it was no big deal.

"Don't you 'what' me," I protested.

He gave me that panty-melting crooked grin, but I was too embarrassed to be affected by it.

"You practically slept on top of me all night. What did you think was going to happen?"

"Go take a cold shower or something," I demanded.

He laughed again, but got up and headed for the bathroom. I couldn't help but watch how his pants tented. *Jesus, how big was he?* I wondered, immediately trying to remove that thought from my mind.

He turned at the bathroom door and his eyes locked on mine from across the room. "You're welcome to join me," he said, sounding cocky as ever.

"Eww, no way," I said. "Make it a very cold shower," I squealed, chucking a pillow at the door as he ducked inside, closing it behind him. I could still hear him laughing when the water finally began to drown him out.

Once he was done, I took my turn getting ready for the day. After I had finished, I went in search of him and found him in the kitchen. Bacon, eggs, and hot toast were waiting for me.

"Did you cook this yourself?" I asked.

"Yeah. I do know how to cook, Lily. This is a farming community. It often means long, hard days outdoors, working with the animals or tending to the fields. Breakfast is the most important meal of the day, so eat up. We're already running very late."

As soon as I was done with breakfast we left the house, driving over toward town. I had promised Thomas I'd spend the day with him. I wanted to get to know the territory, the Pack, and the people. I also wanted to quietly assess just what kind of man and future Pack leader Thomas Collier really was.

I was a little surprised and disappointed when he pulled up in front of the Alpha house.

"I thought I was going to spend the day with you," I said.

"You are," he assured me.

"Then what are we doing at your parents'? I thought you were dropping me off to hang out with Maddie or something."

"Nah. I have a meeting with Dad this morning. I'm afraid you won't be able to sit in on this one, but I'm sure my sisters will keep you company."

I stifled a yawn. "Okay."

"Tired?" he asked.

"Yes. You snore."

"I snore?" he asked with a snort. "You snore," he said matter-of-factly.

He opened the front door and stepped aside for me to pass first. I was too busy arguing to notice the show of respect he was bestowing on me. An Alpha never let someone walk before him, except his mate, or an occasional elder Alpha or Grand Councilman. At the moment, all of that was lost on me, as I was embarrassed by his comment that I snore.

"I do not snore, Thomas. Take it back," I demanded. "You snore."

"Maybe," he conceded. "But you definitely snore, too."

"Do not!"

"Do too! And, you drool in your sleep," he added.

My hands flew to my mouth as I gasped. "You did not just

Julie Trettel

say that."

His laughter infuriated me.

"What is going on here?" his mother demanded as we entered the kitchen.

"He started it," I mumbled under my breath.

"No, I didn't," he denied. "You did."

"Did not!"

"Did too!"

Maddie and Liam were sitting with Oscar at the table, having breakfast. Lizzy was, too, as she held a cooing baby Sara. They all looked to be enjoying the scene a little too much.

"Madelyn, tell him right now. I do not snore."

"Yes, you do," Liam said.

"I do not!" I turned pleading eyes to my friend for help.

"Um, Lil, I love you, but you snore like a freaking lumberjack," MC said.

Betrayed by my best friend. I slumped down into the chair and crossed my arms over my chest. "Well," I said to Thomas, "you snore, too."

He smiled and leaned down to give me a quick peck on my lips, much to my humiliation. "It's okay," he said calmly. "Because you'll certainly never be bothered by it over all the noise you make in your sleep." He winked and walked away as my jaw hung open.

I put my head on the table, cradled in my arms. I knew my face was on fire. I couldn't believe he'd just casually kissed me in front of his family like that.

"Well, there certainly will never be a dull moment of life with you two," Cora said, as the others cracked up laughing.

"Oh, Lily. Lily, Lily, Lily. Mating is the most natural thing in the world. I cannot possibly understand why you would ever fight it," Liam said, throwing my own theories back in my face. How many times had I told my siblings that? How many times had I lectured them for being stupid and not just accepting their fate? I feared that each one of them would gloat in my turmoil.

Straightening up, I rose from the table, punching Liam as hard as I could in the arm. "Jerk," I said under my breath.

Thomas
Chapter 14

I left Lily at the kitchen table. She could fend for herself against Liam and my family. Dad was already waiting for me in his office when I arrived.

"Thomas," he said, sounding a little surprised. "I wasn't sure you were coming today. I expected you and Lily would need a few days to get better acquainted."

I smirked. "That'll take a lot more than a few days."

"She has always been a tad eccentric and impulsive. I had expected that would work in your favor for the mating," Dad said.

"Except you forgot to add stubborn and the fact she hates me to the list, making it a very strange hot and cold effect," I grumbled.

Dad threw his head back and laughed at my expense. "Oh yes, you've definitely met your match then. No one ever claimed mating was easy, but I promise you, she's worth it."

I smiled as warmth spread through me. "I know she's worth it, Dad, if she doesn't kill me first."

We got down to business after that. He caught me up-to-date on the latest Pack news. Two new pups had been born that month, which was cause for celebration. For some reason a lot of packs had been struggling to procreate over the last few decades, and the wolf shifter population had started to dwindle because of it. A few species were even struggling in the wild and heading for the endangered animals list.

Most of the Collier Pack wolves were grey. No one understood why some packs were more prone to specific breeds and others more variety. My mother was pretty religious and believed God placed the species he needed most in each of us. Wyoming was a good breeding ground for grey wolves, and currently the wolf population was thriving.

New wolf shifter pups were a different story, though. While my parents had been beyond blessed with seven pups, the average family had only one, if they were able to conceive at all. I knew several packs were struggling to keep up their numbers.

When I was still just a boy, it was arranged for my sister Lizzy to mate a future Alpha of a South American pack that was struggling to keep numbers. They had been quite hopeful that whatever blessing or genes had allowed my parents to have so many pups would help increase their numbers, too. In the end she hadn't been able to go through with it. A lot of rumors had floated around about her return to Collier, but I still didn't know the circumstances, just that she had never been quite the same afterwards.

Lily came from a large family as well, and I smiled, wondering just how many pups we'd be blessed with. I could envision her swollen with my child as little ones climbed up her legs. If you had asked me a week earlier I'd have said Lily Westin was too self-absorbed to make a good mother, or handle being a Pack Mother. The more I saw her interact with others, the more my opinion of that changed. I had no doubt she was up to the task of both, and I was excited to see her in action and introduce her to the Pack.

Dad cleared his throat. I looked over at him. He didn't seem irritated, just smiling. "Sir?" I asked.

"I know that look all too well, son. You're thinking of your mate," he said.

I grinned, unable to deny it. "It's surprisingly hard being away from her, even knowing she's just down the hall."

"The way she tore out of here last week, I'd say your wolf will be quite uneasy anytime she's out of sight, at least for a while. Go to her. I know you have rounds today. Take her with you; show her our territory and introduce her around. I know you asked not to make a formal announcement yet, but I'll warn you, rumors are already surfacing."

I sighed. "I figured as much." Rising, we embraced and said goodbye.

I found Lily sitting in the living room, chatting it up with Maddie and Shelby. She looked relaxed and comfortable, and it made my heart lurch.

"Hey," she said, noticing my presence, and I was happy to see a smile on her face and no animosity.

"Hey. I've got rounds today. You coming, or would you prefer to hang out with these two instead?" I held my breath, hoping she would choose me.

Lily jumped up, waved a quick bye to my sisters, and linked her arm with mine as we walked outside. "I told you I was sticking with you. Relax. When I set my mind on something, it takes an act of God to change it."

"And you've set your mind on me?" I dared to ask.

She hesitated, and there came the punch in my gut feeling once again.

"Yes. I mean, I guess so. I'm still so confused by all this, but I said I'd give us a shot, so let's do this. Where are we headed?"

I held the truck door open for her before walking around and climbing inside.

"Today we're just going to make rounds. You'll get to see a lot of our territory, meet some people, and get a feel for the Pack. We'll start at the stables. I know Westin's primary income comes through the Foundation, but Collier is a farming town. We have both gardens and livestock. Everyone pitches in and works hard, and it not only sustains our Pack for food, but we have several large contracts to sell off the excess. The profits from that maintain all our needs here and then some. Dad's been working with Liam to invest and grow our funds even further."

I chanced a look over at Lily, who was staring at me in amazement. "That sounds pretty awesome, actually. I love the idea of working the land and being fully sustainable, and to make a strong income off it is all the better. Impressive."

"Maybe," I said, still a little concerned about how she'd handle the sometimes hard life of a farming community. She wasn't exactly used to getting her hands dirty, and while being future Alpha of the Pack afforded me more luxuries and choices than most, when times were tough, everyone pitched in. I could even remember my mother working endless hours under the harsh sun when times were hard. Coming home exhausted, dirt caked under her nails, to clean up just in time to make dinner for us kids, all with a smile on her face. Would Lily live up to that? I was struggling to reconcile the image as she sat next to me in her designer clothes and heels. I looked down to her feet, confused by the boots I saw there instead.

"Where did you get those?" I asked. "I thought you were wearing heels when we left the house. I was just about to suggest we stop and buy you a pair of boots."

"I do need to pick up a pair, I suppose. I brought boots the first time I came here, but must have left them at home when I ran away. I couldn't find them in my suitcase this morning, so I asked MC if I could borrow a pair while you were meeting with your dad." She snorted. "I wasn't sure what we were doing today, but I was pretty sure those shoes weren't going to cut it."

I smiled. Every time I thought I had a grasp on this woman, she threw me another curveball. Arriving at our first destination, I parked in front of the dairy barn and jumped out. Lily helped herself down from the truck before I could make it around to her.

"So," I said. "This is the barn. We don't have a large number of dairy cattle, but this is where we keep the few that we do have. The milk is used to supply the town dairy products. At this time, we aren't equipped to sell in a wider territory. It would require too many upgrades to our current facilities, but is certainly something we're considering in the future. Most of our cattle are classified as free range for beef. We'll take a ride out to the fields to check on them another day. Do you ride?"

"Ride what?"

"Horses," I said. *What else?* I wondered.

She sighed. "Yes, I do."

"You don't sound happy about it."

"It's hard not to feel sorry for the beasts. How would you like it if someone rode your wolf? I know it's not exactly the same, but I still feel bad for them."

I smiled. Under that perfect exterior, my mate had a very kind heart. I wasn't sure why that surprised me so much, but it did.

"Don't laugh. I'm serious," she scolded.

"I'm not laughing. I swear. You just . . . surprise me."

I led her into the barn. She cringed at seeing the cows hooked up to the milking machine. "Ugh, that makes my nipples hurt just looking at them," she said, covering her breasts.

"I'm not sure any woman has ever come right out and said it so forthright and all, but you wouldn't be the first to sympathize with them. I promise you it's not hurting them any."

Lily and I turned to face the man speaking from behind us. Dalton Draper was an old cowboy. A few years back, he had claimed he was getting too old to ride the range, and had taken over the dairy cattle. He oversaw the entire operation and had true love and respect for each of the animals.

"Lily, this is Dalton. He runs the dairy barn and looks after the animals here," I told her. They shook hands.

"Sorry to be so forthright," she said, using the old man's words, but still not quite relaxing. I reached out and lightly rubbed her lower back. I felt the tension leave her almost immediately.

"Little Lily. Last time I saw you, girl, you were all pigtails and knobby knees running with Miss Maddie through my fields," Dalton said.

Lily genuinely smiled, and it was mesmerizing. "Mr. Draper?" she asked. The old man smiled back affectionately and Lily threw her arms around his neck and kissed his weathered cheek. My wolf must have been just as shocked as I was, because neither of us seemed to know how to react. "I can't even believe it. You are as handsome as ever," she continued to gush over him.

"When we were younger, Mr. Draper used to make MC and me the most delicious s'mores ever. We'd sneak out to the fields and join him around the fire until he'd send us back home," she told me, reminiscing about her childhood.

"It's so wonderful to see you," she told Dalton.

"It's funny," I said aloud, "but I don't really remember you here in Collier."

"Oh, that's 'cause little Maddie would get bored when you were traveling with your daddy, or out deep in the range when you started riding with the cowboys. She'd get real sad, missing you something fierce, son, so your mama would always make arrangements for little Lily to come stay for a weekend, sometimes a week. Those two were something else. Like night and day. Miss Maddie with her dark hair and tanned skin, and then little Lily and her pale hair, and skin as ivory as snow even in the middle of summer. Yin and yang, I used to tell them. They complemented each other in every way. It was such a joy watching the two of them grow

97

up together. And then . . ." His voice drifted off. We all knew he was thinking of my sister's disappearance.

Lily snorted, seeming unaware of the shift in nostalgia. "It's true. I still can't tan to save my life. It's white or red. There's no in-between."

Dalton laughed along with her, salvaging the mood back to a more pleasant one, but the memories of Madelyn's disappearance were heavy on my heart and I had a hard time shaking them as Dalton gave Lily a tour of the barn and they chatted like old friends.

I excused myself after awhile and headed outside. I needed fresh air and open space to breathe again. I headed off toward the river and sat on a boulder, alone with my memories. I wasn't sure how long I'd been there before I sensed Lily nearby. I looked up to see her watching me with confusion on her face.

"Where'd you go?" she asked.

I tried to brush it off. "I've been on that tour and heard his stories a million times. I've been right here."

"No, I mean, I know you're right here, physically, but what were you thinking about? Your emotions changed when we were talking about Maddie. Why?"

I didn't want to get into it with her, so I looked back out over the water, trying to compose myself.

"It's nothing," I said with the fake smile I used for everyone who had ever asked me how I was concerning my sister, but I knew by the look in her eye she wasn't buying it. I went to rise, ready to move on to our next site and forget all about it, but before I could get up, she sat beside me.

"Sydney said something the night we were out drinking that's been weighing on me. Can we talk about it?" she asked.

I shrugged. "I guess that depends what on she said."

"She said that Maddie's disappearance had been really hard on you. I hadn't really considered that before. I was just so upset, and it was easy to channel all my anger towards you."

"I've heard that from several people now, but I don't understand it. Why would you be mad at me because Madelyn left?"

She took a deep breath and looked out into the water. She was raw and vulnerable. "I'll explain, if you answer my question first," she finally said.

"Was Maddie's disappearance hard on me?"

She nodded.

"Lily, Madelyn was my sister. We were really close, you know. Not just in age, but in everything. I knew she was sneaking out that night, she told me. I didn't stop her. I should have. I should have gone after her, protected her, but I didn't, and then she never came back. I never told anyone I knew about her plans that night, and I blamed myself for a long time. To make matters worse, Mom got really scared of everything. She went borderline psychotic for a long time. I was fifteen years old. She yanked me out of school to homeschool me. I wasn't allowed to go anywhere without supervision. Do you have any idea what that was like?"

I didn't mean to unleash everything on Lily, but I couldn't seem to stop talking. I'd never talked to anyone about this stuff before, not even Syd. Lily was crying, but I kept talking.

"Dad intervened my senior year, but even still, while others were up partying late into the night, I had a strict ten o'clock curfew and even if I was one minute ahead of that curfew, I'd come home to Mom practically hyperventilating in fear, watching the clock for my return. It was hard. When I went off to college, I went a little wild at first from the freedom. I considered not returning to Collier at all. I was ready to be a lone wolf, but my place in the Pack had been so tightly engrained in me that it only lasted a short while before I came back home."

"But you were never here. Never," Lily said, raising her voice while tears streaked down her face. "I returned every year on the anniversary of Maddie's disappearance. The entire Pack held a vigil, every single year. You missed them all. Rumors said you were in Cabo or up in Alaska living it up with a harem of women at your disposal. You were everywhere but where your family needed you most. Where I needed you most."

The pain in her words cut me like a knife. I wrapped my arms around her and pulled her to me, kissing the top of her head.

"There was never a harem of women. Those were all rumors and nothing more. You're right, though, I wasn't here. I always made plans to be away during the vigil. It was too hard, too painful. I couldn't face it all. The tighter my parents' restrictions were in the early years, the more I resented Maddie for leaving me. I was angry at her. I've never said that aloud before, but there you have it. I was angry at my sister for not coming home. I was angry at myself for not listening to my gut instinct and letting her go out that night. I was young, and I was angry. Mom and Dad understood that, even if they didn't really know the reasons for it. They sent me away to other packs that week, and when I was old enough and on my own, I chose to stay away. I'm not perfect, Lily. There are some demons that are just too great to face and that vigil each year was mine."

Lily

Chapter 15

Never once had I considered things from Thomas's side. His words and account of what he'd experienced and felt contradicted everything I'd imagined in my head. Years of anger and hatred melted away, and I didn't know how to process it all.

"I'm sorry," I whispered.

"You don't have anything to be sorry about," he assured me.

"Yes, I do. I tend to be an emotion feeder. Everyone was always so sad at those vigils, and I never missed them. The only vigil I ever skipped was last year, the day I found out MC was alive and well. Madelyn was never the only one missing at those things. You were. I'd look at your family, so sad and supportive of each other. They were so strong in the face of such devastation, and in my mind, you'd just abandoned that. You gave up on her and you let down your family. Sure, they never said anything like that, and even Ruby and Lizzy tried to argue a case on your behalf a thousand times, but I would never once listen. My mind was made up and you had to be the most evil person alive to do that to them."

"You mean the biggest douchebag?" he said, sadly at first, then smiling bigger and bigger as the pieces seemed to fall into place.

I blushed. "Yup, that's about how it went."

"And now?" he asked, brushing my hair behind my ear.

"Now? I don't know what to think. It's going to take some time to absorb all that," I told him honestly.

He nodded, then stood, grabbing my hands and hoisting me

to my feet. We quietly walked back to the truck. I was thankful we didn't pass Mr. Draper on the way, certain my nose was red and my eyes puffy from crying during his story.

We stopped at another barn. This one was all wood and rustic looking, and I could see the stalls of horses from the parking lot. I quickly checked myself in the mirror on the visor, happy to see I didn't look like I had been crying.

Thomas opened the door and shook his head. "You look beautiful. Stop making a fuss," he said.

His compliment caused wild flutters in my stomach, but when I looked back at him, I was still having a tough time reconciling the man I was getting to know with the boy I had thought he was. I slid from the truck, right into his arms. He leaned in and I knew he was about to kiss me.

"Thomas!" a loud voice yelled, interrupting us.

Thomas rested his forehead against mine and took in a deep, frustrated breath. I liked seeing him all worked up. He kissed my forehead and pulled back with a fake smile on his face and irritation flowing off him in waves.

"Hey man, be up in a sec," he yelled back at a dark-haired, handsome cowboy perched on the fence.

We headed in that direction, and four more gorgeous men in tight jeans and cowboy hats seemed to appear out of thin air. Thomas greeted each of them with some weird handshake.

"We're breaking in the new filly," the one who had yelled at him said.

Ruby came out of the stables and headed our way. I was grateful for a familiar face. It was a little overwhelming being surrounded by all those hot, tanned muscles. My wolf was agitated and didn't like me even near them, but I could still take a second to appreciate the scenery, despite her growling protests in the back of my mind.

"I see you've met the Six Pack," Ruby said, stopping and giving me a hug. "Don't let these boys flatter you. The whole lot of them are nothing but heartbreakers."

"Oh sweet Ruby, I'd never look at another woman if you'd have me," the red-headed cowboy said.

"Austin, that's enough out of you. You know you aren't man enough to handle all this," Ruby teased back. With her own striking, curly red hair they would have made quite the couple. She turned back to me. "Thomas introduce you to the gang already?"

"No, ma'am, he didn't," Austin said, all his attention suddenly turned my way. I felt Thomas take a step closer to me.

"That jackass right there is Austin. This guy up here," Thomas said, pointing to the first one I had seen, "that's Wyatt. And this is Clay, Emmett, and James." I tried to keep track of who was who.

"Hi," I said. "I'm Lily."

"Miss Lily Westin. We'd know that beautiful face anywhere," Clay said, and Thomas growled aggressively at him, taking a step towards him.

"Jesus, Thomas. What the hell's wrong with you?" Emmett asked.

"Poor Clay's gonna shit himself, you do that again," James added.

"Something tells me this girl is completely off-limits, boys," Wyatt laughed, warning them. "Lily, it's nice to meet you," he said, jumping down from his perch. "Any girl manages to get this dick that worked up is fine in my book. How long are you in town for?"

"End of the week, at least," I said. I chanced a look at Thomas just in time to see him wince. *Good*, I thought. I liked the idea of him being affected by that thought. The way things had progressed in the last twenty-four hours, I wasn't sure I'd be able to leave at all, but I wasn't ready to admit that either.

"I'm sure my mate, Kate, would love to have you over for dinner before you leave, if you have the time."

I looked at Thomas and shrugged, seeking his approval. He nodded, and while the others had gone about their business and gotten back to work, I knew Wyatt was observing everything.

"Yeah, okay. That sounds great," I finally told him, and I meant it.

Ruby came back through from wherever she had been headed and stopped to talk some more.

"You'll like Kate, Lily. Sweet girl. Wyatt's the only of the Six Pack to take a mate, so far," she added. "I know Kate will be thrilled for a little female company."

"Why do you call them the Six Pack?" I asked curiously.

Ruby laughed. "Those six have been running together since

they were just small pups. Practically inseparable. They didn't earn their name till they hit high school, though. They all bulked up, working out obsessively for football. They were practically unstoppable. When they rightfully developed six-pack abs and spent an entire summer showing them off, they acquired the name and it's never gone away. They are legendary across the Packs. I can't believe you've never heard of them."

I snorted. "If it started with 'Thomas Collier . . .,' I promise you I tuned it out and didn't want to hear about it."

"Ouch," Wyatt said. "Don't you be going and breaking my boy's heart, now. I kind of got the vibe there might be something between the two of you."

I looked at him in all seriousness. "If you had said that a week ago, I'd have given you a good tongue lashing and probably kneed you in the 'nads. Old habits die hard."

Wyatt chuckled. "Looks like you got your hands full with this one, Collier."

Thomas smiled that full, irresistible, slightly crooked smile. "I'll manage."

"He ain't denying it neither," Wyatt said, winking at me and walking away.

"Ruby?" I asked.

"Yeah?"

"Is Collier Pack as big a bunch of gossips as Westin?"

"Probably even worse," she admitted.

"There's really little point in trying to hide this, is there?"

"You mean, you mating my brother?"

I looked at her guiltily. "Yup."

"Half the town's already abuzz about it, girl. Most are a little shocked. Torn because of . . ." She caught herself and stopped.

"Because of Sydney," I added.

"You know about her?"

"Well, yeah, she's kind of my only friend in town," I confessed.

Ruby put her arm around me. "That's not true. Lizzy, Clara, Peyton, Shelby, and I are all here. I think you'll really like Kate, and many others as you meet people. If you decide to go through with it and bond with Thomas, this will be your home. Your Pack."

"I'm okay with that, Ruby. I've always loved it here in

Collier. It's just . . ." I didn't quite know how to verbalize it.

"My brother is the biggest douchebag on the planet and the last person in this world you ever expected to mate."

"Pretty much."

"I know you channeled all your emotions about Maddie's disappearance onto him. He wasn't around to defend that line of thinking, and you never wanted to hear otherwise. I can't imagine the war waging inside of you right now. At some point you're going to have to talk to him about it."

I gave her a half smile. "We talked a lot about it all, everything really, earlier today. I'm just trying my best to process it. It's a lot to take in."

"It was easier to hate him than to love him, huh?"

"Love?" I snorted. "I don't love him. I can't. No way, that's Thomas!" I protested.

She gave me a knowing look as Thomas rode up on a large white stallion. "Lil, want to go for a ride?" he yelled as he approached.

"This can't be love," I whispered harshly under my breath as Ruby laughed in my ear. "Damn, that might be the sexiest thing I've ever seen," I confessed as he approached on horseback. "When the hell did that happen? Lust? Maybe, but definitely not love," I told her before he was within earshot.

He rode up on that white stallion with a double saddle already in place. He leaned down and grabbed my arm and swung me up in one smooth motion, like something you'd see in a movie. I settled into the seat behind him and gave a quick wave to Ruby as he took off at a trot.

It had been a long time since I'd been on a horse. I was grateful not to be the one in control. My arms instinctively wrapped around his waist as I held on tightly. Wyatt was waiting at the pasture gate, opening it so we could pass through, and closing it behind us. I looked back at him over my shoulder as he tipped his hat to me with a grin.

As soon as we were inside the pasture and in open fields, Thomas kicked and the horse took off at a full sprint. I held on even tighter and felt the rumble of pleasure go through him. I realized then that I was becoming more and more in tune with his emotions all day. It was a sign that the bond was strengthening between us. I stiffened for a moment and let the thought sink in, taking a quick assessment of everything I had learned and observed about him.

Thomas may not have been my first pick as a mate, but he also wasn't the douchebag I had portrayed him as. He was a good man, and it was easy to see he'd be a great Alpha when his time came. I definitely still had some unresolved personal feelings I was sorting through, but the thought of taking him as a mate and spending my life with this man, no longer revulsed me.

My mate, I thought, hugging him instead of just holding on for dear life. I took a deep breath, accepting his scent for the first time without any idea how that small gesture would affect me physically. I moaned in pleasure. It was the most delicious, intoxicating scent I'd ever smelled.

Thomas stopped short and the horse responded in kind, rearing back on his hind legs and neighing loudly. I squeezed Thomas tighter, saying a quick prayer we wouldn't both go flying off. He quickly regained control of the horse.

"I'm sorry," he said in a deep voice.

One second I was sitting behind him, my eyes shut tightly. The next, he had reached around and pulled me off. I yelped as I went flying through the air, though he remained completely in control. When I opened my eyes I was sitting in the front seat facing him. He was staring at me like he couldn't believe his eyes. He gently touched my face and took a deep breath.

"What changed?" he asked.

"Wh—?"

Before I could finish saying the word, his mouth crashed down on mine. I didn't hesitate or stiffen this time. I kissed him back with a desperate urgency, opening fully to him as his tongue swept in and battled with mine. I moaned into him, his arms wrapping tightly around me.

We were six feet off the ground on a horse who had just been spooked. I should have been panicking, but I was lost in my mate's kisses without a care in the world.

He slowed and backed off, giving me a moment to catch my breath. He peppered light kisses across my cheek, nipping at the lobe of my ear. He growled, "Mine."

My entire body shook in recognition. "Yours," I returned, finding his mouth again and kissing him with a desire that overwhelmed all my senses.

Our lips never broke apart as he dismounted, bringing me with him. He paused only a moment to remove a blanket from the saddle bag and spread it across the ground.

I giggled. "You came prepared, I see."

He grinned, and my heart flipped over in my chest. "For a picnic lunch, or so I thought."

I quickly removed my shirt and discarded it on the ground before reaching for his. There was a great sense of urgency. I needed him. All of him. He made short work of his boots, his pants, and my pants. Soon we stood naked in the middle of nature taking a moment to admire each other. He went to remove his hat, but I stopped him.

"You can keep the hat," I said with a smirk.

"Yes, ma'am," he replied, before his lips found mine again.

As we resumed our kisses, my hands explored the hard planes of his chest, the bulging ridges of his arms, and the tight muscles of his stomach that had clearly earned him his place in the Six Pack.

His hands cupped my breasts and his calloused thumbs skimmed my nipples, the contrasting textures causing more pleasure than I could ever have imagined.

"Please tell me you're on the pill, because despite what you think, I did not come prepared for this," he said between kisses.

I grinned against him. "I am, but at this moment I wouldn't give a shit anyway."

He laughed and it became a playful bantering of further exploration that had me panting and ready when he finally took me. I flinched at the sting of his intrusion, and he slowed, giving my body time to adjust and accept him. Taking his time, he led us to a steady rhythm that soon had my head soaring in some unknown plane of existence before crashing back to reality. We were both sweaty, my chest heaving as I tried to regain consciousness.

"That was amazing," I said in wonder as we lay there, still joined as one.

I groaned in protest when he rolled off me, a huge grin on his face. He kissed me softly this time, lovingly.

"Are you okay?" he asked.

I took a quick personal assessment. "More than okay," I assured him, pulling him down for another kiss. I could quickly become addicted to his kisses.

He rolled to his back, removing his hat, and pulled me with him, tucking me close to his side. He kissed the top of my head and sighed contentedly. We lay there talking for a while just getting to know each other, our likes, our dislikes, all those little details of life. I had never felt so perfectly content and happy in all my life. *Complete,* my wolf's voice said. *Mate.*

I sat up and looked around. We were in the middle of a field. The mountains were off in the distance, but otherwise I couldn't see anything or anyone in any direction.

"Um, Thomas?"

"Yeah?"

"I think the horse took off with our lunch."

He laughed, opened his eyes, and looked around. "Yeah, looks like it. He'll find his way back when he gets hungry."

"How about us? What are we going to do?" I asked.

He shrugged. "Want to shift and go for a run? That's the fastest way home."

I loved the idea of running with him. I nodded. "That sounds perfect, actually."

Thomas folded the blanket while I gathered our clothes. He placed them in the center of the blanket and closed it up like a hobo sack.

"Brilliant," I said, and he beamed at my praise. I loved knowing that pleased him.

He shifted first and a very large, gray wolf stood before me.

"Magnificent," I praised again, and could feel his emotions swell even in wolf form.

He walked to me and sniffed me all over as I laughed and pushed him away. He nodded his head, encouraging me to shift. I let the warm sensation flow over me as my body transitioned into my wolf. She yipped and pranced before our mate. I licked him, then turned and took off at a full sprint. I knew I was fast, but despite the time he took to pick up our things in his massive jaws, he caught up to me easily. We ran the entire way back to the truck, clearly both of us needing to work off a little more energy.

With that thought, my wolf filled my head with images of Thomas naked above me. I rolled my eyes, not needing any reminder or further encouragement. If I let myself think about it too much I might freak out. I mean, it was Thomas, after all, but if I just let myself feel instead, all was good. Great, even.

Thomas
Chapter 16

I couldn't believe the sudden change in my relationship with Lily. I felt like things would work out now and we'd be okay. She was amazing, sweet, funny, and really smart, not just smart-mouthed, though she was that, too. The more I really got to know her, the more I liked her.

I knew I hadn't been myself since I lost it back in San Marco. That experience of losing control and having to fight to gain even the smallest bit of control over my wolf had humbled me. Austin had teased me earlier that I was whipped already. Emmett said she might as well put a collar on me. I should have had some witty comment to shoot back at the both of them, but I hadn't.

I knew I could be an asshole. Sometimes it was just because I wanted to be, and other times it was a defense mechanism to keep people from getting too close. Since I'd accepted Lily, my wolf had calmed drastically, and so had I. It was kind of freaking me out, and it had shocked the hell out of the guys. I was trying not to think too much about it.

As we got back to the truck, I was glad to see the guys were gone. My wolf was feeling very protective of our mate, and I didn't think he would have tolerated another male in her presence so soon after making love to her.

I dropped the bag I'd been carrying in my mouth next to the truck and shifted back to my human form. She followed my lead, and I wrapped my arms around her, shielding her from view, just in case I'd been mistaken and someone was around. A quick sniff of the air and another look around made me confident I hadn't.

Still, I encouraged her to change quickly, trying to get her to understand the irrational feelings I was having. She laughed at me, but humored me by dressing.

I needed to get her home. Now that I'd had her, it wasn't enough. I didn't think it would ever be enough. The thought made me grin. Before she had a chance to question my expression, my phone rang.

"Hey, Mom," I answered, seeing her face on my screen.

"Thomas, I'm glad I caught you. Your father needs to speak with you, and I wanted to see if you and Lily could come to the house for dinner tonight."

"How soon is dinner? The horse ran away with our lunch and we're starving," I laughed, as Lily's cheek turned pink and she playfully smacked me and scolded me to behave and be quiet.

"We'll eat early then. Say five?"

"Five?" I asked Lily. She looked at the clock and groaned. It was still two hours away, but she conceded.

"Yeah, that's fine, Mom. We'll see you then."

I hung up the phone and looked over at Lily. She was staring out the window, but smiling, and she felt relaxed. I reached for her hand and linked our fingers together, giving it a squeeze. She turned to look at me, and I suddenly knew there was nothing I wouldn't do to keep that smile on her beautiful face.

"You sure you're okay with spending time with my family tonight? I can call back and beg off if you just want to be alone."

"No, it's fine. I love your family. I don't mind spending time over there, and Patrick, Maddie, Liam, and the kids will only be here a few more days."

I pulled to the side of the road and stopped the car to stare at her. I couldn't let my hopes jump ahead of me in case I was misunderstanding what she was saying.

"Lil, are you saying what I think you're saying?"

She watched with combined confusion and mischief. "What?" she tried to ask innocently, but I wasn't buying it.

"Don't play games with me, I'm being serious here," I said, my tone coming across a little harsher than I meant it to.

She straightened her back, sitting up taller. I noticed she did that when she was being stubborn or defiant.

"I am not playing games, Thomas. I'm simply stating a fact. They'll only be here a few more days and I'd like to spend some time with them."

"But you? Will you only be here a few more days?" That was the question I desperately needed the answer to. "You said a one week trial. Even with all that's happened I didn't want to ask until the end of the week, but I need to know. Are you staying here? With me?"

I tampered down the Alpha demand in my voice that often made me sound like an asshole. I let myself be vulnerable to her because I needed her to tame her own stubborn side and answer me honestly.

Lily lifted her hand and framed my cheek. I leaned into it and her thumb lightly caressed my cheek. "You, Thomas Collier, are the last person on Earth I ever wanted to see, let alone spend my life with." Just like that it felt like a truck ran over my heart, backed up, and hit it again. "But, you are my one true mate. I don't understand it, and if I let myself think about it too much, it sort of freaks me out. I've waited my entire life to find you. I've dreamed of you for as long as I can remember, and sure, it wasn't everything I thought it would be, and I didn't handle anything right at first, but I figure I have the rest of our lives to make that up to you, and besides, you really are cocky, and arrogant, and sometimes an ass. You need me to get that ego in check and . . ."

I cut her off mid-sentence with a kiss, careful not to let it escalate too much or else we wouldn't make it home in time to shower and change before dinner. Suddenly, I very much wanted to be home and naked in the shower with my gorgeous mate.

"A simple 'yes' would have sufficed."

"What fun would that have been? You needed to squirm a little."

I threw my head back and laughed. "Life is never going to be dull with you, is it?"

"Probably not."

"That's okay, because you are mine. Only mine. Always mine," I said in that growly voice that always came through when my wolf was worked up or my Alpha powers were heightened.

Lily just rolled her eyes back at me. "I thought we went through that already out in the field," she teased.

"With everything you've put my poor wolf through this last week, I think I'm going to be reminding you both of that for a long while."

She laughed, then leaned over and kissed me. "Take me home, Thomas. I really don't want to show up at your parents' with grass in my hair, smelling of sex."

"Yes, ma'am," I told her, unable to stop smiling as I drove us home.

When we arrived, Lily didn't wait for me. She jumped out and walked right on into the house. She was confident and comfortable in my home, which would soon officially be our home. It made me want to puff out my chest and strut around for all to see.

When I walked into the house, I could hear the shower already running in my bathroom down the hall. It was a little disappointing how quickly she was willing to wash away my scent, though I understood her reasons as I looked at the time. We didn't have long before we needed to be at the Alpha house for dinner.

Deciding not to waste any time at all, I kicked off my boots by the front door, carefully placed my hat on the rack, and headed for the bedroom. I discarded my clothes, leaving them in the hamper, and walked into the bathroom.

Lily had the radio cranked and was singing and dancing along with some upbeat song I didn't recognize. I took only a minute to enjoy the show before sliding back the door and joining her in the shower.

She screamed and did some crazy ninja chop move with her arms until she realized it was me.

"You scared the life out of me," she said, swearing under her breath as she swatted at me. "Don't do that to me!"

"Calm down, slugger. It's just me—everything's fine," I reassured her, rubbing up and down her arms and pulling her against my chest when it was safe to do so. "Maybe I should change your name to Ninja. Those were some bad moves," I said.

"You mean badass moves," she said with certainty.

"No, I'm pretty sure I had it right the first time."

She smacked me, but there was no malice behind it. "What do you think you're doing?" she finally asked.

"You," I told her, enjoying the look of surprise on her face.

"We don't have time for that, and I'll just have to take

113

another shower afterwards. Dinner, your parents' house, have you forgotten?"

"Nope, haven't forgotten a thing," I assured her. "Figured we'd knock out two birds with one stone."

"What are you talking about?" she questioned, feigning irritation.

I turned her around and pressed her hands against the wall of the stall and held them there for a moment. When I was fairly sure she wasn't going to move, I reached around and grabbed a wash cloth and soap and cleaned her back, her backside, down each leg and back up, trailing my path with kisses and occasional nips as the water washed her clean. She was moaning and starting to pant for me before I made my journey back up, stopping at all the sensitive places I had noted for a little extra attention.

When I stood, she was still bent over with her hands braced on the wall. One thrust and we were fully connected. I wanted to draw it out, take things slowly, but I supposed I had paid her a little too close attention on my explorations. She pushed back hard, grinding against me, seeking her release. I couldn't hold out for long before I was pumping hard, in desperate need of my own release, which came much too quickly. When she started to come, she turned and looked at me over her shoulder. Our eyes locked and for that moment, the only thing that existed was her. My balls tightened and my body shook as I fought not to close my eyes and break the perfect connection between us.

Panting and spent, Lily nearly collapsed in my arms. I protectively gathered her up and just held her as the water beat down on us. We stayed that way until our combined breaths began to normalize again.

"My legs feel like Jell-O," she confessed with a giggle. "But, you were right. That was excellent time management."

I threw my head back and laughed, reaching over to turn the hot water down and add a little cold. "This will help with the lightheadedness some," I assured her.

"You know, I've always been more of a luxury bath kinda gal, but I am seriously rethinking that stance."

I watched her as she reached for the shampoo and began massaging it into her scalp. I had to breathe in deep and try to think of anything else before I gave in to my desires and had her back pressed up against the wall. She gave me a sly look, as if she could read my thoughts. "Next time," I promised.

She laughed as she finished rinsing her hair and turned off the shower. I shook my head and water went flying everywhere. She stopped and turned to face me with both hands on her hips. "Did you just wet-dog me?"

"Did I what?" I asked.

"Did you just shake off the water like a damn dog?"

I could see in her eyes she was teasing and I loved it. "So what if I did? And wouldn't that be wet wolf to you? I'm not a dog, I'm a wolf."

She wrapped her arms around my neck and pressed her wet body against me, kissing me till my head spun. "Correction. You're *my* wolf."

I stood there speechless as she exited the shower and grabbed a towel. I had a dozen witty comebacks in my head, but I couldn't articulate a single one of them.

"Come on, big boy. It's time to go face the family," she said, leaving the bathroom. "I'm never going to live this down, so we might as well get the worst of it over with," she mumbled under her breath.

I shook my head, and finally managed to move my legs again. I dried off and left the towel hanging in the bathroom. She squeaked in surprise when I strolled out of the room.

"We don't have time for another round right now," she said, but the spike in estrogen throughout the room confirmed she wanted to.

"Believe it or not, I'm just grabbing clean clothes."

"Oh, well, then get a move on it. We're going to be late," she reminded me, heading back into the bathroom still wrapped in her towel.

I grabbed fresh clothes and dressed quickly. She still hadn't come out of the bathroom. I peeked in, and my heart nearly turned over in my stomach. My canines elongated and my mouth watered at the sight before me. I took some deep, calming breaths, trying to get control of myself again.

Lily stood at the sink putting the final touches of makeup on. She was wearing a short blue dress that made her legs look a mile long, paired with heels high enough to bring her to the perfect kissing level. Her pink streaked hair lay damp and untouched. She was a vision to look at.

I walked just behind her, grabbing her by the hips. Her eyes met mine in the mirror and she shook her head. "Not this time, big boy. Dinner with the parentals, remember?"

I nodded, and kissed her neck when she stood to full height to stare at the two of us together in the mirror. Watching her turn in my arms, I knew I had been right. I gave her a light kiss on the lips. Perfect kissing height. She sighed as I feathered more light kisses across her cheek and down the ivory column of her neck. Catching me completely off guard, she smiled and bared her neck fully to me.

My breaths were coming in short pants as my canines began to grow again. I took one deep breath, pushing my wolf back.

"You have no idea how badly I want to see my mark on you. Right here," I said, kissing the spot where I knew I would soon claim her. "But . . ."

She stiffened and looked at me with confusion and hurt in her eyes. "But? Did you really just say 'but?'"

I gave her my sexy crooked grin, watching as her pupils dilated. Yeah, I knew the effect I could have on a woman, but that knowledge had never thrilled me more than knowing for certain I could have that effect on this woman, the only one that mattered.

"But, we're late for dinner, and I am not sealing our bond and then heading to the Alpha house to eat with my parents and sisters. When I mark your perfect skin, I plan to spend the entire day and all through the night making very certain you are mine forever."

She shivered in my embrace. "Okay," she said, a little breathlessly and more agreeably than I think either of us expected. She still looked a little dreamy-eyed as I led her out of the house and back to the truck for the drive over to my parents' house.

Lily

Chapter 17

I had always considered myself a dominant person.

I was wrong. Very, very wrong.

When Thomas got all growly or spoke to me with full authority like explaining exactly how our bonding was going to happen, it excited me in ways I couldn't even fathom. And when he took the lead of things so assuredly in the shower, I wasn't certain how I had managed to stay upright.

My cheeks started to pink, and the air seemed hot despite the coolness setting in as the sun dropped. Part of me thought it was a moment I would relive in my dreams over and over, and then reality spoke up reminding me I didn't have to, because he was all mine, and I could have that anytime I wanted.

"You okay?" Thomas asked, sounding concerned. "You look a little flushed."

"Oh, I'm fine. More than fine actually," I assured him. He gave me that sexy grin and I sighed happily.

This is what I had waited for. This is what I had longed for, that moment of complete satisfaction and happiness that only a true mate could ever bring. I was a little disappointed we hadn't already sealed our bond. Once I made up my mind on something, I wasn't one to wait for it to happen. "Lily's like a dog with a bone when she sets her heart on something," my dad always said about me. Perhaps there was a tiny bit of truth behind his words.

I had decided to accept the mating call with Thomas, and oh my word was I ever thankful I did. I had big dreams and ideas of what it would be like, and he had so far exceeded every one of them. I was blissfully happy, and I no longer cared who knew it.

When we arrived at his parents' house, he helped me from the truck, looking handsome in tight black jeans, black boots, and a navy and green flannel shirt that complemented my dress perfectly. We were a stunning match, walking in hand-in-hand.

The entire room went quiet when we reached the living room, where most of the family was sitting around waiting on us. Liam rose and crossed his arms over his chest, but Patrick came over and hugged me.

"Thank God!" he said.

"Come again?" I asked.

"I'm catching a flight back tonight and both Elise and Kelsey have been blowing up my phone looking for a play-by-play. You've given me nothing to tell them," Patrick complained.

"Why are you heading back early? Is something wrong? Is E okay?" I asked, a hundred bad scenarios flashing through my head. Without realizing what I was doing, I clung to Thomas for support.

Shelby laughed. "Yup, they're definitely a thing now."

Lizzy scolded her.

"I wish I'd find my true mate," Peyton sighed, hugging a pillow to her chest.

Maddie wrapped her arms around Liam and he finally began to relax.

"Look, none of that matters. What's wrong that you have to head back early?" I asked Patrick.

"Nothing," Liam said, trying to assure me. "He's just whipped and missing his woman, so he asked if he could return a few days early."

"That's it? Really?" I questioned Patrick.

"That's honestly it. I hate being away from Elise, but especially this long. It's only a few days."

I let go of Thomas and hugged Patrick. A low growl escaped from my mate. I just rolled my eyes and shook my head. "Tell my sisters I'm fine, and to mind their own business."

He laughed. "What the feck are you trying to do to me? They are going to eat me alive for every detail about the two of you, if your mate doesn't kill me first."

"She didn't flinch on 'mate.' Yes! I knew it. Pay up, ladies,"

Ruby said as Cora and Zach walked in.

"Pay up for what?" Zach asked his daughter.

"Ruby has a pool going for when Thomas and Lily are going to seal the deal," Clara confessed.

"What? Ruby," her mother scolded.

Zach looked away and tried to change the subject quickly as his daughters all stared at him. He cleared his throat. "Congratulations, son."

"Wait, wait, wait," I interrupted. "What's the bet up to, and what were the rules?"

"Lily," Maddie started to threaten, but I shushed her because I really wanted to know.

"I think it's over five hundred dollars, and the bets are on when you'd seal the deal," Shelby said as Cora quickly began apologizing to me on behalf of her children.

"Hold up now, seal the deal, as in seal our bond, or just sex?" I asked.

"Oh sweet Lord, what is happening to this family?" Cora said dramatically.

Lizzy choked on a drink and shot water through her nose. Ruby and Shelby just laughed, as Maddie tried to smooth things over.

"Seal the bond," Clara finally spoke up. "The pool has date and time."

My shoulders sagged and I shook my head. "Give them back their money, Ruby," I said, turning my neck to show there was no mark there. Several people groaned.

"Yes," Zach said. "I'm still in it."

"Zachary Collier." Cora turned to him with her finger wagging in his face, but he just snagged her around the waist and planted a kiss on her lips. Her cheeks were pink, but she was radiating with happiness from her mate's attention. I wondered if that's what I looked like to them.

"I was so sure it was going to happen today. What went wrong?" Ruby whined.

"Ask him to explain it. Was not my decision," I confessed.

"Lily," Thomas and Liam both warned in unison.

"What? I thought we came for a nice family dinner. You guys are the ones that bombarded us, not the other way around."

"Lily Ann, we really need to work on getting you a filter," Maddie said, laughing and hugging me. "I'm so happy we're going to be sisters again, though."

I rolled my eyes. "Me mating Thomas does not make us any more sisters than we already are."

Shelby joined in and hugged us both, and so did Peyton. "Maybe not, but it does for the rest of us," Shelby said.

"You guys are really okay with this?" I asked, feeling overwhelmed.

"Look," Ruby said. "Someday we'll have five more brothers added to this family, but we'll only ever have one last sister. You and Maddie have been practically inseparable since you were just little pups. We all watched you grow up. You've always been family. When Maddie was gone, we clung to you every chance we got, holding on to just a small part of her. I think I can speak for all us when I say that there is no one else on this planet that we would rather see Thomas officially bring into this family. No one."

The girls all hugged me, and I was teary eyed by the time Thomas's strong arms wrapped around me. He kissed the top of my head, but quickly tried to diffuse the situation.

"I'm really happy you guys are happy, and I promise we'll make it official soon, but right now, I'm starving, and I know Lily is, too. Can we please just eat dinner?"

"Amen to that, brother," Liam said, giving Thomas a fist bump.

We all settled down to dinner. There was more light bantering and it turned out to be a fun evening. I felt right at home with the Colliers. I always had, but this time it felt even more right if that was possible.

The evening ended much too soon. We said goodbye to Patrick shortly after dinner. Lizzy and Ruby drove him to the airport while the other girls left to head to the bar in town shortly after. They invited me and Thomas to tag along, but we declined, not quite ready for such a public appearance. Maddie and Liam said goodnight when Sara was ready for her final feeding. Oscar had already crashed on the couch, and I watched as my brother carried his son to bed.

My head rested on Thomas's shoulder as we sat on the couch talking to his parents.

"I'm glad the others took off early, son. I needed to discuss something with the two of you," Zach said when it was just the four of us. "Tulok called and said he could use a little help for a few days and was wondering if you were available. He's having a bit of trouble with something, but didn't go into details. I had to explain about your situation, but he assured me that Amka would be most thrilled to meet your new mate. I would be surprised if you didn't already know Tulok and Amka of the Alaskan Pack, Lily."

"Yes, of course. It's been a few years since I last saw them, but I have fond memories of the both of them."

"Would you mind taking a trip up and seeing what we can do to help?" Thomas asked, and it warmed me that he was considerate enough to ask me before making a decision for the two of us.

"That would be fine with me," I admitted. He smiled his approval, and it did something weird and fluttery to my insides.

"We'll fly up in the morning then," Thomas confirmed with his father.

We spent a little more time with the two of them just talking, before calling it a night. Once back outside, the crisp cool night air had me feeling alive and vibrant. We looked too good to just call it a night.

"Are you sure you didn't want to go out with your sisters for a bit?" I asked him.

He seemed surprised by my question. "I assumed you weren't ready to go public. It was only the other day you wouldn't even walk into the deli with me, remember?"

"Yeah, well, a lot's changed since then, I'd say. If I'm not going back with Maddie and Liam in a few days, then word's going to spread really quickly. I'd rather control it at this point, instead of ignoring it, don't you think?"

"Yes, I do think that's for the best," he confessed.

"Well, come on then. Let's do this." I was less certain than I sounded. My mind was made up and I knew Thomas wasn't going anywhere. I didn't understand why I felt so confident about us, but I did and needed to not overthink it. What I worried about the most was Sydney. I had been to the tavern and heard how proud people were to have her as their future Pack Mother. How disappointed would they be to find that role would go to me instead?

I faltered at the door. "Change your mind?" he asked.

"No, just nervous," I admitted.

"Nervous? What do you have to be nervous about?"

I didn't like feeling vulnerable in front of anyone, even if it meant putting up a sarcastic front to cover it, but I couldn't do that with Thomas.

"I know how much everyone loves Sydney around here, and how they all thought she'd be the best Pack Mother ever. How disappointed will they be?"

Thomas smiled and hugged me. "Sydney would have no doubt made a fine Pack Mother, but she isn't you and the mere fact that you are more concerned about their feelings than your own, tells me what an amazing job you're going to do in that role. My Pack wants me happy, healthy, and strong, and with you by my side, I will be. They're going to love you, Lily."

I did some quick meditation breathing and nodded. "Okay, let's do this."

He put his arm protectively around my waist and guided me into the tavern. I spotted the girls quickly, as well as the Six Pack, but not before everyone else in the place noticed me.

It went from a vibrant, loud, music-filled room to dead silence. I looked up at Thomas, but he just smiled and ignored them all. He guided me over to his friends, who were sitting next to his sisters. The guys shook hands and I hugged the girls. Wyatt was there and introduced me to his mate, Kate.

"Don't pay no attention to those staring rudely, Lily. I'm glad you and Thomas came out tonight. I've been dying to meet ya," Kate said, and I felt an immediate friendship bloom.

The place was just starting to recover from our appearance when Sydney walked in. It was total silence once again. Sydney's eyes met mine and she lit up and smiled, walking over to hug me.

"Girl, I sure hope this means you made the right decision," she told me.

"I'm not sure at this moment which one that would be."

"You here with Thomas?"

"Yes."

"You staying when Madelyn heads back home?"

"Yes," I confessed.

"Then you made the right choice. Welcome to Collier. Milly, a round for Lily and Thomas on me. Let those old biddies talk. We needed some good gossip around here."

"I'm pretty sure you're in the middle of that gossip," I reminded her.

"Poor Sydney, lost the best thing she had going for her. Yeah, I've been hearing it all around town and seeing the looks, but you know what? I don't give a shit, and neither should you."

She wrapped an arm around me and we both stared at Thomas. She gave me a squeeze. "I've never seen him look so happy. That's you, not me. I'm going to be just fine, so please don't worry about me."

"I love you, Syd. You're the best," I told her honestly, hugging her tightly.

"Look at that, I didn't even have to get you drunk to hear those words this time," she replied.

I snorted.

Thomas
Chapter 18

The night out had been a little uncomfortable, but not terrible. I had wanted to introduce Lily around, but we stayed close to my sisters and friends. More attention was drawn our way when Sydney arrived, but she and Lily made a quick show of unity and the mood lightened when no fireworks went off between the two of them.

I liked having my mate by my side. I liked that we were not hiding it from others. Overall, it had been a good ending to an amazing day. Even better was coming home and having her curled up in my arms as she slept. I had lain awake just watching her for hours, taking in all that had happened between us.

Morning came much too quickly. I woke up wanting Lily so badly it was uncomfortable, but a quick glance at the clock on my nightstand told me we didn't have time. Sighing, I got up and headed for the shower.

When I was done, Lily still wasn't awake.

"Lily, we have to go," I told her, giving her a shake.

She grumbled and rolled over, pulling the covers up over her head. I dressed, continuing to talk to her, but she didn't budge.

"Lily," I said louder, shaking her harder.

There was a knock at the door and I gave up my efforts so I could answer it.

Opening the front door, I saw Maddie, Liam, and the kids.

"You ready?" Liam asked. "Your dad got tied up and asked if we could pick you up and drop you at the airstrip."

"I'm about ready, but . . ."

Before I could finish, Maddie and Liam both started laughing.

"Let me guess. You can't get my sister up?"

I nodded. "I think she's just really tired. We stayed out too late last night. I hope she's not coming down with something."

"She's not," Maddie assured me. "It just takes an act of God to get her moving. Once she's up, she's usually good, though. Oscar, go wake up Aunt Lily," she told her son.

"Any means necessary?" he asked, looking a little too pleased by that thought.

"Extreme force if you must," Liam told him, and they high fived before Oscar shot off down the hallway.

"Aunt Lily," I heard him yelling.

"End of the hall," I hollered after him.

I heard a screech from Lily and my entire body went into full panic mode. I growled and took off down the hall with Liam laughing behind me. When I entered the room, the tank top Lily was sleeping in was soaking wet, leaving little to the imagination. I quickly moved to cover her when the others walked in.

Oscar came from the bathroom with another cup full of water. "Out of bed or I'll get ya again, Aunt Lily," he said, giggling.

"You wouldn't!" she dared.

"Oh, wouldn't I?"

"Why didn't you just wake me up?" she whined to me.

"What?" I said, exasperated. "I've been trying for half an hour or more. It was like you were dead to the world."

She rolled her eyes and pulled the covers back, getting out of bed. "Well, I'm up now. How much time do I have?"

"You don't," Liam said. "Plane's gassed and waiting."

"No shower?" she whined.

"You'll survive. They do have showers in Alaska, and it's a pretty short flight. Depending on which plane you're on, you might even have one on the flight," Maddie said, trying to be encouraging.

Lily pouted, but she quickly packed and we were soon on our way. We said goodbye to my sister and her family and walked across the tarmac to the small plane awaiting our arrival. I checked in with the captain when we boarded, and escorted Lily to the back to take our seats.

"I can't believe how hard you slept," I teased.

She shrugged. "I get that a lot."

"So, I'm going to have to get an air horn or something just to wake you each morning?"

"Honestly, that probably won't help. It's been tried before."

I rubbed my hand up her thigh. "Perhaps you just need to be persuaded in other ways then."

I watched her gulp and smelled her arousal spike.

"It could be worth a try," she said slyly.

Much to my disappointment, we did not join the mile high club on our flight there, but the time passed quickly with heated innuendos and playful small talk until we were told to buckle up and take our seats for landing.

Tulok met us personally at the airport when we landed. He hugged me, then Lily, kissing her on the cheek.

"Welcome. Welcome," he said. "Amka cannot wait to see you and welcome your beautiful mate."

"How is she?" Lily asked. "It's been quite some time since I was last here."

Tulok stopped and stared at her for a moment. "Lily Westin?" She beamed up at him. He looked back and forth between the two of us. "Zach only said you would be bringing your new mate along. My apologies, Lily. I am caught off guard. Amka will certainly be thrilled. It has been too long since you last visited us, child."

"That it has," she said affectionately. "How is Amka?" Lily asked, taking the old man's arm as he escorted her to a waiting vehicle. Tulok caught her up as they chatted about the Alaskan Pack.

If it had been anyone else along for the trip, and the old Alpha had paid that much attention to them over me, my wolf would have been furious, demanding respect, but he was surprisingly calm. Lily was a Westin. Until then, I never really stopped to consider what that alliance would mean for Collier Pack, or what other connections she would strengthen just because of who she was.

Before that moment, I was too caught up in what she could do for me and how she made me feel. I hadn't given any thought whatsoever to my Pack and her benefit to them.

"What's that look for?" Lily asked me as we settled into the vehicle.

"You're pretty amazing, you know that?"

She leaned over and kissed me. "You're just figuring that out?"

I shook my head. "Nah, just reaffirming."

The ride from the airport to Tulok's home was a short one, but the scenery was amazing. I had always loved visiting the Alaskan Pack, and I didn't mind the snow. My wolf kept me warm in the cold. There were a variety of animals in the area, and they lived peacefully amongst other shifters, too, like the puffins and the polar bears. I had made friends with many of them, tagging along on visits as a pup with my dad, and never turned down an opportunity to return.

Arriving at our destination, I took Lily's hand as she exited the vehicle. Her shoes hit the ice and had I not been holding her, she would have surely fallen. Instead she laughed and grabbed hold of me for dear life. My wolf surged with happiness, and I could have sworn I felt her wolf, too.

Amka came out to greet us as we were still tangled around each other, trying not to fall over.

Lily laughed. "I meant to change to boots on the drive over."

"Those things will never work here, child," Amka scolded over her heels.

"Sweetheart, you will never believe who Thomas has taken as a mate," Tulok told her.

The old woman took a much closer look at the two of us, and gasped. Her hands flew to her mouth and she started talking quickly in a language I didn't know. The Pack lived deep in the Alaskan tundra and had maintained many of their native traditions and language, virtually untouched by the growing world around them. It was a good place to get back to the basics, find your foundation, and connect with your animal spirit on a much deeper level. Dad had sent me to this place on the first anniversary of Maddie's disappearance, and again the summer after my wolf surfaced.

"Lily-girl, is that really you?" Amka asked.

"Yes. It is so wonderful to see you, Amka," she said, risking the short distance between me and the woman to go and embrace her. I nervously stayed close by in case she started to fall again.

Why would she even bother wearing those ridiculous shoes at all? She knew where we were headed, and obviously had visited before, so she had to know what to expect. I didn't like her risking injury over something so stupid, and I would let her know it the moment we were alone.

"You know better than to wear that nonsense here. What were you thinking?" Amka scolded.

Lily blushed and looked my way. I wanted desperately to read her mind just then.

"I, uh . . ." She shook her head to clear her thoughts. "I did come prepared, I just forgot to change my shoes before we landed," she finally said.

"Well, come along then. Tulok will get your things. Thomas, help her into the house," Amka instructed.

She didn't have to tell me twice. I leaned down and scooped Lily up into my arms, cradling her against my chest. She giggled and smacked me, demanding to be put down, but I didn't listen until she was safely inside.

"Why did you wear those stupid things?" I asked as I set her down.

She frowned down at her shoes. "I love these shoes. Plus, someone woke me up rather abruptly and shooed me from the house. And I really love that they bring me up to the perfect height for this." There was a sparkle in her eyes when she closed the gap between us and kissed me.

Tulok cleared his throat behind us.

"To hear this girl talk about you, not that long ago, Thomas, this is the last thing I ever would have expected," Amka said. "You know she used to go on and on about how you were the . . ."

I put up a hand to stop her, knowing what was coming next. Lily buried her face against my chest. "I'm never going to live that down!" she exclaimed.

"Seriously, is there anyone within five packs that you didn't complain about me to?"

"Probably more like ten packs. I know a lot of people," she confessed. Even the tips of her ears were bright pink, which secretly made me happy watching her squirm.

"I should have known, should have seen the signs then. Only a true mate would get that worked up over someone," Amka confessed.

I liked to hope she was right. She pulled Lily from the safety of my arms and placed her hands against Lily's cheeks, looking deeply into her eyes. "Your wolf has always been so restless. She's finally found peace with your mate. I am glad you did not fight the bond, child, for it is strong between the two of you."

Lily dared a quick glance at me. "I didn't fight it that long," she blurted out.

I chuckled. "I think we were both equally shocked at first."

There was casual conversation as we caught up, and Amka fixed lunch for us. The morning passed quickly, and I still had no idea what we were doing there. Dad hadn't really said, just that Tulok had asked for help.

As we were sitting down to eat, their granddaughter arrived to join us. I hadn't seen Karis since she was just a pup, tagging along behind me as I tried to ditch her to play with my friends in the polar bear community. I'm sure she was around somewhere on my last few visits, but our paths just hadn't crossed.

Karis was now all grown up, and it suddenly made me feel old. She had long hair braided into thick dreads dyed red, and had clearly grown into a young woman while I was away.

"Lily!" she squealed, and ran to hug my mate. "Upa only told me Thomas was coming and bringing his new mate. He didn't mention you would be joining them. Why didn't you tell me?" Karis pouted.

"I did not know, child. Lily is Thomas's new mate," Amka told her granddaughter.

Karis turned large oval eyes my way and opened her mouth, then shut it again, before bursting out laughing. "You mated Thomas Collier?"

Lily didn't look so uncomfortable this time, she just smiled happily. "We haven't completed the bond, yet, but we're getting around to it. Just let it be a warning to you, Karis. Don't judge people, period. Trust me on this. No assumptions, and whatever you do, do not openly complain about anyone, especially a boy. I'll likely never live it down, but just like Mom always said, 'God doesn't make mistakes matching mates,' and yes, Thomas is mine."

Lily walked over and hugged me close, and I leaned down and gave her a quick kiss.

Karis and Amka sighed, sharing a look I didn't completely understand, but they looked happy.

"So," Lily said, "catch me up on all that's going on with you."

Karis chatted on and on about how she had finished her senior year the previous spring. She had originally thought she was going to stick around and just take online classes for the first two years of college, but she had been accepted to Archibald Reynolds College, an all-shifter college, for fall enrollment.

Lily told her about her brother, Chase, and his mate, Jenna, who were currently attending the ARC. They had caused quite the uproar around campus the previous semester when his wolf bonded with her panther. Of course, word of their mating had already reached the Alaskan Pack, who had stood with them when Jenna's father had declared war against the wolves in protest of their relationship.

It had been a sad time for the packs. Many good men and women had lost their lives in the battle, but it had also helped to unite the packs stronger than ever.

After lunch, Lily changes her shoes and the ladies took off to join Amka on her afternoon walk visiting others in the area. She was loaded down with a basket full of baked goods to distribute. Each Pack Mother brought their own unique touch to the Pack. I couldn't wait to see what Lily brought to Collier.

Finally, alone with Tulok, we could talk freely. "Tulok, Dad did not explain what you needed assistance with, only that it was urgent and I should go. What is happening?"

The older Alpha hesitated and stared out the window, lost in thought, before finally speaking. "The shifters are under attack. There is no other explanation. A puffin, a polar bear, and now one of my wolves have gone missing. Always just before a fresh snowfall. No tracks, no scent to follow. I am at a loss of what to do. I do not know the enemy we are facing. It has been very disturbing and has my people scared. I reached out to your father for any suggestions, and he offered your assistance to come up with fresh eyes to look over the facts."

I nodded, understanding the gravity of the situation. It was not normal for any of these people to just disappear. The wolves, puffins, and polar bears had lived in harmony for as long as human history could remember in these parts.

"Show me where they disappeared and let me speak to those

who last saw each of them. I am not sure what I can do to help, but I will look over all the facts and hopefully see something that was missed along the way."

"Thank you. That is all I can ask. The forecast is calling for snow again tonight, so everyone is anxious. Do not confuse that for guilt when you speak with them," he warned.

I nodded. "I understand.'

We first headed to a house on the outskirts of the village. He explained this was where Yutu had been taken, one of his wolves. We started there because he was the last to disappear.

Yutu's young mate greeted us at the door. Her small house was packed full with worried loved ones.

"Tulok, have you found him?" she asked, her eyes wide and hopeful.

He shook his head sadly. "I'm afraid we have no new leads yet. This is Thomas of the Collier wolves. He has some questions."

"I do not know anything," the woman sobbed, as three women surrounded her, offering comfort. "He was feeling restless and said he needed to go for a run. That wasn't abnormal; he got like that often. I was sitting on the back porch and I could feel him getting closer. He was coming home. I know he was. There was a strange howl and then nothing. His spirit started slipping further and further from me. I ran out towards the forest where he usually runs, but he kept drifting away from me. I ran and ran, but he slowly faded away and I haven't felt his connection since. Something happened to him out there. He wouldn't just leave like that."

"She called right away," Tulok added. "It was dark by the time we arrived, and a fresh snow overnight covered any tracks that may have been there."

"Trackers?" I asked.

"I brought in two, but they turned up nothing," the old man said.

I nodded. "Can you point me in the direction you felt him heading?"

"Yes, of course," the young woman said, leaving her guests and ushering me outside immediately.

We walked around the small house and down towards the woods. She seemed confident in her actions and the direction we were headed.

She stopped suddenly about half a mile from the house, surrounded by nothing. "This was as far as I went. By the time I arrived here, I could no longer feel our bond, yet somehow I know he's still alive out there. Please find him and bring my Yutu home."

"I'll do the best I can," I promised. I wasn't a tracker and I didn't know this area, so all I really could do was promise to try.

I advised her to head home. I knew there were others waiting who would worry about her. She hesitated but agreed. I continued walking in a logical path through the woods. Not far from where she left me, I smelled a strange metallic odor. Channeling more of my wolf senses, I let him lead me to the source of it. Coming to an abrupt stop, I dropped to my knees and began pushing snow aside.

Tulok caught up to me just as I uncovered a small needle. I held it up and sniffed, confirming what I already knew.

"What is it?" I asked aloud.

Tulok took the object from me and examined it. His eyes shone with fear. I was not accustomed to seeing an Alpha afraid of anything.

"Tranquilizer," he whispered. "Someone shot Yutu with a tranquilizer. They must have taken off with his body, but that would reaffirm everything his mate relayed to us. It's the only thing that makes sense."

I nodded. "Yes, but who? Why?"

"That, I am not sure."

"She said he continued to pull away from her, but that she no longer felt his presence a few yards back. Let's continue on and see if we can determine where they took him. It couldn't be far. If her story is correct, he would have been here when she heard his yelp. She immediately got up and came after him. She noted he was moving away from her the entire time. It took what? Maybe fifteen minutes to get to the spot she said she turned around at? If they were dragging him, she would have walked faster than they would have been moving. Come on," I urged him.

We walked through the woods, following a relatively clear path.

"This is a small creek during the summer months," Tulok said, breaking the silence.

We continued to follow the creek, and within a short time it opened to a clearing.

132

"A helicopter could easily land here," I noted.

"Yes, but we've not seen or heard any such thing in this area recently."

"You don't think we're far enough from the village to come and go quietly by air?"

"No, I do not," Tulok said.

"Okay then, they have to be around here, somewhere. It will likely be dark by the time we pull enough people together to search the area, but tomorrow at first light we start here."

"It's the closest thing to a lead we have. There will be many who will wish to assist in Yutu's search," Tulok admitted.

"How close to here were the bear and the puffin taken?" I asked.

"I am not sure. We will need to go and talk to their people to find that out."

"Now's as good a time as any."

Tulok started to turn back, but we heard some yells and cheers nearby.

"What is that?" I asked.

He shrugged. "Perhaps we should check it out."

We followed the voices, sensing no danger. It wasn't much further until the creek opened up to the river. A group of young puffins were sledding down the hill on their stomachs. Three boys stood at the top of the hill laughing and cheering them on.

"What's going on?" I asked as we approached them.

They looked at me, then to Tulok. They relaxed when they recognized him.

"We're just playing around. Jimmy made it all the way to the river from here. It was awesome!" one of the boys enthused.

"That's pretty impressive," I admitted, seeing how far it was still to the river.

"Who's that, Tulok?" the youngest of the boys asked, pointing to me.

"This is Thomas, future Alpha of the wolves of Collier Pack. He's here to help in the search for Yutu and the others missing."

The boy sniffed and wiped his coat sleeve across his nose. "Lyle was taken, too. He's my cousin."

"The missing puffin shifter?" I asked, and the kid nodded. "I'm real sorry to hear about your cousin. I'm going to do everything

I can to help find him."

The kid launched himself at me, wrapping his arms around my waist. "Thank you."

"Hey," I said, trying to lighten the mood. "Maybe you could help me out with something."

"Me?" the kid asked with curiosity.

"Yes, you. Can you tell me where your cousin was when he disappeared?"

The boy sadly shook his head. "He was heading here to go sledding. We were supposed to come with him, but my friend's chores weren't done yet, so my other friends and I stayed back and helped him. Lyle wasn't here when we arrived. He should have been, but he wasn't. His friends"—the boy pointed down to Jimmy and the others in puffin form—"showed up a little after us. No one was all that worried, but he didn't come home that night. Or the next. Or the next after that. Then we got word that Samson, one of the polar bears, was also missing. That happened almost a week ago. It's like they just vanished."

"I promise you, kid, they didn't just vanish, and we're going to get to the bottom of this. Did any of you see or hear anything odd? Maybe a helicopter?" All three boys shook their head no. "Okay, well, do me a big favor. Keep your eyes and ears alert for anything or anyone strange in this area. And whatever you do, stay in groups. Do not go out alone, anywhere, until we get to the bottom of this. Promise?" They all nodded this time. "Good. There's safety in numbers, and I don't want anything happening to any of you."

I had always had a soft spot for kids. It was clear from the looks on their faces that I had frightened them, and that certainly wasn't my intention. I needed to do something to lighten their mood or I knew it would weigh heavily on me the rest of the day.

"Hey, I think it would be best if I knew for sure that you kids could handle yourselves out here, so I'm going to need to see your best snowball."

They all looked at me like I was crazy, but quickly got to work making the best snowball they could and proudly showed me.

"Okay, now, I need to know you can do more than just arm yourself. I'm going to need to see those snowballs in action."

Before I could get out anything further, three snowballs came flying my way.

"Oh yeah?" I asked. "That's how it's going to be? I was going to say let me see you take out Jimmy and his friends, but if that's how you want to play, it's on."

I ran behind a large boulder and quickly began making snowballs. I peeked over the top only to be whacked in the face with one. Squeals of laughter sounded from all around. I lobbied a few blindly over the rock. When things started to quiet some, I took off after them, my arms loaded down as I lobbed one snowball after the other. Out of nowhere a puffin slammed into me and we collapsed to the ground.

"Get him!" one of the boys yelled as three puffins pinned me down, and the boys each chucked snowball after snowball at me. I got free and tackled two of them to the ground, tickling them as the third jumped on my back. I stood, taking all three kids with me, only to have the puffins grab hold of my legs. I made roaring sounds and walked around, probably looking much like Frankenstein, as Tulok just stood by laughing at the scene, no help whatsoever.

That's when I felt her. My mate. I looked around and across the river stood Lily with Amka and Karis, watching us. I felt her happiness through our bond for the first time and I started hamming it up with the kids even more.

Lily

Chapter 19

Visiting with Amka and Karis was fun, but my spirits lifted and I felt happiness in a whole new way when we reached the river. They had told me it was breathtakingly beautiful, but that wasn't it. My mate was nearby, and I was feeling him on a whole new level. It was a little similar to the first time my wolf recognized him . . .before I knew it was Thomas and things got more than a little weird.

I looked around at the natural beauty surrounding me, and directly across the river was a group of puffins playing. Judging by the man and three boys in the middle of a snowball battle with the puffins trying to join in, I assumed they were all puffin shifters.

The man's laughter rang out across the open air and it made my entire body tingle. Thomas. I looked a little closer at the scene. They were still some distance away, but I could clearly see my mate attempting to walk with three kids on him, and dragging a couple of puffins trying to ride on his feet. It looked like such silly fun, and so unlike Thomas.

"He's always been so wonderful with children," Amka commented.

"He has?" I asked.

She chuckled. "Yes, child. Thomas will make a wonderful father to your pups someday."

My pups? I thought. I tried hard to picture Thomas goofing off with our children as he was with these young boys. My image of Thomas didn't fit that picture at all, but the obvious evidence in front of me said otherwise. That warm tingling feeling washed over my skin again.

"That, Karis, is the look of true love," Amka told her granddaughter.

I snorted. "True love? Yeah, sure. Let's be real, this can't be love. That's Thomas."

"Thomas, the only man your heart will ever covet," she said with certainty.

I sighed. Was it true? Was I falling in love with Thomas Collier? I let the thought sink in, waiting for the disgust to follow, but this time, it didn't. What did that mean?

"I must be heading back now to start dinner for Tulok," Amka said.

"Do you mind if I stay? I think I need a walk to clear my head."

"Of course. But keep Karis with you. She knows these woods very well."

I nodded, accepting her terms.

"What's it like?" Karis asked dreamily as we walked along the river bank.

"What's what like?"

"Falling in love. Feeling the call of the mating bond."

"I don't know how to describe it. If it was anyone else I'd say, amazing; life changing; pure happiness."

"Anyone else? I don't understand," Karis said.

I shrugged. "I haven't always liked Thomas. Okay, I called him the biggest douchebag on the planet and channeled all my hurt, anger, and pain towards him, even though I hadn't seen him since we were kids. I was so shocked to discover he, of all people, was my true mate. I didn't handle it very well. It's still sort of sinking in."

"He's a really good man, Lily," Karis assured me.

"I see that now. I wasn't really giving him a chance."

"And now? Oma is right. You look at him with love in your eyes."

I sighed. "Maybe."

Seeing a series of rocks, I asked her if we could cross the river safely. She told me we could, and like two little girls we skipped across the rocks to the other side. It was a carefree, beautiful moment, and I knew the only reason I wanted to cross the river was to get back to Thomas. I was ready to face the facts. Thomas was my true mate, and he had somehow earned my heart along the way. I didn't want to fight it anymore. I had already told him I was all in, but this time I truly, without a doubt, felt it in my heart.

Karis chatted on as we walked. She told me about how excited she was to be going to the ARC. She confessed she'd never been outside the village and couldn't wait to experience the world.

No sooner had I opened my mouth to tease her about maybe finding her own true mate there than a loud pop rang out from the woods. I felt a sting of pain, and then as if from a far distance, I heard Karis scream. Another pop sounded, but I reacted quickly despite the heavy fog trying to pull me under. I jumped and covered the girl with my body, taking the sting of the second hit.

"Lily! Lily!" she yelled.

"Shh," I said calmly. "They'll be coming. Crawl to the river's edge and hide behind that boulder. Cover yourself in snow. When it's safe, you run. Karis, you run away from here as fast as you can and get help." My words were coming out slower. My whole body felt like it was cast in cement. "Go now!" I managed just before the darkness pulled me under.

When I awoke, all my senses came to full alert. It was dark, except a few lights along what I assumed was a wall. I tried to stand, but the ceiling was too short. I felt around as my eyes slowly adjusted to the darkness. Cold metal. Bars. I felt all around me, my heart sinking as I battled not to vomit. I was in a cage like an animal.

"Hello?" I called out. "Is anyone there?"

"It won't do you any good," a man's voice replied. "They won't be back till morning. At least I assume morning since they already brought us our dinner."

"Who are you?" I asked, my voice sounding stronger than I felt.

"Yutu," he replied.

"Yutu? You went missing a few days ago. Thomas and I were sent here to find you. Amka explained it to me while we were delivering baked goods to her neighbors."

"Well, you found me," he said with no humor in his voice.

"Hi, I'm Lyle. I'm here, too. I've been here the longest. All the cages were empty when they brought me in. Samson arrived the next day, and Yutu a few days later. Now you."

"Who are they?" I asked.

"Don't know," Lyle confessed. "Humans for sure. They've been taking blood, and meals come regularly. Aside from the cramped quarters, it hasn't been that bad in here. But there are cameras everywhere, so watch what you say and do. Got it?"

"Understood," I said, knowing he meant don't talk about being a shifter and do not, under any circumstances, shift.

"Might as well try your best to get some sleep. Nothing's going to happen till morning anyway," Yutu said.

Sleep eluded me throughout the night as I memorized every inch of the cage holding me captive, and the patterns of lights throughout the room. Time lost all meaning.

I must have started dozing off at some point because suddenly the room came to life. The lights turned on, the whirring sounds of machines seemed louder, and the smell of food made my mouth water even before my eyes fully opened.

I was surprised to see several men standing around staring at me. They were all in white lab coats and seemed fascinated by my addition to the other shifters. Surprise registered strongly on the face of the man in the back. He shook his head as if trying to convey something to me, but I didn't know what he was trying to say.

"That's a great catch last night, Kent," one guy said.

"Thanks, Trevor. She's mighty pretty," Kent replied.

The man at the back of the room rubbed his eyes and looked to the ceiling. "Seriously? Do you idiots have any idea what you've done?"

Everyone got quiet as all heads turned towards him.

"What?" Kent asked.

"That's Lily Westin! Her pack will stop at nothing to find her. Give her the memory serum and get her out of here."

"Dave, calm down man. It's all good. The snow fell last night. No one can track her here," Trevor assured him, with more confidence than he had a right to.

I snorted before I can stop myself. "I'm happy to see my reputation precedes me. You clearly realize my family has the connections, resources, and tenacity to find me. And they will. Of that I'm certain. So, run your little tests, and play your little games quickly, because they're coming for you. Every single one of you will pay for this."

I knew I shouldn't provoke them, but sometimes things just had a way of popping out of my mouth before I could assess if they were things that should be said or not. Most of the time I didn't care. And if it wasn't for the challenge written all over Trevor's face at my bravado, I wouldn't be caring now.

"You're certain no one saw you take her?" Trevor asked Kent.

Kent's face blanched white. "Well," he stalled.

"Did someone see you or not? It's a simple question," he said, raising his voice.

"There was a girl with her. She got away."

"What?" Trevor yelled, slamming down the folder he was carrying onto a nearby desk. Papers went flying.

This seemed to bring more attention to the room as the door opened and Jacob Winthrop walked in. Jacob was Madelyn's guardian. She had lived with him for eight years, and he'd practically raised Oscar. He was family. My breath hitched as I fought back the urge to beg for his help. I knew Jacob would get me out of this. I was going to be okay. I looked up and watched him turn a little green as he shared a look with Dave, who subtly shook his head at me.

I didn't know why they didn't want me to react or acknowledge that I knew Jacob, but somehow, I understood that this Dave guy was trying to help me in some weird way. It took every ounce of personal restraint I really didn't possess not to cry out to Jacob for help.

"What's going on in here?" Jacob asked.

"We have a new visitor. However, Kent let a witness go when he grabbed her," Trevor said.

"I see."

"Dave says she's a Westin and we need to get her out of here. I'm thinking we should relocate her to the Philadelphia facility."

Dave and Jacob shared another quick look while the others continued to remain oblivious.

"It's too risky. They'll be on the hunt for her for sure," Jacob said. "It's best the girl stays here," he added.

I shook my head and started to open my mouth to protest, but the look Dave shot me stopped me.

"Don't give them the satisfaction," the big guy in the cage

next to mine said under his breath.

We didn't speak again until the room cleared.

"I'm Lily," I said to my new neighbor.

"Samson," he replied. "You really think they'll come looking for you?"

"Definitely. Hey, reinforcements were already coming in looking for you. That's why I'm here," I confessed quietly. "Do you really think they're recording us?"

He nodded.

I took a good look around the room, matching up the lights I'd memorized the night before in the dark with the camera and various other devices around the room. I took in everything I could about the place. Based on the cold concrete walls, the cement floor, the creepy hanging caged lights in the ceiling, I could only assume it was some sort of shelter, like a fallout shelter or something.

It wasn't long before Dave came back in, this time wheeling a metal cart with our breakfast trays. He passed each of them through a slot at the bottom of our cage. Two above me, which I could only assume were Lyle's and Yutu's, then Samson's, and finally mine.

He didn't say a word, but he made eye contact with me. Again, I felt like he was trying to send me some sort of telepathic message.

He glanced at my tray, then quickly turned and left the room.

"Well, at least the food's good here," Lyle commented with a laugh as the other two men groaned.

I lifted the lid to the tray and inside the lid was a note. It read, "Patrick's been notified. Help's on the way. Just sit tight and keep quiet. They're watching."

I pretended to look at the food while I read it, and carefully set it down on the floor of my crate, certain no cameras would pick up anything suspicious. I wanted to cry in relief, but instead I ate and tried not to show any emotions. Lyle was right, the food was good.

I didn't know if I should remove and keep the note or leave it. When a new guy I hadn't seen before came to pick up the tray, I pretended to want the banana I hadn't eaten and discreetly grabbed the note and fruit at the last minute.

"I might want it later," I said with a shrug when I caught him looking curiously at me.

I didn't mention a word about the note to the other shifters. I didn't really know who I could trust, and Dave had said they were watching. Did that mean they were listening, too? I wasn't willing to take the risk.

I still didn't know what to do with the note, though. It was small, and paper. After a while of sitting there with too much time to think, I started freaking myself out. It was still in the palm of my hand, because I was terrified they'd see it on the cameras.

Paranoid someone would eventually find it, I did the only thing I could think of. Remembering some old spy movie I'd watched with my brothers, I opened my banana, and somehow, without drawing any attention from even Samson, who was watching me, I managed to get the paper in my mouth and took a bite of fruit, swallowing them both down.

I couldn't let myself think about how gross it was that I'd just eaten paper. Fortunately, it wasn't as hard to swallow as I'd feared it might be, and I was relieved to have all evidence gone.

Patrick was on his way and he'd bring the whole cavalry. I just needed to be patient, keep my mouth shut, and wait. Too bad patience wasn't a virtue of mine.

Or keeping my mouth shut.

Thomas

Chapter 20

I was still smiling when I saw Lily and Karis round the bend in the river. I was so busy watching my mate that the kids pummeled me with snowballs, causing me to lose my balance and fall back into the snow.

With the battle back in full swing, I continued to play with the boys as Tulok stood by laughing. Suddenly the easy banter came to a crashing halt.

"Upa! Upa! Help!"

On full alert, Tulok and I turned in all directions, looking for the cry for help. Along the water's edge, crawling on her hands and knees was Karis.

I wouldn't have believed the old Alpha could move so fast had I not seen it with my own eyes.

Karis was crying hysterically. "They took her. I'm so sorry. She saved me, but I couldn't save her."

The hair on the back of my neck stood up as anger and panic began to rise within me.

"Karis, where's Lily? I saw her walking down the river with you. Where is she?"

I didn't mean to raise my voice, or for my Alpha power to flow from me, but I was freaking out and unable to control it. When I went to advance on Karis, demanding she tell me, Tulok intervened.

"Knowing you are a mating male, I will look past your overstep of power, but this is a warning, Thomas. You need to rein in your anger and tone down your Alpha power."

I fisted my hands at my side and took deep, calming breaths, trying to do just that.

"I'm sorry, Thomas. I'm so sorry. They took her. They took Lily," Karis cried.

The boys started to cry, and their fear was evident. They were all looking around for the impending threat.

A large snowflake landed on my nose as I looked up into the sky. I remembered hearing several times that the others were taken just before a major snowfall and therefore they were unable to track them properly.

"Snow is coming. I have to find her before it does. Please Karis, show me where they got her. I need to hear exactly what happened," I begged her.

She was still on her hands and knees, crying.

"Rise, child. We must try and help," Tulok told her.

"My ankle, I think it's sprained, possibly broken. We had just crossed the river no more than half a mile back. Lily wanted to come and join in the snowball fight. She looked so happy, and then there was a pop and she had a funny look on her face. She collapsed. They shot her. They went to shoot me too, but she used her last bit of strength to throw me down, twisting my ankle in the process, but she used her body to protect me. She took the shot meant for me, too. She told me to run and get help, so I did, for as long as I could stand the pain, and then I crawled the rest of the way. You have to go. You have to find her. Follow my tracks back before it's too late."

Tulok took one look at me and nodded. I shifted on the spot, my clothes and coat ripping to shreds across the white-covered ground.

"Whoa!"

"Cool!" the boys exclaimed, despite the impending danger.

I took off at a full run following the river's edge, paying attention to the tracks Karis had left behind. It wasn't long before Tulok's magnificent wolf caught up to me. I remembered being in such awe of him when I was a child, and I was surprised to see he no longer towered over my wolf.

We came to a rocky area and saw the signs of struggle. I knew that must be where they shot Lily. Just the thought made my wolf snarl, but seeing spots of her blood on the snow made me both growl and howl. I caught her scent easily and gave over to my wolf.

The snow was coming down harder and the sky was quickly darkening. It seemed odd at first, but then I remembered where we were. Alaska spent more time in the dark than in daylight this time of year.

Despite Tulok's attempt at a protest, I pushed on until we came to a clearing and I could no longer see footsteps in the snow. Tulok shifted when I came to a halt, looking around and memorizing my surroundings.

"These conditions could lead to a whiteout. Visibility is already bad. We need to head back quickly. I know you want to find your mate, and tomorrow we will resume the search, but for now, we have to go back and seek shelter. Your wolf is not used to this weather, and the temperature will only continue to drop through the night," he said, trying to persuade me.

I knew he was right, but it sliced a deep cut in my heart knowing Lily was out there somewhere, alone and unprotected, possibly drugged. A roar escaped as a menacing growl from within me. Tulok took a step back as I tried desperately to compose myself. The sound of my pulse beating in my ears was like standing near a train at full speed.

As I slowly calmed my heart rate, I turned my face up to the sky as snowflakes continued to fall, and I let a mournful howl.

I'll find you, Lily. Wherever you are, I swear I'll stop at nothing to find you, I swore to myself.

With a slight nod toward the Alpha, I slowly turned around, stopping at the first tree to pee on it, marking the place we last saw their footprints. The snow might wash away the signs of their trek, but it would not wash away my scent. I made sure to stop every few yards and mark the path all the way back to Tulok's. He should have stopped me. I knew it was disrespectful to mark his territory with my scent, but he only nodded his consent at each new stop, until we hit the village line. Seeing where we were, I refrained, and we ran the rest of the way back to his home.

The snow was coming down harder and while it wasn't a complete whiteout, it was close. Amka met us both at the door. We shifted and she quickly covered us each in thick wool blankets, ushering us inside where a warm fire greeted us.

Karis delivered bowls of thick stew with shaky hands. Her

eyes were red and puffy, and she continued to limp, though her ankle was wrapped tightly.

"I'm so sorry, Thomas," she wailed.

"Karis, this wasn't your fault," I assured her. "Are you okay?"

She nodded. "The village doctor stopped by, and he believes it is only a severe sprain. I'll be fine in a few weeks, or I can spend some time in my fur and it'll be good as new in a day or two."

I smiled at her, grateful she was okay, even though everything inside me screamed I should be out there still looking for Lily.

When we finished our meal, the ladies took our bowls to wash up in the kitchen. Tulok hadn't spoken since his speech in the woods.

"You will make a fine Alpha someday, Thomas. Putting your own fears and worries aside to ensure your people are well is important. You demonstrated great restraint today and true concern and caring with my granddaughter."

I looked at him like he had gone mad. "Tulok, that was not me showing great restraint today. I was furious, wild, giving over to my wolf in hopes of finding my mate. I lost it out there on more than one occasion. I growled at you," I said, feeling only slightly ashamed for it as my mind was still analyzing every step we'd taken, ready to restart the search at first light.

He chuckled. "I suppose I should have said that you showed great restraint for a mating male who has not yet sealed his bond. There is a difference. Don't be so hard on yourself. We will find her. Your tracking instincts are impressive, and your tenacity will ensure nothing gets in your way of finding your mate. You are stronger than you give yourself credit for, Thomas."

"I don't feel strong. I feel . . ."

"Empty, like half of you is missing?" Amka asked, entering the room and coming to stand behind her mate.

"Yeah, it does," I admitted.

"That is Lily. A part of you is missing, and you feel it physically as well as emotionally," she told me.

"But we haven't even bonded yet," I protested. "How can I feel her so strongly?"

"You may not have sealed your bond yet, Thomas, but it is

already there and growing. The bond between you is strong. I felt it the moment the two of you walked in the door."

I knew it was still very early, but I needed some time alone, so I excused myself and called it an early night. Laying there in that cold bed without Lily was horrible. My chest physically hurt and at least once I feared I might be having a heart attack. Not knowing where she was or what condition she was in made me think of all the worst-case scenarios.

I was confident Tulok and some of his men would help me in my search, but with or without them, and regardless of what the storm was doing, I planned to head back out at first light to find my mate and bring her home. I knew I would struggle to let her out of my sight again for quite some time, and then it dawned on me for the first time that this is what my mother must have felt like when Maddie didn't come home.

I had resented my mother for her actions after my sister's disappearance. Never had I stopped to consider her feelings or what she must have gone through with the loss of a child. I was getting a glimpse of what it must have been like for her. That terrifying hopelessness, consumed with the need to do something, anything, but nothing would change the outcome.

We lost Madelyn for eight years. I had been young and unable to even help in the search. It had weighed heavily on me for a long time. I would not live with that fear again. This time, I would do everything in my power to make damn sure my girl got back home safe and sound.

With my plan cemented, I tried to close my eyes and prayed for sleep that didn't come.

My phone rang, and I picked it up with a frustrated sigh. Kyle Westin's face flashed across the screen.

"Hello?"

"Thomas? How you holding up, man? And why the hell didn't you call us?" Kyle asked.

That was my breaking point. I wanted to ball up and cry, but I had to be strong for her. I felt like I had let down so many people—Kyle, his family, their pack, my pack, Tulok and the Alaskans who had invited me here to help find their missing people but had another go missing on my watch, and most of all, Lily. My biggest, most important job in life was to protect her, and I'd failed.

"That good, huh? I can't even imagine what you're going through right now, but cheer up some. We've got a lead," Kyle said, after I didn't respond to his question.

"You what? How did you even know she was missing? Did Tulok call you?" I asked, suddenly regaining my brain and realizing I hadn't called and told Kyle that Lily was missing.

"It's a long story. I've got a team deployed just waiting for the storm to pass, they're in Anchorage right now, and they will make the final trek as fast as they can at first break in the weather. We have a man on the inside. He tipped Patrick off and we have the coordinates of Lily's location. It's a human faction we've dealt with before."

I was overwhelmed with relief. We had a lead. We had her location. I'd have her back in my arms tomorrow. That elation was short-lived, though, broken by a flood of thoughts, questions, and concerns.

"Wait. What? Humans know about shifters?"

"Uh, dude, there's a lot we are going to need to discuss, but let's save it till we have Lily back."

"Kyle, I'm sorry. I'm so sorry. I should never have let her . . ."

He cut me off. "Don't do that to yourself, Thomas. I know you aren't the douchebag Lily always claimed you were. And I know what it's like to be a mating male with the emotions coursing through you. I can only imagine how on edge your wolf is, and as an Alpha, there's the added fight for dominance. Kelsey and I were newly bonded when the Bulgarians put a death warrant on her. I do understand what you're going through right now, probably better than anyone else. Just remember not to suffocate her when you have her back tomorrow. Lily has always had this special light about her. Don't snuff that out. She is strong-willed, independent, and she will challenge you every step of the way, but she will make you stronger, too. Keep that in mind tomorrow when every instinct in your being yells for you to lock her away and keep her safe from anymore threats."

I let out a sharp breath. "That's a lot to ask of me, Kyle."

He laughed. "I know that, but my mom says God doesn't make mistakes in matching true mates, which means you, my friend, are strong enough to handle this. Probably stubborn enough to match her, too, but smart enough to know when to pick your battles. I wish I could be there with you tomorrow, but Kelsey's been having some contractions and we're on baby watch here. I hope you'll consider coming here for a visit when things settle down up there. We'll have that talk, and I'll fill you in on some highly confidential stuff you'll need to be aware of as Collier's next Alpha."

I thanked him, said we'd see him soon, and ended the call. We had her location. I'd have her back in the morning. It should have relaxed me, but a few hours of staring at the ceiling confirmed that wasn't going to happen until I physically had my girl back in my arms.

Lily
Chapter 21

By mid-morning I was going out of my mind with boredom. My whole body ached from the cramped space. I couldn't stretch my legs. It was miserable. Plus, they didn't even give us coffee with breakfast, which made me very grumpy.

Kent walked in, and of course he was carrying a fresh, steaming, hot cup of coffee in his hand. I was ready to kill for that cup.

"Is this your idea of torture? Why do you get coffee and not us?" I asked. "I get we're prisoners and all, but come on, isn't there some sort of ethical code here?"

He looked at me with a puzzled look, and I quickly realized he wasn't the sharpest knife in the drawer. "How is coffee against an ethical code?"

"I'm certain it's in the book of war or something marked under cruel and unusual punishment to drink coffee in front of prisoners without offering them some."

He panicked for a moment. "Let me check with Trevor," he finally said, quickly leaving the room.

When the door shut, Samson started to laugh a full belly laugh. "You can thank Lyle up there for your lack of coffee," he said once he composed himself.

"Whatever. I did what I had to do," Lyle said.

"They were sending in a woman named Helen to deliver our meals, but she got close to the cage and as she gave them their meals up there, I grabbed for the keys and Lyle dumped scalding hot coffee on her head as a distraction. I had managed to get out, but not before the others came in from the commotion and someone tased me, before locking me back up once I was subdued. It was worth it just to stretch my legs for those few minutes."

"We haven't seen Helen since," Lyle added. "Or any coffee."

Trevor came in with Kent. "Sorry, Miss Westin, there will be no coffee after the rather unfortunate incident they just explained to you."

That certainly confirmed they were listening to and not just watching us.

"Coke? Chocolate? Anything with even the slightest bit of caffeine?" I was practically begging.

He sighed. "I'll see what I can do. Despite what you must think, our intentions are not to make your lives miserable."

I snorted. "So, these are just your best accommodations?"

He smirked at me. "Touché."

Awkwardly he turned and left. I tried to reposition myself, wondering just how long it would take for this cavalry to arrive and break me out of this prison cell. I didn't really talk to the others much. It seemed too risky, knowing they were listening in. My imagination got carried away with all sorts of secret spy stuff and various escape scenarios. I knew I couldn't just break myself out. No, I'd have to save the others, too.

I felt around in my pockets. Nothing. I found a bobby pin still stuck in my hair. I was convinced I could pick all the locks and ninja fight my way out of there before they could stop me. I took a deep breath, bracing for the exact moment I would enact my plan.

Just then, an alarm went off. It was a loud siren, like a fire alarm. I knew that was my chance. The others would have to be distracted by the noise. I quickly took my bobby pin and squeezed my arms through the cage bars. They rubbed tightly against my skin, feeling like they were burning it off. I bit back a scream and got to work, awkwardly maneuvering the hair pin into the lock and twisting it all around. Nothing. They made this look so easy in the movies. Determined, I still tried to pick the lock, my arms now stuck as far as they'd go through the bars. I never even stopped to think how I'd get them out of there once the lock was popped. I just kept working.

Soon the door burst open and I knew I was busted. They were going to take my bobby pin away and frisk me for more. I hadn't asked what they'd done to Lyle and Samson as punishment for their great escape plan, aside from the coffee ban. Maybe I should have, so I'd know what was coming next.

"What the bloody hell are you doing?" an all-too-familiar voice asked.

"Patrick?" I practically yelled, trying to look up and see him, but with my arms wedged so tightly through the cage bars, my face was pressed up against them and I was unable to move. Tears pricked my eyes at knowing he was there. I was safe. A strange tingling sensation shot up my spine like electrical current. I took in a deep breath from the shock of it. That's when I smelled him. "Thomas?" I whispered. "Patrick, is Thomas with you?"

"Of course. You think he was gonna let us rescue his girl without him? He practically had a path marked to your doorstep. If the snow hadn't come in so quickly last night, he'd have had you home long before we arrived," Patrick told me.

"Thomas?" I yelled. "I'm in here."

"Lily," I heard as footsteps ran towards me. I saw his feet stop just below me. He bent down and looked up at me. "What are you doing?"

Samson let out that full belly laugh of his.

"Not helping, Samson. Are you going to get me out of here or not?"

"Seriously, Lil, what the feck are you doing?" Patrick asked as I heard him unlock the cages above me.

"Since we're stopping to make fun of me, I'm assuming you have the threat under control?" I said, getting a little annoyed.

"Toss me the keys," Thomas finally said. "Your captors are in custody. You're all safe now. Let's see about getting you out of here."

Thomas removed the bobby pin from my hand. He held it up and I could tell he was grinning in amusement without even seeing his face. He unlocked and then removed the lock, but when he went to open the door, I came flying out with it.

"Whoa, there," Patrick said as Thomas grabbed my legs that didn't quite reach the floor below. His contact calmed my wolf for the first time since the whole nightmare began, but my arms were tightly wedged between the bars and they weren't budging.

"Get a chair for her to stand on," Thomas ordered. "What did you do?"

"I was trying to escape. I heard the siren go off and thought this was our chance."

"And what? You were just going to pick the lock with a hair pin?" Thomas asked.

I could hear humor in his voice, but I also felt his underlying nerves. He was keeping it light so as not to freak me out–or anyone else.

"I saw it in a movie Chase made me watch once. They made it look simple." The room exploded in laughter. I groaned. "Laugh it up, but get me out of here."

"Can you pull your arms back through?" Patrick asked.

"Don't you think I've tried that?"

"We may need to soap them up." Yutu offered. At least he was trying to help.

All they could find was some antibacterial hand gel. It was cold as they squirted it, coating my arms. It burned from the abrasions the bars caused, but it gave a little, then evaporated much too quickly.

The next round they lubed me up, and Samson tried pulling me from behind. I cried out in pain, causing Thomas to growl at him. Patrick decided that was a perfect moment to snap a picture on his cell phone and send it off to Kyle.

"What? Kyle asked me to send a pic as proof you were safe and sound."

"You'll pay for that, Patrick," I threatened.

"Slugger, I know it's going to hurt, but I really need you to pull your arms through this time," Thomas said. I could feel his wolf close to the surface. He was going to lose it if I didn't get free soon.

"Okay, let's do this," I said. As soon as my arms were coated once again, I pulled back with all my might. I heard my elbow pop as pain shot up through my left shoulder, but I kept pulling until they both popped free. I looked down and saw the ugly red marks left behind.

Thomas crushed me to him, pulling me down from the chair. I whimpered against him, just before his mouth crushed down against mine. Feeling his wolf begin to calm, I pulled back from him. The edges of my vision were beginning to darken.

"Thomas," I gasped. "My elbow."

He carefully examined it, quickly realizing what I was telling him.

"Patrick, I need your help. Please hold Lily tightly, her elbow is dislocated and needs to be set," he said.

"Why don't you let me do that?" Patrick offered.

"No, she's in pain, and my wolf is far too worked up right now. I'll likely rip the head off anyone who hurts her. It has to be me."

I shivered at the thought, closed my eyes, and braced back against Patrick as he held me. Thomas straightened my arm and pulled. I didn't scream, but I wasn't sure how I'd managed not to. There was an awkward pop again and the pain almost instantly subsided. I opened my eyes, feeling Patrick's arms relax, and I launched myself onto Thomas.

Having him back in my arms righted my whole world. My wolf growled possessively, and I nibbled at his neck. We were ready to complete our bond, and if my wolf had her way we'd be doing it right then and there.

Patrick's phone rang and broke the moment. I pulled back a little, my cheeks flushed. I didn't let go of Thomas, keeping one arm around him and resting my head on his shoulder.

"It's Chase," Patrick said. "Sorry Lil, looks like Kyle sent that picture to the whole fecking family."

"Put me on speaker," I heard Chase say. With enhanced wolf hearing, he really didn't need to.

"Lily? Lily, are you okay?" he asked once on speaker mode.

"I'm here, Chase. I'm fine."

"Aw, don't be too hard on them. I'm glad you're safe. I didn't know any of that was going on, so I'm little angry at them both right now for not telling me you were missing."

"It wasn't even twenty-four hours, and there's nothing you really could have done. One of the guys here helped me. They sent me a note with my breakfast letting me know Patrick was coming with help."

"They did?" he said excitedly. "What did you do with it? Did the bad guys find it? Please tell me you ate it. Please, please, tell me you disposed of all the evidence."

Thomas watched, fascinated, as I blushed furiously. I was willing to bet that even my hair looked a shade pinker.

"Yes, I ate it with a banana. I couldn't let it fall into their hands, and I didn't know who to trust," I blurted out as the several remaining people snickered around me.

"And that pic Kyle sent? You were trying to pick the lock, weren't you?"

"I'm going to kill Patrick, then Kyle, for sending that."

"Are you kidding? That's awesome. A few more minutes and you'd have had that lock picked, I'm sure of it. Just like . . ."

I cut him off. "Don't ever mention that movie to me again! We should sue them for false advertising or something. That shit does not work."

"We'll practice when I'm home for Christmas, just in case you ever need it again," he offered.

"Chase, it's never happening! Plus, I imagine I'll be in Collier for Christmas anyway. Maybe you and Jenna could come visit for a few days on your break."

"Collier? Why would you be in Collier?"

I turned wide eyes towards Thomas. I couldn't believe no one had mentioned our mating to Chase, even though he was away at college. How could he not know?

"Um, that's a conversation for later. I really want to get out of here. I promise I'll call you when I'm settled in. We have a lot to talk about."

Thomas
Chapter 22

We stuck around the old emergency shelter where the humans were keeping Lily and the other shifters in until Patrick's team had thoroughly gone through every bit of research being done there. Unfortunately, it was a new facility and they were only just getting started.

When Patrick arrived at Tulok's, the sun hadn't quite risen yet, so he took some time in a closed-door, confidential meeting with myself and the Alaskan Alpha before we went to rescue Lily to fill us in on some pretty crazy stuff that was going on. I had never heard of the Verndari before, a human faction that discreetly monitored shifter activity worldwide. I didn't even think there was a shifter group that kept up with that sort of information.

I was a little pissed that Kyle had been keeping all of this from us. If these humans were a threat to the packs, all Alphas should have been notified about them, yet he'd chosen to keep it on a need-to-know basis. Earlier this year the ten biggest packs had joined together to stand with Chase, the youngest of the Westin children, when his panther mate's father declared war on the wolves. We were all together then, and he had still mentioned nothing about the Verndari.

Some rational part of me knew that wouldn't have been the time or place to release such a bombshell of information, but had I known about these people, I would have taken drastically different measures when I went looking for the missing shifters. I would have never let Lily out of my sight until they were found to save her from the nightmare she'd had to endure.

Patrick told us he had strong alliances on the inside—humans. The current group we are dealing with are the new generation of the Verndari, the new generation who believed their parents were wrong in protecting and observing the shifters. They saw our enhanced gifts and strengths as things to be studied for the benefit of humans. I couldn't argue with their logic, just the method they chose to obtain it.

Patrick's human friend on the inside had tipped him off with the coordinates to Lily. I would be forever indebted to him, and I hoped I'd get the chance to at least shake the man's hand and thank him properly. I was still in shock with this new information, and by the quick response of the task force that Kyle had sent. He hadn't mentioned who exactly they were, but they clearly were not just a bunch of random Westin wolves helping out. I still had a lot of questions, but they had to wait as my need to ensure my mate was safe was stronger than anything.

I had been told to hold back while the team went in first to clear the bunker. They were heavily armed and obviously trained. Again, I wondered who they were, but I was too busy trying to keep control of my wolf to press the issue.

Since the moment Karis crawled into sight the day before, my wolf had been on edge and fighting to break free. The brief time tracking when I'd let him have control only made him harder to restrain him when we didn't return with our mate. Seeing that we had stopped a mere twenty feet from the hidden door to the bunker made me physically sick. We'd been so close. I couldn't stop the feeling that we had let Lily down.

Seeing her locked in that cage made me see red. Patrick had to take the lead to free her because my body was vibrating in anger and I was seconds away from sprouting fur. I kept my voice light and so much calmer than I actually felt as we got the cage unlocked. It wasn't until she almost fell from the damn thing, dangling there, stuck, and I'd wrapped my arms around her to support her that my wolf started to relax. She looked ridiculously cute, but she wasn't in danger and it felt like my heart began to finally beat again.

Now that I had her back and she was safe, I was struggling not to touch her, grateful when she didn't pull away from me, staying by my side. Even when she moved to give Patrick back his phone after ending the conversation with her youngest brother, Chase, she held my hand and never lost contact with me. I wondered if maybe her wolf was more on edge than usual, too.

I knew I was ready to get out of that place. It gave me goosebumps just thinking about it and what could have happened there. Even with my mate's touch, I knew I couldn't fully relax until we were out of there. Going back to Tulok's was not an option. I needed to get us home.

Patrick and his men were still busy working when I pulled him to the side. He hadn't introduced the team he'd brought with him, and from what all I had learned, I wasn't sure I was ready to hear more, so I didn't bother asking who they were or where they came from. I wasn't even sure if they were shifter or human.

"Your guys look like they have things under control. How bad would it be if I ditched and got Lily home?"

Lily looked confused all of a sudden. She stared around the room. "Your guys? What's he talking about? These guys are with you, Patrick?" I could see fog slowly lifting, and questions began to pour out of her. "Wait, how did that Dave guy know you? He warned me you were coming. He knew exactly who I was and told them to let me go. But how? Why? And Jacob Winthrop was here. I kept my mouth shut about that and didn't question it because Dave was signaling me not to, but seriously, what does Maddie's dad have to do with any of this?"

"Wait, Maddie's dad? My sister? Are you saying my father was here?" I asked, suddenly needing to know what was going on.

"No, sorry, I meant her father-like figure. Jacob and his wife, Annie, took MC in after . . . the incident. . . and helped her raise Oscar all those years. He's been like a dad to her and every bit the grandfather to Oscar. I shouldn't have said 'dad.' I don't really know what else to call him, though," she explained.

Patrick scrubbed his face with his hands. He looked exhausted, and I was certain it had been a very long night for him. "Jacob's also a Verndari."

"Come again? Vern-what-ya-said-ie?" Lily asked.

"Verndari," I repeated for her. "Patrick was explaining them to me this morning that they're some sort of human faction that monitors shifter activity."

Her eyes widened at the implication. "So, are all these guys

Verndari?"

"No." Patrick answered. "We learned about the Verndari more or less through Maddie, or rather Jacob. Turned out Liam was doing business with several of them, but we had never heard of them. We were caught off guard and didn't like it. Most of them are actually good people. They are sworn to keep our kind secret and it's been cool to learn about the various things they've done throughout history to throw humans off our tracks and allow us to live in peace, but there's a small rogue group, mostly young people, that are taking things to a scary new level. Last year Maddie and I had freed a bunch of shifters they were holding captive. The facility was a lot bigger and more state-of-the-art than this place, but you can imagine. They were running all sorts of experiments. Raina was being held there, Lily. That's why I got involved, for Kelsey."

"Who's Raina?" I asked.

"Kelsey's aunt from Bulgaria. She was supposed to have come to visit in time for Zander's birth, but never showed up. I know Kelsey was worried sick about her. If you saved her, where is she now?" Lily added.

"The packs are still monitored closely. We couldn't risk tipping them off by a sudden appearance in San Marco. Jacob helped us fake her death to get her out of there, so she's lying low in a facility we built just outside our borders. It was done in secret alongside the new lodge."

"So like, the lodge was a cover-up for this place?" Lily asked, sounding surprised.

"Exactly," Patrick commented. "Kyle and I thought it would be best if we started keeping a closer eye on these people and mapping out shifter activity on our own. When we faked Raina's death and got her safely out of there, she was supposed to be the only one, but Maddie couldn't stand the thought of leaving the others, so she freed them all. Several of the shifters had been there for years, kidnapped from all over the world and had nowhere to go."

"They live at the lodge?" I asked, starting to put the pieces together. I knew the lodge they were talking about. I had been there earlier that year when the Grand Council had called a meeting regarding Chase's mating situation. The place was huge, and there were several areas marked as "Under Construction. Do Not Enter," but I had seen a few people walking in that direction, and they didn't look like the construction worker type.

Patrick seemed surprised that I had put it all together so quickly. "Yes. They live at the lodge. Raina lives there, too. Kelsey's seen her and rests at ease knowing she's safe and sound, but we cannot allow the Verndari to know she's alive. She works with several of the other rescued shifters and a few others we've brought in. We call them Westin Force. Most are just in observation and information fields. These guys," he said, pointing at the team that had accompanied them, "are our elite forces. This is Bravo Team. Most are ex-military, mercenaries, or moles."

"Moles? Like double agent spies?" Lily asked, sounding more excited by the second.

"Well yeah, a few actually, but I mean moles, as in mole shifters. Those guys are into everything and already had the infrastructure in place. They just needed better funding. It's scary how much they know."

"Let me guess, the Foundation is funding this?" Lily asked, rolling her eyes.

"Of course," Patrick said. "Where the hell else do you think we'd find that kind of financial backing and the means necessary to fecking hide it? You both do understand this is all one hundred percent confidential, right? Word can never get out about these guys, or the work they are doing."

"Why are you telling us now?" I wondered aloud.

Patrick rolled his eyes this time. "You, you're probably smart enough to keep your mouth shut and not ask, but this one," he said, pointing to Lily, "she'd never let it go without details."

Lily shrugged and nodded. I couldn't help but laugh.

"Wait," Lily said. "What about Dave? Do you know him through Jacob? I had the impression he knows you well. I mean he did contact you with my location and had me rescued in less than twenty-four hours. How? Or really, why?"

Patrick sighed, "Dave and I met awhile back. Do you remember when Elise was trying to hide from me and we went to that spa and she was kidnapped?"

Lily nodded her head. I nodded mine too, because I had been privy to that information. We had been cautioned to be on the lookout at the time.

"Wasn't that the Bulgarians, though?" I asked.

Patrick nodded. "Yes, but the Verndari were monitoring the Bulgarians' movement. It was flagged as out of the norm. Dave and two of his buddies were there. They were only supposed to be there for observation and to ensure there were no issues with the local humans, but they helped me. They helped me save my mate and I will always be indebted to them for it. I didn't know who or what the Verndari were at that time. That all came about through Jacob, when Liam found Maddie, but I already knew Dave. We've worked together a few times since, and he always gives me the heads-up when trouble's heading for Westin Pack."

"Is that why my brother made you Beta?" Lily asked.

Patrick shrugged. "Could be. I don't know, but I'm grateful he did and security for Westin strengthens more and more each month. We aren't quite where I want us to be, but we're close." He turned to look at me. "We monitor Collier just as closely. If there's ever any issue or concern flagged for your pack, I promise you'll know it."

I shook his hand. "This is all crazy, like something out of a movie. It's going to take some time to process, but thank you."

It didn't seem like nearly enough, but when I put my arm around Lily and pulled her close to me, the other man smiled and I knew he understood. I would be forever indebted to him, and this crazy militia program of his, and even his friend, Dave.

Lily

Chapter 23

We said goodbye to Patrick. Thomas made it clear we were heading home to Collier and not sticking around. I didn't argue. Even though nothing had seriously happened to me—they hadn't even gotten around to taking my blood yet—I still couldn't help feeling violated and more than a little humiliated. My brothers would pay for their part in that.

We headed back to Tulok's. Amka and Karis ran out and tackled me in hugs before I could get the door shut on the SUV Thomas had borrowed from them.

"Look at me, child, I need to know you're really okay," Amka said.

It felt like she was staring into my soul, and I struggled not to cry. "I'm fine," I said as convincingly as possible.

Tulok came out to meet us, too. "I'm sorry, there's another storm brewing that is disrupting flights. I spoke to your father, and your pilot is unable to reach you at this time. I'm afraid you'll have to wait out the storm."

"Honestly, I'm not sure my wolf will tolerate it, Tulok," Thomas confessed. "How bad would driving be in this storm?"

"You could probably make it into British Columbia before the worst of it hits. Twelve to fifteen hours max."

"If it's that far away, why can't the pilot make it?" I asked.

"It's a strange one, coming in from the south. They'd have to fly through it to reach us, and that just isn't going to happen. It's big, so there's no way around it. You'd likely end up stuck in a hotel for a few days during and after the storm until the roads are clear enough to pass," Tulok said.

"Best you just stay here," Amka said, sounding worried.

The two men shared a serious look.

"Take the SUV, Thomas, and leave quickly. It'll handle well for you. Just heed my warning: When the snow starts, seek shelter quickly. Some place warm and safe that you can spend a few days to let it pass."

"Thank you," Thomas said, shaking the old man's hand before jogging into the house and returning quickly with our bags.

Amka continued to fuss over the decision, but in the end, she hugged us both and wished us well. I promised to keep in touch and to let her know we were safe along the way, until we reached Collier territory.

Before I could think straight, we were off, heading out on a fifty-some hour road trip.

Thomas remained quiet for the first hour, though he hadn't let go of my hand since he put the vehicle into drive. I had visibly seen the tension in his shoulders ease the moment we were out of Alaskan territory.

"I'm sorry for this," he finally said, softly. "I'm sure you must think I'm a freak for insisting we venture out with a massive storm in our path."

I shrugged. "I have brothers. I've watched them all go through mating, and even beyond. I mean, they say it's supposed to ease up and get better the stronger the bond is, make you less crazy and all that stuff, but really, I don't know if it's an Alpha thing or just a male thing, but it just seems to never go away. Not just with their spouses either. They've all pulled the Alpha card on me before. I know when to pick my battles over it."

I watched him as he stared forward, not commenting, but giving a slightly crooked grin.

"I saw you relax when we left Alaskan territory. I'm guessing my disappearing caused your wolf to go a little crazy, and being in someone else's territory wasn't helping, huh?" I knew the answer, but for some reason I just wanted him to confirm it.

"Yeah, something like that. I would have gone nuts stuck there a few more days. Everything in my being is screaming to protect you, get you home, and keep you safe. I'm not sure it's a healthy obsession, but I can't seem to stop it." He looked apologetic when he chanced a quick glimpse my way.

"Stupid bond. It makes you and your wolf crazy. Mine really wasn't much better. She just wants to rub all over you, so forgive me for touching you so much. I can't seem to help it."

He glanced over with a smoldering look in his eyes. The moment felt much longer than should have been safe while driving, but I couldn't break away. He gave me that damn smirk again. "I really don't mind."

Oh boy. I suddenly couldn't wait to find that hotel I'd be cooped up in with him for a few days. I had plenty of brilliant ideas on just how we could pass the time, starting with completing this bond, once and for all.

Just the thought of truly being alone with him, especially after all that had happened, was making me seriously horny. I couldn't help it. I scooted uncomfortably in my seat, really wanting some relief. *Couldn't he drive any faster?*

Thomas laughed, okay, really it was more like a deep, sexy chuckle. "If you don't calm down, we aren't going to make it much further. Tulok said we had about twelve to sixteen hours before the worst of it hit. I thought we'd try to get as far south as possible, but babe, your scent is driving me crazy over here."

I watched him squirm in his seat and my eyes dropped to see him straining against the zipper of his pants.

"I could take care of that for you," I offered.

The wheel jerked a little as his head whipped my way. "Are you trying to kill us?"

I threw my head back and laughed, some of the tension between us easing, until I felt his hand on my breast. He pinched my nipple, causing me to groan. "Not helping," I murmured through clenched teeth as he moved to attend to my other side. "Thomas," I said, meaning it as a warning, but it came out in a strange, breathy voice.

His eyes were still focused on the road as he drove with his left hand, and his right moved lower, rubbing me through my jeans as I moaned, feeling pressure build between my legs. He unbuttoned my top button, and slowly unzipped my pants as he worked his fingers inside, and I nearly shot off the seat at first touch.

I needed to protest. This was insane. We were driving down a dark highway in the middle of nowhere, but no words would come as his fingers began working his magic over me. Soon my hips were bucking off the seat in rhythm to his hand, which earned me a smirk that melted my heart. His eyes never left the road, yet he was there with me every step of the way. My body tensed, then let loose like a rubber band that had just snapped, and I screamed his name.

It took my breathing some time to return to normal, and my heart beat heavily in my chest. Thomas looked quite proud of himself.

"That was the sexiest thing I've ever seen in my life," he said, and just like that my body tensed up again. I knew I must be addicted to him and wondered if all couples felt this way. I couldn't imagine it possible. No one would ever leave the bedroom except to pee and eat if they felt half as good as he made me feel.

I remembered watching him playing with the young puffin shifter boys, and how my heart had swelled with happiness. I had been on my way to see him, to tell him.

"I love you," I blurted out.

I heard the screeching of tires and felt the car come to a halt as he pulled over on the side of the road and turned to look at me.

I smiled and shrugged. "I don't know when it happened, but I was on my way to tell you when they took me." A single tear ran down my cheek, but I didn't want to cry. I didn't want to let go of the emotions bottled up from the experience. I just wanted to feel. I wanted my mate.

He wiped the tear away with his thumb as he lovingly cradled my face. He didn't have to say the words, I could feel them. My breath hitched as he leaned in and kissed me. If I'd had any doubts that he loved me before then, he showed me with certainty in that kiss. I was panting for breath when he finally pulled back, kissing his way across my cheek and down my neck. I didn't hesitate to bare it to him.

I felt my canines elongate and froze.

"Stop," I said, perhaps a little more aggressively than I meant to. My emotions were jumping all over the place.

Thomas pulled back, looking confused. "What's wrong?"

"What's wrong?" I asked, giving him a big toothy grin to show him my canines. As I suspected, he smiled, and I could see his, too. "What's wrong is that there is no way in hell I'm telling our children that I bonded with their father in the front seat of a car in the middle of nowhere Alaska, or are we in Canada? See, I don't even know!"

Thomas stared at me for a moment. "Is that all?"

"Yes, that's all."

He looked at me, then at the time on the dashboard clock, and back at me. "We've only managed about eight hours so far but screw it—we'll stop at the very next hotel we find."

I laughed as he gave me one more kiss before pulling back onto the road. We had truly been in the middle of nowhere, because it took nearly two more long and frustrating hours to find a place to stop. We couldn't even find a hotel; instead, we ended up at Bunny's Bed and Breakfast.

The tinkle of a bell on the door sounded as we entered the foyer. The owner came out, yawning in a long nightgown and robe, complete with bunny slippers.

She clapped her hands together gleefully. "Oh, just look at the two of you. Newlyweds, I'm sure of it. I'm Bunny." She looked at the registry list and frowned. "Oh no, looks like Gino booked the last room an hour ago. I'm afraid the only thing we have left is the guest cottage. People have been stopping all day to hunker down before the storm hits."

"We'll take it," Thomas said.

"I'm afraid it's quite costly," Bunny warned him. "And just three exits south are several of those big hotels, if you'd rather," she said with disdain in her voice.

"Oh, we've seen how far apart your exits are, we'll take it," I insisted.

"Very well then. I'll drop the price to two hundred and fifty dollars a night, given the circumstances and all, but that's as low as I can go, I'm afraid," she apologized.

"It's fine, we'll take it," Thomas assured her, turning over his credit card.

"How many nights will you be with us?" she inquired.

"Just till the storm passes," he told her.

"How about we do a day-by-day payment then?"

"That's very kind of you, thanks," Thomas said, but something in his voice screamed, "Hurry up already!"

Bunny finished checking us in, Thomas grabbed our bags

from the vehicle, and we followed her around the side of the house to a small guest cottage in the back. It was much larger than a hotel room and had a small kitchen, a living room area with a fireplace, and a huge bedroom with an equally large bathroom, complete with a two-person hot tub.

Bunny left without a word. Thomas and I were finally alone, but before we could even move the bags into the bedroom, she was back, loaded down with bags of food. There was a man with her carrying even more bags. While Bunny loaded the refrigerator, the man set about starting a fire.

"Okay," she finally said, seeming satisfied that her work was complete. "Breakfast, lunch, and dinner are served in the main house dining room every day; however, if this storm is as bad as they are claiming, you may not want to venture out, so the kitchen is now fully stocked with food, though I'm afraid you'll have to cook for yourself then."

Thomas wrapped his arms around me and pulled me back against his chest. "We'll manage," he assured her.

"Oh Gino, aren't they just the most precious couple ever?" Bunny gushed to the man stoking the fire.

"She says that about everyone," he said, lovingly watching her blush. Then he spoke to Thomas directly. "It will get very cold tonight and tomorrow. This fire will help if you keep it going. There's a wood stove in the bedroom, too. I'll help you get that one started before leaving. It's easier to keep through the night. There's a fresh pile of wood on the front porch, dry, and enough to last you several days. I'd advise carrying more in tonight, just in case," Gino said.

"I understand," Thomas said. "Thank you both for everything."

I bit back a smile at his dismissive tone. Gino recognized it too and simply grinned at him, slapping him on the arm and wishing us well. "Come on, my sweet Bunny. Let the lovebirds be."

When they left for real, I first went to the kitchen to see what she'd left that we might be able to eat right away. I was surprised to see two containers packed full of the most delicious smelling pasta I'd ever smelled. My stomach grumbled loudly. It was still warm and required no preparation.

Thomas brought a stack of wood inside and quickly got the

wood stove going. The place was toasty warm in no time. I motioned for him to join me on the couch as we feasted on the wonderful meal.

"I'd come back here again just for this," I said, regarding the food and feeling gluttonous for having eaten so much.

"And I'd come back again simply for this," he said, hugging me closely as we kissed.

I hadn't expected Thomas to be so sweet and affectionate under that Alpha exterior. There was no mistaking it, he was all Alpha. It was in the way he walked and talked. He commanded attention the moment he walked in a room, and he struggled to keep it in check around other Alphas. With me, he didn't seem to have those same issues. He didn't have to be in charge all the time. It dawned on me that it made him vulnerable. I did that to him. I was his weak spot, the weak link in the Collier Pack.

He frowned, watching me puzzle out this new revelation. "What is going through that pretty little head of yours right now? You just transitioned from happy to carrying the weight of the world on your shoulders."

"It's nothing," I assured him, not certain how to vocalize the feeling of despair it caused, knowing I would weaken him and potentially the Pack, too. It wasn't too late, though. I didn't have to complete the bond. Just the thought of it made me wince in physical pain.

"Lily?" he asked, sounding even more concerned. "What is it? Tell me." His last command came with an Alpha punch. I watched him wince when he realized. "I'm sorry. I, I never want to command you to do anything. Sometimes it just happens when I'm upset, scared, or pumped up."

"That's who you are, Thomas. You are an Alpha, and you're going to be a great one for Collier when your turn comes."

"Why do I feel there's a but coming here?"

"But," I said dramatically, trying to lighten my mood a little, "I'm worried about what will happen if we complete the bond."

"If? Lily there's no 'if.' You already said you love me. You have to know I love you, too. What's all this about?" His voice had shifted and I could tell he was trying to stay calm, but his body was tense and emanating stress.

"With me, you have a vulnerability. I'd make the entire Pack vulnerable. You did a great job of holding it together back there, but let's face it, there's a reason we're stuck in the middle of nowhere in some crazy storm."

"Yeah, my wolf is very strong. He's hard to control at times. It leaves me temperamental, irrational, and quick to make rash decisions. That's not you, that's me. We've always had our struggles."

"You let your guard down with me. Your wolf, too. I can feel it, and I can see the differences. That gives you a weakness, Thomas. A mate should make you stronger, not weaker."

He smiled, and I felt his entire body relax as he reached over and pulled me across the couch and onto to his lap. He cradled me close and kissed the top of my head. "Is that all this is about?"

"Is that all? That's pretty major, don't you think?"

I looked up at him and he looked so happy. "Lily, the kind of weak you make me is a good thing."

I smacked him. "I'm not talking about sex right now, Thomas."

He laughed. "Neither am I, slugger. My dad used to tell me my mate would be my biggest treasure and greatest weakness and I must always protect her above all else, even the Pack. It's the burden every Alpha must bear. This isn't something new or exclusive to us. I remember the first time he told me that, I laughed in his face. Told him no woman would ever weaken me. I was too strong. And he said that was the whole point."

"The whole point of true mates is for one to weaken the other? That's bullshit." I couldn't believe he could really think that. Kelsey didn't weaken Kyle, she strengthened him. Mom didn't weaken Dad, did she? I always thought she was so strong and contributed so much to the Pack. Was I wrong? Did she bring down my father and leave him vulnerable, too?

"Not weaken," he said, caressing my cheek and forcing me to look at him. "Balance. Without you to ground me, I'm a loose cannon. I'm arrogant, cocky, and prone to anger and aggression. What you perceive as vulnerability isn't. It's bringing me back down to earth, shrinking my ego some, making me focus on someone besides myself. That's not the same as weakness. It's more humbling. You make me see the world differently."

I considered his words. He was arrogant and cocky. I'd seen

his aggression flare, but I seemed to be the cause of it more than the tamer of it. Did I humble him? Seeing the world differently didn't sound so bad. And earlier he had said he loved me.

"Wait, back it up. Did you say you loved me?"

He threw his head back in a deep sexy laugh. "Yes, Lily Ann Westin, I love you. I didn't expect it to happen so quickly, but I do. I love you. I don't just need you to calm my wolf and keep me grounded and make me a better man, but I want all those things and so much more. I want to spend my life with you."

I kissed him deeply, overwhelmed with emotions. "I love you, too."

"So, we're good?" he asked, looking a little relieved.

I gave him an evil grin and moved so that I was straddling his lap. I didn't wait for my canines to elongate, instead calling them forward, and my wolf happily obeyed. I brushed my hair to one side, exposing my neck to him. When I smiled, showing him my teeth, I heard his quick intake of breath. "Almost," I whispered before kissing him again.

I felt his teeth sharpen and grow, running my tongue against the new sensation and change in his mouth as I smiled against his lips. He was breathless when he pulled back to stare into my eyes.

"There's nothing more permanent than this. We can wait if you need more time." I shook my head. "You're certain?"

"I'm sure, Thomas, so stop talking and claim me already." I was still protesting when the sting of his teeth sinking into my neck hit me. It didn't hurt, quite the opposite. I almost lost myself in the crazy sensation he was invoking and forgot to bite him back.

He paused, hesitating for a moment as reality came back to me and I followed his lead, letting my teeth sink into his neck. Heat spread through my body, sending tingling sensations up and down my spine as I sucked on him.

I thought Thomas had made me feel as incredible as was physically possible in the few times we'd been together, but as our bond sealed, a new level of ecstasy came with it. I reached down and pulled his shirt up, needing to feel him. I rubbed myself against him and protested when his canines finally retracted and pulled away from my skin. I eased up on him and smiled at the sight of my mark on his skin. I licked it and planted a kiss there, soliciting a moan from my mate.

He eased my shirt off me and quickly discarded my bra. I supposed he felt the same all-consuming need as I did, like a pulsing that thundered through my body. We couldn't seem to stop kissing, though I pulled back long enough to lift his shirt over his head. I moaned as his lips found me again and worked magic across my body.

We hadn't even disposed of our jeans or shoes yet, but I was throbbing all over and seeking release. Thomas carefully stood, carrying me with him. I wrapped my legs fully around his waist as he carried me to the bedroom. It was warm, almost too warm, thanks to the wood burning stove. The added heat only contributed to the crazy sensations of the moment as he laid me on the bed and carefully removed the rest of our clothes before joining me.

"Mine," he growled, nibbling on my ear as he took me with no further foreplay.

I aggressively met him stroke for stroke until I reached my climax, growling out his name. He slowed his pace only long enough to kiss me before flipping me onto my stomach and claiming me fully in the most Alpha way possible. I didn't think I could come again so quickly, but the telltale signs began building almost immediately. He reached around to stroke my breasts as he picked up his pace, causing us both to shudder in release.

Thomas
Chapter 24

Lily lay beside me, watching me with a look of wonder on her face. I had been a little rougher with her than I had meant to be. I couldn't even put into words the driving need to make her fully mine.

"Mine," I said softly, leaning down to brush my lips gently against her swollen ones.

"Yours," she replied happily. "I can't wait to see your mark, but at this moment, I'm not sure my legs would hold me if I tried to make it to the bathroom."

I laughed, and as quickly as I could, I climbed off the bed and scooped her up into my arms and carried her to the bathroom, carefully setting her on the counter to admire my bite mark in the mirror. I turned my head to the side to get a full look at the one she had left on me, too.

"It's perfect," she said, touching the spot on her otherwise flawless skin. We stood there looking at each other and admiring our marks for a while. It seemed so surreal. Our bond was complete. Lily Westin was mine forever.

"I love you," I told her, staring into her eyes through the mirror.

Her face brightened as she said, "I love you, too." Then the moment was gone as her face contorted. "Okay, get out. I really have to pee."

I shook my head and helped her down to the floor before leaving. I checked on the fires as she finished up and opened the front door to see that snow had begun to fall. She joined me, hugging me tightly. It never dawned on us that we were standing there, still naked, until my wolf ears picked up a human gasp and I looked up at the main house just in time to see a couple walk away.

A low grumble sounded in my chest, but Lily just shook her head, unable to wipe the smile from her face.

"Hope they enjoyed the show," she said.

Life with Lily would always be interesting. You just couldn't predict what was going to come out of my girl's mouth.

"Doesn't look too bad so far. Maybe we'll luck out and be back on the road tomorrow. That will require sleep though. Come on, back to bed . . . to sleep this time."

She groaned in protest, the little minx.

It took a good hour for me to finally fall asleep. Lily had done everything in her power to provoke me into another round, until she finally crash out, leaving me in an awkward and uncomfortable state, but at last sleep did find me and I spent the remainder of the night dreaming of a future with the beautiful woman snuggled next to me.

When I awoke, Lily was draped over me and the room was chilled. I knew I should get up and stoke the fire again, but she didn't exactly leave room for me to move. Pinned to the bed, I tried to rouse her. I already knew waking the dead was easier than getting Lily to move in the morning. She snored softly, her breath tickling my chest.

I let my hands roam over her back, memorizing the curve of her sides and hips. I kissed the top of her head and rolled her gently to her side. The proper thing to do would have been to get up, take a cold shower, or handle things myself in there, and then put more wood on the fire. Too bad there was a little validity to her douchebag nickname for me. I was hungry for my mate, and curious just how long it would take me to wake her properly.

With an evil smirk, I let my hands trail further north to the peaks of her breasts. There were a few faint pink marks left behind from our lovemaking the night before. I leaned down and kissed each one in turn before sucking one nipple into my mouth. She whimpered softly, but still did not wake. I moved to the next nipple and nothing. A few sexy sighs were all I could elicit from her.

I stared down at her beautiful naked body and grinned evilly.

Kissing my way south, I explored every inch of my mate, tasting her for the first time. Soon her breath was quickening, and she was bucking against me. I could feel her muscles begin to tighten as she let out a loud moan. Her eyes shot open, wide in shock, as she looked down at me. I smiled against her, humming appreciatively as her head flew back and she screamed my name. I stayed with her until her body calmed and the quivering subsided.

"Oh my God! What do you think you're doing?" she asked, her breathing not quite back to normal yet.

"Good morning," I simply said.

"Uh yeah, it's a great morning, but what was that all about?"

I laughed. "You are impossible to wake up, but you looked so damn sexy, I couldn't help myself. I figured it would be a better option than Oscar's cold water method. And look, it worked."

She started to argue. I could see in her eyes it was her first instinct to do so, but she shut her mouth before she spoke and caught me off guard when she did finally reply. "Best wake-up call ever. I'm going to expect that every morning from now on. That was better than a triple grande peppermint mocha."

I laughed and felt it rumble through my entire body. I didn't remember laughing or being so genuinely happy before Lily waltzed into my life and turned it upside down. It felt good. It felt right.

I stood and stretched. I knew I was standing at full attention, and I watched her lick her lips as she openly admired me.

"Perhaps I should repay the favor. You look like you could use some help with that."

I knew then and there this woman was going to be the death of me in the best ways possible.

"As amazing as that sounds, I need to get this fire restarted, and see about breakfast."

"Fine," she huffed. "You tend the fire, I'll get the breakfast."

By the time I had the fire roaring again, the cottage smelled of mouthwatering goodness. Lily had fried up eggs, bacon, and potatoes, and she made toast. It was all delicious, though not quite as delicious as my beautiful mate.

When the meal was finished, and the dishes done, I grabbed the comforter off the bed and wrapped us up before opening the front door. There was nearly two feet of snow with the door imprint clearly marked on it, and it was still falling fast and thick.

"Guess we're going to be here a while," Lily said, not sounding disappointed at all.

To pass the day along, we spent time continuing to get to know each other. It was a rare opportunity where neither of us had anything better to do. She had insisted on repaying me the favor of her wake-up call, and then requested a do-over when she thought she could do a better job. Who the hell was I to argue with that?

Clothes had been a non-issue as we made love and talked, with some occasional food thrown in. Day one was hands down the best day of my life.

Day two, I awoke Lily in the same manner, deciding I could get addicted to her quickly, and the smile on her face instead of the snarl, cursing, and anger I had previously experienced from a Lily Westin morning, was much improved.

Lily was a little sore from where we'd overzealously gone at it the day before. We found some cards and board games in the cabinet under the TV to help pass the time. I learned quickly that she cheated at both and had an obsessive need to win.

After lunch, I drew her a hot bath in the enormous tub, and though it took more willpower than I knew I possessed, I left her alone to relax with a book she had found.

I took the time away from her to call Dad.

"Hello?" my father answered. "Son? Is that you?"

"Hey, Dad."

"It's Thomas," I heard him say, likely to my mother.

She confirmed my suspicions quickly by joining in the call. "Thomas, sweetie, are you okay? Lily's with you right? Tulok called and explained what happened. I've been worried sick about you both. Where are you? He said you insisted on driving and wouldn't wait out the storm."

"We're fine, Mom. Lily's with me and we're holed up in some bed and breakfast waiting for the storm to break. I promise, we're both safe."

"It's a fifty-hour drive, Thomas. What were you thinking?" she continued. as if I were a small child.

"I was thinking that even with Lily found, my wolf wasn't going to settle down as long as I was in Tulok's territory. I was thinking I really needed to get the hell away from there before I did something I'd regret."

"Leave him alone, Cora," my father said. "He's a grown man and he knows his wolf better than men five times his age. If he was that agitated—and with Lily's disappearance, I imagine he was—then he did the right thing."

"I know, I know. I just hate knowing they are stranded out there like that."

My father snorted. "Something tells me he's not minding that one bit."

I laughed.

"Do you think they finally bonded?" my mother said excitedly.

"I'm right here and can hear you, you know," I chimed in.

"Well?" my mother asked, waiting for a response.

"Yes, we bonded. I was calling so Dad could officially start the stupid mating challenge clock."

I heard their excitement through the phone as Mom relayed the information for the others.

"Congratulations, son. I'll get the news out immediately."

"Thanks, Dad."

I heard him walking away, the voices growing more distant, and then a door shut.

"What happened?" he asked seriously.

"Have you spoken with Kyle?"

"Westin? No, why?"

"The Westins know a lot more than they've let on. They knew exactly who took Lily and were tipped off on how to find her. There's a lot to catch you up on, but it's probably best to wait and do it in person. I don't even have all the details yet, only what Patrick O'Connell filled me in on."

"Who did this, Thomas?" he asked, using his most serious tone.

"A human faction, Dad. They know about shifters."

"The Verndari?" he said, sounding surprised.

"You know about the Verndari?"

"I do, but kidnapping shifters? That doesn't sound like them."

"Patrick said it was a small group of their young people going rogue," I confessed.

"I see," he said. "I'll reach out to our contacts and find out what I can."

"Why didn't you tell me about them, Dad?"

"All in good time, son. You take care of your new mate and leave the rest to me. I also think a visit to your new in-laws would probably be a good thing. Since you and Lily are off on this wild road trip anyways, how would you feel about swinging over to the coast and paying a visit to Kyle to find out all you can?"

"Are you certain you don't need us back sooner? I'm sure Lily would love to visit her family."

"I'm sure. And I think it will do you both some good. Get to know each other better and all."

I grinned as we said goodbye. I had already gotten to know Lily in every way imaginable, but I was up for the challenge of learning more.

"What are you certain I'd love?" she asked, standing in the doorway of the bedroom wrapped in a towel to keep from dripping on the floor.

"Dad thinks we should consider rerouting and heading for Westin. He thought maybe talking to Kyle and getting more details on what's going on would be a good thing."

"Really?" she asked excitedly. "Can we stop by the ARC and see Chase and Jenna on the way?"

I shrugged. "Don't see why not. We don't have anything to rush back for at the moment, so might as well enjoy it."

She jumped in glee and clapped her hands before running and tackling me in kisses.

"Thanks," she said breathlessly.

We spent the rest of the day in bed, and I realized quickly, I'd do whatever it took to always keep her that happy.

On day three, the snow finally stopped. Gino cleared a path from the main house to the cottage, which allowed us to walk over and have lunch with the other guests in the dining room. Bunny fussed over Lily and made certain everything was fine. We assured her it was great. I squared up on our payment and didn't care one bit what she charged me. It was worth every penny. I had no doubt we'd be staying at Bunny's Bed and Breakfast for many years to come. It just seemed like it became our place, and I was already making plans to book the cottage for our one-year anniversary.

"The main roads are all clear, and those from here to there

should be soon, too," Gino informed us.

"Great," I said, turning to Lily. "Do you want to leave tonight, or wait till morning?"

She blushed and I knew that meant her deliciously dirty mind was going to places that would make me very happy later.

"Tomorrow it is then," I said, without waiting for an answer. She elbowed me in the side, but didn't retract my statement.

I paid for one final night, and we thanked Bunny and Gino. I informed them we'd be heading out early in the morning, and they wished us both well. Bunny winked at me as she hugged Lily goodbye.

"I have full belief that our paths will cross again," she told my mate, knowing full well I had already booked us for exactly one year from the date we arrived.

"I hope so," Lily said.

I would surprise her with the news much later.

The night passed quickly and when I awoke the next morning, I smiled as I moved to wake my girl. Afterwards we shared a quick shower that took a little longer than I'd planned, and packed up to head out. We were both sad to say goodbye to the cottage, but I knew a year would pass quickly and we'd be back for another amazing stay.

The remainder of the day was spent driving. We were back in the States by nightfall, stopping to catch a few hours of sleep before hitting the road again. Late the next day we pulled up to Chase and Jenna's house.

Lily
Chapter 25

I didn't bother calling ahead. Maybe I should have, since they were still basically newly mated. I just thought it would be more fun to surprise them. It was later than I expected, long after dark, but they were in college. I was sure it would be fine. Plus, I really didn't want to explain Thomas over the phone to my younger, but still way too protective, brother.

I jumped from the car when Thomas stopped. I really did have to pee, but I also needed to give at least a five second notice before Chase said something we'd all regret. I glanced back to watch Thomas wave me on as he got our bags from the back of the SUV.

I pounded on the door. I could hear Chase grumbling before it even opened.

"Surprise!" I said, quickly hugging him and noticing I'd woken him. "You were sleeping? You're in college."

"Lily? What the hell are you doing here? And we have early morning classes. What time is it?"

"I don't know, eleven maybe? I really have to pee. Be nice to Thomas, he's my mate," I said quickly before pushing past him. Jenna was in the living room wrapped in a robe, looking equally sleepy-headed. "Hey Jenna, please point me to the bathroom!"

"Lily?" she questioned in surprise as she led the way.

"She didn't tell you we were coming, did she?" I heard Thomas ask Chase as I peed.

"It's fine, really," Jenna said. "We're always happy to have you. I'm Jenna," she added as I rejoined them. I gave her a quick side squeeze.

"Jenna, this is Thomas Collier, my mate," I said proudly, surprised to find I was officially introducing him to the family and I wasn't embarrassed in the least bit.

Chase nearly choked, and Jenna had to run and grab a glass of water for him.

"Your what?" he finally gasped out.

"I didn't want to tell you over the phone, and I knew you'd question it if I called and asked if you had room for two. So, I thought I'd just surprise you instead. Surprise."

"Thomas Collier, as in heir to Collier Pack? Maddie's brother?" Chase spit out.

"Yes, and yes," Thomas confirmed. "It's okay, go ahead and say it. I kind of miss hearing it."

I rolled my eyes, but Chase looked exasperated.

"The biggest douchebag on the planet? You hate this guy," he reminded me.

"Correction, I hated this guy. That was in the past, and to be fair, I didn't really know him or give him a chance." I saw Thomas cringe at my words and hated that I was hurting him. "I will spend the rest of my life apologizing for it, I'm sure," I told him, rising on my tippy toes to kiss him. "I love you. That was in the past."

He calmed, and I loved that I had that kind of power over him.

"Aw, you two are adorable together." Jenna sighed.

Chase shook his head. "I don't even know where to start with this. I guess welcome to the family," he told Thomas, offering his hand, which he accepted. "Guest rooms are upstairs. Pick whichever you want. We'll talk in the morning, okay?"

"We have an eight o'clock class tomorrow, but we should be back around ten. Just make yourselves at home. The kitchen's stocked. I went shopping this afternoon. I'm so excited you're here," Jenna said, hugging me.

Chase and Jenna had come home for the summer. They both were working at Westin Foundation, and Jenna had started making a name for herself taking portraits—families, couples, and especially children. She was so passionate about her photography that I often envied her.

She and I spoke on the phone several times a week, which

was way more than I called Chase, and I was happy to add her to my list of sisters. I knew she would be confused, and maybe even a little hurt that I hadn't mentioned Thomas to her, but I was also certain she would be happy for me, for us.

It seemed weird to think we were in Chase's home. My baby brother shouldn't be old enough to have settled down and bought a house, yet here we were. It was totally surreal.

As I busied myself, unpacking and us settled into the room, I knew Thomas was watching me.

"What?" I finally asked.

"You really didn't tell them?"

"I wanted to surprise them," I defended.

"Oh, you certainly did that. Poor guy didn't know what to do when I walked in."

I laughed. "He's family. He'll be fine."

I did put my foot down and refuse to have sex in my baby brother's house when Thomas tried to make a move my way. I just couldn't. Instead, I snuggled up next to him. I liked using his chest as my personal pillow. He sighed contentedly and was soon snoring. I let the sounds of his breathing lull me off to sleep.

The next thing I remembered was the glorious feel of Thomas's tongue. That man had a magical tongue and I was the lucky girl who got to wake to it every morning. I moaned and stretched as my body convulsed in shock waves of ecstasy. Every night I went to sleep wondering if he'd wake me again the next morning and so far, he hadn't disappointed. I had never been a morning person, but it was by far my favorite time of day now.

"How long you think you'll be able to keep this up?" I asked.

He leaned down and kissed me. "How about for the rest of your life?"

"You are too good to be true," I said, running my hands through his hair. A conscious thought began to upload to my brain and I remembered where we were. I shot up and looked around the room. "Oh my God, are they home?" I mouthed.

He looked at the time on the clock next to the bed and shook his head. "It's nine, so they should be at school still. Want me to hunt up some breakfast?"

"I have a better idea," I said, waggling my eyebrows at him and pulling him closer to me.

My breathing was still erratic as we lay naked in bed after a morning quickie when I heard Chase's Jeep coming up the driveway.

"Shit, they're back," Thomas said.

"My thoughts exactly," I confessed. "I thought we'd get at least one more round in."

"Dammit, Lily. I swear you're going to be the death of me."

"Yeah, yeah, yeah, at least you'll die happy," I said as I got out of bed and started to dress, tossing him clothes and loving the simple things in life, like just seeing our clothes in the same drawer.

Our lives had intertwined so quickly, yet in some ways they'd always been that way. We just hadn't known it yet.

Jenna and Chase were just walking in when we descended the stairs, hand-in-hand.

Chase stared up at us, still looking confused. "You know, Jenna had to convince me this morning that I hadn't dreamed this up," he said, pointing to my hand linked with my mate's. "I just don't know how this could have happened, and you never even bothered to tell me."

I sighed, and Thomas threw his hands up in surrender. "This is a sibling issue, slugger. He's your brother, talk to him."

"Have you two eaten yet?" Jenna asked as we both shook our heads.

"Um, okay, I'm going to make breakfast then."

"I'll help," Thomas offered, letting me go and following Jenna into the kitchen.

"He's your brother now too, traitor," I mumbled under my breath, but all it did was earn me a wink before Thomas disappeared from sight.

"I'm sorry I didn't call you. It's kind of a long whirlwind story, and it's not like you ever called and told me about Jenna. I had to learn about her from Liam."

"So this is payback? I was confused. She has an identical twin and I didn't know it. I couldn't tell which was which, but I didn't know there were two to tell apart. It was making me crazy. I didn't know how to talk about it," he said.

"And I discover my best friend's brother, whom I've labeled my sworn enemy and the biggest douchebag alive, is my true mate. Don't you think that kind of freaked me out a bit? I didn't want it to be true at first. I got scared and ran home with my tail between my legs. He came after me and I had to face the facts."

"You said last night that you loved him. The bond doesn't make you love him."

"I know, but it does help. Once I stopped fighting it, I don't know. He's not at all the guy I had painted him to be. Like not even close. He's a really great man, and he's going to be an amazing Alpha someday. I'm terrified I'm not good enough to live up to Pack Mother next to him, but we're worth trying. And I did fall in love with him somewhere along the way. I don't even know when it happened, but I can't imagine spending my life with anyone else. Don't listen to what I've said in the past, Chase. Give him a chance. Get to know him, and decide for yourself."

Chase shrugged. "I can do that. And wow, you're going to be a Pack Mother."

I hugged him. "I know. It's crazy. And thanks. Now catch me up on what's going on around here."

Breakfast was soon ready and Chase filled me in on life with Jenna at the ARC. He was in his final year, and she still had one more to go, but was taking a few online classes to try and speed up her graduation. They were excited to start the next stage of their life together. And they loved the cabin so much that they had an identical one built back home, awaiting them.

They skipped the rest of their classes to hang out with us. Chase and Thomas were becoming fast friends. When bedtime came I was sad to see the day end, knowing we would be leaving early the next morning and heading for San Marco. I was excited to get home, but sorry to see our time with them was over. They promised to come see us over the winter holiday and I promised to do a better job of keeping in touch. It had been a great visit.

In comparison to how far we had already traveled, the drive from the ARC to San Marco was a breeze. Excitement built as we headed up the mountain for the final leg of our trip. I knew my wolf would calm and peace would find me as soon as we entered Westin territory, but as we pulled up to my family home I still didn't find that sensation I had been bracing for.

Exiting the vehicle, I stretched, tense from another day of driving. Thomas walked around the SUV, giving me an appreciative look. He wrapped his arms around my waist and my arms naturally fell to his neck. He leaned down and kissed me.

I sighed happily, then took his hand and led him into the house. I could smell food cooking, which made my stomach rumble.

"What day is it?" I asked Thomas, feeling stupid for not even knowing.

"Tuesday, I think."

"Really?"

He counted up the days in his head. "Yeah, I'm pretty sure it's Tuesday."

"Hello?" My mother's voice called out from further in the house. "Who's there?"

"It's me, Mom," I hollered back as I dragged Thomas towards the back of the house heading for the kitchen which I knew was the only place my mom would be on a Tuesday afternoon. "She's going to be so excited," I told Thomas. "We made it for Tuesday night family dinner."

He stopped, and I jerked to a halt. I looked up to find a condemning stare. "You didn't tell her we were coming, did you?"

I gave him an apologetic look just as Mom came out of the kitchen. "Lily!" she exclaimed. "What a pleasant surprise." She hugged me and glanced up at Thomas, then pulled back and looked back and forth between the two of us. "All the craziness is finally sorted, I see."

"Mom," I started, but she cut me off.

"I've been around a long time, and I know what a bonded couple looks like versus a mating one. When? And why didn't you call and tell me?" she chastised.

"I wanted to surprise you," I said sweetly as Thomas groaned and dramatically rolled his eyes.

"Well, I'll take a surprise visit from the two of you anytime. Come on back to the kitchen and I'll put you to work."

"We've been on the road so long, I honestly didn't realize it was Tuesday," I confessed.

"On the road? Vacation or business?" she inquired.

I shared a look with Thomas. Certainly my mother knew where I'd been and what had happened to me.

"We've been to visit the Alaskan's. Tulok was having an issue he needed my help with. Lily and I decided to make it a road trip home. We stopped by Chase and Jenna's to surprise them, too," Thomas filled her in for me.

"Well, it's a great surprise, and I'm happy you're both here. I've missed my girl," Mom said with a tear in her eye. "I'm blessed to have four of my babies stay in Westin, but I'm gonna miss my Lily girl so much." She stopped what she was doing and came over to hug me.

"Oh, Mom. I love you so much. That's never going to change, and I promise I'll visit as often as I can."

"I know you will, sweet girl, but I'll still miss you every day you're away. I'm so proud of you though, and I know you will make an amazing Pack Mother someday."

I grinned proudly as I hugged her tighter. "I did learn from the best."

We spent more time catching up and she got to know Thomas better as we helped finish the meal. I felt like I should have been nervous, officially introducing him to the family, but I wasn't. It just felt natural having him there.

"Mary?" Kelsey yelled when the front door opened.

"Kitchen," she replied. It was a normal scene in the Westin home.

"Grandma, look!" Z squealed as he ran into the kitchen, coming to a complete stop when he saw me. "Aunt Weewee!"

"Hey Z-man. How's my favorite youngest nephew?" I said, picking him up and snuggling him close.

"He's your only youngest nephew, silly," Kelsey said

"For now," I said, noticing her enormous belly protruding. "Still no baby I see."

"What are you doing here?" she asked, setting down the bag she was carrying to hug me.

"Apparently, we're on a road trip of surprises," Thomas said sarcastically.

Kelsey looked him over. "Well, I see you made the cut. Good luck keeping this one in line."

He laughed. "Oh, I'm finding my ways."

"Maddie and Liam just got home about an hour ago. I stopped and grabbed some extra food, just in case they decided to show tonight," Kelsey said, passing the bag to Mom.

"That's about as close to having all my babies under one roof as I can ask for right now. I'll give Maddie a call," Mom said as she set the groceries on the counter, and then left the room to no doubt harass MC into coming for dinner.

My phone dinged a few minutes later.

MC: You're here and didn't even tell me?

LILY: I thought you were still in Collier.

MC: Why aren't u in Collier. U didn't leave Thomas already, did u?

I snorted as Thomas looked over my shoulder to read my text.

He pulled out his phone.

THOMAS: It's not going to work. Lily left me. Need to talk.

MC: Seriously?? Want me to kick her ass for you?

Thomas laughed and showed me his phone.

THOMAS: Whatever it takes.

I grabbed my phone and furiously started typing.

LILY: You're brother's a douchebag. I'm sorry. I tried.

MC: But he's your true mate!!!

LILY: So? You actually liked Liam and tried to call it off. I thought you'd understand.

MC: He's texting me. He sounds devastated. U sure bout this?

LILY: Absolutely.

MC: Sara's waking up, I'm on my way.

Thomas's phone rang not thirty seconds later. I tried to tell him not to answer it, but he did anyway.

"Hello?" he answered, sounding pathetic.

Kelsey was trying not to laugh out loud. "That's so pitiful," she mouthed.

"He's good," I mouthed back.

"I don't know what happened, Mad. One minute everything was great, the next she's flying off the rails like a rabid wolf. Is she bipolar?"

Kelsey held her stomach with one hand and her mouth with the other and started dancing around as she ran out of the room.

"Hey, sis, can I call you back? Something just came up . . . Yeah sure . . . Love you, too."

He hung up the phone quickly and I burst out laughing.

"What was that all about?" he asked.

"Kelsey's bladder is like the size of a dime when she's pregnant. I think you made her pee herself a little. MC's going to murder you for this."

"You started it."

We moved into the living room and sat side by side on the couch waiting. The front door opened and slammed shut.

"Madelyn? I thought you all were going to lie low and take it easy tonight?" I heard my mother say. Thomas and I shared a look and laughed as Kelsey walked in, shaking her head at us.

"Lily's upset about Thomas. I needed to come over and check on her."

"Oh really?" my mom asked from the doorway, giving us both that deadly mom stare. I'd always hated that look. Even as a grown woman it made me squirm in my seat next to Thomas.

Maddie walked in and set the carrier down, too distracted with baby Sara to take notice of us.

"Oh, give me, give me," I begged when Sara was finally free.

MC turned to pass the baby to me and froze. One hand went to her hip as she too gave us the mom face, causing Kelsey to giggle.

She handed me the baby and I cuddled the sweet little girl. She was so precious, and I suddenly couldn't wait to be pregnant and have one of my own.

"Say hi, Uncle Thomas," I said in a gooey voice reserved only for babies and puppies.

"You played me. Both of you," Madelyn confronted us. "It was all made up, wasn't it?"

"I nearly peed," Kelsey confessed. "They're terrible."

"So you guys are okay?" she asked, still sounding concerned.

"Never better," Thomas said.

MC flopped down on the couch next to me. "I was about to take a hot bath while the baby slept."

"Oh please," I snorted, passing Sara to Thomas and turning to face Maddie. "You'd much rather hang out with us tonight anyway. You just needed a little prodding to get here."

She smacked me in the face with a throw pillow. "Maybe, but you still suck. Both of you. Are you really okay?"

I nodded. "We're good."

She blew out a breath. "I'll just be happy when you're officially bonded and can no longer pull this crap on me."

Thomas and I both laughed. "I promise you, we'll still pull this crap after we've bonded."

"So you're going to go through with it? Like this is it? You're serious and not teasing me?"

To put it all to rest, I pulled down the collar of my shirt and showed her the bond mark he'd left there. "Done deal. I'm afraid you're officially stuck with me as family . . . again."

Madelyn squealed and launched off the couch to tackle us, baby and all, in a huge hug.

"And you're happy about it, right?" she questioned, sobering for a minute.

"Extremely," I admitted.

"Both of you?" she asked, looking at Thomas.

"Never happier," he told her.

"I'm calling Liam right now. He took Oscar over to the office for a bit so I could have some quiet, but he'll want to know about this for sure." When she hung up the phone after animatedly telling my twin about us, Maddie yelled into the kitchen where Mom had escaped to. "Mary, Liam's on his way. We're staying for dinner."

Thomas
Chapter 26

Maddie and I actually sat down and talked, really talked. It was both awesome and therapeutic and made the entire trip worth it. Mary Westin's infamous Tuesday night family dinner was certainly an experience. I felt like I was being drilled by a firing squad between Lily's father and brothers, but in the end, I passed their tests and was welcomed with open arms to the family.

Kyle had been a little put off that he hadn't been informed sooner, but Dad's notice to the packs was going out the next day. I apologized to Kyle for coming into Westin territory uninvited, but I genuinely thought Lily had taken care of it. He assured me that I was welcome anytime and not to worry about it. Formal invitations were not necessary amongst family.

The Westins were very different from my own family. They were loud and wide open with each other. Nothing seemed off-limits, and Mary knew everything there was to know about each of her children.

With my parents, especially my mom, I always felt like I had to walk around on eggshells. I didn't like upsetting her, and maybe it was a product left over from the days of Maddie missing, but I never felt like I knew for sure what would set her off and send her running away in tears. It was kind of refreshing not to have to deal with that here. Mary seemed to take as good as she gave.

It wasn't until Wednesday afternoon that I was finally able to corner Kyle and really talk.

"Hey, you got a moment to talk?" I asked him.

"Sure man, anytime. Come on in," he said, ushering me into his office. I closed the door behind me, knowing he had a dampener in the room so the others couldn't hear us. "What's up?"

"Tell me what you know about the Verndari," I said, cutting to the chase.

"I knew you'd get around to asking eventually. Honestly man, Patrick's my go-to for them. Whatever he told you, I probably can't add much more to it."

"Fair enough. So tell me about Westin Force then."

"How about we go for a ride and I show you instead?"

A few minutes later we left the house and drove down the mountain to the lodge just outside Westin territory. I had been there before and had already pieced together that they were housing the unit there.

"Patrick explained what the Force does?"

"More or less," I confessed.

"So you know the Force is not only watching the Verndari, for any signs of rogue activity, but also shifters worldwide, right?" he asked as we were walking into the lodge.

"Yes, he did mention that. But he didn't explain how exactly that was taking place, or whether or not I needed to be concerned for my Pack."

"You wouldn't be in line for Alpha if you didn't ask that, but you have nothing to fear from us, Thomas. Collier is safe and will remain so under my watch. A month ago, heck a few weeks ago, I probably wouldn't have given you the time of day regarding all this, but you're family now and we take care of our own, and we do try to help those that aren't, they just don't know it."

Once inside, we turned down a hallway that I knew was filled with nothing more than hotel-style rooms. I had stayed there myself during the Grand Council gathering. We walked through the roped-off construction area, and once on the other side it looked no different than the rest of the floor.

"My men stay in this wing," he informed me as we got on an elevator. Kyle swiped a card and punched in a combination of numbers on the pad. The elevator started to descend.

I knew we were on the first floor. I hadn't even noticed there was a basement. The elevator seemed to be dropping even lower than that, though. When it finally stopped and the doors opened,

Kyle said, "Welcome to Base 1."

I was not prepared for what I stepped into. There was a dozen or so people all sitting at work stations with at least three large monitors, each tuned to nearly every news station on the planet. One window looked out into a data center filled with thousands of servers.

"What is this place?" I asked.

"Who's that, boss? I don't have any visitors on the schedule today and no time for tours," said a short, portly man with glasses too big for his face as he approached.

"Thomas, this is Archie. Archie, this is Thomas Collier," Kyle said, making the introductions.

"Thomas Collier, wolf, future Alpha of Collier Pack, official notice of bonding with Lily Westin was just released this week. Congratulations." Before I could say thanks, he turned to Kyle. "Now what's he doing here?"

"Be nice, Archie. Thomas is family now," Kyle warned. "They took my sister right under our noses. I don't ever want that to happen again. Thomas will protect Lily, but only if we give him the knowledge and resources he needs to do so. Plus, we always talked about spreading out to include our ally packs. You know that."

"Yes, but we're not ready for that yet," Archie argued.

"Well, too bad. We're there. Collier Pack is our first official ally, and privy to all information. Got it?"

Archie nodded, causing his too-big glasses to bounce on his face. "You're the boss."

He started walking away, but Kyle followed, so I did, too.

Archie sighed, stopping at the window looking down into the data center. "So, this is Base 1, headquarters. The moles have been monitoring shifter traffic for many generations. Joining forces with Kyle and the Westin Foundation has allowed us to bring our facilities up-to-date with all the latest and greatest technology. What you're looking at here is a new state-of-the-art data center, housing super-computers that allow us access to nearly every private and government agency in existence, as well as major satellite systems, to aid in our efforts."

"The moles?" I asked, trying not to snicker and hoping I heard that wrong.

"Yes," Kyle confirmed. "Archie is a mole shifter. It was

sheer luck that had us stumbling across the moles as we began start-up of Westin Force. Jacob had passed along copies of documents of known shifter families throughout history, and we started mapping out last known locations and researching old family names in the areas."

"My boys flagged the activity during their online searches, and we basically stumbled right over each other," Archie concluded.

"After some initial hesitation on both our parts, we made a pact and joined forces. Our combined efforts give us so much more reach and knowledge," Kyle explained. "The moles already had the infrastructure in place, to a certain degree."

"We have underground facilities and tunnel systems through most major cities across the world. What can I say? It's in our DNA, and what we do. Some moles were designed for building, some were built for designing. I keep a small team of six of us here, all designers, like me. We excel in coding and keeping a low online profile. We can dig into code, break through firewalls, and place tracker software with virtually no footprint, which helps us monitor top secret government and private systems."

"So you're highly skilled hackers is what you're saying?" I asked sarcastically.

Archie glared at me but continued as if I hadn't spoken. "Kyle insisted on having headquarters close to home, and who were we to argue? My boys had been itching to dig, something that hadn't been done in decades aside from upkeep and repairs. Let's face it, we can't exactly get away with digging in today's modern world with all the red tape, permits, and humans watching. Fortunately for us, my ancestors took care of everything we would ever need in that regard. But this place," he said, looking around proudly, "this is a masterpiece. It's fortified, virtually undetectable by satellite even. The project was covered by the building of the lodge and entirely protected behind the greatest firewall system ever invented."

"Let me guess? You designed it," I said, starting to understand the ego of this guy.

"Of course I did," he snapped.

"Okay, you get the gist of the monitoring side of Base 1. Thanks, Archie. I'll take it from here," Kyle said as the mole shuffled off, talking to himself. "I know, he's a strange one, but the things he can do with a computer would blow your mind."

"I have no doubt about that," I said, trying to wrap my head around it all.

Kyle led me to the end of the monitoring room and through another door. There was a long hallway with several doors off to either side. Kyle told me they were offices and emergency escape routes. We didn't stop till we reached the door at the very end of the hallway.

"They'll be in training right now, so we need to be quiet, but I wanted you to get a glimpse of Bravo Company. This is also their headquarters. There are also Charlie and Delta teams. For security purposes each elite forces unit has a different operations headquarters. Bravo is our top team. They're the ones that went in to help rescue Lily."

He opened the door and we walked out to an observation deck. Below, the team was working out in formation. I saw an indoor shooting range, more tactical gear than I could ever fathom, a full gym, and a room with chairs and a white board. The men were big, built, and looked mean as hell. I recognized one or two of them from our adventure in Alaska, but I had been so focused on Lily that I hadn't stopped to really give them the time of day. Somehow, they looked even more intimidating here.

Kyle waved to the one I assumed was the team leader and then motioned for us to leave. He didn't speak until the door was closed behind them.

"I don't really mess with those guys. So far, I really haven't needed them for much. They've assisted with things like the roundup of some rogue tiger shifters that were harassing Chase last year after escaping a Verndari facility, and of course, most recently, the helped with Lily's rescue. Archie sends them out to acquire information that even he can't get online. They also have their own private mercenary jobs for extra money. As long as it stays on the up-and-up and doesn't interfere with Westin Force business, we have the understanding that they are free to take on those type of assignments. Right now it's a win-win for all of us."

"And the Verndari—you've mentioned them a few times. You work with them? But aren't they the ones who kidnapped my mate?"

"Now don't get all worked up. Yes, we work with some Verndari. Not all of them are bad, Thomas. We have our inside guys and they are great at sharing much needed information with us, like the coordinates to Lily's location. They've helped save Elise in the past, and the couple that your sister lived with all those years are also Verndari. They love her like a daughter and would never do anything to hurt her or Oscar. Somehow, they never knew about Maddie. The trauma of the rape meant her wolf never surfaced, but they knew her rapists were likely tiger shifters and they've protected Oscar his entire life. It's brought us a unique connection to the Verndari."

I growled, hating to hear him speak so candidly about Maddie's attack and her time away from us. I still hadn't fully resolved my feelings about it all.

"Calm down. I understand. It took a lot of restraint not to rip their throats out last year when we crossed paths with those tigers."

"You crossed paths with the tigers that raped my sister? And they're still alive?" I growled between gritted teeth.

"Maddie's doing. I get how you feel, but it was her choice. All but one is locked away for good in a Verndari stronghold that they will not escape from. I hate sending any shifter there, but for them, I'd make that exception a hundred times over."

"What do you mean all but one? You let one get away?"

"No, MC did. He was the youngest and, well, you'll have to ask her the reasons, but she asked us to give him his freedom. I still have extra eyes on him, though. She doesn't know that, so I'd appreciate it if you didn't mention it to her."

I took a deep breath. Talking about Madelyn's rape was enough to send my wolf into stress, putting me on edge.

"Do you have any questions, or was this enough for now?" Kyle asked.

"I'm good. It would be best if we head back."

"Yeah, I was sensing your wolf's discomfort with this topic. Your mate will calm him quickly."

I nodded, smiling in spite of the situation just at the mention of Lily.

Kyle laughed. "You've got it bad."

I shrugged, not bothering to deny it.

"We'll be keeping a closer eye on the Verndari from now on. I don't want you worrying about them coming after your Pack or anything. Ninety-five percent of them are truly harmless. Their mission is to observe and protect, not interact. Westin Force will keep the remaining rogues in line. With the take down of the Alaskan site, we've got the last of the information we needed on them. If that changes, or any threat to Collier comes up on the radar, you'll be the first to know."

"Thanks, Kyle. I really appreciate that. If there's ever anything you need or any way I can help, just ask."

On the drive back to the house we spoke amicably about family, and he shared funny stories about Lily as a kid. He warned me about how difficult she was to wake in the morning and how I better have coffee ready. I just nodded and tried to hide my grin. I had no problems waking my girl each morning.

When we got back to the house I found Lily and Maddie talking in the living room. Maddie was pacing the room and Lily was sitting on the couch, hugging a pillow to her chest. They both shut up when Kyle and I walked in.

"I don't want to know," Kyle said. "I'll be in my office." He left.

"Where is everyone?" I asked.

"Out," Maddie said a little too quickly, glancing at Lily with a look that begged her to be quiet.

"So? What's going on?" I asked, unable to help myself.

"Nothing," Mad said, a little too quickly once again.

"You know I can't exactly lie to him, MC. Don't put me in that situation, because you know he's going to ask," Lily said, talking like I wasn't even there.

"It's nothing," she said, a little too forcefully while staring at Lily. "Besides, it's not his problem or concern."

"Hey," I said. "I'm right here. If you don't want to tell me, Madelyn, fine. Just tell me you're okay and I'll walk away and leave you two alone."

"I'm fine," she said with a straight face.

"Liar," Lily chimed in, under her breath as Maddie glared at her.

"You're going to tell him everything anyway the second I leave, aren't you?" my sister challenged my mate. My instincts were to jump in and help Lily, but I knew they were closer than sisters even, so I held back.

Lily sighed and gave me an apologetic look. "Thomas, can you please leave us alone and don't question or ask me about all this later? It's personal and it's her business, but it's not bad, and she really is okay."

I couldn't say no to her, so I leaned down and gave her a quick kiss, then nodded my head and turned to leave without another word.

"Wait," Maddie said just before I left the room. I slowly turned to face her.

"I'm just nervous. Come back. It's still kind of weirding me out a little seeing the two of you together, but Lily's right. You're her mate. You're my brother, and while this isn't necessarily any of your business, I know she'd never ask me to keep anything from Liam, and it's not fair to ask her to keep this from you."

"Maddie, it's okay. Whatever it is, I'm sure you have your reasons," I told her, turning to leave again.

"Thomas?" she said softly, and I turned to meet her eyes. There were tears in them and my instincts were split between turn and run, and go and comfort my sister.

"Ah Mad, it can't be that bad. Come here," I said, crossing the room and wrapping her into a big hug. I hadn't really had much contact with her. We'd made baby steps on eggshells back home, but this felt like the start of a new phase in life for us.

"I'm okay. I'm okay," she said with her face buried in my chest. I gave her a few minutes to gather herself together before pulling away. She wiped a tear from her cheek and motioned for me to sit, so I joined Lily on the couch.

"This really isn't easy for me to talk about," she started. "How much do you know about what happened to me the night I disappeared and why I never came home?"

I sucked in a sharp breath. "Enough," I said.

She nodded. "And do you know that Oscar is half wolf, half tiger?"

"Yeah," I admitted.

"Last year I helped rescue some shifters, and in the process, I inadvertently let loose the tiger pack that attacked me that night. I know it was stupid, but I didn't know they were there. Anyway, last spring they showed up at Chase and Jenna's place. The bad ones are back in custody, but I let the youngest of them go free."

I already knew most of that from what I'd pieced together from Kyle. "Why?" I asked, trying to keep judgement out of my voice.

"Because it was the right thing to do. He was just as much a victim to his brothers as I was. Yes, he acted that night too, but they got him really drunk, possibly drugged, and basically forced him on me. I have it from reliable sources that he really isn't a threat and I was willing to give him a second chance at life, in exchange for a blood sample. I had samples taken from each of the tigers and"—she waved an envelope in her hand—"I have the results in."

"It's the DNA results to identify exactly which one of them fathered Oscar," Lily added. "We were just about to open it when you came in."

"I see," I said. "Are you sure it matters?"

"It really doesn't matter, but I need to know for closure. Oscar may have questions about his biological father someday, and the answers are here in this envelope."

I nodded. "Would you like me to open it for you?" I offered, surprising both the girls.

Maddie stared at me for a moment, then she nodded as she handed the envelope to me with shaky hands, and I slid over so she could sit next to Lily. The two girls hugged.

"Are we rooting for anyone in particular?" I joked.

"Jack," they both said in unison.

I opened the envelope and quickly read through it. "The results read by 99.9998 percent probability of paternity, Jack Simpson is Oscar's biological father."

Both girls started crying. Maddie grabbed the results and they looked them over for themselves.

"Shouldn't Liam be here for this?" I finally asked.

"He didn't want to know," Maddie confessed. "Says it doesn't matter because he is Oscar's father, his only father. He's not wrong, but what if Oscar turns out to be a tiger shifter? He may need someone to talk to. He may want to know his biological father. And I can't tell you how relieved I am it's Jack."

"Are you going to tell him?" Lily asked, seriously.

Maddie shook her head, then shrugged. "I don't know. Maybe someday. I'm just relieved it's him and not one of his brothers. I won't go behind Liam's back, or invite him into our lives unless Oscar asks us to. I'm not real sure what to do with the news exactly, but I'll talk to Liam and we'll decide together."

Lily hugged her tighter. "I know you're relieved it's him. In some really messed up way, I'm happy for you. Not that it's something to be happy about, but well, you know what I mean."

The girls both laughed. There were tears still in their eyes. Maddie reached across the space between us and squeezed my hand.

"Thank you for being here and reading the results, Thomas. I know things have been really strained between us, but I hope that we can find some common ground again. I mean, you mated my best friend, and maybe I don't deserve it, but we are still family."

I snagged Maddie around the waist and pulled her to me as she yelped. I hugged my sister as she grinned against my shoulder. I let her go and took a serious look at her.

"I'm not going to lie and say I didn't harbor some resentment towards you all those years, but if I've learned anything lately, it's that no good comes from channeling negativity towards someone you love. It's too easy to do and hurts more than anything. I was angry you left, and even angrier that you didn't return. I was young, and I had my reasons, but none of that matters now that you're back. I don't want to be the biggest douchebag on the planet any more than I want to resent you for those lost years. I say we start a clean slate right here, right now. I don't really know you anymore, and you don't know me, but I'd like a chance to fix that."

Lily was crying with a huge smile on her face as she nodded at me.

Maddie and I hugged just as baby Sara sounded off from the nursery upstairs.

"I'll get her," Lily volunteered, jumping up and quickly leaving the room.

"You're really good for her, you know?" Maddie observed.

"You think?" I asked.

"I know. She's happy, like really happy. I think you are, too. And you're right. It's been a long time, Thomas. I'm sorry. I'm sorry for everything, but I'd really like to get to know the man you are today." She snorted. "Man? How did that happen? My little brother is a grown man, mated and everything. It's crazy!"

"And you? You're a mother, Mad. How insane do you think that is?"

"They're good kids. You're going to love them, and I bet you'll be a wonderful uncle."

"You think? I do like kids," I confessed.

Lily walked back in cradling Sara. I had a momentary flash of her holding our future child as she rocked her and cooed sweet nothings. Lily was going to be a great mother. She was a natural, whether she realized it or not.

As if channeling some weird psychic connection from just thinking of the Pack, my phone rang. I looked down to see it was my dad. Swiping the screen, I quickly answered it.

"Dad, what's up?"

"Lily's been issued her first challenge. I need you both to return home immediately."

Lily

Chapter 27

Thomas had been a nervous wreck ever since his dad's call came in. I was getting a little annoyed. I told him to have some faith in me. I was a Westin. I had trained my entire life for this. I wasn't worried one bit. Sure, fighting was not high on my fun list, but I was fast and strong enough to hold my own against any she-wolf.

The closer we got to Collier, the more relaxed I felt. It was the feeling of home, of Pack. It was what I'd expected to find going home to San Marco, but it never came. I sadly realized for the first time that my wolf's allegiance had already shifted. Maybe it came with the bond. I wasn't sure. But I wasn't a Westin anymore. I was a Collier.

When we arrived at the Alpha house, Zach met us and quickly ushered us into his office.

"Who, Dad? Please tell me it's not Sydney . . . but who else would do this?" Thomas said, clearly upset by the challenge I'd received.

"It's not Syd, son. It's Jessie."

I hadn't met a Jessie. I was certain of it, but by the way Thomas grabbed the back of a chair and braced himself, I knew it had to be bad.

"Has her wolf even come in yet?" he asked his dad.

"What?" I demanded. "I'm being challenged by a pup?"

"Her wolf surfaced just last month," Zach informed us. "She has the right to challenge. I'm sorry, I couldn't talk her out of it. Maybe you'll have better luck, son."

"When can we meet with her?" Thomas asked.

"The both of you? Together? Do you really think that's wise?"

"Yes sir. I think it's the only way."

Zach considered it and nodded. "You know her best. I'll make the arrangements."

When Zach left the room and we were finally alone, I turned on Thomas with my most burning questions.

"Who's Jessie, Thomas, and who is she to you exactly?"

He turned worried eyes my way. "She's Syd's kid sister."

Within the hour, Zach had arranged for us to meet with Jessie. I wasn't sure what to expect, but the small child who hadn't yet grown into her features was far from it. She was just a kid. How was I supposed to kill this pup? It wasn't right, and I didn't know if I had it in me. What if she kept pushing back, like that kid from the New York Pack that Kyle had to face? It had affected my brother being forced to do that, and let's face it, he was a million times stronger than I was.

"Hi, you must be Jessie," I said, trying to keep my concern from my voice and take her seriously as an equal. Her waif-like features made it difficult.

Her eyes widened. "You're Lily?"

I nodded.

"You're prettier than I expected," she said, like that mattered any.

"Thanks, you're very pretty, too."

"What's all this about, kiddo?" Thomas asked, cutting to the chase.

She glared at me, wanting to hate me, but it fell short like she didn't know what to think now.

"How could you, Thomas?" she asked. "Syd won't challenge her, so someone had to step up and do it. That should be Sydney by your side. You know that."

"And if you beat her, Jess, if you kill her, it still won't be Syd by my side. You do realize that right?" Thomas said calmly. "You know I love you and Sydney. That's never going to change, but I'm not in love with Sydney. I haven't been for a long time. She knows that, kiddo. Lily's my one true mate. To challenge her, hurts me. Is that what you really want?"

It didn't hurt me to hear him say he loved them, not even Sydney. Something in our time away had shifted things. I was secure in my relationship with Thomas. Maybe it was the bond, but I thought it had more to do with our trip and truly getting to know each other.

I remembered Kelsey had still struggled heavily with other she-wolves near Kyle during their challenge period, even after they had completed their bond, not that I'd ever compare myself to Kelsey. With her Alpha witchy powers, she had plenty of additional things she was dealing with, too.

Thomas had taken a seat directly across from the girl, so I took the chair next to him. I thought it would be best if I were on the same level as her. A part of me wanted to scare the shit out of her so she'd come to her senses and drop the challenge; but the other part of me didn't want to provoke her further. Taking my seat and allowing my leg to rest against my mate's, helped keep my wolf calm.

"Jessie, you understand what happens if you were to beat me, right?" I asked.

She looked at me. "Of course. You'll be dead, and Thomas will be free."

"Sorry kiddo, it doesn't quite work that way. If you beat Lily, you take her place as my mate," he informed her.

I bit back a smile at the look of disgust on her face.

"No, I'll be in charge and then and I can decide. I can give Sydney to you in my place."

"Technically, only if she kills you to take your place in pack order," I chimed in to the girl's horror.

"You mean I'd have to . . ." She gulped heavily as she turned her wide eyes toward Thomas.

"Afraid so, kiddo. You would become my mate, in every way," he added.

"But I'm only seventeen. That's not even legal!"

Sydney had walked in during the conversation and stood at the door just behind her sister. "I'm sorry," she mouthed to me. Aloud, she finally spoke. "Hey Jessie, what's this really all about?"

The girl turned to face her sister with tears in her eyes. "It's supposed to be you. You're supposed to be our Pack Mother. You're supposed to be Thomas's mate. He always comes back to you. She's just an outsider. She doesn't belong here. Someone has to stop her."

Sydney hugged her little sister. "I love you, Jess, and I love that you're so worried about me and our pack, but you have to drop this." She pulled back and I saw the shock on Jessie's face. Sydney reached across the table and grabbed my hand. "Jess, this is my friend. Lily is a good person. She's going to be a great Pack Mother."

"But . . . "

"No but's, kiddo. Thomas was never really mine. All I've ever wanted was for him to be happy. Look at him. He can't even glance her way without smiling. I barely recognize him because he practically glows when Lily's around. I deserve to have a man that looks at me the way he does her. Don't you think? I'm not his true mate, she is. I'm begging you to pull out of this challenge and really give her a chance."

Jessie was crying and hugging her sister again. "But it's always been you and Thomas."

Syd looked at the two of us sitting across the table and smiled. "He's my best friend, Jess. That's not going to change just because Lily's in his life now."

The door opened again, and their parents walked in. It was easy to see the resemblance without anyone having to tell me who they were.

Sydney squeezed my hand one last time. "It's okay," she mouthed.

"We should go," Thomas said. "Give them some time to talk." His arm was possessively around me when he spoke to Jessie. "We'll be awaiting your final decision, kiddo."

Once we were out of earshot, I spoke again. "Say a prayer she changes her mind, Thomas. I'm prepared to defend my place by your side no matter what, but I really have a hard time stomaching a fight with a child. Did you see her? She's truly just a kid. I don't want to kill a kid," I confessed.

"Sydney will get through to her if we haven't already," he said, more confident than I felt.

We left the house and walked down the street to the Tavern. When we walked in, everyone got quiet and shot death glares my way. I was finally feeling at home in Collier, but the evil eyes staring at me reminded me I was little more than an outsider.

I would be their Pack Mother one day. That was my role, and as such I had to win these people over. I couldn't cower or show weakness, so I held my head high, smiled politely, and grabbed hold of Thomas's arm for dear life.

We took a seat at an empty table and Thomas called Milly over. "Hey Milly, two sodas and a couple menus. What's the special today?"

I was amazed by the commanding presence he carried. It was strange. I had gotten to know the real Thomas Collier, my mate, but now I was seeing him in a new light as Thomas the future Alpha.

"Special's meatloaf," Milly told him, still not looking my way.

He nodded. "Babe, what are you having?"

"Cheeseburger please," I said, smiling at Milly, who still wouldn't look at me. Thomas ordered the special. As Milly went to leave, I reached out and touched her arm. Her eyes flew to mine. I smiled. "Thanks, Milly."

She sighed, gave a hesitant smile, and nodded.

I felt like I was living in a fish bowl the entire time we were there. Thomas acted oblivious to it all, so I did too. I concentrated on my mate and tried to enjoy a normal meal together, even if everyone continued to glare at me.

Later that night, when we were back in the safety and quiet of our home, I felt like I could finally relax.

"You okay? You seemed a little tense at dinner," Thomas acknowledged.

"Ya think?" I asked sarcastically, rolling my eyes at him. "I'm pretty sure I'm the most hated person in all of Collier."

"Don't be silly. No one hates you. They just don't know you yet. Maybe some of them did once, or remember you as a child, but give them time to get to know you now. They'll warm up. Just be patient."

I sighed. I knew it wasn't going to be easy. The challenges were still in full swing and even if Jessie backed out, there was still a target on my back. It was clear to me that no one inside the pack was going to challenge Thomas, so unless it came from an outside wolf, he was safe. That actually gave me great relief. I was a Westin and as such, I always knew I'd mate well, and had been preparing for this literally my entire life. It didn't matter what their opinions of me were at the moment. I was going to be their Pack Mother. No one could take that from me. I'd earn their trust the hard way and do whatever it took to prove to every wolf in Collier that I, Lily Westin, was fully capable and deserving of the title of Pack Mother, and that no one was better to stand by their Alpha's side.

The following days were not easy. I continued to endure glares and rude remarks everywhere I went, but I didn't back down. It was a humbling experience as I bit my tongue each time I would normally lash out in response.

I had quickly learned that the Tavern was the hub of Collier Pack. It was also the hardest to endure. The addition of alcohol made tongues even looser, but I forced myself to have at least one meal a day there with or without Thomas. When he called to apologize because a Pack Council meeting was running late, and they'd be working through dinner, I knew it was time to face the Pack.

I put on my big girl panties and headed into the wolf's den. I took a table in the center of the room and called Milly over to order, just as Thomas would have if he were there. She looked a little put off, but I was friendly and cordial to her and I always left her a bigger tip than was necessary, so she was slowly warming up to me.

"Can't believe she'd have the guts to show her face around here without Thomas to protect her," someone said from the table next to me.

I snorted and tried to bite my tongue. I told myself not to engage, but it wasn't in me to back down from a challenge. "I don't need Thomas to fight my battles for me."

"Ohhh," came from a few instigators, as if a challenge had just been issued.

"Ignore them, Lily," Milly warned me. "Been in here all day and already two sheets to the wind and looking for a fight."

"I'm not looking to fight anyone," I assured her.

"Well ya better be," the same guy said. "'Cause you don't belong here, and every she-wolf in Collier is going to stand up to challenge you until you realize that or are good and dead."

My heart stilled for a moment, but some little voice inside my head told me he was just drunk and trying to goad a response from me. "Maybe," I said. "But I certainly hope that won't be the case. Collier Pack will be a lonely place if I'm to be the only remaining she-wolf in it."

Shocked sounds came with hushed whispers throughout the room as the man bellowed out a laugh. "You definitely have spirit, girl. I'm Hewitt. Welcome to Collier Pack."

He offered me his hand, and I shook it. Maybe trying to be humble and keep my mouth shut wasn't being true to me. It dawned on me then that maybe Mom was right. God doesn't make mistakes in matching mates, and I didn't need to try to be anything I wasn't. Just being me was enough, and I vowed to stop biting my tongue so much and just do me.

Most of the place settled down and went back to life as usual after my brief encounter with Hewitt. Sure, I still got stares, but there was a curiosity to them now, until Sydney came in. She spotted me immediately and made her way to join me.

"Hey Lily," she said sweetly. "Mind if I join you?"

"Hi, Syd. Not at all, take a seat."

"Thanks."

Before we could get past the basic greetings, three women came to our table.

"Sydney dear, we heard about Jessie. Is she really going through with the challenge to *her*?" the first asked, emphasizing "her" and nodding my way as if I wasn't sitting right there, too.

"Yes, is it true?" the second one asked.

"It is true that Jessie issued a formal challenge to Lily, but she didn't really understand the implications of that. She hasn't officially reneged on her challenge yet, but my parents seem confident she will. She seemed to be under the impression that if I wouldn't challenge Lily, then Jessie could at least, and then give me her place after she won the battle. We had to explain to her that things don't work that way. She's a little freaked out right now, but I think she's going to be okay." She turned and smiled to me. "Lily did a great job of talking her down before I got there."

The third woman's face scrunched up in disgust. "Of course she did, Sydney. She's only protecting her own tail. Beat her psychologically before they even reach the arena."

I gawked as my mouth dropped open and this time I was struggling to shut it. "She's a child," I said. "Her wolf came in only a month ago. I've been training for this my entire life. Do you really think I'd take any pleasure in beating a pup? I don't take pleasure in killing anyone, but certainly not a young girl who's confused and upset because things aren't going the way she expected them to."

The women looked a little taken aback by my outburst, but I couldn't bring myself to regret it.

"Lily's right," Sydney said. "Jessie is no challenge for her, and I don't want to lose my baby sister over some warped sense of obligation."

"I still don't understand why you haven't issued your challenge and staked your claim as Pack Mother. You belong with Thomas, Sydney. The entire Pack is behind you," the first woman said.

"You're wrong, Edna," Syd said to the gasps of all three old biddies. She reached across the table and squeezed my hand in show of support. "Thomas is my best friend, and I get that everyone around here has had the two of us paired off since we were in diapers. For a short time, I had even believed we could go through with it, but that compatibility approval has been hanging over our heads for more than a year now. Don't you think there's a reason we never went through with it? If you guys could just get your damn heads out your asses for five seconds and really take a look at Thomas, how happy he is, how she smooths out those rough spots and calms his wolf, you'd know without a doubt that she is what's best for him, and what's best for all of us."

"You can't possibly mean that, Sydney," the third woman said.

"I do, Edna. Thomas is my best friend. Until Lily, I was closer to him than anyone, but I can't be her. She is his one true mate, and quite frankly I deserve mine, too. I don't want to be second best. She's the daughter of Jason and Mary Westin. She knows what it takes to be a Pack Mother. She knows what Thomas will need as Alpha better than I ever could. God doesn't make mistakes pairing true mates, and I will not come between that. If you're all seriously waiting for me to challenge her, then stop. I'm telling you now and you can go spread the gossip throughout the Pack, but I will not be challenging Lily. I cannot be your future Pack Mother, and I don't want to hear any more about it."

As their shocked faces took in all she'd said, I squeezed her hand back in appreciation and grinned. "You know, my Mom has always said that."

"What?" Syd asked.

"About God not making mistakes with true mates." I snorted. "You were there the night after our wolves connected. I don't think it will come as some big shocker that I was questioning that statement then. I didn't want it to be true. I had spent years channeling all this anger and hatred at him, when really he was just my scapegoat for missing Maddie."

The ladies were openly listening now and others began to join them, surrounding our table. I ignored it and stayed focused just on Sydney.

"Madelyn is my best friend in the entire world. Despite being from two different packs, we grew up together. We attended the same camps, she'd visit me in San Marco, and I'd spend weeks here in Collier with her and her family. This place has always felt like home to me. The Colliers have always been family, and when Maddie disappeared, a part of me died. I needed some way to channel those emotions, and whenever I'd come back for her annual vigil, Thomas was gone. I built him up to be this uncaring beast and I called him a lot of harsh names and said some really bad things about him over the years, but I was wrong."

Sydney laughed and gave me a quick hug, understanding that it wasn't easy to talk about, but I had the attention of the entire room, and they needed to hear my story. She encouraged me to go on.

"I rarely admit I'm wrong about something. My mom says I'm too stubborn for my own good. Maddie coming back into my life was a great gift. To find she was mated to my twin brother was even more incredible. We were finally sisters, for real, but a piece of my heart was still broken from all those years of missing her, and only Thomas could repair that. I had to let go of that anger and hatred, and that wasn't easy for me. He embodied that to me, and I definitely wanted God to be wrong when I realized that Thomas, of all people, was my true mate, but you're right. My mother was right. God doesn't make mistakes. We've worked past old prejudices, despite how unfounded they truly were. Thomas is a great man, and he's going to be an amazing Alpha. He needs a strong woman by his side." I looked out across the room, making eye contact with as many as possible. "If you let me, I can be that woman. No one else can ever truly take my place because I am his true mate, and with that comes a strength I didn't know was possible. I've been groomed for leadership my entire life, but never really fit in anywhere. I've worked dozens of jobs at Westin Foundation. I'm adaptable and good at all of them, but I could never commit to any one. That's because my place was never meant to be there. I'm supposed to be here, in Collier, by Thomas's side, and supporting all of you, because that's what a Pack Mother does. And quite frankly, I'm gonna be a damn great one."

Sydney laughed and hugged me. "Yes, you are."

I had built up my speech expecting some major change to occur, but they all just continued to stare at me.

"Come on, give her a chance. I promise you won't regret it," Sydney told them, breaking through the silence as murmurs started throughout the room. "They're gonna be talking about this for years," Sydney whispered to me.

"I didn't say anything too embarrassing, did I? I have a problem keeping my mouth shut sometimes," I confessed.

"Your speech was just what we needed to hear," Edna assured me. "Change is hard, and we won't go easy on you, but if you survive the challenges, we'll come around."

"Thanks, I think," I said with a chuckle.

Several women came up and introduced themselves. A few even wished me well. The aggression towards me was already subsiding, and I believed everything was going to be okay.

I saw Lizzy and Shelby make their way through the crowd.

"Wow, what's going on here?" Lizzy asked.

"I think Lily has decided to just campaign for Pack Mother in order to win over the old biddies," Sydney teased.

I covered my face with my hands and shook my head, knowing my cheeks were burning.

"That's not necessary, you know," Lizzy said.

"Unfortunately, I think it might be," I confessed.

"Um," she started, uncomfortably bouncing from one foot to the next. My face dropped. I knew something was wrong. "Can you come back to the house? Dad wants to talk to you."

"You've got another challenge," Shelby blurted out, and the whole room quieted again.

Thomas
Chapter 28

I was pacing back and forth across Dad's office since the call had come in. Wanda Larken had challenged Lily. My instincts to protect my mate were high, and my wolf was agitated. Dad had sent two of my sisters to get her, but it should have been me.

"You need to stay here and calm down. I know this is tough on you both, but every mating couple goes through this, and as future Alpha, son, you knew the probability was high she'd be challenged."

Lily walked into the room with Lizzy and Shelby, who was looking rather guilty, and I knew she'd spilled it and already told Lily of the challenge. I stared at Shelby and watched her squirm in guilt. They were supposed to just say she was needed back at the house so I could be the one to break the news to her.

Lily threw her hands up when I started to embrace her. "Just tell me it's a real challenge this time and not another pup paying tribute for Sydney."

I pulled her against my chest and wrapped my arms around her, letting her soothe my wolf's nerves. "It's a legit challenge, babe. I'm so sorry."

Lily pulled back and looked up at me like I was crazy. "What are you sorry about? It's not like I didn't know it was coming. Future Pack Mother is the highest position a she-wolf can obtain in the Pack. Of course I've got a target on my back. I'm ready," she insisted. "Who is it, sir?" she asked my father.

He threw a file down on his desk. "Wanda Larken. Everything you need to know about her is in that file."

Lily picked it up and thanked him. "When?" she asked, a little too calmly.

"Standard three days."

"Got it," she said. "I'm going to go study up on this information, if you'll excuse me."

"Of course," Dad said.

"Wait," I ordered. "You can't seriously be this calm about the situation." She was being challenged by a Larken, the most ruthless I'd ever met of our kind, and she was acting like Dad had just told her to go bake cookies. Where was the fire and the passion in my girl? She was freaking me out.

Lily stared at me like I had two heads. "It's fine, Thomas. Don't worry." She grinned, and I saw just a hint of mischief in her eyes. "I've got this."

"Don't you even want to know about her?" Shelby asked, sounding as shocked as I felt by how well Lily was excepting this challenge.

"Sure," she said. "What can you tell me about Wanda Larken?"

"First," Shelby started, "she's a Larken. That alone should concern you."

"Explain," Lily said.

"She's a Larken. What more is there to explain?" Shelby insisted.

"The Larkens were once part of Collier Pack. Her uncle, Jedidiah Larken, had a falling-out with Dad when we were just little pups. He pulled his allegiance and left. A few other families followed him. They still live in the area, just on the other side of the railroad tracks in a rundown trailer park. They're bad news, Lily," Lizzy added.

"Oh," she said sounding surprised, then her whole face lit up. "She's not actually a Collier wolf then?" The girls shook their heads. "Great! Well, that's certainly an improvement then. Thanks!"

Lily turned to leave, looking much too happy.

"Why are you okay with this? Why aren't you freaking out, Lily?" I asked, trying not to freak out myself. "This is a challenge to

211

the death. I need you to take this seriously. She's lethal and won't back down."

Lily turned to me and there was fire in her eyes. "Thomas, you need to have a little faith in me right now. I've prepared my entire life for this. I've been training since I was a pup, and my wolf and I are in perfect synch. You may think her lethal, but that's only because you've never seen me fight. I need you to just support me right now. I am capable of taking care of myself, you know? And quite frankly, I did not just confess way too much to the entire pack to just give up and die. I'm slowly gaining respect, but I still have a lot to prove to them, and apparently to you as well. I need some time alone to go over these notes and to train. Is there a place I can do that?" she asked.

I gulped. She seemed cold and disconnected, and I really didn't like it, but I nodded.

"I can show you a place," Lizzy offered. "I use it when I need to just get away. No one will bother you there."

I was probably the only other person on the planet who knew where she was talking, but I didn't say it. Lily would be safe there at least, and I knew Lizzy would keep a close eye on her.

"You have nothing to prove to me or the Pack, Lily. They'll come around," I told her.

She smiled, but there was still a cold feeling behind it that made me shiver. "They will, but you're wrong. I have everything to prove."

Lily and Lizzy left and I was once again alone with Dad. He chuckled and shook his head. "I understand you want to protect her, son, but she's a Westin. I guarantee Jason and Mary have personally seen to her training. She'll be ready. She needs your support more than your protection right now."

"I get that, Dad, but that's a lot easier to say than do. My job is to protect her. I hate this challenge bullshit. What is even the point? It's such an archaic system."

"I don't entirely disagree with you, but we fall under Grand Council law. It can only be changed by them."

My mind was already going a million miles an hour, thinking through scenarios and petitions that would be necessary to get the challenges dismissed. The previous night while Lily lay sleeping in my arms, I had scoured through the full text from the Grand Council regarding mating challenges, searching for any loophole possible to get her out of this. I knew it was too late for us, but I never wanted our children to have to face this, and I would do everything in my power to rally enough support to ensure they'd never have to.

"Look, Thomas, I know it's not ideal, but it is tradition and part of our heritage. I really need you to just hold it together for a few more days. Jedidiah is bringing Wanda over to meet you in a little while. I'm expecting them anytime now."

"And you just thought to warn me about this? Should Lily be here, too?"

"She wants to meet with you, not Lily. Besides, your mate asked for time alone. We should give her that. The less stress on her or her wolf, the better shape she'll be in to fight. I do not need Wanda agitating her and making things worse, and mark my word, that's exactly what these Larkens will pull."

I had been so young when Dad and Jedidiah had their falling out that I still didn't know all the details, or even why it had happened. All I really knew was that Jedidiah had sworn revenge on the Collier Pack, and if this was how he planned to enact it, he was in for a major disappointment.

A knock on the door of Dad's office alerted us to their arrival. He answered it personally.

"Hello Jed."

"Zach," the man said just as curtly. You could feel the tension thickening in the room as the two Alphas watched each other closely. "My niece, Wanda," Jed finally said.

"Hello, Wanda." My father nodded toward her then looked to me.

"Yes, hello. Welcome. I'm Thomas Collier," I said, following Dad's lead and not bothering to extend a hand to either of them.

"Wow, you're a lot sexier than I imagined. This isn't going to be such a bad gig after all," the woman said. She was tall, much taller than Lily, with luscious curves that once might have tempted me, but all I felt was disgust towards her.

"Come again?" I asked, not sure what she was getting at.

She stalked over to me and placed her forefinger at the top of my chest and proceeded to move it down. I growled and took a step back.

"Thomas," my father warned.

"No," I insisted. "Meeting her is one thing. She has no business touching me. My wolf will not stand for it."

Wanda laughed. "When I kill your mate in the challenges, you'll reconsider that. After all, I am going to be your new mate and Pack Mother of Collier Pack."

She sounded so certain that I wanted to smack the smirk off her face, but I knew Dad would never tolerate it. His wolf was barely holding on to sanity just with Jedidiah in our territory. Even I could feel his heightened stress.

So I smirked back at the audacious woman instead. "Actually, I won't."

Her brow furrowed. "I knew he wouldn't go through with it," she told her uncle. "Where's your pretty little mate hiding, Thomas? She too scared to face me? Think you can bully her way out of the challenges? Well, think again."

I smiled again. This one was a hothead. I filed that away to tell Lily later. "Actually, Lily is busy training and preparing for your challenge, and I have full faith my mate will defeat you and hold claim to her rightful place by my side. I was simply referring to us, of which there will never be an us under any circumstances."

"When I beat your mate, you'll have no choice," she threatened.

"Actually, if you were to beat my mate, and I highly doubt that possible, you will assume her role within the Pack. You will have your title of Pack Mother, but you will never have the title of my mate."

Dad glared at me as if I were a small child being warned to behave, but I brushed him off.

"It's in the rules, Thomas," she laughed. "You can't deny me as your mate once I kill yours and take her place."

I turned to Dad's desk and pulled off the copy of the Book of Wolves I had borrowed from him the night before to study. It was already open to the page I needed.

"Section 8, clause 7 under mating challenges, clearly states that in the case of true mates amongst Alpha males, where a dominate wolf loses his mate and refuses to take another, the winning she-wolf will live side-by-side and assume her predecessor's title, without expectation of mating. She will not have the option to take a mate, as it would cause conflict with the Alpha. This only occurs in rare occasions and is reserved exclusively for Alphas and future Alphas.

It's all there, read it for yourself. I promise you, my wolf is strong. He's aggressive, loyal, and very, very stubborn. There is zero chance that he or I will take another mate, ever. If Lily dies before our bond is secure enough to ensure I follow her in death, then my wolf and I will mourn her for the rest of our life. You can have your title, but I promise you it would be a lonely, empty life, and that's only if you can actually defeat my mate, which I highly doubt. Consider your options, Wanda. The ball's in your court," I told her.

Dad's face was somewhere between proud and shocked as he and Jedidiah set their differences aside for a moment and studied the Book of Wolves. I'd done my homework and I knew my rights and what stand I'd take, and I would make damn sure to let any she-wolf daring to threaten Lily, know it.

"You're going to do what you feel you have to do, and so will I," Wanda said. "You best enjoy your mate while you can, as she only has three days left to live." She looked down at her watch. "Make that two and a half."

I growled at her and felt my dad's Alpha power press down on me, but my wolf didn't want to concede to him.

"Jed, get her out of here. He's getting stronger."

Jedidiah's eyes widened as he stared at me. "Wanda, come on, it's time to go. You have a challenge to prepare for."

"As if I'll even need it," she said sarcastically. "I already saw his little pink-haired Barbie doll. She's no challenge for me."

When the door was closed behind them, I was still seeing red. Dad amped up his power, which continued to do nothing more than piss me off.

"You will calm down, and you will concede," he said, staring me straight in the eyes. My knees shook and tried to buckle, but I held out a little longer before collapsing into a chair.

My breathing was erratic and I was sweating, struggling to calm down even after giving in.

"You wolf is growing stronger. He won't tolerate my commands much longer, Thomas."

"What does that mean, Dad?"

"It means I may be out of a job sooner than I expected," he said, smiling down at me.

"I don't want your job. Not yet, it's just . . ."

"It's just your wolf is very powerful and has always been quite opinionated. I have always known you would need to assume control at a younger age than most, and I know you are ready."

"Dad . . ."

"Son, it is my greatest privilege to pass the reins on to you. You'll understand that someday. I cannot get Lily out of this week's challenge, and I pray to God she survives it, because I truly fear what will happen to you if she doesn't. Two Grand Council members will be here to oversee the fight. With your permission, I'd like to discuss this with them. I know it will be difficult for you to sit there watching and remain neutral. I need to explain what's happening here, that we're heading into transition and how unstable that could make you during the challenges. If Lily wins this, there's a very small chance we may be able to end the challenges for you after that. You will have shown your willingness to comply and that may be enough."

"Don't tease me, Dad," I said stiffly, still trying to regain full control.

"It will mean that you will advance to Alpha without contestation. Is Lily ready to take over as Pack Mother?"

"I'm positive she is, but I'd like the chance to discuss with her."

"Yes, your mother has questions and concerns as well that we will need to discuss," he said, pointing to his head, letting me know she was already well aware of the situation.

A part of me felt terrible that Dad would even consider giving up his pack position for me, but mostly I felt relieved that he was willing to help and that there was a possible solution to end this nightmare. I knew it would take every ounce of personal restraint I could muster just to sit through Lily's challenge. The thought alone made me feel sick to my stomach and completely helpless.

Lily

Chapter 29

Thomas sent me a text to meet him at the Tavern for dinner. I was still in my workout clothes, my hair was pulled back into a half ponytail, not long enough for a full one, but enough to keep it from falling in my face. Normally I took great care about my appearance in public, but I had too much on my mind and too much to do to be concerned.

I had one full day left to prepare for this battle. I'd taken my time and done my homework on my opponent. Wanda Larken was ruthless, but she was also noted as emotional and unstable. I could work that to my benefit.

I had called Kyle to see what he could give me on the Larkens. It was more than I hoped for. They were into some pretty shady stuff, and there was no way I was going to allow that into Collier. I had to protect my Pack and that meant focus, something I wasn't great at to begin with.

Lizzy had proven to be a great sparring partner. There was this sort of sadness surrounding her, but once we broke past that, I saw glimpses of someone entirely different. She always appeared to be the quietest, most reserved, and weakest of the Collier girls. I was wrong about her. Her inner strength and stubbornness when she set her mind to something was astonishing, and I couldn't wait to dig deeper and get to know the real woman beneath the façade she carried.

When I walked into the Tavern, there was only a brief pause this time and then everyone went back to their conversations. It sort of freaked me out. Was I finally starting to fit in? Or had they just written me off as "soon to be dead, so don't waste the time?"

I took a high table for two near the bar because it was the first I saw. My leg muscles were still burning from my workout, and I just couldn't muster the energy to move any further.

"Just one tonight?" Milly asked.

I couldn't help but smile, feeling no more animosity from her. "No, two. Thomas should be along soon."

She nodded. "Coke while you wait?"

"You know, I could really use some whiskey tonight." She gave me a look, like she remembered what happened when I drank, and I grinned. "Okay, okay, one Whiskey Sour, and a Coke. I'll behave tonight, I promise."

She gave a quick laugh. "I'm going to hold you to that just one, but you definitely earned it. Heard you've been working your ass off training for your upcoming battle. It's not against little Jessie, is it? No one 'round here seems to know for sure who the second challenger is."

Gossip ran rampant in the Tavern, and Milly was the ring leader of that crazy circus. I wondered why she hadn't heard about Wanda. It should have been public knowledge already.

Before I could respond, Edna and her two friends that always seemed to be with her shuffled over to join in the conversation. Feeling a presence just behind me, I turned to see Emmett and James standing just behind me, glaring at the gathering crowd of gossipers.

Clay walked up into the middle of them. "Would y'all just back off and leave the girl alone? She has enough to deal with without you up in her business."

"We just want to know who the challenger is with," Milly insisted.

"It's okay, Clay, thanks." I meant it, too. Having Thomas's friends show their support was everything. "To put your minds at ease a little, I have not been given a challenge date for Jessie Parker. That's not to say it won't come, because I also have not been told that she has officially reneged on the challenge, but at this time, there is no challenge."

Murmurs and sighs of relief went through my captive audience.

"We heard there was another challenger, though, and look at you. Clearly you've been preparing for it," one of Edna's old crows said.

I looked down at my attire and frowned, wondering if I should have taken a few minutes to clean up before dinner. I'd been so hungry and excited to spend a little time with my mate that I hadn't even considered it.

"You look fine, child, just different than usual. No one was judging," Edna insisted.

I snorted. "Y'all have been doing nothing but judging."

She gave me a knowing grin. "Yes, but not over how you look or what you're wearing now," she added.

"I do like your candor, Edna," I confessed, earning myself another true smile from the old bat.

"So? Who is it then?" Milly asked excitedly.

"Wanda Larken. I battle her in two days," I told them, surprised at how loud and angry the voices grew as the information spread around the room.

"That bitch has the audacity to show her face in Collier territory?" Edna said just as I took a drink of my whiskey. It burned through my nose as I tried not to choke.

"There's a reason Alpha didn't make a public announcement," James leaned down to whisper in my ear.

I shrugged. "They have a right to know. Challenges are public information."

"No Larken is going to take down a Collier," Hewitt loudly yelled to the agreement of others.

I snorted. "Thought I was nothing more than an outsider. I'd think you'd want someone a little closer to home for your Pack Mother, the way you've all been acting."

The room quieted.

Edna was the first to speak. "Child, we were all shocked when you showed up. Everyone loves Sydney, and no one wanted to see her hurt."

"I'm right here, you know," Syd said from across the room. "And I'm not hurt. I'm happy Thomas found his true mate. Maybe a little jealous that I haven't found mine yet, but Lily's a great person and she's what's best for him. That's all that matters to me, and that's all that should matter to you guys, too."

"Thanks," I mouthed to her, and she nodded.

"Of course, we know all that," Edna said, blowing her off. "We protect our own around here. Sydney's Collier. You, Ms. Lily Westin, are not . . . yet. Most of us remember you as a young pup, running around with Madelyn. We've seen you grow up into a fine young woman. We aren't even questioning your capacity to care. You just have some mighty big shoes to fill as our future Pack Mother, and we're not going to go easy on you because we need to know you're tough enough to handle the job."

I nodded. "Okay, I can accept that. Time will tell on that one."

"Time, shime," Hewitt said, swaying when he stood to walk over to my table. "No offense, Syd, but you were always too sweet and too quick to appease everyone to make a truly good Pack Mother. You need a pair of balls for that job, and you, missy," he said, putting his arm around me, more for his own balance than as a show of comradery. "You have a big set of balls, a smart mouth, a quick wit, and still a kindness to everyone, despite how poorly you've been received. You will make a fine Pack Mother, and have my full support. Now kick some Larken ass to seal the deal."

Cheers actually went up to his speech, and I shook my head, laughing.

Edna had to add her two cents. "Far as I'm concerned, if it's a match between you and a Larken, you have my full support, too." Her friends nodded their heads in agreement.

"Thanks, Edna. That means a lot coming from you," I admitted.

Thomas walked in and looked confused. Several said hello to him and began to scatter. He stopped to talk to Clay for a moment, and I had no doubt Clay filled him in on all that had just happened. James and Emmett were still standing guard at my back. When Thomas finally got to me, he surprised me by leaning down and kissing me for all to see. Hewitt started hooting and hollering his approval. Somehow I'd made a strong ally in the town drunk.

Emmett finally left his station to help Clay pull another table over and my three Six Pack guards joined us. I could feel Thomas's wolf was agitated, so I scooted my chair closer to his so that our thighs touched. He didn't calm immediately, so I turned and placed my hands on his chest and leaned closer to whisper, "Are you okay?"

He looked as if he were studying me, and then leaned forward till our foreheads met. I sensed the shift within him as he finally started to calm. "I am now," he confessed, stealing another quick kiss.

Milly showed up and took our orders without any further fanfare.

"Thanks for watching my girl's back," Thomas said, speaking to Emmett and James.

James was sitting next to me and nudged me with his elbow. "She ain't gonna need our help. Hewitt's right, this girl's got a pair."

"I assure you, she doesn't," Thomas mumbled under his breath as my cheeks started to burn and I turned to scold him, but he was grinning and looked happier than I'd seen him since our return to Collier.

Dinner was pleasant, and despite the weight of the challenges, the evening passed in lighthearted fun as I got to know this half of the infamous six-pack. They were loud, often vulgar, very animated, and sexy enough to gain the attention of every eligible she-wolf in Collier, as woman after woman stopped by to say hi, under the guise of introducing themselves to me, all the while staring at them. It really didn't bother me though. I genuinely liked the guys.

As we finished up and said goodbye, Thomas and I made our way back to the car to head home. Several people stopped us along the short walk to wish me well in the challenge. Many of them had not been at the Tavern that night, only showcasing just how fast gossip spread through Collier.

Thomas was quieter than usual on the drive home. It wasn't an uncomfortable silence, just different, and I knew he had a lot on his mind.

"Are you okay?" I asked when we were in the house and able to speak freely.

"No," he said honestly, looking vulnerable. "We need to talk."

My initial response was to overreact and start second-guessing everything that had transpired between us, but I took a deep breath, letting his scent soothe my nerves as I reached for his hand

and led him over to sit on the couch. I sat first, patting the space next to me.

"Okay, talk," I said.

He hesitated, like he was puzzling out what to say, or how to say it. "I met with Wanda today." An unexpected growl erupted from me. Instead of causing added tension, Thomas laughed and leaned forward to kiss my lips. "That's my girl. I may have angered her and she's certain she's going to win this battle, but I assured her she'd never actually win me. She's a hothead, Lily. You can use that to your advantage."

"Already did my research on her. It was clearly documented. I'm ready for this, Thomas. I've got this, and I don't want you worrying about it."

"I'm going to worry, slugger. I love you. I hate that there is literally nothing I can do to stop this nightmare. I've gone through every word in the Book of Wolves about the mating challenges and my hands are tied. I can't get you out of the fight. I need you to know that if she were to win, there is a section of code I will invoke that will ensure she will never be my mate."

"What?" I asked, not sure I was hearing him correctly.

"It's an Alpha-specific clause. My wolf and I will never take another mate. For us, it's only ever going to be you, no matter what."

I sighed. "Thomas, the last thing I'd ever want is for you to be lonely. Your wolf needs companionship too. It's what feeds our emotional connections. You have to know that."

"We'll survive, Lily, but we'll never truly live without you."

"And you told Wanda that?"

"Yeah, I was sort of hoping it would make her rethink through this and back off, but it backfired on me."

"Because, unlike me, you didn't do your homework and know who you were dealing with. I won't make that mistake, and besides, none of this matters anyways, because she won't beat me," I said with a certainty I felt deep down in my soul.

"There's something else," he said hesitantly, giving me an apologetic look that made my stomach flip with nerves. "My wolf lost it today, Lil. He tried to overtake Dad when he went to make me submit. While you give him a peace I've never felt before, you've also empowered him, and Dad feels like it's only a matter of time before he'll refuse to submit at all."

"What does that mean, exactly?" I asked. It didn't sound good, but I didn't know where he was going with it either.

"Dad thinks it's time," he said simply. "And I didn't want to agree to anything without discussing with you first."

"I'm not following you, Thomas. You're not a danger to the Pack. If you're having trouble controlling your wolf's aggression, we can work on that. What do you mean it's time? I don't understand."

"It's time for Dad to step down and for me to advance to Alpha," he said, taking in a sharp breath and waiting for my response.

"Now?" I asked. "In the middle of challenges? Don't we have enough on our plate without adding that?"

He smiled. "I tell you that you could be Pack Mother within a month's time, and you're concerned about the trials? Lily, if this happens the way Dad thinks it should, he'll petition the Grand Council for approval when they are here for your battle against Wanda."

"Since when does the Grand Council have to approve a new Alpha?" I asked, still not fully understanding where he was going with this.

"They don't, but we need their approval to request the exemption for any further battles. Our mating challenges would effectively end as we assumed our new roles within the Pack. What do you think? If it works, you'd only have to fight Wanda." He said her name through gritted teeth.

"You and your dad didn't come up with this idea just to get me out of battles, did you?" I said, suddenly worried that he truly thought I wasn't capable of fighting my own fights.

"No, babe, that's not the case at all. Actually, I'm afraid it's me, not you. My expectation during a battle is to sit there and watch without showing favoritism. It's just not possible. He's already got plans in place to contain me and even remove me if necessary. My wolf isn't handling a threat to you well at all." He sounded regretful, embarrassed, not realizing how relieved it made me.

I never understood how they could expect that of a mate. It's not like we were potential mates, we were bonded. If they wanted to continue their stupid trials, they should be issued before a couple bonds.

"I hate that these stupid challenges even exist at all," I admitted. "But Thomas, I'm a lot stronger than you think. Maybe I need this battle to prove that to you and to the Pack. Our Pack, and to answer your earlier concerns, if stepping up sooner, rather than later, is what's best for you, then it's what's best for me too."

The relief on his face at my words made tears spring to my eyes. Time for talking was over as he carried me to our bed and showed me just how much he needed me.

The next day I was on full focus. Lizzy came by her so-called secret place to spar with me some more, but apparently it wasn't that big of a secret, because we quickly had a growing audience. We had already discussed the importance of basics, so nothing fancy was happening to the disappointment of those in attendance.

By lunch time I was drenched in sweat and starving. I had asked Thomas to stay away, despite his need to spend every second with me before my battle the next day. We compromised. He would give me the space to train and prepare until six o'clock, then we would head home and spend the night alone.

When the five remaining Six Pack showed up with lunch, I made a mental note to add them to the off-limits list.

"What are you guys doing here?" I groaned. "It's bad enough we've gained an audience," I grumbled.

"Relax, Lily," Wyatt said. "We come in peace, bringing lunch and offering our help."

I snorted. "Besides running interference with the ladies, how are you boys offering to help, exactly?"

"Well, she still has her spirit, that's a good thing," Austin said. "Now we want to see if you can really fight."

"Huh?" I asked, no doubt giving them a comical look.

"Wanda Larken is ruthless. She's going to come at you with all she's got, and she won't be looking to play fair," Clay added.

"We're here to make certain you're ready," Emmett explained.

"Yeah, I was talking to Thomas this morning, and our boy is losing his shit over this battle. I'm sure you've trained for this, probably your whole life, and no offense to Lizzy, but walking through basic combat moves isn't going to cut it. We need to see for ourselves where you stand. We won't go easy on you because Wanda won't tomorrow. We have less than twenty-four hours to guarantee you are ready, and make no mistake, you will be ready," James said. I suspected he was trying to intimidate me, like they didn't think I was taking it seriously or anything. I'd show them.

"You're on. Who's up first?" I challenged, to their surprise.

"Austin," James said. "Enjoy your lunch, warm up, and prepare to fight Austin. I'll referee. Austin, when you hear that whistle blow, you back it down immediately. Are we clear?"

Austin nodded with a smirk. I quickly assessed he was a cocky show-off. I suspected by his build and easy gait that he was agile and likely quick on his feet.

"Wait," I said, as I was strategically thinking through the scenario. "Are we fighting in human form or wolf?"

"You'll be expected to fight in wolf form tomorrow," James reminded me.

"So wolf it is then," I said, finishing the last bites of my sandwich and getting up to stretch out the kinks of my morning workout. My wolf was already primed and ready to be set free. Austin might not go easy on me, but he had no idea what I was truly capable of either. I already knew that my biggest advantage was their underestimation of me and I was counting on that being the case with Wanda tomorrow as well.

Austin warmed up mostly by flirting with a few cute girls who were watching. I rolled my eyes at him, but didn't let it dull my concentration. When the time came, I stripped out of my clothes and shifted quickly to my wolf as I watched him do the same. He had a large grey wolf. I knew most of the wolves of Collier Pack were grey, making my white one stand out.

Our makeshift arena was a round, fenced in area they used to break in wild horses. James called us to the center and had us bow towards each other since it was too late to shake hands. He listed off some safety rules, clearly favoring the reminder towards Austin, the biggest of which was not to kill me. *Thanks, James.*

When he blew his whistle and jumped back out of the way, I hung back and let Austin come to me. As I had predicted, he was fast on his feet, showing off with quick movements meant to intimidate me. I held my position and waited. He looked towards the girls for only a second and I sprang into action. It took no effort to pin him to the ground and sink my teeth into his vulnerable neck with just enough pressure to let him know I wasn't playing around.

James blew the whistle to end the match as I backed away. Austin's eyes were filled with confusion when he stood and shifted back to human form, to the delight of his fans. Emmett jumped the fence and came our way.

"Mama wants to play, we'll play. I'm next."

I nodded as Austin left the paddock to face his friends, who were already heckling him for losing so quickly to a girl. I ignored them, focusing instead on Emmett, who had already shifted. His wolf was much larger than mine. From size alone, I knew he wouldn't be as fast on his feet as Austin had been, but he was far stronger.

When James blew his whistle this time, I didn't stay put. Instead I began circling Emmett slowly, assessing his movements and watching for his weaknesses. He wasn't going to go down easily, that much I was certain of. He started following my lead, and I grinned. He wasn't a leader. I could lure him in and take advantage of that. I tested my theory first and sure enough, he followed my lead the entire time, watching for my weaknesses. Too bad for him, he didn't realize that my only weakness and distraction was Thomas and that was something I was trying to come to grips with for tomorrow's battle, knowing he had to be there.

I didn't want to put the burden on Thomas, but if he lost it and they had to restrain or remove him, I wasn't sure how my wolf would handle the situation.

Emmett finally made his move, but as predicted he was slow and I easily sidestepped his attack, ducking and dodging as he came after me again and again. I saw his weakness with growing clarity. He was easily frustrated when things didn't go his way. I used that to my advantage and continued thwarting him until his movements became sloppy, then I went in for the kill.

He wasn't easy to take down, but I managed well enough, and regretted the slice across his front shoulder in the process. James blew his whistle, and Emmett was bleeding a little when he shifted back.

I tried to relay how sorry I was, but he looked at his shoulder, wiped off the blood, and smiled at me. "Good move, mama. You're a hell of a lot tougher than you look, I'll give you that." I nodded my thanks, waiting for my next opponent.

Wyatt jumped the fence, then leaned back over to kiss his mate as she cheered him on. I watched him closely and waited. Wyatt was a lot tougher to read. He was the largest of the six-pack, taller even than Thomas, and clearly strong from the obvious signs of his defined biceps and chiseled waist. I gathered from a few looks Clay and Austin shared that they had not expected Wyatt to challenge me. I only hoped he hadn't seen some weakness I wasn't aware of while fighting the others.

One thing Mom had always told me was to never fight the same fight twice. Every opponent was different, and a good opponent would vary their attacks and battle strategy, so I had to also. Even if Wyatt thought he knew what he was coming after, he didn't. I was ready for him.

I didn't hesitate with Wyatt. He was too big for me, so I figured I had two options: One, strike quickly before he knew what was coming, or two, toy with him until I wore him down some. I opted for option number one.

Where I had held back on the whistle even with Emmett, I made my attack swiftly and immediately with Wyatt. I plowed into him with a force great enough to send him flying into the air and lose his footing on the landing. I heard the crack. I knew he had broken something, but I pinned him quickly anyway and forced my teeth down against his neck as James quickly blew the whistle, running over to us.

This time I shifted immediately. "I'm so sorry, Wyatt. I didn't mean to hurt you."

Austin, Clay, and Emmett stood there laughing at him.

Kate jumped the fence and was by his side before he could shift back. James thrust my clothes at me as I forgot I was still naked. It didn't bother me, but we both knew Thomas wouldn't like it. His wolf was too unstable right now for me to egg it on, so I got dressed while Kate checked Wyatt over.

"You changed your strategy. Why?" he asked, clenching his teeth in pain.

"I'm so sorry, Wyatt. I was trained to always change my strategy. Every opponent is different. Assess his or her weakness and go in for the kill when they're most vulnerable. Your wolf is huge. I could have worn you out or struck quickly and unexpectedly. I went for the surprise element, just didn't expect it to work *that* well. Is it broken?"

Kate felt his leg and found the break. "His leg is definitely broken, but he's tough, he'll be okay. This wasn't your fault, Lily. You can't let this psych you out for tomorrow."

"Psych her out?" Austin asked. "No way. She's ready to kick ass tomorrow! If you can do that to Wyatt, Wanda Larken doesn't stand a chance against you."

"Thank you," I said. "That's what I've been trying to tell everyone."

Training was over. My next opponent would be Wanda. The crowd partly dispersed and partly followed us as James and Emmett carried Wyatt to the truck, then climbed in back with him as Clay and Kate jumped in the front and drove him to the clinic. Lizzy and Austin rode with me as we followed behind.

"I could have warned them and saved him this pain, but they came in so cocky I couldn't resist letting you have at them," Lizzy said with a gleeful smirk.

Austin rolled his eyes. "We've been watching you. There's no way you knew she was capable of this off the drills y'all were running."

Lizzy and I looked at each other and laughed. While the area was still "secret." before everyone caught wind of me training with Lizzy, she had sparred me full on. She was a tough opponent, but I had defeated her in the end and earned her utmost respect. It had given us a new bond and she had confessed she hadn't been too sure about the idea of me bonding with her brother, though she also admitted that Thomas was her baby boy and always would be. She was like his little mother growing up and they had a uniquely close relationship because of it.

Austin just shook his head at us. "Well, you're definitely ready for the challenge tomorrow," he grumbled.

Thomas had gotten word of an accident at my training and was seeing red and sprouting fur on his hands when I arrived. Several people were trying to talk him down and explain it was Wyatt that was injured, not me, but his wolf wasn't hearing it.

With hands on my hips, I walked right up to him. "Thomas Collier, I told you to have some faith in me. I'm more capable than you realize and I'm perfectly fine."

Through glossy eyes he stared at me, then reached out and pulled me to him, crushing me against his chest.

"Can't breathe," I grumbled as he loosened his hold.

He was on the verge of hyperventilating, but he placed his nose in the crook of my neck and sniffed deeply, then breathed his scent on me, and kissed his mark on my neck. Still a little shaky, his wolf finally began to calm.

"Shit, Thomas, you have got to keep that in check tomorrow. She wasn't even hurt. Kicked Austin and Emmett's asses, and then broke Wyatt's leg. That's why we're here numb-nuts. She doesn't even have a scratch on her," James told him.

"I can't say the same." Emmett chuckled, pulling up his sleeve and showing off the deep scratch I'd left on his shoulder.

"Sorry Emmett," I finally said.

"No big deal, mama. You got this tomorrow. Let Thomas take you home and just relax tonight. Wanda has no idea what she's getting herself into," Emmett said, grinning proudly.

I turned to Thomas. "That sounds perfect to me, but I really need to make sure Wyatt's okay first."

Turned out he needed to be rushed in for a fracture reduction. The doctor explained it would take a couple of hours because they had to sedate him in order to properly set the break. I must have apologized a hundred times to Kate, but I never left her side through it all, and Thomas never left mine.

Thomas
Chapter 30

It had been a long night, but I'd gotten a glimpse of Lily in a new light. She wasn't "Lily, my sister's best friend." She wasn't "Lily, my mate." Last night, she'd been Lily, Pack Mother of Collier Pack. She didn't have to sit there, holding Kate's hand for half the night. Wyatt was going to be fine, maybe a little annoyed that he got beat so badly by a girl, but fine.

The guys had passed the time recounting over and over how they'd gotten their asses kicked by Lily. She had continued to remain humble and say it was nothing instead of joining in with the smack talk.

People came and went all evening, checking in on Kate and Wyatt. Lily had been the cornerstone of it all, filtering inquiries, assuring people he was fine, comforting his poor mother, and of course Kate. I knew that in times of crisis, this is who she'd always be. The Pack responded positively to it, too. Those that returned didn't try to speak with Kate, or even the nurses, they went straight to Lily. Somehow, she had earned her position in the Pack and I was lucky enough to have a front row seat as it all unfolded. The most amazing part to me was that she had no clue it was happening. As always, she was simply being Lily.

It was late into the night when she finally agreed to go home. Wyatt had been out of the operating room for hours by then, but she had stayed, continuing to be the pillar and comfort needed by everyone who stopped by.

"You're amazing. Do you even know that?" I asked her in awe.

She snorted, undressing for bed. "For breaking Wyatt's leg and leaving claw marks on Emmett? I don't think so."

"No, for just being you. I was worried about pressuring you into Pack Mother too soon, but I shouldn't have, because you are a natural. I don't even think you realize it."

She shrugged. "In times of crisis I always ask myself, *What would Mom do?* She was a pretty awesome Pack Mother, so I figure I can't go wrong with that thinking."

Lily was restless all night long, despite an exhausting day. I lay awake worrying about her challenge, until finally, in the wee hours of morning, I drifted off to sleep.

For the first time since our bonding, Lily was up and ready before I woke. I frowned when I saw the bed beside me empty. A few minutes later Lily came out of the bathroom, her hair dripping wet from a shower.

"Good morning," she said, much too cheerfully.

"You're awake?" I grumbled.

"Couldn't sleep," she confessed.

"I didn't even get breakfast in bed this morning," I mumbled under my breath, causing her cheeks to match the color of her hair. If I were being honest, the taste of my beautiful mate first thing in the morning and waking up to her moans of approval had become far more addictive than the strongest coffee.

She leaned down and kissed me, and it wasn't nearly enough, but I could sense her hesitance to escalate things beyond that. I looked over at the clock, surprised to see it was already eight o'clock. Her fight would begin in just two hours.

Every instinct in me told me to grab her and spend that time showing her how much I loved her while marking her with my scent and love bites to remind every other wolf that this one was mine, but she had other plans.

"I'm meeting Lizzy in half an hour to warm up, so we don't have much time," she said sadly. "I need you to know that, no matter what happens today, Thomas, you have to stay in that seat and not react. I'm not going to lose this battle. I'm not, but that doesn't mean I'm going to come out entirely unscathed, either. Promise me. If the rules didn't say you had to be there, I would ask you to stay away."

Just like that, my little slugger bashed my heart into pieces once again. I had thought that after our bonding, she wouldn't have that effect on me anymore, but there it was.

"You don't want me there?" I asked. It was all I truly heard her say.

She rolled her eyes. "You only ever hear what you want to hear. That's not what I said, and it's not possible anyway." She was stalling, trying to find the right words. This was Lily, anything en route to her brain shot out her mouth. She wasn't restrained, especially with me, so why now? It was freaking me out a little.

"What is it?" I finally asked, unable to stand it any longer.

"Our bond is strengthening," she said slowly. "I can feel it, Thomas. I can feel you. My wolf has started feeding off your emotions and I'm worried that if you start to freak out today, so will she. I'm used to being in perfect harmony with her. It's one of my biggest battle strengths, but if she's emotional because you are, I don't know how that will affect our fighting. I didn't really realize it until last night. I was wrong not to bring you to training. So I'm asking you to please try and remain calm, no matter what happens today. I'll make it as quick as I can, but I have no doubt that word has already spread with how quickly I took Wyatt down. She'll be waiting for that. She'll be arrogant and think she's got me. I have to alter my strategy again. She's strong on the offensive, but she fights emotionally. I need her to lose her temper out there, and you need to sit there and let that happen. Do you understand me?"

I nodded. What she was asking was impossible. My wolf was already agitated just knowing she was going to be at risk, and I wasn't strong enough to subdue him.

She climbed into bed and cuddled up against me. Peace washed over me, settling my wolf. We didn't talk further, and despite the desire welling up in me, I didn't act on it. I simply held her until the last second.

She wouldn't let me say goodbye, only "see you later." It broke my heart to watch her walk away. This stupid mating challenge went against everything sacred to our bond. It defied my wolf's patience level and would test me as much as her. I needed to protect my mate. It was engrained into every ounce of my being. Why couldn't the Grand Council understand that? The members making up the stupid rules never even faced the same challenges, because they didn't bond or have families. It was one of their requirements as Grand Council members to supposedly allow for objectivity. There was no way they could fully understand what they were asking for.

I again solidified my position to challenge the rules. No wolf should ever have to go through this. There were already pack placement challenges. The idea that it was better for those challenges to come during early stages of mating was ridiculous. That was when our wolves were most vulnerable and irrational. I knew I couldn't do it alone, but I would see to it that my children never had to suffer through this. It would be my highest agenda as Pack Alpha, and I was confident that my allied Alphas would fall in line on this one.

A knock at my door had me jumping out of bed and throwing on a pair of sweats to answer it. Austin, James, Clay, Emmett, and even Wyatt on crutches were standing there, a bag of food in Clay's hand.

"Thought you could use the company this morning," James said.

"You damn well better have a pot of coffee on," Austin grumbled.

Clay hugged me when he passed by on his way in.

"We knew today was going to be hard. Just want you to know we got your back," Emmett said.

"Trust me," Wyatt said, frowning down at his casted leg. "Lily's ready for this."

"I know," I sighed. "It just doesn't make it any easier."

Breakfast with the boys was just what I needed. Looking around me, I realized that I might have been abundantly blessed with sisters, but I also had five of the greatest brothers imaginable. They might not have been my blood brothers, but they were my life brothers, and they stayed by my side until the last second. If they could have joined me on the platform for the battle, I know they would have, but more stupid rules kept me segregated from the others. I was only grateful that as Alpha, my dad got to stand by my side, and I prayed that if I did anything stupid, he'd be strong enough to subdue me.

There was excitement in the air as the entire Pack came out to watch Lily fight Wanda. A small section had been marked off for the Larkens in an attempt to contain any old resentments that might arise in conflicts outside the arena. My wolf was growling in my head just having them in my territory.

When I got to the top of the platform overlooking the arena, Mom and Dad were already there, as were two of the Grand Council members and all four members of Dad's Pack Council.

I had known Titus and Victor my entire life. They were allies of Collier and had served well in their time on the Grand Council. They were also the first two I planned to hit up with invalidating the challenges entirely, but I would need to bide my time for that one. It was a strategic matter that could take years to campaign enough support.

I shook the men's hands, hugged each in turn, and thanked them for coming.

"Your father has warned us of your unique situation," Titus said, the more diplomatic of the two. "We do hope there are no issues with today's challenge."

I knew it was both an affirmation and a warning.

"I'm trying, Titus. Impartiality here will be impossible, but my mate has asked that I sit tight and let her do her job, and I certainly intend to try. The last thing I want to do is distract Lily during the battle," I assured him.

"I see what you meant, Zach," Victor told my father. "I can feel his power just being in his presence. It's amazing, so commanding."

"Amazing?" I snorted. "That's not exactly how I'd describe it. Hugely problematic when you're about to put my mate in danger of her life, is more like it." Titus raised his eyebrow in question. "I said I intend to try, Titus. If my wolf becomes too agitated, you'll have to be prepared to subdue me. He's been known to see red quickly whenever she's in danger, and this disaster you call tradition is most certainly putting her in danger."

"He's rational, yet his aggression is borderline dangerous," Titus commented, as if I were in a clinical study.

My father nodded. "Yes, but as I told you, I fully believe it is because his Alpha side has evolved. He's ready to take over the Pack. I'm certain of it."

"But you cannot expect him to do so in the middle of his mating challenges," Victor said.

"Which is why I've petitioned Titus to forego any future challenges and allow him to promote immediately," my dad said to Victor's astonishment.

"You're serious? He's still young to take over a Pack this size."

"Maybe, but it is my greatest honor to hand it over to him. I've trained him personally since the day he was born, and I'm telling you, he's ready," Dad said proudly.

"And what will come of you then?" Victor inquired.

Titus and Dad shared a look that made me uncomfortable. "Oh, I'll find my new place in the Pack. Look how well it's worked out for Jason." They all chuckled, knowing the former Alpha had been struggling to find his place, but finally settled on grandpa as his favorite new title. "Perhaps Thomas and Lily will bless me as well in the near future."

"Dad," I scolded as they all chuckled, then sobered as a hush came over the crowd.

Lily and Wanda walked out of the arena doors and into the center. They turned and looked up at where we stood. Dad clapped a hand on my shoulder and gave an apologetic look before stepping forward. He welcomed them all, went through the formalities necessary to start the fight, and before I knew what was happening, I'd been pushed down into a chair with Titus and Victor standing guard on either side of me. Dad took up his place just behind me, a hand resting easily on my shoulder which I knew would give me a blast of his Alpha power should I step out of line.

Lily stripped, as did Wanda, and they waited for the signal. On my dad's order, they both shifted and the fight was on. Wanda immediately retreated. Lily had been right—she was ready for a quick attack. Wanda's grey wolf shook off the confusion as Lily's white wolf started to circle her.

Lily toyed with her just enough to slowly draw her in. Wanda started making close, quick jabs for Lily, who easily dodged them all. There was a sudden commotion from the Larken section. Wanda didn't falter, but Lily did, and the second she did, Wanda dove in for the attack.

Lily hit the ground with a thud and my heart stopped. My vision blurred and a low rumble started deep in my chest. Just as

Wanda went in for the kill I felt a jolt of Alpha power surge into me from Dad.

At the last second, Lily jumped up and plowed into Wanda, knocking her off balance and avoiding her kill move. Lily took one look up at me and I felt terrible for distracting her. She had the upper advantage and should be using it, but she didn't. Instead, Lily walked slowly over to Wanda, who was quickly regaining her footing. She lifted her head towards the sky and howled.

My wolf immediately responded before anyone could stop me, but more than that, she had affectively called to the entire Pack as shifter after shifter joined her. When I looked back down, Lily was in full focus. I knew at the moment she howled that she'd given herself fully over to her wolf, something I had heard she never did in battle.

I rose to my feet and walked to the railing for a closer look. The others didn't stop me, but the Pack followed my lead as they all rose to their feet. The howls had been signs of respect and acceptance. Lily had officially just become Collier and it was clear to see the Larkens knew it, as did Wanda, whose fighting became defensive and sloppy.

Exactly as Lily had explained, she patiently waited until Wanda was so angry that she was acting irrationally and emotionally. The first moment she left her neck exposed, the beautiful white wolf leapt in for a swift kill. It happened so fast I wasn't even sure the grey wolf knew what was happening until it was too late.

With Wanda dead, Lily sat back on her hind legs and howled once again, this time in both grief and victory. Those from Larken made a quick exit as the eerie sounds of Collier Pack followed her lead.

"I told you," Dad said to Titus. "They're both ready."

Titus nodded. "We'll make the call tonight and let you know."

"Am I free to go to my mate now?" I asked, not wanting to screw anything up with the challenge, but desperately needing to feel for myself that Lily was okay.

"Yes, son. She's all yours. Go get your girl," Dad said with a smile.

I didn't bother with the stairs. It was a straight drop down to the arena floor from the platform, which I easily landed. Lily's wolf jumped in surprise, as she turned to face me. I hadn't spent a ton of time with her wolf, and not at all while still in human form. She happily greeted me, tail wagging, and rubbed her scent against my leg. I leaned down and hugged her as Lily shifted back into her beautiful flesh and bone in my arms.

I lifted her up, cradling her against me as our Pack cheered. The noise was deafening, yet somehow when I leaned down to kiss her, it grew even louder. Lily threw her head back and laughed, wrapping one arm tightly around my neck, and the other she used to wave to the crowd.

"I told you I had this," she reminded me. "This little slugger didn't even need a bat to finish the job."

"Slugger, don't ever scare me like that again. When you went down like that, I thought . . ."

"Nope," she said, pressing her lips to mine. "No what ifs. Just let me enjoy my victory. I think the Pack may have finally accepted me."

I laughed. "You think? You had everyone on their feet howling, babe. That's typically only something an Alpha or a Pack Mother can do."

She shrugged. "I am still the future Pack Mother."

"Yes, yes you are. Now let's get you dressed and go home to celebrate properly."

I watched the blush creep into her cheeks. "You really think they'll let us?"

I looked around, feeling a little disappointed. No one had left. They all still stood around chatting and watching us. She'd just taken her place in Collier. There was no way they were going to let us just leave. *Dammit.*

After Lily had thrown on some sweats, we tried leaving the arena, but we were both practically tackled by Sydney as she hugged Lily. Jessie was with her. She nodded to me, and then bowed to my mate, baring her neck.

"Two battles in one," Syd whispered as Jessie rose.

"I'm so sorry, Lily," she started.

"Stop," Lily commanded her. "You were only doing what you believed was right. You were protecting your sister. There's nothing wrong with that, Jessie. You were very brave."

"Really?" Jessie asked with wonder in her eyes.

"Really," Lily confirmed, before being attacked by Shelby next in another bear hug and swarmed immediately by the remainder of my sisters. They were all there, except Maddie. I knew Lily would have loved for her to have been there, but somehow knowing she was safe and sound in San Marco made her absence more bearable.

"You kicked ass, girl! I knew you had it in you," Lizzy praised. It dawned on me that I hadn't seen my oldest sister look quite so happy in a very long time. Even the haunted look in her eyes was temporarily gone.

Clara and Ruby recanted every second of the battle, as Peyton offered to bring meals for us throughout the week, assuming correctly that we'd want some time alone after everything that happened.

The arena, like most things in Collier, was within walking distance of the Alpha house. I felt like we were leading a parade or something as everyone followed us back to my parents' house where my truck was parked.

Numerous invites had been shouted out along the way. It was going to be a full day of celebrations and it wasn't even lunchtime yet. I had casually dismissed each of them, just wanting to get Lily home.

It was finally Hewitt that intervened and left no room for negotiations as I found we were being ushered towards the Tavern for celebration drinks. That turned into lunch which consumed much of the afternoon as people continued to come back and offer their congratulations or simply welcome Lily to the Pack. She was smiling so brightly that despite my barely controlled need to just have her to myself, we stayed until each and every one of my packmates had time to speak with us.

It was late afternoon when a break came, and I felt it would be safe to finally move on. We said goodbye to Milly and a few others. I thanked my friends for sticking around and for all their help leading up to the fight. We made plans to go riding the next week, and then, suddenly we had escaped.

The streets had largely cleared and I was making a mad dash for the truck, dragging Lily along with me, knowing that if we stayed too much longer it would roll into dinner. I was opening the door when Ruby poked her head out of the house and yelled for us.

"Thomas. Lily. Dad wants to see you both before you leave."

I slammed the door shut again and banged my head on the glass as Lily giggled.

"Come on, the faster we get in there, the sooner we can leave," she said, wrapping an arm around my waist. I stopped her and looked down, framing her face with my hands, I leaned down and kissed her. I didn't give a damn who was watching us, I kissed her like we were the last two people left on Earth.

"Is it too much to ask for just a few minutes alone with you?"

She gave me a quick peck on the check, though she looked a little dazed from my kiss. "No, it's not, but today meant a lot to them, too."

"I do love that you always put our Pack above all else, but let's try to never prioritize them above us."

She laughed. "You're just super horny right now because you didn't get any action this morning. You'll live, I promise, and this will all be behind us soon."

I groaned, knowing she was right and followed her into the house. My wolf was still a little agitated from everything going on, and the only way I felt I could keep it in check was to touch to her. She didn't seem to mind, though.

Mom greeted us in the hallway and hugged Lily. For some reason, the sight of the two of them embracing finally hit me. This was real. Lily was here, she was fine, and this nightmare was temporarily behind us. The last of the fight and aggression balled up within me released.

We were soon ushered into Dad's office. Titus and Victor were waiting there for us, along with the full Pack Council. Seeing them all there, Lily started to excuse herself, assuming it was a meeting just for me.

"Lily, I'd like for you to stay please. This concerns both of you," Dad told her.

She looked at me with concern, but held her head high and stood strong by my side.

"What's all this about?" I asked when an awkward silence came over the room.

"Son, have you had a chance to discuss with Lily what we talked about the other day?"

He was speaking cryptically, and I didn't like it. "I'm not sure what you're referring to."

"Your father is ready to step down as Alpha, Thomas," Titus said.

"We have discussed that," Lily admitted.

"And did you have any concerns? You are very young to assume the responsibilities of Pack Mother," Dad said.

Lily nodded. "I am, but no younger than Kelsey was when she took over in Westin Pack. Plus, you must remember, I was raised by a Pack Mother. I know exactly what this duty entails."

"And you feel that you're ready for such a role in the Pack?" Victor asked her.

Lily looked at me, and winked. "Victor, what I know is that my full allegiance has already shifted to Collier Pack. If I had any doubts in that, they were put to rest today. There is nothing I wouldn't do for my Pack. Whether the call to Pack Mother comes in twenty years or twenty minutes from now, I will be ready, as long as that is what is best for the Pack."

The men looked around the room at each other, nodding. It took a lot to hold my tongue, but I wasn't a hundred percent sure what was going on.

"Thomas, the Grand Council voted this afternoon, and we agree with your mate. The two of you will be a fine legacy to Collier Pack. At your father's insistence, and upon validating his concerns personally, as I have expressed to the Council, it was also agreed that the transfer of power should begin immediately."

My chest tightened as his words sunk in.

Titus continued. "The process will occur over the next six months, and as such, we are canceling your mating challenges. You two will have more than enough to deal with, without that hanging over your heads." He paused and smiled, then nodded. "Congratulations!"

I knew my mouth was hanging open, but I couldn't seem to shut it, until Lily looked up at me, shook her head with a snort, and shut it for me. "Thank you," she said graciously, for the both of us.

I shook hands with each of the men present, still unable to form a coherent thought.

"Take the rest of the week off and spend some time with your mate, son."

I hugged my father.

"I'm really proud of you. Both of you."

"Okay, then. It's been a really long day. With a whole lot to process. I think I'm going to take this guy and head home now, if that's okay," Lily said, and they all smiled and nodded their approval.

This time we didn't quite make it back to the truck, when Clara stopped us. "Hey, I hate to tell you this, because I'm sure you just want to get home and, ew, do whatever it is you do, but your boys just started a big bonfire out in the field and the whole town is headed that way. Apparently it's turned into a potluck celebration and they're talking about a midnight run as well."

I growled softly as Lily elbowed me in the chest.

"Six Pack parties are legendary," I warned her. "It's sort of their way of saying welcome to the family."

"So we should go?" she asked.

"Yes, you should at least make an appearance," Clara confirmed as I nodded with a sigh.

We were greeted like royalty this time as Dad and the Council somehow managed to arrive before us and had already made the official announcement regarding him stepping down as Alpha. I wasn't prepared for the response, and in truth, Lily handled it better than I did. Her hand never left mine and she gave me encouraging squeezes at exactly the times I needed them.

From the moment we arrived, people came up, offered their congratulations, and bared their necks to us. It was overwhelming after an already emotional day.

After the initial shock of it all, we blended in with the rest of our Pack and enjoyed a fun, stress-free, challenge-free, celebration. It was even fun, but at the first chance to take off, I grabbed Lily's hand and made a run for it. We got a few giggles and knowing stares along the way, but I couldn't have cared less.

When I pulled up in front of our house, we sat there in the truck for a few minutes not even talking, just taking in all that had happened in the absolute longest day of our lives.

"You okay?" I asked, breaking the silence.

"Yeah, it's just a lot. You know? And I am exhausted."

I'm sure I gave her a wild-eyed look as I jumped from the truck and ran around to her side. I swung open the door and threw her unceremoniously over my shoulder. "Too bad, you're all mine now!" I said as she laughed and kicked while I raced us into the house, carried her over the threshold of our home, and took her to bed where we finally got to truly celebrate.

Lily

Epilogue

10 years later

I looked over towards the field, watching my daughters play with their cousins. Every year since Thomas and I bonded, we had brought together each of our siblings and their families. It had certainly grown over the years.

I leaned against Thomas with a happy sigh. "This is my favorite weekend of the year. I love having us all together."

He laughed. "Yes, I know. You tell me a thousand times every year."

We had taken over Collier Pack as Alpha and Pack Mother at such a young age that we'd been forced to grow up quickly. We'd had our battles, both of us being too stubborn for our own good, but things always had a way of working out for us. Overall, I'd say that Mom was right, God really did know what he was doing when matching true mates.

"I wish we could all get together more than just once a year like this," MC said.

"Me too," Kelsey agreed. "We never get enough time together, Lily."

I smiled at her sadly. "I know, but thank God for video messaging, right? I don't feel like I've missed out on quite as much in all your lives because of it."

Elise raised her wine glass, filled with sparkling cider. "Cheers to that! I don't know how I'd have survived this pregnancy without you," she said, rubbing her round baby bump. Thanks to modern technology, we were able to see each other every single day.

After more than a decade, Elise and Patrick had sworn they just weren't meant to be parents, much to our mother's disgust. One trip to Paris and forgotten birth control later, and they'd come home with the surprise of their lives. It had been a shock at first, but as her pregnancy was quickly coming to an end. They were both ecstatic with their little oops and couldn't wait to meet their son or daughter.

Oscar came over to join us where we sat, all the grown-ups sprawled out on blankets and in lawn chairs just catching up. I was mesmerized watching the young man before me. He wasn't a child anymore and it was hard to imagine when exactly that had changed, but at eighteen, going on nineteen, he was a full-grown man now.

"Oscar, you still haven't shifted?" Thomas asked him.

I noticed he squirmed at the question and tried to avoid it. Pinned down by a dozen eyes waiting, he shrugged. "Still no wolf."

"Could be a tiger," Jack offered, sounding hopeful. As Oscar's biological father he had somehow been incorporated into the family. Maddie and Liam had made their peace with him, so I had, too. MC actually seemed genuinely okay that Jack had taken an interest in Oscar's life and chosen to be a part of it, despite everything that happened.

Liam initially had a harder time accepting him, but Oscar had come to my brother and asked him to reconsider. He told Liam that he, and only he, would ever be his father. Oscar still didn't call Jack "Dad." He had always just been Jack. I knew that meant the world to Liam, who loved the kid as his own.

Something seemed off with Oscar, so given the chance away from the others, I cornered him, and the interrogation began.

"Spill it. What's going on?"

His eyes widened. "What do you mean?"

"You're eighteen, and you've always had signs of a shifter for as long as I've known you. You're healthy, and—" He squirmed under my close scrutiny—"You've already shifted, haven't you?"

Oscar turned his big brown eyes on me. I'd always been a sucker for those eyes. "Aunt Lily, you can't say anything. I'm not ready to admit it. I know Mom's going to be disappointed."

"Tiger, huh?"

He shrugged, his head dropped, and he slowly, sadly nodded.

"How long?"

"Huh?"

"How long since you're first shift?"

Oscar looked around uncomfortably. "Almost two years."

"What? You've been keeping this from them for almost two years?"

"They're so certain I was going to be a wolf. I just, I don't want to disappoint them."

"Oscar Westin, you look at me right this second." I waited until he looked up. "You are not a disappointment. You never will be. Your mom isn't going to care that you shift to a tiger instead of a wolf. She's going to be proud of you no matter what . . . though I'd probably leave out the 'I've known for two years' part for a while."

"But Aunt Lily, I'm a cat in a pack of dogs. How can they not be disappointed?"

"Aunt Jenna is a cat in a pack of dogs. Do you love her less than me because of it? Wait, don't answer that, of course you love me more, cause I'm your favorite aunt. So, do you love her less than Aunt E?"

Oscar laughed. "No. I love you all equally."

"But me just a tiny bit more, right?"

He hugged me. "I love you, Aunt Lily."

"Love you too, tiger."

He groaned. "I don't want to ruin the weekend, but I promise I'll tell them soon."

"I'm going to hold you to that, you know."

He rolled his eyes. I never realized just how annoying that could be till I had little ankle biters mimicking me with it. I hated an eye roll now.

"Hi, Oscar," a voice called, and I looked up to see a pretty blonde girl wave our way. She looked to be about sixteen or seventeen, and was obviously happy to see my nephew.

"Who's that?" I asked. "She certainly doesn't seem to mind that you're a . . ."

"I get it. I'll tell them. Mind if I bail and go hang out with Bailey?" he asked.

"Bailey, huh? She's cute."

He grinned, looking back at the girl and waving. "Yes, she is."

"Go on. I'll cover for you."

He gave me a quick kiss on the cheek. "That's why you're my favorite," he said as he ran off to catch up with the girl. I smiled after them. *I always knew I was his favorite.*

"Where is your mother?" I heard Thomas ask one of the girls.

The poor guy had been surrounded by six sisters growing up, only to father four daughters. Lucky number five was on the way. I rubbed my protruding belly. I loved being pregnant, but I was done after this one. Girl or boy it didn't matter to me, but I knew Thomas was secretly hoping it was a son, even though he swore he was destined to only be surrounded by beautiful ladies.

"Lily?" he called.

Where the hell did she go this time? I clearly heard him say, but I was staring right at him and his lips never moved.

Thomas? I thought, and he turned my way.

"Oh, there you are. Kelsey needs you to help Peyton set up for dinner. Something about Zander daring little Jason to climb a tree and now he's stuck."

We walked back over to where the group was congregated. I laughed as Kelsey passed by.

"You know how many times I've told him wolves don't climb trees? He looks up to Z so much, but all Z wants to do is terrorize his little brother. Be thankful you have girls," she murmured.

"It really doesn't help that the twins take after their mother and taunt him from above," Chase added proudly. He and Jenna had a son, followed almost immediately by an adorable set of identical twin girls.

Thomas? I thought in my head as he turned around to face me.

"Yeah? What is it, slugger?" he asked, still using the nickname he'd granted me since our initial mating. All these years and he still wouldn't tell me why he called me that.

"Why do you call me that?" I asked him aloud.

He smirked, giving me that sexy crooked grin that could still melt my panties or piss me off at any given time.

As if I'd ever tell her. My little slugger, whose mere words could cut me down and smash my heart into a million pieces. Man, if she knew what kind of power she truly had over me, I'd be screwed!

It would tear her up if she ever learned just how bad her initial rejection of me had hurt during our mating period . . . so bad that I granted her the nickname that I still use just to bug her.

He called me slugger because I'd hurt him? Did I say something to hurt him every time he used it? I thought back through the years. No, that wasn't possible. He used it too frequently and usually with a smile on his face, but knowing it all stemmed from me hurting him was too much to bear. I started to cry and walked away, hoping he didn't notice.

Shit! Damn pregnancy hormones. What's wrong with her this time? Thomas thought, and once again I heard him loud and clear.

He walked up behind me and hugged me. I turned in his arms and cried into his shoulder. *I'm sorry. Stupid baby hormones.* Before I could stop myself I thought, *I never wanted to hurt you.*

"What are you talking about?" he asked, pulling me back so he would look at me. "You could never hurt me, babe. What's all this about?"

I looked at him and without opening my mouth to speak, I said, *because now I know why you call me slugger. I never wanted to hurt you, not even all those years ago. I'm sorry.*

His eyes kept staring at my mouth that wasn't moving. He shook his head in confusion. "What did you just say?"

I gave him a watery smile. *You heard me, big boy.*

Lil? he asked without speaking.

I smiled and nodded.

Shit, you set me up, he accused.

I grinned and shrugged. *Maybe you should pay a little more attention to your mate.*

It's really happening. I can't believe it. Our bond's complete?

Looks like, I admitted, jumping up and wrapping my arms around his neck and kissing him. *This is the coolest thing ever!*

He pulled back and didn't look so convinced. *This is going to take some getting used to.*

Just think, now I don't have to give subtle hints that you often miss when I want the girls to go to bed early so I can have you all to myself. I can just secretly tell you. I had a momentary flash of him naked, making love to me.

He grinned from ear to ear. *I saw that, you know.*

You did? How about this one? I remembered how he used to wake me up every morning pre-kids. Certainly put a smile on my face.

If you can convince Cammie to actually sleep in her own bed, I'd be happy to reinstate that particular tradition.

Liam walked by us and stopped. "Why are you two just standing there staring at each other with those goofy looks on your faces?"

Oh, wouldn't he like to know? I thought, cracking both of us up.

"Jesus, you'd think you were newly mated or something," Liam continued. "You're supposed to be helping Peyton in the kitchen, Lil, remember?"

"Oh yeah, I'm on my way," I told him, giving Thomas a quick peck on the lips and turning to leave for real.

I had an instant flash of my behind walking away. *Damn, I'll never get sick of looking at that.*

I turned and grinned, shaking my booty for him. *Even though I'm fat and gross?*

Girl, you are incredibly sexy carrying my child. You have no idea what that does to me. All round and beautiful. He growled in my head.

Good to know, but this is still our last pregnancy.

We'll see about that.

I laughed.

Once upon a time I dreamed of my perfect mate. He would be strong and handsome with eyes only for me. My life would be filled with love and laughter and we'd live happily ever after. Those were the simple pipe dreams of the young girl I used to be. The life I'd created with Thomas in the last decade was nothing like I'd imagined.

It was even better.

Dear Reader,

I hope you enjoyed Thomas and Lily's story. I know many of you have been excitedly waiting for her story since One True Mate was first released. I truly hope it didn't disappoint. If you enjoyed it, please drop me a quick review here:
https://www.amazon.com/dp/B07DCCRB58

I am sorry to say that this concludes the Westin Pack Series. BUT... keep reading for a couple SNEAK PEEKS of where we're headed next. TWO new spin off series are coming this fall. Collier Pack with plenty more of Lily and Thomas, and ARC Shifters as we head back to Archibald Reynold's College from Confusing Hearts, book 4 in the Westin Pack Series. Two distinctly different series, but many of the characters you already know and love, and so many more waiting to meet you!

For further information on my books, events, and life in general, I can be found online here:

Website: www.julietrettel.com

Facebook: http://www.facebook.com/authorjulietrettel

Facebook Fan Group:
https://www.facebook.com/groups/compounderspod7/

Instagram: http://www.instagram.com/julie.trettel

Twitter: http://www.twitter.com/julietrettel

Goodreads:
http://www.goodreads.com/author/show/14703924.Julie_Trettel

BookBub: https://www.bookbub.com/authors/julie-trettel

Amazon: http://www.amazon.com/Julie_Trettel/e/B018HS9GXS

Much love and thanks,
Julie Trettel

SNEAK PEEK

BREATHE AGAIN

A Collier Pack Novel

By

Julie Trettel

Coming September 2018

COLE

Chapter 1

When Westin pack started aligning more closely with Collier pack, I knew it was only time before I'd end up back in Collier territory. Escorting Liam and Maddie Westin to visit her family, ahead of her brother's celebration ceremony as he assumed the role of Alpha of Collier Pack, was not something I had looked forward to, even knowing Lily Westin would be there to flirt with and help ease my nerves.

When Lily found her one true mate in Thomas Collier, the alliance between the packs was sealed. Sure, the two packs had always been on amicable terms, but with the Westin twins mated to two of Zach Collier's children, the alliance was tight and virtually unbreakable.

What did that mean for me? More time spent in Collier territory, the one place I dreaded more than anything.

It had been over a decade since I had last seen Elizabeth Collier. I wasn't that same kid anymore. Once upon a time, I had been just as enamored with finding my one true mate as the Westin children had been. Jason Westin, our Alpha before he was injured in a battle against the Bulgarian pack that had transferred power to his son, Kyle, had always made it an important part of Pack. Of course, every wolf shifter had free will to fall in love, or not, with whomever they chose, but Jason had always stressed the strength and power of true mates, so Westin pack had a much higher number of them than most other packs.

Finding your one true mate took time. Some would go years, decades or a lifetime even before crossing paths with that one soul that would complete them and set their animal spirit at peace. Jason made it feel like it was worth the wait. Because the odds could be high against it, many Alphas stressed the importance of mating and growing the pack, regardless of whether they were true mates. We called those compatible mates. It was only one of the things that set Westin apart from other wolf shifting Packs.

A shifter could have numerous compatible mates, but only ever one, true mate. I used to believe in the power of true mates. I believed it when they said you would know immediately, and it would alter your life the moment you met, like some sort of ridiculous fairy tale. Yes. I, Cole Anderson, Westin's resident elusive bad boy, standing at six feet four, weighing in at two hundred and forty pounds of solid muscle, and covered in tattoos was once upon a time a true romantic. That was then, before Elizabeth Collier.

I had just celebrated my eighteenth birthday. I was a clean cut all American teen with high hopes and promising expectations. Jason Westin had recognized me as with alpha potential at a young age, confirmed when my wolf surfaced at only sixteen years of age.

My parents were good people and raised me to be considerate, dependable, and yet not take any shit from anyone. I loved them deeply, and as an only child, I had a closer than average relationship with them. My parents had been true mates. My dad was killed in a car wreck, and because he and my mom had been fully bonded, I lost them both to that accident.

I remember the day clearly. Mom and I were cooking dinner together and laughing and talking. I had just graduated high school and had already been accepted into university. They had been enormously proud of me. She hugged me tight telling me just that, and then she was just gone, collapsed in my arms.

I didn't know what was happening. We had been waiting for Dad to return from a business trip. He worked for the Westin Foundation and had been out of town. I couldn't wake her and when I realized she wasn't breathing, I started to freak out.

I called Jason, only to find he was already on his way, having received a call from my dad's partner. He had been driving when their car was T-boned on the passenger side. He had lived, my dad had not. I was suddenly an eighteen-year-old orphan.

Jason had encouraged me to take an internship with Zach Collier. They had started doing that in an attempt to strengthen both packs. He thought it was best if I got away for a while, and I couldn't have agreed fast enough. I spent that whole summer before my freshman year at university in Collier territory shadowing Zach Collier.

I would never forget the day I met Elizabeth. She was sixteen years old with long brown hair that fell in waves halfway down her back and she had bright blue eyes that mesmerized me from the first moment I saw them. She stirred my wolf in a way I had never imagined, and I was convinced she was to be mine.

It had freaked me out a little, in a very excited way. I took leave that night and drove an hour to a hotel. I had called my Alpha and told him what was happening to me. I explained how I felt, how the hair on my arms had literally stood up and my whole body tingled with nervous energy. He was happy at first, until I told him I thought my one true mate was Elizabeth Collier.

Lizzy, as everyone always called her, was two years younger than me. Jason was quick to squash my hopes and dreams telling me that he knew for fact that her wolf had not yet surfaced and that there was no way that my wolf could possibly recognize her before then. He told me I needed to be patient and wait.

I waited and watched her all that summer, never acting on the emotions I felt. Elizabeth was the eldest daughter of Zach Collier. Her mate would someday be second in line to the Alpha. She was highly protected, as were all the Collier daughters. . . all six of them.

A week before I was due to leave, Lizzy wanted to go shopping for the upcoming school year. She was heading into her Junior year and finally an upperclassman. Zach asked me to escort her, which really meant he was entrusting me to protect his daughter. It was a big moment, and the first truly responsible thing I was given that summer.

I was nervous, sweaty palms, the whole bit, just sitting next to her in the car. Her scent overwhelmed my senses and I couldn't think straight, let alone carry on a coherent conversation, so I didn't even try. She didn't last long in the silence though before she began to babble on about this and that and asking me questions. To my surprise I even managed to answer then without bumbling like a complete idiot. It made the drive go by much too quickly, and by the time we arrived at the mall, over two hours away, we were on comfortable, friendly terms.

It amazed me how easy she had been to talk to. Once I let go of my nerves, being with her was truly as easy as breathing. I opened the car door for her upon our arrival and she reached for my hand, pulling herself up. The fire that shot through me felt like I'd been hit by a lightning bolt, and I was again convinced this girl had to be my one true mate. Yet she looked entirely unaffected.

She wrapped her small hand around mine and kept it there as we headed in to shop. I had imagined that shopping with any girl would be a nightmare of an experience, but not with Elizabeth. It didn't seem to matter what we did or where we went, life was just better with Elizabeth Collier.

That shopping experience was only the first. The next day she had told her dad she hadn't found everything she wanted, despite having a new wardrobe that would clothe half her pack and asked if I could escort her to another mall a little further away this time. He didn't even hesitate to say yes to her.

Elizabeth had not shown any signs of recognition, as Jason had warned would be the case, because she hadn't yet shifted, but that didn't seem to stop the chemistry between us. I was trying to tell myself it was all one-sided. My wolf didn't want to hear it. He wanted this beautiful creature, there was no doubt in my mind that it was not just my personal infatuation with her.

Busying myself with reminders that she did not feel the same, or anything at all for that matter, I ignored all the signs she continued to send out. The fact that she always held my hand when we walked through the stores, or the way she'd look away and blush when I caught her staring at me. I couldn't let myself give in to the internal turmoil my wolf was causing that told me she was our mate, when it wasn't even possible.

She had gone into the dressing room of a department store to try on a few things when I heard her yell out my name. Fearing the worst, I immediately ran to her dressing room door.

"Elizabeth, what's wrong?" I demanded, my wolf already on high alert.

"Nothing," she said sweetly. "I just need your opinion on this outfit."

She opened the door and I hesitated but entered. It was the largest dressing room I'd ever seen, with a long bench that ran down one side, but that was all missed as I stepped in and stared at

Elizabeth Collier standing in the middle of that room in nothing but a sexy black lace bra and thong panty set.

I froze, certain my mouth hung open in shock. My tongue felt dry and sticky just before I started salivating. Still over a decade later, it was the sexiest damn thing I'd ever laid eyes on. No moment before or since has ever been as great at that day.

"Close the door, Cole," she said in a huskier than usual voice, and I obeyed without question.

She watched me closely. My hands twitched to reach out and touch her. I wanted to close the gap between us more than I'd ever wanted anything in my entire life, but I just stood there like a statue.

She twirled around, a mischievous twinkle in her eye as posed.

"So? What do you think? Do you like it?" She sounded innocent in her question, but there was nothing at all innocent about her in that moment.

I growled in response and watched the fire it caused ignite in her eyes. I smelled her desire and heard the quicken of her heart. In two seconds flat, I had her pressed up against the wall of the dressing room, my mouth devouring hers. She opened to me and my tongue explored, memorizing every inch of hers.

When I finally pulled back we were both panting hard and my need for her was a thousand times stronger than it had already been. I had never experienced anything like it before.

She gave me a slow, sexy smile, wetting her lower lip with her tongue, as I stared transfixed.

"So, I'm going to assume, you like it?" She giggled, but not in a nervous way. No, Elizabeth was one hundred percent in control, or at least that's what it felt like to me.

I shrugged, "I think it would look a hell of a lot better on the floor over there." I shocked myself by my audacity. I was a good boy, and that was not something I had ever imagined could come out of my mouth. Her cheeks flushed, and she nodded. I didn't need further invitation to strip off that tiny lace lingerie and give her my virginity right there on the bench in that dressing room. Turned out, it had been her first time too, which had only heightened my desire to make her mine.

Walking out, with my arm proudly around her, we passed a tattoo parlor.

"We should definitely mark this day with matching tattoos," she had said.

"I don't know, Elizabeth. They're so, I dunno, permanent. And the needles? I don't know if I could do it. I'm not really a fan of them. Besides, don't you have to be eighteen or have your parents' approval."

She just grinned and shook her head. "Come on, it'll be fun."

I knew in that moment that I was screwed. I would never in my life be able to say no to this girl. Before I knew what was happening, she had flashed my id and a fake one of hers claiming she was nineteen, and we were in chairs next to each other as she pointed out which one she wanted, and I walked away with a black silhouette of intertwined wolves howling at the moon on my right upper arm. She had a tiny version of the same thing just inside her bikini line. She had tried to talk me into getting it in the same spot, but the dude had told me that was okay for girls, but I needed a real tattoo.

It was now ranked amongst the top ten dumbest things I had ever done. At the time it had burned like a son of a bitch, but I was convinced Elizabeth and I were destined to be together forever and I wanted the whole world to know it. That was the real reason I had gone all in, proudly showcasing the tattoo that only I knew matched hers.

The remainder of that week we snuck off every chance we had to be together, while trying hard not to bring too much attention to it. By the time we had to say goodbye and head off to college, I was head over heels in love with Elizabeth. I had even considered staying, just to be with her, but she was level headed and practical as well as passionate and sometimes impulsive, and she still had two more years of high school to complete.

For the first month we spoke on the phone every day, but as school for her started and she settled into a new routine, the calls were fewer and further between. I had even considered calling her father a few times just to check on her, but he didn't know about us and I wasn't sure how he'd take the news.

By Christmas break, I wasn't sure there was an us. It all felt more like a dream. Depending on the day, that stupid tattoo was either heckling me or holding my sanity, confirming it all really had happened. Jason had insisted I spend the holidays with his family, so

I was unable to see her and she no longer answered my calls. My wolf was restless, and I started growing more irritable.

The next summer I was sent to Texas to shadow the alpha at Longhorn, despite my protests and requests to go back to Collier. It would be two more years before I'd see Elizabeth again. This time I was twenty-one and she was nineteen.

I had heard the news the moment her wolf had surfaced just before her eighteenth birthday. It had taken every ounce of my restraint not to run to her, confirming what I had already known. Elizabeth and I were true mates.

Finally, the moment had arrived. I would look upon her again and we'd know. I hadn't been with another female in that time. It was only her for me. I had grown bigger and stronger during our time apart and I was used to deflecting women on a daily basis. For me, there was only one, and I would wait forever for her.

I was traveling with Jason. One of the Collier wolves had taken a mate, and as w as custom with our kind, the mating trials were opened. The mating challenges were a fight to the death. Any wolf could challenge for a mate and pack position. One of our Westin wolves had chosen to do that. I was just grateful I had an excuse to finally see Elizabeth again.

The moment our eyes met, it was like seeing her again for the first time. I had wished we were not in such a public place, but I had prepared myself for the impact a best as I could. As I knew it would, the mating call flared wildly within me. My wolf was excited and immediately recognized hers. The physical response to seeing my mate again was stronger than anything I had ever imagined, but Elizabeth was on the arm of another man.

I fought back the urge to growl at him and warn him off of her. I was on foreign territory, representing my pack. It would not bode well with Jason or Zach if I caused a scene, especially one involving Elizabeth.

I waited until the moment came that I could steal a few minutes alone with her. I didn't' say a word or give warning as my lips crushed against hers. She sighed and started to kiss me back. Next thing I knew, she was pounding my chest and pushing away from me. I was shocked and confused.

"Cole, stop it," she demanded. It hurt on a cellular level.

"We can't do this. Santos is the future Alpha of a pack in

Venezuela. We're together now. You can't just go around kissing a girl like that. I know we were friends once, but we haven't even seen each other in years. You have to stop it."

I was so confused. Everything inside me was screaming *this is your mate,* but she didn't seem to feel it at all. There was no way it could all be one sided for me. I did not wait three years for her just to be rejected.

"Friends? Elizabeth," I started, and she cut me off.

"My name's Lizzy, Cole. Everyone calls me Lizzy. Why do you insist on calling me by my full name?"

She was changing the subject, trying to start an argument, but I didn't understand why.

"Lizzy reminds me of a little girl in pigtails." I looked her up and down and saw her skin flush. Knowing I could illicit such a response despite her protests, encouraged me. "And you are no little girl, Elizabeth." Rendering her momentarily speechless, I continued. "I know who you are to me. I've always known, and I know you have to feel it to."

She gulped, and her pupils dilated. It was the only sign that I might be right.

"What do you know?" She asked softly.

"You are my one true mate, and I am crazy in love with you. I've known it since the first moment I laid eyes on you, and I have waited for you all these years."

Yeah, I was that sentimental sap, and what did it get me? Nothing. Elizabeth had laughed in my face. She told me she felt nothing of the sort. My heart broke into a million pieces that day and I swore from that moment on, I would never go looking for love, or allow it to affect me again. If Elizabeth Collier wasn't my one true mate, I didn't want one. No one would ever get close enough to hurt me the way she had that day.

Since then women came and went. I kept them at a distance, used them for my personal pleasure, and then I sent them on their way. I preferred human women as they were much less clingy with no idea what it meant to mate. Many ladies over the years had tried to capture Cole Anderson, but I would never allow myself to be vulnerable to anyone like that again. She had shattered my faith in true mates, and even seeing friends and people I cared about finding their happily ever afters would not thaw my heart and leave it vulnerable to love ever again.

SNEAK PEEK

PACK'S PROMISE

An ARC Shifter Novel

By

Julie Trettel

Coming October 2018

Karis
Chapter 1

I could barely contain my excitement as we loaded up the truck with all my possessions and headed south. I'd never even been out of Alaska. California seemed like an enormous feat, especially since we were driving, and it would take a few days to reach the destination—Archibald Reynolds College, affectionately known as the ARC.

I didn't think I'd be able to go. I didn't even think Oma and Upa would allow it. Upa was my Pack Alpha and I was a proud Alaskan wolf shifter, only surviving heir of Tulok. It wasn't supposed to be this way. I had been small child when my parents went packed up the truck, loading up my three older siblings and headed off on an adventure. My brother was fourteen, the eldest of us. He was ten years older than me and being groomed for to take over as Alpha someday, second in line behind my father. He had been my hero and seemed larger than life, then in the blink of an eye he was gone. They all were.

The truck had skidded on some ice and went down a ravine. Dead. My mother, my father, brother, and two sisters, all dead. I didn't even know where they were going or what they planned to do, only that I was very little and had come down with some sort of sickness, and they'd left me behind at the last minute. I grew up believing that I was supposed to have been in that truck too. I should have died that day, and I never understood why I was allowed to survive without them.

Upa told me many times over that only God truly knows his

plan for us, but that there was a promise to the pack straight from God himself that a <<find a tribe name>> heir would always reign as Alpha over the Alaskan wolves. I reminded him many times over that a she-wolf could not assume the title of Alpha. His answer had always been that God would find a way.

My grandparents were true believers and revered God's nature and provisions above all else. Respect the land, respect the animals, bring harm to no one. That theory was preached to me for as long as I could remember.

It wasn't that we lived entirely off-grid and I was completely out of touch with the real world. I wasn't. We had cable and the internet. I wasn't naïve, exactly, just very inexperienced. Simply driving down the highway on the journey of the destination to my new path in life, was an adventure for me. Everything was new and exciting.

I had read up everything I could on the ARC and my new roommate and I had spoken numerous times on the phone and texted daily. I felt like I already had a kindred spirit waiting for me.

The excitement of the drive became underwhelming quickly as one day blurred into another. I was beginning to think we'd never arrive. It didn't help that in the last remaining hours we were stuck in back-to-back traffic as students from all over arrived to start the new school year.

As we passed through the campus gates, my nose was pressed against the window taking it all in. I had registered online and already had my class schedule and boarding assignment, so we passed by the administration building and wound through campus, passing the quad, Greek row, the lake, numerous academic and residential buildings, until we finally arrived at Fenrir Hall.

"Child, calm yourself," Oma warned, but I was just too excited to listen as I pushed open the door and finally set foot on the campus of Archibald Reynolds College.

"Can you believe it? I'm actually here!" I squealed in excitement, hugging Oma.

She gave me a stern look, but I could see the sparkle in her eyes. I knew my grandparents were not only proud of me, but happy for me, too.

I didn't have a lot to unload. I didn't really need that much to get by. But I loaded up what I could in my arms, took a deep breath for confidence, held my head high and marched right into my dorm, making my way up to room 301.

The door was slightly ajar. I would have been concerned, but my roommate had texted me the night before letting me know she'd gotten in early and couldn't wait to meet me. Butterflies filled my stomach as I walked in and looked around.

"Eeeee!" came a loud squeal as I entered the room. "You must be Karis!" Before I knew what was happening, I was pulled into the biggest hug of my life as we rocked back and forth. "Oh em gee, I'm so excited you're finally here! I'm Sabrina Walters, your new roommate."

I laughed as we ended the embrace, the load I was carrying now strewn across the floor, and I finally got a good look at the bubbly redhead I would spend my freshman year with.

"Hi Sabrina, I'm Karis, and I'm so excited to meet you in person, finally."

"Girl, I know. I'm sorry if that was a little over the top. I've just been waiting all day for you to get here and I can't believe it's really you. You're here. We're here. We're in college!"

This time when she hugged me again I was more prepared for it. We both jumped up and down squealing. I pulled back and settled as I caught Oma's disapproving eye.

"Um, Sabrina, these are my grandparents, Tulok and Amka."

She shook each of their hands. "It's so nice to meet you both. Karis speaks very highly of you."

They said very little in exchange as Sabrina and I calmed down enough to get my things unloaded. Oma insisted on helping me unpack, despite Upa wanting to hit the road as quickly as possible ahead of all the others. Basically, he didn't want to sit in anymore traffic if he could help it.

Until the moment came to say goodbye to them, I didn't know how hard it would be. It wasn't like I was losing them, yet the little girl within me was terrified of just that. I had tears in my eyes, but I put on a good show and kept it together for their sakes. They promised to call when they stopped for the night.

I thanked them and hugged a dozen times, before Upa announced they really had to go. I stood on the curb and waved until they were out of sight, then turned slowly and walked back into the building, up the stairs, and into what felt like a whole new life.

"I'm sorry if I got a little overwhelming and excited when you arrived. People say I talk a lot, and that it can be annoying at times, but really I'm just excited that we're both finally here," Sabrina said as I walked into the room. She was laid out on her bed which was covered in bright pink. Everything on Sabrina's half of the room was pink, and she had little fairy lights hung on the wall above her bed.

I looked at my side and realized just how very plain it was in comparison. I'd chosen greens and browns as they reminded me of Alaskan summers and made me feel a little more at home. It may not have been as ostentatious as Sabrina's side, but it was all mine, and my heart swelled with pride.

I squealed and flopped backwards onto my bed. "I can't believe I'm actually here!"

"I know the feeling. I kept saying that to myself all last night," she said.

I looked up and grinned at her. "So, what have you been doing since you arrived? Found anything awesome yet? Have you walked around campus or anything?"

Sabrina shrugged. "Only a little. I got in late last night, then was worried I'd miss you if I ventured too far out today. Besides, I kind of thought we could do that together?" she asked, awkwardly. "I know just because we're roommates doesn't mean we have to hang out all the time, but I do hope we can truly be friends and not just share a common space."

I grinned at her. "Same. I don't know anyone here, well, I sorta know one person, but I haven't seen him in a long time, and he lives off campus with his mate, but I promised his sister I'd look him up at some point. Definitely not today. Today, it's just you and me. Let's go check this place out!"

Sabrina and I were in perfect synch and everything was going better than I'd anticipated. We walked around campus each pointing out what we knew about the place. She'd clearly done her homework too.

"I love the lake. I can really see us hanging out there, but then I love the water," Sabrina said.

"Me too," I confessed. "But the quad seems pretty cool too, especially in between classes since a lot of the academic buildings are off it."

"Definitely. Have you done your class schedule yet?"

"Yes, I did it online before we left. How about you?"

"Yup, but I want to try and change up two of my classes. My parents sort of pushed the issue and I really want to get out of them quickly."

I smiled, missing my own parents. I liked to think they'd be proud of me. Sometimes it was hard to even remember what they looked like, let alone what it felt like to have a mom and a dad, but I couldn't let myself dwell on it and become sad. This was too important of a day.

"Are you getting hungry? Because I'm starving," Sabrina finally said.

I looked at my watch, surprised to find it was almost eight. The sun was beginning to set low in the sky, something I wasn't quite used to seeing again, as it stayed light nearly all day in Alaska during the summer months.

"I'm hungry," I told her, and we headed off towards the cafeteria.

"There are other places to eat on campus, but this place is one swipe of your meal card and then all you can eat. I think I'm going to be frequenting it here."

"Let the freshman fifteen begin," I joked.

Sabrina looked me over and snorted. "As if. You could gain fifteen pounds and still look fabulous. Me on the other hand, may need to stick to the salad bar."

I crinkled my nose. As a wolf shifter I preferred meat to veggies any day.

Sabrina laughed. "They aren't that bad, carnivore."

"Technically, I'm still an omnivore, I just prefer meat is all," I pointed out. "And you aren't going to eat salad all year and we both know it," I teased.

I knew from previous conversations that Sabrina was a red fox shifter. I assumed that's where her red hair came from. She was short and curvy all over, but with a bit of an athletic build. She had bright blue eyes, the bluest I'd ever seen, and despite her small stature, she seemed larger than life and practically invincible to me.

Walking into the cafeteria, the two of drew the attention of several boys sitting at a table. Sabrina seemed to grow a foot as she strutted before them. I grabbed a tray and quickly followed after her.

There weren't a lot of boys my age back home, and the few that were there were more like brothers to me since we'd all grown up together. There were a few cute polar bears I had started flirting with, but they weren't wolves, and I could never get serious with anyone that wasn't a wolf.

I had a promise to keep to my Pack. I was the last of my bloodline, and knew it was my responsibility to carry on my family's lineage. It was a heavy burden to bear, but I vowed to see it through and make my family proud.

It was strange not knowing what kind of shifters these people were. Back home the shifters: polar bears, moose, puffins, and wolves, all lived peacefully together, but I knew everyone within twenty miles.

I loved the mix of species at the ARC. It was the biggest things that drew my attention to it when applying for schools. Archibald Reynolds College prided itself on interspecies relationships. Growing up the way I did, I didn't really get the whole exclusive thing. Sure, I could understand when it came to mating, but that was different, and my opinions on that had been shaken to the core when Chase Westin, a friend from an ally Pack found his one true mate to be a panther.

A panther! I couldn't even imagine. My future mate would be Alpha of the Alaskan wolves. He couldn't be anything but a wolf. I laughed to myself just thinking about it. Imagine, a panther, a freaking cat, as Alpha to wolves, or maybe he'll be a rabbit, a cute little bunny. That would go over wonderfully. No, I would befriend anyone, regardless of their species, but when it came to dating I knew it would be best for me to stick to wolves.

"What are you thinking about? It looks pretty funny judging by the expressions on your face."

"It's nothing," I said and changed the subject quickly.

We met a couple other girls at dinner and talked to a few people here and there. Too many names were mentioned for me to keep track of anyone. We were invited to a few parties and compared schedules with some of them. Sabrina had a class with one of the girls, but no one matched mine.

When we finally finished up at dinner, it was time to head back to the dorm. Arm-in-arm Sabrina and I practically skipped across campus, laughing the entire way. It was going to be a great year. I could just feel it and I couldn't wait to really get things started.

Damon
Chapter 2

A sense of doom still loomed over the doghouse. It was going to be a long, hard year, and I wasn't looking forward to it. Last spring we'd all gone to battle against the big cats in support of our brother, Chase, and his true mate, Jenna. Jenna was a panther shifter, her father an elitist prick hellbent on killing Chase. No way would any of us have let that happen. In the end the dogs won, but at a great loss.

Matt Williams had been my roommate, my fraternity brother, and my friend. He died in that battle, and life in the doghouse hadn't been the same since. I was still a proud brother of Delta Omega Gamma, but the sadness of the place was hard to take.

Senior year. Finally, just two more semesters and I was out of there. When Chase moved off campus with Jenna, I moved into his room. I couldn't take staying in mine knowing Matt was never going to return. It was too much to bear, too many memories, and too much sadness.

I had stuck around campus through the summer figuring it was better to deal with it all alone than being inundated with sympathy back home. And while I was happy to have my boys back, I was already feeling overwhelmed by the constant chatter of my new roomie, Chad.

Chad was an interesting character. First, he's a squirrel shifter who pledged D.O.G. at another school where they didn't take the acronym quite so serious. Nearly all of the D.O.G.s were canine shifters of some sort, then there had been Matt, a rebel cat, jaguar shifter determined to hold his own with the big dogs. Now we had Chad, the squirrel.

That kid talked more than anyone I'd ever known, and his habit of hiding chips throughout his half of the room was downright annoying at times. Still he was a pretty cool kid. I'd never have believed a squirrel could be that badass. Seeing him fight in the battle for Chase had been a unique, eye-opening experience.

His transition since his arrival had been the talk of the school. Heck, it even trumped the Chase and Jenna saga. Who knew squirrel shifters fattened up in the winter, then slimmed down in the warmer months? Dude had been an overnight sensation around campus, a total chick magnet, not that D.O.G.s ever had a problem catching the ladies.

Still, with everyone back at school for the start of the new year, my wolf was becoming more and more restless. I found myself going for runs daily and searching out places just to be alone. It wasn't normal behavior for a wolf shifter. We were communal animals by nature. I knew Chase was worried about me being depressed. Maybe he was right, but damn, I think I had a right to be.

I just wanted the year to fly by quickly, so I could be done with the place and the haunting memories of Matt everywhere I turned. I wanted to be angry at someone, I wanted to yell, scream, and pick fights with anyone who got in my way. But there was no where to channel that anger. I couldn't blame Chase. Matt was his best friend and Chase didn't even ask us to fight alongside him. It was Matt's idea. He had insisted we stand up next to our friend, or die fighting, and he'd done just that, but Matt wasn't around to be mad at, so it all bottled up and fell empty.

I was in bed staring at the ceiling, consumed in darkness once again, when Chad walked in.

"Hey, man. We're all heading over to Jack's for a celebration round, then maybe over to Theta. Hear they're having a wicked party tonight. You joining us?"

"A round of what, kid? You're not even old enough to drink," I teased.

"Pfft, since when did that stop me?" he asked.

It was true. The punk could get away with nearly anything since his transformation. Still, I knew he was only joking. I'd never seen anyone stay as level headed as Chad in the brink of all that attention. He told me once that the girls he followed him around during the summer were fun enough to hang out with for a while, but far too shallow for him. He needed a girl that would stick around through the winter months and love him for who he was and not what he looked like in swim trunks. Had to hand it to him, he was far more mature than he'd lead one to believe.

"I think I'm gonna pass," I finally told him.

"Damon, it's the last night before classes begin. Come out. Celebrate with us."

"Right, last night before classes and I have an eight a.m. Sorry. Pass." I saw the disappointment on his face. I'd been seeing it a lot on the faces of all my brothers since they returned. I knew they were worried about me, but I was fine, at least as fine as I was going to be. "Hey, look, I promise, Friday night. We'll do whatever you want, okay?"

Chad perked up and smiled. "Yeah, okay. Sounds great. Enjoy your night."

He changed his shirt quickly and left without another word. The house had gone quiet and I suspected I was all alone. The walls started closing in around me, and I knew I needed to get out there. I changed into gym clothes and headed outdoors. I meant to actually go to the gym, try to at least be around other people, but when the woods came into few near the lake, I found myself venturing off course.

I sighed, stripping at the edge and setting my wolf free. I wasn't the only one depressed these days. We ran until past nightfall. It was easier for me in my fur. I could give myself over to the wolf and temporarily forget everything that had happened.

I was exhausted when I finally shifted back to my skin and headed home, collapsing into bed the moment I entered my room. Chad was already snoring softly in how own bed. It felt like I passed out the second my head hit the pillow and the first time in a while I slept peacefully.

When the alarm clock woke me, I groaned and pounded on it till the noise stopped. I wanted to curl up under the blanket and go back to sleep, but I knew it was first day of classes. Why the hell had I signed up for a eight a.m.?

I begrudgingly got out of bed and hit the shower, dressed for the day, and grabbed my backpack to head off to my final year of college. I was so ready to be done with this place.

The walk across campus was refreshing. New faces, and a new buzz in the air. I normally loved freshman, especially those dumb enough to pledge Delta Omega Gamma, but this year the usual excitement for new recruits was waning.

I heard whispers about my friends along the way. Trying hard not to roll my eyes or engage. Chase and Jenna were interspecies true mates, a rarity that many of us didn't even know was possible till it happened to them. They'd become instant campus celebrities. By end of last semester the shock and gossip had calmed down, but I supposed with the new class, word was spreading again already.

I didn't blame him for moving off campus. Missed the shithead, but still couldn't fault him for it. If I had the money Westin had, I'd have left too. Chase came from Westin Pack, a large and influential Pack. He was among the upper elite of wolf shifters. I, on the other hand, came from a very small, virtually unheard-of Pack in Italy. Not that you could tell by my accent.

My Alpha sent me to the States to study when I hit my teen years. I lived mostly with the Longhorn Pack of Texas. I'd picked up a bit of the southern drawl quickly. My Mediterranean coloring was about the only thing that set me apart at this point. No one would have guessed I wasn't born and bred in the USA.

For a little extra cash I worked as a teacher's assistant in the Italian department. It was a pretty sweet gig. Afterall, it was my primary language even if I was equally fluent in English. I had spoken with the professors and we all agreed I wasn't needed for the first two weeks of school. I was grateful for it a it gave me time to settle in to my own schedule before taking on theirs as well.

I walked into my first class, Intercultural Communications. I was an International Relations major. I was hoping it would help me with Pack status down the road. For the moment I wasn't sure if I wanted to return to Italy, change my allegiance to Longhorn or some other Pack. I really didn't know where I would go when I graduated. Maybe a few years as a lone wolf would do me some good. Only time would tell. I had put off all inquiries surrounding that question throughout college and can no intentions of trying to decide on an answer anytime soon.

Looking around the classroom, I was surprised to see Chase

and Jenna there. They were sitting down front, and I quickly made my way across the room.

"What are you guys doing up here?" I asked.

Jenna smiled and gave a little wave.

"Liam thought it would be a good class for us. Verdict's still out, but we're here," Chase said. Liam was his older brother and CEO of the Westin Foundation, their family business. Chase would assume his role in the company after graduation. Both he and his mate would be heading up their communications department, specializing in social media. I didn't think the class was exactly what they were looking for, but I was all for a couple of friendly faces.

I took the seat next to Chase as the professor called the class to order. He handed out the syllabus and discussed the expectations for the semester. Nothing looked too difficult and I knew it would be an easy class for me.

The hour passed quickly and soon as I was off and running to my next one, and then the one after that. I'd loaded three back to back Monday, Wednesday, and Friday, then a lunch break, and three more in afternoon into evening. It was a heavy load, but freed up Tuesdays and Thursdays for me to work or study.

By the time my last class ended, I was exhausted, and it was only day one, the easiest day of the semester. I was wondering if I would grow to regret this schedule. It certain made for three very long days in the week.

Walking back across campus to the doghouse I felt a tingle run up my spine. It made me stop in my tracks, and my wolf became aggressive and excited, fighting me to take control. That rarely happened and freaked me out a little. I looked around in search of the cause of it, but didn't see anything unusual. I was standing outside Fenrir Hall. It had been my freshman dorm. I chalked up the weird feeling to nostalgia and headed home.

Check out more great books by Julie Trettel!
The Compounders Series:

Start with Book 1!

In the wake of terrorist attacks, economic collapse, and martial law, America has become a nation at war and a country at odds. Mike Jenkins was well prepared, and moved his family and friends to his totally secure compound on a remote mountain in western Virginia.

After several years, Holly Jenkins couldn't wait for the elders to open the bunker doors, allowing her to roam at will, and feel free once again. Escaping to the sanctuary of her hidden cave would set in motion changes in her life heretofore unknown.

The AMAN presented a threat to the compound and the nearby towns; a threat that could not be ignored. They were prepared for war, but nothing could prepare Holly for her own battle between the two men she had grown to love… and the third she might be forced to marry.

Chaos will reign! Will love survive?

The Compounders: Book1
http://www.amazon.com/dp/B018HKIU7O/?tag=kp-jtret-20

DISSENSION
http://www.amazon.com/dp/B01N6FSGLE/?tag=kp-jtret-20

DISCONTENT
http://www.amazon.com/dp/B07215QYL1/?tag=kp-jtret-20

Westin Pack Series:

Start with One True Mate

Kelsey Adams is alone, and has been since childhood. Running away is all she knows and necessary to preserve her deepest, darkest secret. She can not afford for anyone to get close, or know about the monster within. But when she lands a lucrative job as an administrative assistant to Kyle Westin, CEO of the Westin Foundation, her life changes and everything's at stake. Can she conceal her growing feelings and her true self from this enigmatic, strong willed man, or will her world fall apart?

Kyle Westin, an alpha male who always gets what he wants, has watched and waited for the little she-wolf he knows is his perfect mate to show any signs of recognition. For two years he endures her unnecessary formality and daily rejections with a patience he did not know he possessed. But even Kyle has his limits . . . Can he make Kelsey notice him as someone other than her boss and break down the walls she built around her heart? Or will Kelsey do what she has always done—run?

One True Mate
https://www.amazon.com/dp/B071HXL3R2

Fighting Destiny
https://www.amazon.com/ dp/B07575HC9T

Forever Mine
https://www.amazon.com/dp/B077V9WHMG

Confusing Hearts
https://www.amazon.com/ dp/B07BP9XL9W

About the Author

Julie Trettel is author of the Compounders and Westin Pack Series, a full time Systems Administrator, wife, and mother of 4 awesome kids. She resides in Richmond, VA and can often be found writing on the sidelines of a football field or swimming pool. She comes from a long line of story tellers. Writing has always been a stress reliever and escape for her to manage the crazy demands of juggling time and schedules between work and an active family of six. In her "free time," she enjoys traveling, reading, outdoor activities, and spending time with family and friends.

Visit
www.JulieTrettel.com